Mutti's Dream

Beverly Hopper

Clink
Street

Published by Clink Street Publishing 2021

Copyright © 2021

First edition.

ISBN: 978-1-913568-55-9 - paperback
978-1-913568-56-6 - ebook

*To the memory of those whose plight history has chosen to ignore,
I dedicate this book to the many thousands who lost their lives on
30th January 1945 on The Willhelm Gustloff.*

The Position of East Prussia within Europe pre 1945

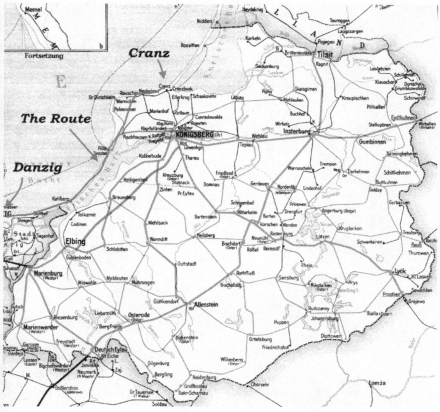

Map of East Prussia up until August 1945 including the route taken in the escape

The Family Line

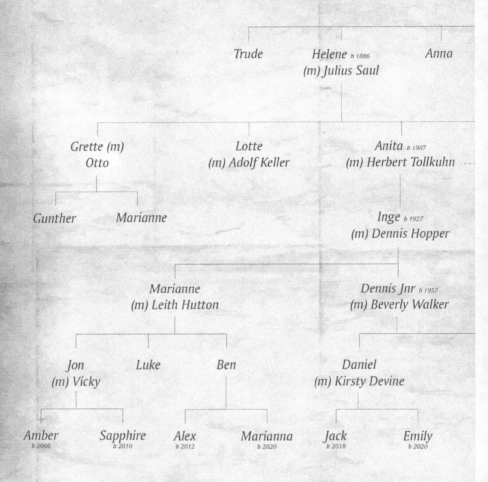

Trude   Helene b 1886   Anna
(m) Julius Saul

Grette (m)   Lotte   Anita b 1907
Otto   (m) Adolf Keller   (m) Herbert Tollkuhn

Gunther   Marianne   Inge b 1927
(m) Dennis Hopper

Marianne   Dennis Jnr b 1957
(m) Leith Hutton   (m) Beverly Walker

Jon   Luke   Ben   Daniel
(m) Vicky   (m) Kirsty Devine

Amber   Sapphire   Alex   Marianna   Jack   Emily
b 2006   b 2010   b 2012   b 2020   b 2018   b 2020

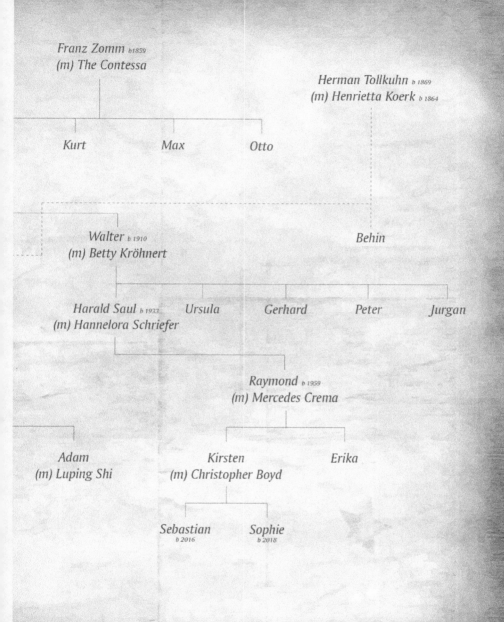

Prologue
Summer 2002

They assembled from all over the world, including Canada and England but most now lived in Germany. Some brought their children, all adults of course, as those making the trip were in their late 60s or 70s – with one over 80.

Our journey started in Hannover, where my mother-in-law, Inge, once lived with her mother, Anita, who was always referred to as Mutti. We had made many trips to Hannover when Mutti was alive, she never spoke a word of English, and so my pidgin German was frequently tested. A ferocious lady, I didn't relish our visits if truth was told and Inge, my mother-in-law, was in constant fear of one of her mother's tongue lashings. She was never forgiven for leaving her mother after the war. That said, we all had a deep level of respect for Mutti, her intelligence, her foresight and wisdom and not least and probably most significantly, her sixth sense!

We were a party consisting of Inge (pronounced Inga, with a soft G, for the benefit of uncertainty), her daughter and husband, Marianne (pronounced Marianna) and Leith and my husband Dennis and me. I don't apologise for the emphasis on the 'e' being pronounced 'a', as it is in the Germanic tongue, as shortly you will be introduced to many similar names ending in 'e'.

It was a warm summer day and we wore short-sleeved tops and cropped trousers as we walked towards Mutti's grave in the local cemetery with flowering bushes between each gravestone. She had died just six years earlier in 1996 and this was a solemn event as these occasions always are. It was a joy to see how well kept her grave was, considering her immediate family lived in the UK. We were still so grateful to the loving care that her friend Lilo showed in looking after her old friends' grave. Every week she would tend the grave, place fresh flowers and polish the black marbled headstone.

Following this graveside visit, we returned to Lilo's house and enjoyed the traditional German spread of kaffee und Küchen. The table was spread with a conventional German embroidered tablecloth and in the middle was an inviting feast of käseküchen, apfel and Mohnküchen. My mouth waters at the very thought. This delicious traditional afternoon spread of cake and coffee is something I am most certainly in favour of when visiting Germany. We tucked in enthusiastically and heaped compliments upon our host, Lilo; in reply she beamed the gracious smile of a cook who had complete confidence in her cooking expertise.

The following day we met the coach in Hannover, many others on the coach who were once refugees already knew each other from a previous trip. Warm embraces; old friends reunited. The younger among us shook hands with new acquaintances before boarding the coach, stopping to make another pick up in Berlin, before making our way through Poland. The expedition was well planned with regular stops and an overnight stay in Poland. Excellent hospitality awaited and every meal was washed down with a small glass of vodka, which even the teetotallers respectfully accepted from the hoteliers, their hosts.

One poignant stop was in Poland which was once part of West Prussia. We visited the Fortress Ordensburg Marienburg, the world's largest brick castle and the Teutonic Order's once headquarters and now known as Malbork Castle it has been declared a UNESCO world heritage site. Of course, to everyone making this trip, they were arriving in Marienburg!

The coach stopped at the side of the broad, gently flowing River Nogat glistening in the sunshine. The usual peddlers of various types of merchandise met us as we disembarked. However, one very old lady stood out, shabbily dressed and with an extremely weathered complexion. She gathered a crocheted shawl around her stooped shoulders before holding out her cupped hands and calling out "Meine kinder, Meine kinder."

Many of the party were saddened to see this old lady who remarkably had survived – having failed to leave her homeland when everyone else had made their escape and instead remained to become no more than a beggar in the street. It was a stark reminder to everyone how lucky they were to have been cared for by vigilant family members who took them away from a nightmare experience to go on and build a new life.

Shortly everyone re-boarded the coach, and the journey continued. The rendition of old school songs entertained the younger ones among us. Sheets of words were hastily handed round for those who may have forgotten the lyrics, but nobody failed to remember the tunes. Every single member of the party sang heartily, song after song taking them back to the school he or she once shared in Königsberg, East Prussia.

The singing continued until someone shouted from the front of the coach that we were arriving at the Russian border, the coach fell silent. There was palpable anxiety among the coach party; I felt my mother-in-law tense as we made our approach towards this significant section of the journey. Nervous glances were exchanged around the coach, and Werner, the organiser, stood up as if sensing the tension emanating from the passengers. His outstretched arms flaying downwards in a calming gesture, and he spoke softly to assure everyone that he had everything under control. We younger members of the party ultimately recognised the significance of this border, but we could not possibly share the complexity of emotions this next experience would stir in the older travellers.

Only about three or four years before had the Russians reopened their borders, allowing the Prussian people access to their homeland. This encounter was a poignant moment for many as it was the first time that many of the party would set foot in the country of their birth for over 55 years.

The Russian soldiers advanced towards the coach in full uniform bearing machine guns. They ordered the driver to switch off the engine. Immediately the air-conditioning cut-out, and in searing heat, we sat in the coach for nearly 20 minutes while our passports were collected and paperwork checked. Modern coaches rarely have many opening windows, and soon some of the older party members started to gasp for breath. The air was stale, and the heat was choking.

Eventually, we were ordered off the coach and into a waiting room; at least the air here was fresher even if the heat was still well into the 30s. One by one each person was forced to enter through a door into a small room, one metre square, where two fully mirrored walls stood with a door at either end and then we were ordered to stand spreadeagled, arms aloft. The mirrors were, of course, two-way. Then the second door would open, and we were met with a body search. Female soldiers searched the women and likewise, male soldiers, all carrying machine guns, searched the men. A heart-breaking exemplification for this elderly group ushered at the point of a firearm as they go back to their homeland, much like the conditions under which they had left, over 50 years ago.

I glanced over to my mother-in-law Inge whose face bore the expression of incandescent fury as she slowly turned to speak to me in her still strong

Prussian accent, "They take our land, steal our possessions and this is how they treat us." She felt utter and complete contempt and practically spat the words out.

Chapter 1
The Family Early 1900's

Grete, was an attractive, elegant girl, always pristine in her appearance. Her warm brown hair carefully curled and lifted onto the top of her head, framing her large green eyes. Grete was not ambitious, she loved the village where they lived and often helped out at the local kindergarten, loving children as she did. Grete was kindness itself and indicated that becoming a wife and mother was her intended path. She was an upright, strong and proud young lady; she took her time to look her best and was always a dutiful daughter to both her parents. When Grete was just two years old, she was presented with a beautiful baby sister, Lotte. Grete doted on her from the very start, she spent hours gazing into her crib, playing with her tiny fingers and chattering away in baby noises and the occasional comprehensive dialogue that she was only just developing herself. Lotte was christened in the local church and all the family and friends came to see the baby and celebrate in the family garden afterwards.

Lotte was the quietest of the children, and generally reluctant to be placed in the spotlight. She was a shy and gentle soul, and her eager smile radiated warmth. While eager to please, she held less maternal instincts than her older sister Grete, rarely playing with dolls and wanting to help her mother in the kitchen, albeit generally getting in the way. Lotte, was just two and a half when she found her mother, Helene, one day writhing in agony in the garden… she was terrified and ran into the house to find her big sister. Grete came running and although still under the age of five, knew exactly what to do. Grete ran for the doctor and as she did so, shouted to their neighbour to fetch their father from work. Lotte clung to her mother's skirts as her cries rang out across the garden and they slowly made their way through the back door of the house and into the kitchen. Lotte screamed as water flowed out from under her mother's skirts onto the floor. Fortunately another neighbour close by heard the commotion and was on hand to assist Helene and whisk the tiny child away from the immediate scene.

The doctor had been deeply concerned about Helene throughout the whole labour, he felt that the child was stuck. He was a young doctor and had only ever assisted in a caesarean, never having performed one on his own. He became flushed with panic until eventually he could feel the head of the baby. Panic turned to relief as he knew the baby had entered the birth canal and he reminded himself that he was dealing with the mother of a third child. The anxiety returned as the head was out but not the shoulders. The cord needed to be manipulated and the doctor was about to perform an episiotomy when he felt the shoulders release, the perspiration on his brow matched Helene's as the baby finally slipped out and immediately belted out a huge cry. On this day, 17th May 1907, facial tensions turned to expressions of astonishment – this was an enormous baby. The doctor reached for the scales and announced that Helene and Julius were the proud parents of an 11lb little girl, and they christened her Anna after her aunt, Helene's sister.

Quite quickly, Anna's name, as with that of her aunt, gave way to Anita and she grew up as cherished as her siblings, yet her manner was different, she was often aloof and would take on new learnings with ease, It was recognised within the family that Anita was gifted musically, also her perceptions on life and those around her astonished the family on a regular basis. The trauma of Anita's birth might have been enough for most women to throw in the towel and say "No more." Yet Helene knew how much Julius longed for a son and they decided that they would try one last time to see if they could produce a much longed for little boy. Their patience and prayers were answered when on 9th May 1910 Helene gave birth to Walter, Julius was immensely proud to have a son to carry on the family name and quietly thought about all the future plans he wanted to map out for his son. Setting him up in business, going to university, imagining him becoming a local dignitary perhaps, someone that everyone would look up to in the local community.

Growing up, Anita reacted to most situations quite differently from her sisters and thought them to be overly emotional and lacked stimulating conversation most of the time. Anita would make an early judgement on people and conditions and cared little whom she may offend. As far as Anita was concerned, they preferred spending too much time working to look pretty, plaiting their hair, and giggling about the young men in the village. All very shallow thought Anita. Even given the age gap her relationship with her brother was often challenging, their views differed on many things and Anita was never afraid to express her views strongly on a vast array of subjects.

Often the family would witness the end of an argument between the two siblings and it would be Walter that stormed out of the room in frustration and indignation at his sisters' differing views.

On a trip home from boarding school, Anita persuaded her mother, Helene, to trim her hair short; she wasn't concerned so much about her appearance. Why mess around wasting time styling hair. She would rather play the violin or practice on the piano. Anita could play almost any musical instrument and would often be heard humming the tune to a wordless classical melody. Music flowed through her body, making her feel spiritual, enlightened, excluded from all those around her. Only listening to music and a higher level of conversation brought Anita to life. Otherwise, she would be practising a musical instrument or reading a book. Her poor mother despaired that her daughter would ever find a man that would take her on, being of below-average height and never to be seen with a ribbon in her hair. It appeared to all who knew her that she had no interest in becoming a wife or mother.

Anita's sisters were less academic and schooled locally as was her brother, yet he had extra private lessons Julius paid for to ensure that Walter would achieve the highest grades possible. The family lived in a spacious cottage in the large village of Kaukehmen in the North-East part of East Prussia. Later to be renamed Kuckerneese from 1938–1945, it was initially called Kuckernesse by the earliest settlers in 1530. Formerly the administrative headquarters for the district of Elchniederung and originally a pagan centre of worship. Around 1903 the Church sold and leased much of the land to the local community to build more roads and houses. A school, shops and cinema were erected in the following years; it soon became quite a self-sufficient community of around 354 residential buildings and about 4500 inhabitants around the time of the Second World War.

Significantly Kaukehmen stood remarkably close to the Lithuanian border. Although this had been an independent state since the end of the first world war, the proximity to Russia was still a matter of concern to those who lived so close to their volatile neighbours.The village stood surrounded by fertile agricultural land, and local farmers regularly sold the produce in the bustling marketplace. The broad market stood centrally to the town, encompassed by substantial, well-built buildings of sophisticated architecture. On market days the municipality would significantly increase in numbers, and local gossip was often exchanged for farming advice. The knowledgeable elders would share their life's experience with the younger members of the community while sitting on benches or the back of farm trailers strewn with hay.

With a river and canal close by, individuals would often take lunch sitting on the banks of the river on sunny days, having collected fresh bread or cakes from the bakery. Few people had a fridge so buying regularly and when produce was at its freshest was paramount to the discerning housewives. The beating heart of the community was set firmly in the past. On the edge of the square on market days, farm vehicles and tractors littered the side roads in testament to the fact that the produce was fresh from the land to the table in just hours. The family home had an immaculate front garden, which was tended to daily. A white picket fence surrounded the whole property, including the back garden, within which Anita's parents, Helene and Julius grew fruit and vegetables. Not enough to sell but adequate for their needs in the summer months. Often much would be pickled for the winter. Winters were harsh with temperatures falling to minus 20–30 degrees, and summers were baking hot.

Chapter 2
Anita 1925

"Our Beautiful Kingdom of East Prussia has had a chequered history. Centuries ago it was part of the monastic state of the Teutonic Knights of the Northern crusades along the Baltic states in the 13th century…"

Anita's pen was poised as she sat attentively during this history lesson; she treasured hearing about her heritage. Especially as her grandmother loved to exalt the fact that she was born of nobility, a contessa in fact. Fräulein Schmitt had covered the content of this lesson with her pupils many times and today took the form of a revision session. She recounted events and dates to the class spanning the centuries, ensuring that the critical periods remained entrenched in the minds of her pupils. She continued to recount historical facts through the eighteenth century. The teacher, looked up from her notes, needing to know that she still held the attention of her class.

"Klasse – who can tell me the year that East Prussia became part of the German Empire?"

Anita held up her hand,

"Fräulein Schmitt, was it in 1871 during the unification of Germany led by the Prussians?" she responded quizzically but was quite confident of the answer. After all, she had read up on this topic assiduously.

"Liebe Anita, das ist gut, The Kingdom of Prussia ended with the abdication Wilhelm II, and the kingdom being succeeded by the Weimar Republic's Free State of Prussia. Do we all appreciate how advanced we were in that by 1900 we had extensive electric tramways in operation too? Ja?" Fräulein Schmitt scanned the room for nods of agreement. *"Regular steamers worked the Baltic coast towns of Memel, Tapiau, Labiau, Cranz, Tilsit, and Danzig; we should not forget how important our trading port of Königsberg was too – and still is. Also, since 1901, our economy has benefitted with the completion of the canal to Pilau. The canal has helped to increase our trade of Russian grain."*

Ten years later Königsberg had reached a population of 246,000 many of whom were Jews who began to prosper in the culturally diverse city.

"So today," the teacher continued, *"As you know West and East Prussia stands between Poland and Lithuania and Russia. Our land is rich in arable farming, our country is recovering quite well after the war and is the envy of Germany,"* Fräulein Schmitt smiled as she nodded to her class in knowing recognition.

Anita understood well that while Prussia's peoples were mostly Germanic, they were also made up of Polish and Russians as well as other nationalities. They considered themselves to be a separate race – a superior race. The aristocracy fought hard to maintain a high standard of living. During the lesson, Anita found herself lost in thought once again. She held her pencil tightly as she glanced out of the open window. Anita viewed across the fields of wheat swaying in the spring breeze to the Manor house where a noble family lived. Anita knew the family owned a large estate and were known as Junkers. She felt that should have been *her* birthright, and she should be living among them.

Her grandmother led a privileged life as a child as she was born a contessa. However, she had to relinquish her nobility when she fell in love with a commoner, Franz Zomm. The fact that he was also a Jewish refugee of Russian descent only served to complicate the situation still further in the eyes of her family. Many Russian Jews fled their homeland at the end of the nineteenth century when it became troublesome for them to openly practise their faith in a country which had little time for Jews.

Her family looked after her financially, but she was rarely allowed access to the life she once knew living among the aristocracy. The contessa's values and views of the world were fed down to Anita like a child takes food from its mother. Anita, christened Anna Gertrude Saul, soaked it all up. Anita often observed her grandmother's poise and thought her to be entirely majestic in her deportment, unlike Anita, who bore an altogether less graceful posture. She felt frustrated that her grandmother had betrayed her birthright and as a consequence denied Anita a better life, or so she thought. As far as Anita was concerned, she had lost out, and she felt piqued about that.

The contessa and her husband bore three sons, Kurt, Max, and Otto. Also three daughters, Trude, Helene and Anna, the latter Anna was known as Anita or Nita. By some strange twist or maybe design, Anita was named after her, Anna, and she also was known as Anita. Fortunately, Franz Zomm was the beneficiary of a moderate Russian Estate after their flight, and his benefactor had the foresight to extract as much of the fortune into Prussian banks before their getaway from the impending backlash on the Jewish community. The Zomm's fortune dwindled as each child took a portion resulting from their various financial obligations yet they still lived a comfortable life, and the contessa was not afraid to share her affluence with her preferred children and grandchildren.

Helene married Julius Saul (although not a practicing Jew, Julius was also of Jewish descent), they were both dedicated to their family and each other, a perfect match. Each of their children regarded their parents as the epitome of an ideal marriage and Grete and Lotte had every intention of emulating them in every way they could. Their family consisted of three daughters and a son, whose childhood was happy, and both parents took an active interest in each of their children. Always taking great care to accept and account for all their differences, particularly in the case of Anita, who was entirely unlike her other siblings.

Anita was, later in the year, to leave the prestigious boarding school her grandmother funded, as she was approaching her final exams. Her grandparents had recently taken her to Vienna to watch the Vienna Strauss Philharmonic Orchestra, encouraging her to practise hard for her forthcoming music board exams. It had been her dearest wish to attend the Vienna School of Music, but finances would not stretch and her grandmother, now in failing health, was all too aware that she had other grandchildren to consider plus her husband who remained in good health and would not appreciate their resources being unnecessarily drained.

Everyone had high hopes for Anita, being musically gifted, but she was a non-conformist and always going to do things her way. Anita was highly opinionated, and with growing maturity, she emerged a level-headed albeit strong-willed and ever so slightly arrogant young woman.

Chapter 3

Anita and her siblings at various stages of their development and age were introduced to Königsberg society. Königsberg has the literal meaning of "Kings Mountain" and being the capital of East Prussia was where those who wanted to be seen needed to be and Anita loved it. Walter would venture into the city quite regularly but her sisters were happier living in their village. Anita loved to look at the beautiful statues in the city and appreciate the architecture of the tall buildings and most significantly take in the beauty of the Königsberg Schloss (castle), a significant landmark of the town since 1255 and a great symbol of Prussian rule .

Anita was fortunate to be included in the guestlist of a summer debutante social gathering at the Schloss. There would be dancing and the opportunity to meet potential suitors, her grandmother still had some influence and used it on occasions. Anita's parents and grandparents spoke in depth about how they should affect Anita's future – without her assuming they had coerced her into meeting a respectable young man. Fortunately, Anita was oblivious to this conversation, or she may well have elected not to attend the event that night. Significantly she chose to wear a dress for the party and while quite plain, her mother, for once, approved of her appearance. Helene grinned with approval as Anita left for the station that late afternoon accompanied by her young brother. Walter promised to keep a strict distance from her once they arrived. In truth, Walter welcomed any opportunity to visit the capital city. Anita had no high expectations of being particularly noticed on arrival; she certainly did not want to be seen hanging on the arm of her brother.

They made their journey in the small narrow-gauge trains that ran in East Prussia; only the large cities had the benefit of two tracks. So often there would be long waits for signal changes and another train to use the track in the opposite direction before they could continue their journey. Anita felt slightly frustrated that her younger brother should be accompanying her, so spent most of the journey staring out of the window until they eventually arrived at the central station and started to walk through the streets of the capital city of East Prussia.

As they approached the stone bridge leading to the entrance to the Schloss, Anita looked up in awe at the craftsmanship and architectural design of the building. The Castle tower, which formed the Coronation site for Prussian kings, stood tall before them. Anita was excited as she turned to her 16-year-old brother and said,

"Look Walter, it is hard to imagine this beautiful Castle has been around since medieval times, don't you think it's a wonderful part of our heritage Walter?"

Covering a vast area of around 160 hectares and standing on the banks of the River Pregel, the Castle could be seen for miles around and was the focal point for the city. Anita loved it so much yet Walter's reply was much less appreciative.

"It is merely a reflection of a bygone era Anita. There was much ignorance in those ancient times. You would do better to look towards an ideology that cleanses the society in which we live rather than looking backwards at old buildings."

Anita shook her head as she cast her brother a confused sideways stare and then walked on ahead, shrugging her shoulders.

Anita saw some girls she knew as they entered the grand hall. They were prettily dressed and ready to flirt. Acknowledging Anita they beckoned her over. Without further words being spoken Walter and Anita parted company and Anita moved quickly to find her friends. She glanced back to Walter with a slightly sarcastic grin to indicate she would be fine. Walter stood and looked after her for a few minutes. Accepting that parties were not for him, he turned and walked out of the door, back over the bridge and drifted off into the back streets of the city.

Anita comfortably chatted among this group of female acquaintances when, after a few minutes, a group of handsome young men approached the assembly. Not being the flirty type, Anita felt wholly confident and held her own in the conversation. She was educated to debate political views of the day, and she could articulate her argument with great conviction. As a consequence, the influential men in the group found her stimulating and listened attentively to her views. They talked about the after-effects of the First World War. Although it had ended just seven years earlier, many of the young people knew friends and family members who had fought. Prussia had suffered the invasion of Russian forces from August to September 1914. Despite having overwhelming superiority over the Prussians in terms of numbers; the Russian armies remained separated and were finally defeated in the battles of Tannenberg and the Masurian Lakes. The famous Prussian aristocrat Manfred von Richthofen was known to some of the partygoers that night. They were reminded of his 80 air combat victories and that since his death in 1918 he had become renowned as The Red Baron of Germany.

One of the young men, while being particularly good-looking, was less impressed by the pretty girls mingling with his party of friends. Instead, he watched Anita intently as she spoke, and when she finally paused, he smiled at her, confidently and quite deliberately. She felt startled for a moment and then slowly smiled back. Without looking left or right, the young man held her gaze as he closed the gap between them and politely held out his hand to introduce himself.

"I am Herbert Tollkühn, what is your name?" he slowly asked.

"Anita" was the reply.

"My father is Prussian, and my mother is Italian," he made the statement quickly as if expecting an inquisition. Instead, he heard,

"Oh, how very interesting." Anita half-smiled back. She observed the softness of his skin during the gentle yet perfect squeeze of his handshake, which lingered just a second longer than necessary.

Anita took note of his dark hair and the fact that his face was not so round as traditional Prussian faces. His dark eyes and strong eyebrow line made him look distinct. He wore an ever so slightly olive complexion, and it was quite evident that he had Italian blood in him. Herbert explained that he was born Herbert, Erich, Gerhard, Tollkühn on 27th January 1907. Anita calculated that made him 19 years old, four months older than her. Anita had turned 19 on 17th May earlier that year and now just standing and listening to him she experienced an interest in this young man.

Their conversation soon began to flow, and they found that they had many things in common, a love of music, boats, art and intellectual debates to name a few. Anita talked about her grandmother, the Contessa who was no more a Contessa. Herbert spoke of his love of art; his father was a renowned artist in the city, Italian coffee and how much he loved the Italian Lakes. It was as if there was no one else in the room. Anita shone, her eyes lit up as he talked, and then when he asked her to dance, they waltzed, and she floated around the dance floor feeling light on her feet. For the first time in her life, she felt attractive, it was a strange emotion, and she enjoyed it, Herbert made her feel good.

During the following days, they took every opportunity to see each other. Herbert lived in a village a few miles away, but they were fortunate to both reside close to the train route. They met at the station cafés or waiting rooms. They were finding ingenious ways of getting notes to each other via the postal service – even friends of friends were happy to go slightly out of their way to deliver their envelopes. Herbert also used the family's pony and trap to make short visits to rendezvous with Anita. Anita bewitched Herbert. He had never been able to relate to other girls in the way he could with her on such an intellectual level. She excited him, and Anita was smitten with this good-looking young man who genuinely liked her for herself. Herbert was not a man who was impressed just by a pretty face, and for that Anita was very grateful.

As the weeks rolled on, their visits became more frequent. Herbert, having met with Anita's parents' approval, felt the time was right for her to meet his family, his parents and sister. Herbert being the gentleman, made the trip over to collect Anita, who was quite nervous meeting this Italian rather hot-headed lady, as her son described her. When they finally arrived back at his family home, they discovered a note. His grandmother had been suddenly taken ill. At short notice, his parents and sister had made the trip over to Johannisburg in the south of East Prussia and made no mention of when they expected to return. Herbert was somewhat at a loss at what to do next. He gathered his thoughts and swept his arm to gesture towards the paintings that hung around the room. Herbert explained that his father Herman was a great artist and his paintings were displayed in the art gallery in Königsberg. His father spent much of his time painting. Anita glanced around the walls of the house and marvelled at Herman's work; she was very impressed. She considered the style to be along the lines of Monet. The sweeping brushstrokes looking casual yet well intended, coming together as building blocks of paint flowing like running water. Herbert stood and thoughtfully observed Anita as she surveyed the array of artwork.

Today was the first time that they found themselves alone together and in private. Herbert could not take his eyes off her. Anita blushed when she realised he was watching her so closely. Their eyes searched each other intently. Any initial embarrassment at finding themselves in this predicament of being alone together was soon overtaken by the overriding urge to fall into each other's arms, and they kissed passionately for the first time. The sensation was everything that Anita thought it would be, having imagined Herbert's arms around her as she lay alone in bed at night. Anita felt a sensual desire rising through her body, an irresistible urge to press her body close to his. Herbert was powerless to resist. Neither had experienced feelings like this before, nor could they stop even for a moment to defend their actions. After a few minutes of passionate embrace, he slowly led her to his bedroom where they remained for the rest of the afternoon.

Chapter 4

Anita did not meet Herbert's parents that day, and the next opportunity was three weeks later when they were all at home. His grandmother had sadly passed away, Herbert attended the funeral, with Anita not included, of course. It was an anxious meeting for Anita; she was less sure of herself in the company of Herbert's family and anticipated that there could be a degree of friction. To add to the significant unease, she had been due her period a few days before and was beginning to feel concerned. All the same, she was praying hard that all would be well. In confirmation of the anxieties within Anita, the meeting started badly. Anita shook the hands of Herbert's mother, father and sister. Herbert's mother took one look at her and openly exchanged a grimace with her daughter. Behin, in turn, smiled awkwardly at Anita who stood stiffly, already feeling self-conscious. Both mother and daughter dressed in their Sunday best, Behin wore her hair up in a relaxed style, her curly locks resting gently around her eyes and looking like a prissy young lady. The starched collar on Henriette's dress matched her stern facial expressions, and her searching eyes flicked between her son and his girlfriend.

It was a bright September afternoon, and there was enough warmth in the sun for them to take kaffée und Küchen in the garden. Anita grabbed the opportunity to take some deep breaths in the crisp afternoon breeze to calm her nerves. Henriette had made an excellent Käseküchen and delicious Mohnküchen mit streusel that Anita loved even though the poppy seeds always got stuck in her teeth. Anita's unease continued as they held polite conversation while making every effort to ingratiate herself with the family. She complimented Herbert's mother on her excellent Prussian cooking. The reply was sharp and less than gracious.

Henriette pronounced,

"A good cook can always turn her hand to different cooking styles, but I enjoy Italian cuisine mostly."

Her accent was strong, and Anita listened carefully, amidst the simmering hostility, so as not to miss a word or at least the context in which she spoke.

Now feeling decidedly awkward and needing to substantiate her position, Anita began explaining her heritage albeit lapsed now. Nevertheless, she felt instinctively that her efforts to impress were falling on stony ground. After a further half an hour of polite, if strained conversation Henriette stood up from the table and pulled Herbert to one side. They moved towards the house and stood in the canopy of a large cherry tree; at this point, his sister rudely followed in hot pursuit. Anita remained seated at the small garden table feeling distinctly embarrassed. She could not overhear what was said, but she was astute enough to recognise the body language. Anita guessed that she had not met with his family's approval. Hermann remained seated opposite her. They tried hard not to meet each other's gaze, but when they did, he smiled awkwardly, quickly looking away and struggling for something to say.

Anita saw Herbert throw down the napkin still in his hand and storm away from his mother and sister. The point was made evident in no uncertain terms that Anita was no match for the pretty young girls in the village, and he should end this relationship immediately. His mother's blunt indiscretion sent Herbert into incandescent rage. He walked back towards Anita and gently took her hand and led her away from the table without allowing her to thank his mother and say her goodbyes. Herbert whisked Anita through the gate onto the lane before he turned to her and took both her hands. He was apologising profusely for his family's insulting response to their introduction as a couple. He felt embarrassed beyond words and so ashamed. Looking deeply into her eyes he spoke,

"Meine Liebe, can you ever find it in your heart to forgive my family for their indiscretions?."

Anita looked up at him, and her eyes twinkled as she sympathetically smiled in recognition of his awkwardness. In response, Herbert kissed her firmly on the lips and then placed his arm reassuringly around her shoulder as they walked together towards the railway station.

By mid-October, an unusually warm month for the time of year, Anita and Herbert had not been able to spend time together since the unfortunate encounter with his mother and sister. Herbert had been sent away by his family on the pretext that his grandfather needed him. He thought he knew the real reason was to keep him and Anita apart. After two weeks, Anita was relieved when she finally received a letter from him. He asked after her wellbeing and explained that he had missed her terribly. Anita's heart nearly leapt out of her chest as she read the words in the letter. Herbert went on to say that there was still a reasonable degree of boat activity on the river in Königsberg. He suggested that they should go punting on the river with a large group of mixed friends and take a picnic when he got back, as it was so unusually warm.

Anita was excited to see him again, she dressed appropriately for the late season in consideration of the temperature and felt that she might pass as pretty for once. After receiving parental approval at her appearance, she caught a train to the city of Königsberg. Herbert met her as she arrived at the station. He had been staying at his parents flat in the city. They walked the short distance to the river where they chatted with friends. The group drank sparkling local wine and posed for photographs. A friend was fortunate to have a newfangled more modern version of the box camera and keen to show it off and practice his newfound hobby.

Anita's mother had become increasingly concerned about her daughter's moodiness of late. Following a brief squabble about her abrupt attitude towards her sisters and brother, she instilled a curfew of 8pm if she were to go to Königsberg. Helene promised severe consequences if Anita violated her curfew as she was only just 19 years of age. Anita had little choice but to comply and so reluctantly agreed. Her mother was astonished at the lack of argument in response, quite unlike Anita, Helene thought, she must be sickening for something.

The group, as usual, was vocal and enjoyed sharing liberal argument between them, one, in particular, Hans, held the attention of the group. He was exultant as he explained that he had recently spent time in Germany, and was familiar with the political repercussions lately around a bombastic young political activist in the National Socialist party. This radical young man believed that the victorious allies had ridiculed the German Weimar government after World War One and he attempted a coup d'etat in 1923. This action resulted in a nine-month prison sentence for high treason. While in prison the extremist read any book he could find on history and philosophy which consolidated his own beliefs at that time. He was encouraged by his business manager to write an autobiography as a way of passing the time. A young man, Rudolf Hess, was imprisoned alongside him, he also contributed to its writing, and so he dedicated the book to him. It was initially to be called *Four Years of Struggle Against Lies, Stupidity and Cowardice*. On advice, the name of the book was altered to a more marketable title *My Struggle* in the end, the book was a part autobiography and part political manifesto and more familiarly recognised as *Mein Kampf*, the author was Adolf Hitler.

The book, which was long and repetitive and difficult to read, laid out his visions for Germany as an innate superior race known as Aryan. He wanted to win back the land they had lost to Russia in the Great War and illustrated his political views against 'Bolshevist-Jewish' Communism. Adolf had fanatical beliefs that the Jews had aspirations to take over the world, and relied on a false composition called *The Protocols of the Elders of Zion*, written by anti-Semites, to 'prove' his case. Most significantly, Hans recounted during his running commentary, how he was picking up some rumblings from his Jewish friends that there seemed little appetite on the part of the main political party to quash this young activist after they had imprisoned him. Many thought him no more than an agitator, yet it was a source of discontent among the Jewish community. Anita listened intently, her family was of Jewish descent in Russia, and while she did not consider herself a Jew, she bore the name of one. Also, her mother's maiden name was Zomm, clearly a Jewish surname. Anita visibly shivered as Hans shared this knowledge, she felt a strong sense of foreboding about this man she heard about, Adolf Hitler.

As the afternoon drew on, Anita knew that she needed to take the opportunity to speak to Herbert alone and so she persuaded him to take her on one of the smaller boats and pontoon out a short way. She did not want to be overheard by the others. They drifted a few hundred yards down the river as Anita gazed in admiration at the beautiful Schloss and all that it stood for. She was enjoying the fading sunshine, and Herbert was, of course, standing. He gazed down into her eyes, and as if he was anticipating her next move said, "Meine Liebe – what is bothering you? You are so distant today; you must tell me what is the problem, did Hans upset you with his ramblings?."

Anita saw no point in dressing this up and so blurted out

"I am pregnant, and I don't know what to do." Her eyes were teary, but she held her control as her hand reached up towards her face. Herbert's face, on the other hand, turned to a paler shade of grey. His stomach did a few somersaults, his heart pounded furiously, and he reached for his chest with his right hand – an action that caused him to lose balance and the boat to rock from side to side. Anita held on tightly, a hand grabbing each side of the boat.

Feeling shellshocked, Herbert struggled to regain control of the vessel, and himself. This extreme reaction was not really what Anita had hoped for; she knew that Prussian society in the 1920s was not what one would call broad-minded when it came to childbirth out of wedlock. Also, Herbert's status in the community was unlikely to benefit from the unexpected news. However, their choices were slim. She had hoped for a more favourable response from Herbert.

Malbork Castle, in Marienburg

Contessa and Franz Zomm

Helene (nee Zomm)
and Julius Saul

Kaukehemen

Königsberg Schloss (castle)

The Saul Family Home

Anita, Herbert and friends

Chapter 5

After the initial shock that day, Herbert considered the situation over the next week and knew that he had to do the honourable thing and marry Anita. She, in turn, felt determined they should come to terms with the news in their own time and was grateful for his integrity. So they spent over four long weeks discussing and coming to terms with their predicament before deciding that it was time to share the news with their families.

Both parental encounters were not pleasant; there were tears, lots of shouting and most of the time, Anita placed herself in a protective bubble. Helene sat and cried, Julius clasped his chest as if he needed to protect his aching heart. Greta and Lotte stood in stunned silence, not knowing whether they should comfort Anita or their parents. Walter bore a look of utter disdain, shaking his head as he uttered disparaging words towards the unfortunate couple. Anita was catching only odd words, she knew the expected outcome; she had to look positively to the future and needed to get past this period of pain and disappointment on the part of her family.

Herbert's family reacted similarly, his father was heartbroken and his mother took herself into a state of apoplectic shock, continually chanting in Italian

"Mama Mia, perché, perché," why why? Such was her disbelief.

One thing on which everyone eventually agreed was that Anita should have the baby in Königsberg away from the prying eyes of local people. Herbert's parents owned a top floor apartment at 28 Schleiermacherstrasse, Königsberg, a respectable area where they would be away from prying eyes. This tree-lined road was situated in an affluent area of the city, where a renowned school called the Hans Schemm Schule stood close by. Its academic results held testament to the high standards the local community demanded.

The flats in this area were well built to withstand the ravages of winter, and many enjoyed double-glazing with the additional benefits of the insulation that an apartment offered with fewer external walls. The entrance to the flats was often strewn with prams and bicycles. Stone steps lead down to the basement cellars and upwards to the three or four-storeyed apartments. So plans were hastily made to pack all that they would need during the harsh winter months. Anita did not dare show her mild amusement that it was more important that they should be moved away from the villages where they lived, than actually to commit to marriage as soon as possible.

December arrived. Anita and Herbert were devoted to each other. Herbert bought matching wedding rings and had the date of their engagement inscribed on the inside, 24–12–26, Christmas Eve. They considered that at least delaying the wedding might give their parents more time to come to terms with the idea. For his part Herbert believed he was doing the right thing, and his initial shock had long–since lapsed into wild exuberance at the thought of becoming a father, and nothing could change that now. However, as was the intention, the neighbours living in the other flats at 28 Schleiermacherstrasse assumed the young couple were already married, as they of course prematurely wore their wedding rings.

In Herbert's eyes it was his duty to keep his wife warm and safe in this treacherous winter; fortunately, the flat had a form of double-glazing with a sliding second window, which made a significant difference compared to those who did not and certainly more than she had previously at home. Without this benefit, they would have to do the same as others and break the ice every morning from the inside of their windows, particularly when the temperature dropped below -20 degrees. The icicles hanging from the tall buildings were three, four, even five feet long and presented a danger to passing shoppers. In case one fell from the roof, shop owners scrambled to climb ladders and also hang out of windows to detach the offending weapons from the eaves.

Herbert's mother, Henriette, was happy to delay wedding proceedings as long as possible. She hoped that her son might even have a change of heart while they were living together in the apartment in Königsberg. She wondered if perhaps they might discover that they were not suited or maybe the baby might not reach term, then all could be saved! As the winter started to thaw, Henriette had to accept that Anita was blossoming and there would indeed be a baby in a few months. Reluctantly she agreed to participate in the wedding plans. Frantic exchanges occurred between the two families to pull together a half-decent event – a small family gathering after a civil ceremony at the Town Hall Administration Office in Königsberg. The wedding day on

7th March 1927 was a small family affair. Henriette and Behin looked on stiffly as the proceedings developed. Anita wore a pure coffee and cream chiffon gown gathered loosely just under the waist as was the fashion of the day and gave adequate space for a bulging tummy. Her mother forbade her from wearing any veil as this tradition, of course, was intended for virgin brides. But her dress design did not warrant one in any case.

Anita's grandmother was now in failing health, and the family felt quite concerned for her wellbeing. The shock of Anita's predicament had taken its toll, and she questioned the years of support going to waste. Nevertheless, Anita's grandmother wanted her to have a small dowry. Her husband kindly reminded her that they had other sons, daughters and grandchildren who might benefit from their assistance. With a heavy heart, she agreed they should only pass a small dowry over to Herbert as a demonstration of support. When Anita's siblings discovered this news, they reacted in differing ways. Walter was furious that his wayward sister should be rewarded for bringing disgrace upon the family; he kicked the ground with his feet and subsequently retreated into the background. Grete and Lotte looked at each other in dismay. Grete, was now engaged to be married to Otto, and Lotte had recently met a charming local boy called Adolf Keller. Both recognised that when their time came, the same generosity was unlikely to be extended to them.

After sharing a knowing glance, Grete squeezed Lotte's hand and smiled at her sister as if to say, 'we will be Ok', and that they just had to accept the situation for what it was. They were pleased that their sister's beau was doing the right thing. They secretly wondered at Anita's prowess in finding such a handsome young man.

The next three months flew by and regardless of Herbert's family being remote from the situation, Anita's parents Helene and Julius made frequent trips to Königsberg, to help make preparations for the baby. Their first disappointment and embarrassment about the prospect of explaining their daughters' situation to local people had subsided as she was safely tucked away in an apartment in Königsberg. They were to become grandparents, something to look forward to. Especially as the family had sadly suffered the recent loss of Helene's mother, the Contessa, who gradually deteriorated until her ultimate demise in early spring.

Anita had taken the news badly and felt a degree of guilt. She held the notion that her actions may have speeded the otherwise inevitable passing of her grandmother. She even asked the local doctor for advice on the subject but was offered the reassurance that the causes of her declining health were unavoidable. She had heart failure, and there was nothing anyone could do. Her Grandfather Franz was bereft and needed support from the rest of the Zomm family who were keen to run to their father's aid, as did Lotte and Grete.

Anita's short frame expanded and with the heat of the spring months, her legs and ankles swelled. Some of the neighbours further down the street where they lived made cruel remarks after she passed by one day, saying that she resembled a barrel from the city brewery. On one occasion when Anita overheard such a comment, rather than run home and cry, she turned on the older women gossiping in the street and tore such a strip off them that one of the perpetrators remained in tears. Anita heard no such remarks from any spiteful locals after that!

The flat enjoyed a view of the wide tree-lined street from the lounge window. Anita often looked out onto the scene and watched the world go by as she patiently waited for the imminent arrival of her baby. In the second week of June, labour started, Anita's waters broke as she carried a basket of brötchen, fresh from the bakery. If it weren't for the fact that her mother was present and able to take the basket from her, as she cradled her stomach, the small bread rolls would have ended up rolling down the road. Fortunately, Anita was only a few yards from the entrance to the apartment. She had requested that her mother should come to stay with them from late May until after the baby was born just in case it came early. She was also just a little concerned at her lack of maternal feelings for the baby growing inside her and hoped that her mother's influence would encourage her to feel the emotions that one expects during and after childbirth.

The midwife was concerned that the child was likely to be large. Not least because Anita was 11lbs at birth and with Anita's relatively small build, the birth had the propensity to be complicated. Herbert was summoned from work at the water-testing laboratory, and an ambulance whisked her quickly to Katarina Hospital. Anita had read avidly about the childbirth process, almost as if she was entering an exam. She felt she owed it to herself to know all there was to know. She also recognised that having a large baby was likely to present difficulties, and she hoped that the baby would not cause her too many problems. Even more, whether the child would be able to cope with its journey into the big wide world unscathed.

The labour was long, and Herbert became increasingly concerned as he paced the hospital corridors, interspersed with frequent walks around the courtyard garden outside to steady his nerves. He heard Anita's screams through the open window and felt powerless and desperately wanted to be at his wife's side. He was even prepared to be present to witness the birth and offer moral support, but this just was not protocol and therefore, not even worth discussing. Anita was becoming exhausted as labour continued through the night; there were concerns for both mother and child. Just as the topic of forceps was discussed, Anita overheard the dialogue and became determined that she would not undergo a minefield of intervention. With that, she found a final burst of strength and energy, and with one mighty decisive push in the early morning of June 9th 1927, a beautiful daughter was born. Weighing just over 9lbs, they called her Inge Helene Doris, and Anita revelled in the calls of 'Bravo'.

Chapter 6

Herbert became a doting father and Anita took full advantage of the support of her mother and sisters, even Walter appeared on the scene and proudly announced to the world that he was now an uncle. Anita failed to bond with her daughter entirely and was just a little bit jealous of how Herbert fawned all over her. She was the one who had gone through all the discomfort of pregnancy and the pain of childbirth. All the attention went towards this demanding baby. Yet Inge was a good baby and soon settled into a routine. Helene was overjoyed to be a grandmother, and nothing was too much trouble. Herbert's family paid a token visit to see the baby, and after that, their contact was quite minimal. Impressively they passed over the deeds to the apartment to the young couple and became resigned to the situation and wished for a discreet veil to be drawn over the circumstances of their son's marriage. Their attention had turned to Herbert's sister. They felt determined that they would have maximum influence in their daughter's nuptials once, of course, they had scrutinised the list of suitors!

As the months rolled by, Anita and Herbert divided their time between Königsberg and Kaukehmen. Inge developed into a lovely dark-haired bundle of fun. Anita realised that her life choices were now more limited. The child was preventing her from exploring a career in music, so what was she going to do now? The prospect of being a full-time mother did not enthral her. Herbert was working, and when he wasn't, he was wholly absorbed with his daughter. Never had Herbert felt such complete and unconditional love for another human being. He was aware that his wife had not taken to their child to the same extent as he. Consequently, Herbert overcompensated whenever he could. He did not want Inge to feel that she was not wanted and loved.

Anita focused on building a future for them and felt a degree of responsibility towards the money that her grandmother had left her. She was not insensitive to the fact that her sisters and brother had not benefitted to the same extent and felt a duty of care to the family as a whole. She was intelligent and single-minded and even as a young woman, held an intuitive knowledge that she was the mistress of her destiny. The responsibility did not lay heavy on her shoulders; moreover, she relished the accountability that she took upon herself to decide the future of her family. What happened next was mostly down to Anita, and she knew that she could persuade Herbert to support her in whatever developed.

As the hot summer days drew to a close, Anita's family in Kaukehmen prepared for winter. It was as usual very harsh, and life was a ceaseless ordeal to stockpile enough firewood and bulk buy local produce to feed the family. Of course, much food had been pickled and placed in jars during the summer months. Bottled sauerkraut and bratwurst sausages then formed part of the staple winter diet. Anita felt the need to be near her family with a young baby in the winter, and so Herbert travelled daily into Königsberg to his job in the laboratory, which was quite a trek. When the weather was particularly bad, he was forced to stay overnight at the apartment and away from his beloved wife and daughter.

It felt like an eternity coping with the adverse weather conditions and willing the deep winter to thaw. The gentlest spring rays finally melted the thin blanket of ice glistening on the rivers. Everyone looked forward to spring, and when summer arrived shortly after Inge's first birthday, they decided to take a few days family holiday to the Baltic coast. Walter elected not to join his family, instead preferring to spend time with his newly formed friends and associates, leaving the rest of the family to visit a beautiful seaside holiday resort called Cranz. Formerly a fishing village, it was a growing holiday destination and better still it was only 35 kilometres from Königsberg.

They took the steam train from the city, and when they got to the station in Cranz, they realised that it was the end of the line. They then walked the short distance to the hotel that Anita's parents had booked for the family's holiday. They passed by the busy open-air market stalls mostly selling fresh produce intermingled with trestle tables of amber. Local people were selling it after they had collected it on the beaches, so abundant were the surrounding areas with this semiprecious stone. The roads were straight and crisscrossed between the houses and eventually led onto the wide promenade between the beach and the hotels and café's lining the seafront. New businesses bartered for positions either close to the road from the station or near the long wooden pier; entrepreneurs were emerging in this growing town.

The edge of the white sandy beach was interspersed with flagpoles each bearing the Prussian flag and lining the promenade. Their emblem was of considerable significance to the Prussian people. It bore the primary coat of arms of Prussia, a black eagle on a white background, and helped set the nationality apart from Germany. As far as they were concerned they were *their* race and did not want to be mistaken for Germans. Scores of holiday-makers relaxed under the glazed porches of the pavilions along the promenade looking out over the Baltic Sea. Gentlemen wore suits and hats as arm in arm they promenaded their ladies dressed in short-sleeved mid-calf length dresses. Dress length was suitably shorter now in the late twenties, and it was perfectly acceptable to be seen displaying a well-turned ankle. Anita preferred to wear trousers and keep her chunky legs hidden. It made for an altogether more straightforward wardrobe choice and far less expensive than having to keep up with the new fashion trends.

The family stayed in a large hotel overlooking the promenade and naturally the beach. Anita managed to negotiate an upgrade to get a sea view. She intended for this to be partly a belated honeymoon for her and Herbert. Helene had already recognised that fact and promised that Inge would sleep in her grandparent's bedroom to afford her parents' maximum privacy. Anita had a vigorous sexual appetite and Herbert, as a healthy young man, was happy to acquiesce to his wife's demands. The first two days of the holiday was spent mainly confined to their hotel room, only meeting the family at mealtimes. Grete and Lotte were denied the company of their beaus, as it would not have been suitable to have brought them along before their marriage. One errant daughter was quite enough for any family in Helene and Julius' view. As a result, the young sisters felt indignant and were quite scathing of the limited time that Anita devoted to her daughter since their arrival.

Finally, Herbert, who liked to maintain a good observance of social norms, felt the need to join the rest of the family on their outing scheduled for the third day. Plus, and most significantly Herbert was missing his father-daughter cuddles. Inge, in turn, kicked her legs and smiled broadly upon seeing her father that morning. Anita looked on, experiencing a vicarious thrill as he knelt towards Inge as she sat in her pram. Herbert beamed at his daughter as he proceeded to pick her up gently. He lifted her, his arms outstretched and swung her round in a circle. Inge laughed contagiously.

Helene had asked the hotel staff to prepare a picnic, and so armed with a small hamper basket and a selection of blankets they slowly set off making their way along the promenade. There was laughter, and playful exchanges between the family members and the ladies did not mind that the gentle wind tousled their hair as they enjoyed the gift of the present. As they walked further from the heart of the town, the buildings became smaller; the three to two-storey buildings then became bungalows or holiday chalets. The flag-poles disappeared; the promenade was reduced to a pavement and eventually, a sandy path.

Ultimately trees interspersed with dunes replaced the buildings. They saw a small sign on the side of the path, Rosehnen, the name of this area marked on a wooden plaque. The family admired the clean sand and the gentle Ostsee (Baltic Sea) lapping against the shore. Just a few fishing boats bobbed up and down gently on the water. The sea's music took control of Anita's senses momentarily, and she stopped to absorb the sunshine on her face and the taste and smell of the brine wafting in the sea air. Few holidaymakers were evident in this area, and it was peaceful. Only a young couple were visible close by looking down intently among the dunes and, using a small spade, they were occasionally digging and sifting the sand as if in search of something. Anita stood, intoxicated with the atmosphere when she heard her mother's voice,

"Anita, stop dreaming, come on."

Julius reminded the group that there was still copious amounts of amber along the shoreline in this area. Several contained the fossils of small insects, and many carried a considerable value. Much of it was made into jewellery and Grete and Lotte decided that after lunch they would go and explore the area to chance their luck finding amber.

At this point, Inge woke up and became fractious, and Anita suggested she needed her lunch. They made camp among the dunes, offering a degree of shade in which to place the pram and the food. As they lay their tablecloth on top of one of the blankets and carefully put the other quilts on three sides of the cloth, Anita said,

"I love it here, I feel at peace here."

She looked at her mother as she spoke and in return Helene smiled as she said:

"I am so glad that you are happy Anita, that means the world to me."

They positioned themselves to allow a view of the sea through the undu-lations of the dunes. Everyone said how much they were looking forward to lunch. Nothing was forgotten, and each tucked into the smoked eel, bread rolls with meat pate, boiled eggs, and cheeses. Followed by apfelküchen and some fresh fruit, all washed down with bottles of beer and lemonade. Inge loved the meat pate, and Helene carefully mashed a banana in a small bowl and fed it to her on a teaspoon. In response, the happy little girl gave her grandmother a cheerful smile and chuckled between every mouthful, watched on by her doting father.

Herbert stayed with his daughter and mother-in-law while the three restless sisters, along with Julius, decided to walk towards the trees on the edge of the beach and across the path they had just walked. The sun was beaming down, and Anita was grateful they had left Inge in the relative shade. The trees were little more than a copse really, hardly what you could call woods. However, as they approached, they looked through the thin branches of the trees and observed a building. They moved closer and on further inspection considered it to be abandoned. The area around the building was overgrown, the windows were blackened as if fire damaged. There was evidence of smoke damage on the outside of the two-storey building as well. It looked to be a large house, with one gable end looking out over the Baltic Sea and the other end looking over woodland. There was a single storey extension to one side of the house in a lean-to style that ran the length of the house. It looked like a hotel to Anita and when she glanced up to the wall of the gable end she could see the name, Blaue Möwe, (Blue Seagull).

Anita was intrigued and desperately wanted to explore further. Her father beckoned her back towards the beach, but she was adamant she should uncover the secret that this house held.

"Papa, it's enormous, we simply must see inside, Come here, Papa,"

Anita implored her father to venture further and look inside the building. Grete and Lotte were equally curious and joined Anita in her appeal to their father to which he relented, and the four of them explored the building as far as they could. They discovered evidence of a fire at every turn and yet it was as though the fire had not managed to get a full hold on the property. The brick was blackened, especially at the front and side and the wood around the doors and broken windows were little more than slightly charred. Julius concluded that most of the damage was from smoke and the fire must have been extinguished before it was allowed to gain a hold on the property.

During his assessment of the circumstances of the building's damage, Julius muttered that being left open to the elements had left it at risk of further damage. Anita was trying the handle of the front door – firmly locked, as was the back door. She then, without a word to anyone, ran round the side of the hotel and quickly turned to see a small set of steps going down into what could only be the cellar area. The door was hidden behind overgrown brambles and blackberry bushes. It was at that point she turned to look at the back garden and saw all the cherry trees. They were laden with cherries, most just ripening, but the crop would be substantial she felt sure. There was even a small band-stand in the garden. They looked at each other in awe.

The others now came to look to where Anita was, and just as they arrived, she turned the handle of the door. It turned, yet she could not open it. She pushed and pushed and then realised the wood must have swollen in the heat and with age. She pushed harder and just as her father shouted,

"Stop, Anita stop," the door swung open.

They were greeted by a musty smell, and so much dust was disturbed that they all gasped for breath as fresh air entered the cellar for what must have been the first time in many years.

"No, Papa, we are here now, and I need to see inside the rest of the house."

Such was her enthusiasm; Julius knew his daughter and her determination would not be curtailed. Grete and Lotte decided that this degree of devilment was not for them and they stayed at the cellar entrance, happier to stand in the sunshine and fresh air.

Anita felt excited; she could not explain even to herself what had taken hold of her in the minutes since setting sight on this large old building. She climbed the stone steps from the cellar to the house and expected this door would probably be locked. To her amazement and gratitude with one pull of the handle, the door opened toward her, and she stepped up into a large hallway. Anita noticed the inside of the front door was blackened, and most of the downstairs windows. There was a decent-sized kitchen, still pretty well intact,.The fire had not managed to damage this part of the house. She then moved into what she guessed was the study or owners living room. This room was very severely damaged, and the freestanding stove had evidence of damage all around. The floor was covered in a thick layer of ash and most of the furniture was severely charred if not wholly burned. Julius and Anita concluded that this was the epicentre of the fire and everywhere else really only suffered the damage of smoke. Then they walked into a larger room with a smaller room attached with a room divider between them. After venturing upstairs, they noted the damage was limited to the smoke residue, and after a few minutes they could hear Grete and Lotte calling them from the garden outside.

Once they were all back outside in the garden and looking up at the building, Anita turned to her father and said,

"Papa, will you help me to find out more about this house?" The reply was simple,

"Why my child, there is nothing for you here, why waste your time on something so unimportant?"

Anita said no more to her father for now but went into deep thought as they walked back through the trees towards the beach. Herbert and Helene were now starting to feel somewhat anxious for their whereabouts. Anita excitedly told Herbert all about their find and how she thought she just had to know more about the circumstances of the building. Herbert, who was always keen to placate his wife in any way possible, agreed wholeheartedly that they would indeed establish the status of the property. Anita smiled in recognition of his acceptance and reached to kiss him firmly on the lips.

The next hour was spent running down to the water's edge and, for the first time, letting Inge feel the seawater on her legs. She squealed when the cold water stroked her skin as it gently lapped against the seashore. Grete and Lotte went looking for amber. Julius and Helene soaked up the ambience and watched their family having a lovely time. They felt both proud and grateful for what they had. Soon it was time for Inge to have a nap and so she was handed to Oma (grandmother) for a cuddle and some nursery rhymes. She quickly closed her eyes and drifted into a light slumber resting in between Oma and Opa.

Anita continued to feel restless and persuaded Herbert to go back to look at the house with her. He needed little persuasion, and without telling anyone else where they were going, they sloped off into the tree-lined area of the beach and Anita led the way towards their exploration. She took the same route, and Herbert was at first a little reticent to break any rules and trespass. He soon appreciated his wife's eagerness to show him, and so he relented and followed two steps behind her into the building. From room to room, they ventured with Herbert hearing the possible accounts of what might have happened and tending to agree on the evidence that he saw. They ventured to the upper floor and looked down at the beach below and sunlight dancing on the sea, the old wooden stairs creaked as they walked back down. Spiders scurried into dark corners, and their worn webs flapped in the disturbed atmosphere.

Once they came back out of the cellar and into the sunshine, Herbert stood for a moment and looked at his surroundings, turning 360 degrees as he did so. He asked Anita if she had explored further in the other direction. Just as he was talking, they heard the sound of a train coming closer. They both turned to look quizzically at each other and without a word moved forward in unison through the overgrown bushes, quickly appreciating they were on the concrete platform of a small railway station. They stood in aston-ishment as the short train with two carriages rattled past and stood open-mouthed as they saw the train slowing down into what could only be the central station at Cranz.

"I didn't even know there was a coastal track running this way" Anita exclaimed,

"Neither did I, " replied Herbert.

All of this only served to increase Anita's intrigue, and as they turned to go back towards the house and through the trees to return to the beach, Anita stopped suddenly and turned taking a couple of steps to the right towards a large bush. Herbert almost bumped into her as she stood so still.

"Anita, what are you looking at? Why did you stop?" Herbert asked her,

"I am not too sure," she replied. She continued to stare in the direction of the large bush. Looking more intensely, she moved closer taking small steps, unsure of her intent. Suddenly she found she was staring down at a battered and muddied sign on the ground amongst the undergrowth. Anita stood motionless as she read the words out loud,

'Zu verkaufen', for sale, the house was for sale, or at least it had been. Her pulse quickened, she felt flushed, and an overriding sense of exhilaration came over her. She picked up the sign and held it in both hands, showing it to Herbert as if proof were needed. This hotel was their destiny, she just knew it, and she would pray hard tonight.

Chapter 7

2002 Kaliningrad (Königsberg)

Our coach entered this Fortress city, which was once home to so many of our group of reluctant tourists. The significant Brandenburg Gate standing proud is the only remaining gate you can still walk or drive through. Situated in Bagrationa Street, I was amazed to learn that there was more than one Brandenburg Gate, the more famous one being in Berlin of course. I marvelled at the architecture, it was as impressive as Inge said it would be. My mother-in-law had loved this city. She had spent much of her childhood here, and it held so many happy memories. The coach was quiet, each sat looking out of the window with their own thoughts. They were the indigenous population by birthright, yet the surroundings had lost their familiarity. New buildings had sprung up of course. That should be of no surprise after 50-odd years, and yet it added to the sense of resentment that this stolen land should bear any hallmark of change.

Upon arrival at the hotel, the coach swung into the small turning circle in front of the reception – everyone was relieved to be able to stretch legs and arms. It was good to take in a few deep breaths to prepare us for the inevitable scramble to retrieve the suitcases from the hold of the coach. The driver being eager to please, and earn a decent tip at the end of the holiday no doubt, offered extra assistance where needed, particularly to the older members of the party. The reception was more polished than I had expected. Why had I assumed it would be any different? I am not sure, but the hotel presented itself in a favourable light, modern and much as we would expect in the rest of Europe.

One significant point to note was the rather large polished wooden desk sitting just left of the entrance; it was accommodated by a couple of somewhat large burly gentlemen in dark suits. They were keen to be of service to us in any way possible. I later found out they were the Russian mafia. Should we have needed cigarettes, alcohol, or I daresay any other invited service, they were on hand to deliver, or at least their minions were. A carefully selected variety of young boys were beckoned at whim to provide whatever service had been requested. And they delivered without delay, eager to please or maybe desperate not to displease! Light-heartedly we jested between ourselves that these young boys were the trainee mafia of the future. Joking apart I rather suspect we may not have been far from the truth. They were keen as mustard and appeared from nowhere the moment we sat outside, and ordered a drink. Did our shoes need cleaning? Did we need anything from the shops? As small children like to perform for the entertainment of adults, these 8–12 year olds attuned themselves to what might elicit attention and created amusement. Plus of course the little tip as each bill was settled on every occasion we sat in the outside bar area.

One of the most thought-provoking things I came to notice and quite apart from the primary aim of the journey, of course, was how very slim all the young girls were, really thin. It was so apparent that at that time (and I might say luckily for them) they had yet to succumb to the vagaries of fast food joints opening everywhere and as a consequence, they still enjoyed a more healthy diet. The downside for we shoppers was, of course, looking in the shops to find few clothes that would fit we more portly Western Europeans. The shops were fascinating as they lacked shop windows. One almost needed to guess what was behind. Mostly they were boarded up. Sure enough, the little mafia boys were always on hand to advise, for a price of course.

The lake area was well geared up for tourists and fully equipped with ice-cream sellers, stand-alone bars and cafés, all situated close to the lakeside and positioned on artificial grass. It was the first time I had witnessed this used over such a wide area, and I suppose I considered it quite contemporary, although why I hadn't considered the Russians were capable of modern, I am not entirely sure.

A tour of the city and the port highlighted that there was much that had not changed. Significant landmarks were still recognisable, such as the Prussian churches we visited.

My mother-in-law was naturally keen to visit the apartment where the family once lived. As we walked towards Schleiermacherstrasse, Mum talked about the beautiful grand piano that lived in the flat with them. So many memories came flooding back, and she just talked and talked and talked and of course we patiently listened. Even though we had heard these accounts so many times, there was often a new snippet of information not previously recalled, an interesting fact about her early life. She had lived in England for nearly 60 years at that time and only spent her comparatively shorter time of 17 years in Prussia. We all know that those are the years on which our childhood memories are built and remain with us our whole life long; Inge was no exception in this.

Inge recognised the street as soon as we approached, and within seconds we were standing outside the apartment block where she had lived when in Königsberg. She entered the hallway and showed us aspects of the stairways that led to her flat. We could go no further as Russian families occupied the now dilapidated apartments. As with so many other areas we were to visit later, it seemed as though the houses were unloved and possibly lacked real significance in the lives of their occupants. Or were we merely witnessing scenes of abject poverty? I suspect the latter.

From Schleiermacherstrasse, we visited the school that most of the party of travellers had attended, Hans Schemm Schule. We watched as Mum smiled walking down the buildings broad wooden stairs from the first floor. Something she would have done many times as a young girl and teenager. The outing concluded with a visit to her classroom, remarkably little had changed in the subsequent years.

In 1946, out of the old city of Königsberg, a new one was created, Kaliningrad, it was named in honour of the late Mikhail Kalinin, the powerless Soviet head of government under Stalin. There was much architectural vandalism committed by the Soviet authorities, and without a doubt, the worst one has to be the one building which had previously dominated the whole landscape. The beautiful Schloss was no more. There had been significant damage in the closing days and weeks of the Second World War, but unlike many of the other medieval buildings, it remained mostly structurally intact. There had been a degree of fire damage and significant neglect. Nonetheless, a decade later, the Kaliningrad authorities made plans to renovate the castle into a museum of local history; however, Moscow disagreed.

A Soviet statesman and co-leader in the early 1960s Alexei Kosygin, was heard to say

"A museum? What kind of museum? A Museum of Prussian militarism? I want it gone by tomorrow!"

The final instruction came from Soviet Premier Leonid Brezhnev, and the beautiful Schloss that had stood since the Teutonic Knights of the 13th century was destroyed. In its place, they erected a concrete carbuncle, which was never finished and was designed to become The House of Soviets. The locals refer to it as a robot; it has no design, lots of empty holes, is square and grey and desolate looking. Standing today as it does, a complete embarrassment to the local population. Surely it should stand in good stead for an award as the most ugly building. *I*, for one, should like to nominate it for such an accolade.

Chapter 8
1931 Building a Future

"Mutti, Mutti,"

Inge called to her mother. She played in the garden of their hotel in Rosehnen near Cranz and had found a frog in the bushes. Anita came down the steps from the kitchen door to see what all the fuss was. The sight of the frog fascinated Inge. She loved hedgehogs equally, which was a source of amusement to her father in that she never seemed phased by the vast diversity of small animals. Similarly, her Papa took his time to explain the peculiarities of every creature she came across.

Anita reached her little girl in the garden and then when she saw the cause of the commotion, scolded her for distracting her from the essential tasks in the kitchen. With a bottle of kirsch in hand, she was, among other things, making a schwarzwälder kirschtorte (Black Forest gateau) with bottled cherries from their garden from the previous year. She had much to prepare; a new group of guests were arriving that day. Lotte was not present as she would normally have been as she was tied up with her wedding plans. Herbert was due to come home that evening from Königsberg where he spent most of the week, going over to Cranz at the weekend since they had moved into the hotel for the summer months 18 months ago.

The family had worked hard over the past 18 months to turn the old property they stumbled upon in Cranz into a thriving hotel once more. There was a considerable degree of negotiation with the Estate of the previous owners to agree on a sale. It transpired that the hotel occupants at the time of the fire, were quite elderly and the fire had begun accidently when burning rubbish. It happened during the First World War, and so there were no staff in residence either. In the absence of any children of their own, nor known living relatives, it was a matter for the local authorities to liaise with the couple. The hotel was not operating at that time and it was agreed to move them to a nursing home where they would receive better care. The authorities concluded that they were potentially a risk to themselves should they be left in the hotel alone. They were quite wealthy, and so there was no issue concerning funding the move; however, their removal had a detrimental effect on their overall wellbeing. Within three months sadly, both passed away, and the Estate placed the house on the market. The war had broken out two years previously, and nobody was able to make such a commitment to purchase for the next few years. The solicitors were quite neglectful in their duties and allowed the house to fall into disrepair. They also claimed to be searching for any known relatives, but to no avail and consequently for over ten years, the hotel was left to deteriorate.

Subsequently, Anita, with the support of her father, was able to negotiate a low price for the property. She needed little in the way of borrowing thanks to the generosity of her grandmother, and she was delighted when she also received the approval of her grandfather Franz Zomm. Much of the work that needed to be done to bring the hotel back to its former glory was cosmetic. So armed with scores of paint tins, the family set to work, each taking a role. Walter played a great part in the heavy lifting and enjoyed the unity that working together in a team had brought to the family. The larger downstairs room with a smaller room attached served perfectly as a dining room and it was with immense pride that Anita hung a large blue / grey seagull hanging from the ceiling.

Although a baker by trade, Lotte's fiancé, Adolf was also a keen gardener. So his role was to trim the trees, bushes and branches and tend the fruitful cherry trees, cultivate the rose bushes back to good health and plant new shrubs were they were needed. Taking into account their proximity to the sea and of course the very sandy soil, Adolf did a decent job. He grinned with delight when everyone heaped praise upon him after his six solid weeks of work. Grete, Otto and Lotte decorated the inside of the house. Paying particular attention to the six letting bedrooms, all a proportionate size, two of which had an en-suite and the remaining each had a sink in the room. The girls made privacy curtains, and Anita and Herbert painted pictures to decorate the walls. They worked hard and enjoyed every minute of their toil. The private quarters were somewhat cramped, and Inge slept in a box room that could occupy no more than a bed and a tiny table. Her father made her some shelves for her toys and books. At the age of four, she was already reading stage one schoolbooks, and her parents actively encouraged her reading. They had also introduced her to Anita's violin last Christmas which they had spent in Königsberg in the family apartment.

Christmas Eve was when Santa Claus came and brought presents to all the kind children. Shortly after lunch, Inge was told by her mother to sit and read with Oma and Opa. Papa was busy putting the finishing touches to the Christmas tree and the rest of the family shortly assembled in the room. Inge radiated delight at the sight of all the people she loved most in the world, but where was Mutti? she wondered. Suddenly all went quiet, and the door of the room opened, and there was Weihnachtsmann (Santa Claus) with a large sack of presents. Inge squealed with delight, and the family applauded Santa as he gave out gifts to everyone. Inge sat on his lap, and Santa bounced her up and down on his knee, before he sipped a Glühwein and bid his farewells and wished everyone a happy Christmas. Within three or four minutes Anita entered the room upon which Inge exclaimed,

"Mutti, Mutti, Santa Claus came and brought me all these presents, and you weren't here, Oh Mutti you missed him." Anita responded,

"Nein, Nein Inge it is all right, I saw him as he was leaving." Inge smiled back at her,

"Oh, that's all right then Mutti."

After the festive season the weather started to improve, most of the family relocated to the Hotel Blaue Möwe (Blue Seagull), where preparations continued for the coming season. As far as Anita was concerned, the hotel not only helped to support her more extended family, but it also provided them all with somewhere to live. This gave her an enormous sense of satisfaction, and she was happy that she had been so confident in her outlook from the beginning.

Grete had married Otto and was happily settled back in Kaukehmen, although they spent much time helping out in the hotel too. Spring was upon them and summer a few weeks away. Lotte and Adolf were finally planning to be married in a week after a long engagement. Anita was keen on making sure the reception, which was due to be held at the hotel, would meet the aspirations of her sister. Anita felt it was the least that she should do to provide a reception venue and pay for the costs of the nuptials. After all, she had done the same for Grete the previous year; she owed them that much at least.

She was also keen to take the burden of responsibility off her father, who was not a healthy man. Nobody could identify what the problem was. Julius was not an admirer of doctors or traditional medicine and wanted to improve his health with natural remedies, good food and copious amounts of vitamins now marketed in bottles in tablet form. He felt sure that he would cure himself of whatever ailed him.

Back in 1928, the family had discovered some devastating news. Walter had joined the National Socialist German Workers Party. This party was by then over 150,000 strong and gathering momentum under the leadership of Adolf Hitler. The rising levels of unemployment disillusioned Walter, and his beliefs had caused the family an enormous amount of distress. Walter's covert activities were not shared with any of the family. However, his late-night meetings and strange behaviour all came to a head when Helene one day found her beloved son wearing a uniform of the Sturmabteilung SA, often referred to as the Brownshirts. This wing was in effect the original paramilitary arm of the Nazi party. Walter's deportment on this revelation indicated that he was proud to be a Brownshirt. Helene's face crumpled, and she felt sick in the pit of her stomach.

"NO, Walter, surely not, why?"

"You cannot possibly understand Mother; it is complicated; you should know that the rest of the world persecutes Germany; something has to happen; I believe in the party and I have already proved myself to them."

"Why, Walter, How? What have you done?" His mother started to become emotional.

"It is better that you do not know the details." Helene stepped back, she felt repulsed by her own son and his belief system, her hand covered her mouth, and she remained silent. She did not know much about the National Socialist German Workers Party, but what she had heard about them was not good.

Although their power was not immense in the early days of the Nazi party, Walter had been involved in a large amount of Ball Room brawling and was considered one of the bully boys. He often returned home with black eyes and a bruised face. The revelation of Walter's political leanings did nothing to improve relations between him and his sisters, particularly Anita. However, for the respect she felt for her parents, she tried hard not to argue too loudly with Walter in their presence.

Now in 1931, Walter was on hand for the early wedding preparations of his sister and he brought his young fiancé, Betty. The atmosphere when they arrived was tense to say the least but fortunately everyone liked Betty immensely. The family hoped that she would keep Walter on the straight and narrow and maybe even change his political beliefs. Walter tended the garden in preparation for the wedding. Anita wanted to keep her distance from her brother and asked him to be sure that the cherry trees were pruned;

in her opinion, they looked too sprawling. Also, he should make sure the pathway to their little railway station was clear, and any branches and shrubs were clipped and tidy. It was apparent that Anita was taking the opportunity to order her brother around. Such was her resentment toward him. Walter was biting his lip much of the time, but keen not to cause an upset, he did as he was bid by his sister.

Adolf worked in the kitchen where he felt at home, Anita considered Adolf to be somewhat hapless but an agreeable sort and certainly a grafter and he certainly knew his way around a kitchen. Lotte loved him dearly, and so Anita was pleased that they were finally to be married. Adolf had worked hard all day preparing the wedding cake as well as meals for the new guests' arrival.

Anita could not have the visitors arriving by train being anything less than entirely amazed at their first impression. After all, she had taken six long months to negotiate with the railway company to permit the trains to stop at their little station once more. They needed to uphold the standards that she had now set for the guest's arrival on each occasion. Guests would slowly inhale the fresh sea air as they walked from the little train platform to the hotel. The path way was wide and clear now from the platform to the hotel and, there were many compliments about how relaxed they felt leaving behind the frenetic lifestyle of the city as they entered the well-tended garden, drinking in the fragrance of cherry blossom and Jasmine.

Inge adored Tante Lotte und Onkel Adolf and never wasted an opportunity to spend time with them. They, in turn, cherished the little girl and Lotte along with her sister, Grete, took turns whenever they could to brush her hair and put it in ribbons. More often it would be scooped up in a large bow at the back of her head. Inge saw Onkel Adolf in the kitchen and offered to help him. Adolf knelt and stroked her cheek, giving her a broad smile. She beamed back at him as he instructed her to go to the bathroom and wash her hands before kaffee und küchen, Tante Lotte would be home shortly. Adolf could turn his hand to most things and kaffee und küchen was his speciality. He was a gentleman and unlikely ever to be found in an argument. His trade was as a Bäcker (baker), and he and Lotte also owned a small sweet shop in Kaukehmen so they were a busy couple. Adolf's baking skills were put to good use now they were occupying a hotel as well.

Helene and Julius arrived that evening too, and together the family sat and enjoyed a meal around the large kitchen table. The dining room, of course, was reserved for the hotel guests. Only after they were served dinner and their needs suitably attended to were the rest of the family permitted to relax. Helene chatted about local life in Kaukehmen and shared how Grete was worried at not having been able to conceive a baby since her marriage. Helene was anxious that her eldest daughter was excessively fretting and did not feel enough time had elapsed since her marriage to become so distressed. Grete and Otto were soul mates, pure and simple, two halves that complemented each other perfectly, and they both felt that a child would complete them. Lotte promised to go and spend time with Grete once her wedding had concluded. That appeared to ease her mother's apprehensions somewhat.

Anita was eager to grasp an opportunity to speak with her father about his health. She indicated this to him after their meal, to which with a hollow laugh, he waved his hand, as if sweeping away the concern. He subsequently met with a crisp response from his daughter and a promise that tomorrow they would discuss the subject whether he approved or not, no arguments.

Anita tended to their guest's requirements for the night before withdrawing to spend the rest of the evening with her family. Herbert arrived home on the train and apologised for being late; he had work to attend to that had taken far longer than he had intended. Inge looked up at her parents and grinned a cheeky smile. She was feeling so completely loved as her father scooped her up in his arms and hugged her tightly.

"Come on darling, bed, it is late. Tomorrow we play and have fun, but now it's time for sleep," He beckoned her to follow her mother towards her bedroom,

"Gute Nacht meine Liebe Inge."

Once most of the family and guests had retired for the evening, Anita, and Herbert sat and discussed the real reason that Herbert was delayed that evening. He had accompanied one of his seniors and his friend Gustav Sauf, the leading Königsberg newspaper's executive editor, to a meeting at the headquarters of the Social Democrats. They went to listen to a debate about the political views of the day. They had been discussing the struggle to recover in much of Europe since the Great War. Also the changes in Russia from the time when Stalin had come to power in 1927, following the death of Lenin in 1924. They discussed the effect Stalin was having on the unification of Russia. Prussian people always had a vested interest in any political unrest with their divided and authoritarian neighbours – even though Lithuania separated them in between. Likewise, the Italians were witnessing the rise of a fascist leader in Benito Mussolini who was starting to cause political turmoil in that country. Herbert had concerns for his cousins living there. His mother and sister visited regularly and had recently told of anxieties at the changes taking place in their homeland.

Anita listened intently to what she heard from Herbert, her gaze on him as he spoke did not falter. Anita gathered that what she was hearing was a cause of great concern to all of them. Most significantly, Germany saw an undercurrent of movement around the activities of the eccentric known as Adolf Hitler. Many saw him as a saviour, and he was beginning to gather opinion among the accepted society of the day. He had a lot in common with Mussolini's ideology, including radical anti-Marxism and fierce prejudice in the form of anti-Semitism along with a passionate nationalism. The meeting had concluded that Prussia was fairing quite well. Nevertheless, there were the beginnings of an exodus among the Jewish people, and undue emphasis that all should be 'on their guard' against any political unrest.

Anita tried to compute the overall message she was hearing; she felt the dawning realisation that her brother upstairs was a part of all this; she felt sick. How could she face him in the morning? The likely consequences of this unrest had the potential to be catastrophic. She did not want Herbert to become too politically active and potentially place himself at risk. However, equally, she wanted to know what was happening outside their comfortable little realm. The newspapers were only able to report so much; Herbert tried to pick up what he could from his friends and colleagues. However, the propaganda was stable and controlled.

Herbert did his utmost to convince Anita that things would blow over and she should not worry unduly. She desperately wanted to believe him and was at least grateful that their business was doing well. This fact was a great relief, but equally, Anita needed to understand if she should change course with their business plans. Herbert reassured her that they were fine as they were, but it was undoubtedly a time for them to consider how they were going to spend the next few years. Inge was to attend school shortly, and in a few weeks she would be five, and in the coming September, she would be at school full time. Anita was not keen that she should attend school locally; Cranz had a reasonably good school but was not equal to Königsberg. However, that presented them with a problem, how would they run the hotel and manage Inge needing to be in Königsberg? "Tomorrow my darling Anita," he said as he kissed her forehead, "now it is time for bed. We will discuss this tomorrow." Herbert spoke gently as he led his wife towards the bedroom.

The next day started with the usual hustle and bustle, including serving guest breakfasts and someone needing to visit the bakery down the road for fresh brötchen. Walter had left early with Betty, leaving a note on the kitchen table to say he had business in the city to attend to and they would return in time for the wedding. Anita read the note, showed it to her husband and just said,

"I am glad he is not here, but what is he doing Herbert? I cannot trust my own brother any more. This is getting serious and he needs to keep his distance."

Herbert looked saddened and perplexed but before he could spend too much time contemplating the situation, Inge ran down the stairs from her room to the smell of fresh coffee and warm bread rolls.

"Danke Oma," she shouted back to Helene in hot pursuit.

"Wait, child, I haven't finished doing your hair." Anita glanced across with disdain, if she had her way her daughter would have short hair and be done with it. However, Helene was adamant her granddaughter would look as pretty as she could.

With breakfast cleared away and the beds made, Anita went to speak with her father in the garden where he sat on a bench with his back to the house looking through the now very green copse of trees leading to the beach.

"Papa," she spoke quietly and with a concerned voice, "talk to me," as she sat beside him. However, this still took the form of instruction rather than a polite request. Julius turned to look at Anita, at which point she saw he looked teary. She immediately took a sharp intake of breath and sat up straight as if to prepare herself for something she might not want to hear.

Anita was right. She would have been grateful to be spared the technical details as he spilled his heart out to her. He was dying. He had cancer, and there was no positive outcome. All the doctors had agreed and had come to the same conclusion. Julius had looked at natural remedies and recently resorted to traditional medicine, but the cancer was too active. His pancreas, she heard, had now been affected also and he knew there was no cure. Anita held her breath for the entire time it took for her father to explain his predicament.

"Does Mama know?" she breathed out the question. The reply shocked Anita,

47

"No, your mother doesn't know nor must she or anyone else… Anita, you must promise me that you will not divulge any of what we have just discussed with anyone, do you hear me?… Anyone!"

Anita was stunned, heartbroken and very shaken as she made a commitment to her father. After hugging him tightly, she managed to determine that he only had a few short months left to live. She had to pull herself together and successfully avoid her mother as much as possible for the next few hours; she had a wedding to plan.

Chapter 9

The wedding procession meandered across the village of Cranz. Lotte and Adolf Keller radiated happiness to onlookers as they made their way from the church via pony and trap to their reception so ably put together by Anita, Greta and Helene. Walter had remained on hand in case it was too much for his father to give his sister away, but in the event Julius was strong and held onto his daughter with pride. Lotte wore a two-piece suit and a cross-over white blouse, with pearl earrings and matching necklace, Adolf wore a dark coloured lightweight suit and a handkerchief in his breast pocket. Dozens of people cheered the happy couple along the tree-lined road running adjacent to the coastline towards the Blaue Möwe Hotel.

Everyone had helped in some way to make the day special; Grete had contributed with both her time in decorating the hotel and making the wedding cake. She brought flowers from her home village of Kaukehmen to make Lotte's bouquet and dress the wedding table. The initial disappointment of not holding a wedding in her home village soon subsided as Lotte saw all the effort that had gone into making it a special day. Even her father looked better that day, Lotte thought; perhaps he was on the mend at last.

Anita's birthday was the previous week, and she insisted it should be overlooked in favour of all the arrangements that the family needed to do in preparation for the wedding. As, it was almost summer they enjoyed a beautiful garden reception. There were nearly forty friends and family, including each of the relatives from the Zomm side of the family, all well catered for and enjoying the bright sunshine of late May.

The usual speeches followed. Julius stood proud. It was a short speech but with no economy of sentiment when he wished the happy couple a long and blissful life together. As the merriment drew to a close in the late afternoon, some people wandered off to the beach. Anita was tired and thought about how well her father had coped with the occasion. The secret was a tough one to keep. She adored her father and found it heart-breaking now seeing him slumped in a chair at the end of the day, trying desperately to maintain a smile and knowing that he must be in pain. She felt so desperately sad for him and guilty that she held such a secret, but she had to remain strong and uphold all that she had pledged to her Papa.

There was no respite for Anita. As soon as the wedding was over plans were made for Inge's impending fifth birthday. She and Herbert were proposing to divide their time between Cranz and Königsberg to satisfy Herbert's job and also run the hotel. They decided Inge would benefit from being schooled initially in Kaukehmen. Helene wanted to spend more time with Inge, and it was the school that they had all started their academic lives attending. It also meant that Inge would receive one on one attention. Inge was happy to live partly with Oma and Opa as she loved them dearly. Tante Grete could play a role in looking after her and with Julius not being well, it offered him a positive distraction. Lotte and Adolf helped to manage the Hotel with Anita when she was there and with the addition of staff. Anita missed Königsberg desperately. She dearly wanted to spend more time there now that her mission to build a business in the Hotel Blaue Möwe was coming to fruition.

It was still July, and the school's new academic year had not yet started. Inge enjoyed spending time on the beach with Oma or Tante Lotte or whoever else could spare some time for her in her father's absence. The family were grateful to be away from the hot city for a little longer. During the week Herbert worked at his job in Königsberg where he worked at the water treatment laboratory. He was responsible for ensuring that the drinking water was safe for the public to drink. It was not a job Herbert hoped to remain in for too long. His dream was to develop his artistic skills and spend more time with his wife and daughter.

He had been asked to provide an account of his role for an article in the weekly newspaper. It was some vain attempt to assure the population of the cleanliness of their drinking water supply; there had been recent spurious reports of a contaminating leak. Unusually, Herbert had been requested to attend a Sunday evening meeting to assist the journalist who was preparing the article. The journalist was also reporting on a meeting that night at the Otto-Braun-House. They were expecting to listen to a significant politician Max von Bahrfeldt, and the journalist needed to be there too, so Herbert agreed to meet him at the venue.

On Sunday 31st July on a warm summer evening, Herbert bid his farewells to the family and gave his daughter a big hug and made his way to the station. As he did so, Anita, uncommonly, came running after him imploring him not to go. She could not explain why she just felt that he should stay with his family and not go to the meeting that night. Herbert argued that it was part of his job and he must get to the meeting. His boss would be furious if this article were not printed. They needed to try and calm a small fraction of the sceptical public. Anita became more and more distressed at the prospect of him leaving her. Herbert not being used to seeing such uninhibited emotion in his wife, finally relented. While feeling utterly confused, he walked back to the Blaue Möwe with Anita, hand in hand. She was looking straight ahead as he carefully observed the indomitable expression on her face.

Herbert managed to get a message to his boss that evening to say a family member was ill and he would make the journey in the morning. He would go straight to the editor's office to assist with the publication of the article. His boss was amiable to the situation and agreed between them that Herbert would take the earliest possible train into Königsberg the next morning. As they slept, Herbert awoke to the ringing of their newly installed telephone in the Hotel at about 5 am. He was shocked to hear the devastating report. On the previous evening, there was a bomb attack on the headquarters of the Social Democrats in Königsberg, at the Otto-Braun-House, the leader Gustav Sauf was killed. Also, the Königsberger newspaper's executive editor along with the politician Max von Bahrfeldt was severely injured. Herbert would have been at that meeting, and he was shaken to the very core. What was happening in their city? Had he been there, he would have been severely injured or worse, killed. The biggest shock came from remembering the previous evening, and the hysteria that his wife demonstrated so that he did not make the journey to Königsberg that night. That action may well have saved his life. He went back into the bedroom and looked down at his sleeping wife, and was in awe of her intuition. Was it intuition? Why had she become so hysterical at the prospect of him leaving his family last night? The question washed around his mind until he decided to wake her and inform her of the dreadful news.

Chapter 10

In Kaukehmen, Julius held Helene's hand as tightly as his diminishing strength would permit. She mopped his brow as he lay in their bed, she, sitting apprehensively by his side, looking anxiously into his eyes. Helene knew she was losing him; nobody had confirmed that to her, she instinctively knew. His eyes were heavy as he tried to hold her gaze, and each breath grew increasingly shallow. In silence, Grete opened the door of their home to the other family members as Anita had discreetly summoned them, even Walter, although it pained her to do so. And one by one they slowly and respectfully gathered at the bedside. With a heavy heart, Lotte read a few choice verses from the Bible. Her words shattered the silence in the room. Inge remained in the living room with Adolf and Otto who ably amused her with a few toys and games. While upstairs, her dearest Opa rattled out a final breath and closed his eyes for the last time; his hand fell limp in Helene's. Her face crumpled, and she dropped her head onto his chest, sobbing uncontrollably.

The funeral was sombre; everyone wore black and had white waxy faces and red-rimmed eyes. The event was well attended, and on a dull day in late August, Julius Saul was laid to rest in the cemetery in Kaukehmen. The girls had been quick to comfort their mother who's grief tore at her insides like a tornado. The three sisters were relieved when Julius's brother and wife and Helene's father, sisters and brothers made the journey for the funeral. Some of them brought their children as well, it was rare that Inge would see her cousins and their presence brought some light relief to the otherwise solemn occasion.

After the funeral tears were shed, the memorial party gathered back at the house for the wake. It was a tight squeeze, but everyone accepted it and welcomed the closeness that the occasion forced upon them. There was nowhere to hide, emotions were raw, and the hugs were plentiful. Anita and Adolf took on the responsibility of catering, and between them they turned out a very respectable spread. Anita achieved a successful Käseküchen and was proud that everyone remarked it was as good as her mothers, not, of course, within Helene's earshot.

Anita, Grete and Lotta welcomed their Zomm cousins warmly. Their children played well together. Innocently naïve of the solemnity of the occasion, their joyful antics did break the atmosphere. Helene sat and watched them, gently nodding her head in recognition that she was looking at the future now, and how in Inge her legacy would live on when she eventually passed into the next life. Her deep thoughts were soon broken as one child screamed at another for pinching a toy and their parents instantly rushed to calm the moment. However, minor squabbles were of no matter to Helene. Her heart ached. She realised how life had to continue for the young ones. Quietly she took herself away to her room mumbling a request for some solitude for the rest of the afternoon. Downstairs the gathering caught up with each other's lives and remembered their loved one, recounting stories of times gone by until one by one each of the funeral party gradually slipped off to resume their daily lives.

Coping with the new adjustments to their world was challenging for the family. Grete looked after her mother, and they spent time in Cranz in the summer, helping Lotte and Adolf when the hotel was open. Grete was making daily visits to Helene, being a dutiful daughter, and dividing her time between Cranz, and most of the time remaining in Kaukehmen. She never lost the opportunity to be with Inge and considered the little girl to be the light of her life. Her husband Otto was a loving man, and together they desperately yearned for a child of their own since their marriage. Grete regularly cared for other people's children in a subconscious attempt to fill the void that she experienced in her own life. The absence of a regular monthly cycle was the real reason for her not having conceived she was told. As the months rolled into years, the desperation turned to an awkward acceptance that this was her destiny, and she should spend her time helping others, and that is what she did.

Helene had needed tender loving care after Julius died, and all the family felt the loss of him terribly. He had been the source of such great advice and instilled stability within the family that they now appreciated what they had lost. Grete took it upon herself to be at his graveside for long periods, and Otto often found her there, lost in thought and blinded by the tears in her eyes. Otto understood her sadness and desperately wanted to help his wife come to terms not only with losing her father but the absence of the children she so yearned. His heart ached for her pain to cease and Grete, in turn, battling with her demons, did her best to hide what she was going through. Grete desperately wanted to avoid a chasm opening up between them. She felt that she had failed him as a wife. Maybe if she permitted him to confront her with how he felt, he might admit that she was a disappointment and decide to leave her. Grete couldn't bear that, and so she bottled up her emotions and decided that was the way things would be, and that was the end of it.

The hotel in Cranz was a great source of accomplishment to Anita. She was very grateful that both Adolf and Lotte had gladly accepted the role of housekeeper, cook/gardener and general management even though they also had a business to run, albeit with staff, in Kaukehmen. They needed only a few staff at the hotel, and as the season changed, the guest numbers fluctuated. Anita was a keen financier, took complete charge of the accounts and tenaciously kept the overheads to a minimum. She was prudent with the hotel purchases and 'make do and mend' became her motto. She looked for economic alternatives wherever possible. The deliverymen who went out of their way to supply the Blawe Möwe, although it was slightly off track, were always greeted with kaffee und küchen. But never a tip.

The local farmer would deliver his fresh food and appreciated the custom. On occasions when Anita was on the premises, they could be heard holding loud arguments about the price and quality of his produce. Ultimately, with inflamed cheeks, he would throw his arms in the air and exclaim that only Anita, with a withering stare and well-intended reasoning, could bring down the price of eggs to an all-time low. They would always finish as friends and laugh at themselves afterwards. It was accepted by the community that Anita was an intelligent lady and a consummate businesswoman for someone so young. The locals respected her even if some were a little frightened of her. Yes, her family were in awe of her too, and her opinion mattered to them. Anita was quite capable of influencing others with her sound reasoning, and only the brave would argue back.

On rare occasions, Inge was permitted to go on day trips with family members, a few miles up the coast to Rauschen. These trips were wonderful, and every day she spent there felt like a weeks holiday to Inge. Mostly Inge went there with her Papa and their time spent together formed many of her happiest memories. They had caught the train along the coast and upon arriving at the train station, they would grab an ice cream and look at the market stalls where her father would often treat his daughter to a trinket or a little summer dress. They would then stroll the streets or perhaps take the funicular railway down through the forest. The minutes that it took to travel from the top of the cliffs to the bottom and across the dunes to the sea gave Inge time to admire the forest and watch the squirrels as they jumped from tree to tree like little miniature acrobats. They would then take a walk along the promenade where they would stand and appreciate the sea. It always felt rougher here than at Cranz, probably due to the cliffs, Inge thought. The coastline was quite different here, and Herbert felt the benefit of getting away from Cranz and the endless chores, which often prevented him from spending time with his precious daughter.

The whicker changing huts on the beach always amused Inge, and they were scattered everywhere. There were many holiday villas dotted around the area and the health spa attracted many to the resort. A visit to the Arboretum to visit the beautiful and unique plant collection where the local citizens and seamen brought plants back from their travels would complete her day. Then they would hurtle back on the train to Cranz in the evening.

Grete had been helping at the local school that Inge went to as she generally did two mornings a week. One particular morning, she felt unwell, wondering if one of the children had passed a bug on to her. Grete felt quite queasy, and lightheaded, so left early, walked home and sat down with a cup of tea. The next thing she heard was Helene knocking on the door quite concerned that her daughter had not called round that afternoon as she always did. Good gracious, she must have been asleep for hours. Realising that, Grete jumped up in alarm and shame that she had let her mother down. She Immediately felt faint and lightheaded as she reached for the door handle, Helene grabbed her arm at the sight of her and assisted her back into her seat. After Grete gave her account of how she had been feeling that day, her mother summoned the doctor. He came round within the hour.

The doctor was diligent in his assessment of her and spent a good 25 minutes with Grete and asked her some very pertinent personal questions as well as giving her a full physical examination, after which he gave her his diagnosis. Grete sat stunned, hardly daring to take in the news. "You are pregnant my dear and by at least three months." How could she have not known until now? His advice was quite stern. "Due to your previous history, you should take things very easy and ensure you take plenty of rest"! It became clear that Grete's many duties looking after so many people and family members must categorically take a back seat. Her priority was now to nurture her growing child.

When Helene arrived from picking Inge up from school, she came into the room. On hearing the news she was ecstatic. "This is the boost that we all need," she exclaimed and wasted no time in sending Grete to bed to acclimatise herself with the news and avoid any symptoms of shock. She waited for Otto to come home from work and warned him "She is in bed, but do not worry, I will be up shortly with a cup of tea."

On hearing the news, Otto clung to his wife as they both cried their tears of joy, and then both prayed to thank god for their little miracle. Within the next 48 hours the rest of the family had been informed and little by little the news sank in. Everyone was elated, particularly Inge. She was so excited to be gaining a cousin, better than a doll any day..

Inge still attended school in Kaukehmen, and while Anita wanted to offer as much support to Grete as possible, she was finding her life complicated with a Hotel In Cranz, a life in Königsberg, a daughter, mother and pregnant sister in Kaukehmen. It was a struggle even though they had secured extra staff for the hotel.

Fortunately, the pregnancy was straightforward and as the due date loomed all the plans were in place for when Grete finally went into labour. The same doctor who diagnosed the pregnancy was present at the birth, ably assisted by the local midwife. Or moreover it was the other way round, as the midwife took control of most of the proceedings. After the relatively short labour of just nine hours, Grete safely delivered a healthy boy. His earthy cries resonated down the corridors of the hospital in Kaukehmen. Otto cried as he held his son for the first time, and Grete was the epitome of a proud and doting mother. They called him Günther, and he was the light of their lives.

Chapter 11

Inge loved living in Kaukehmen and Oma was a guiding light in Inge's life. They often walked along the canal, which linked the rivers Russ and Gilge. Helene remarked that most children are usually too distracted to appreciate walking and nature. It was clear to Helene that the very essence of Kaukehmen was completely exemplified in Inge. She noted how the countryside stretched out before them like a quilted blanket of corn as it swayed first one way and then the next in the gentle breeze. Helene and Inge would often have the whole day mapped out before them. They were only a short distance from the Lithuanian border. Often they would visit the border and look across the steel bridge to the country beyond, imagining the lives of the people who lived there. They Climbed over stiles and rambled through pastures, talking to the farmers as they passed them on the lanes on their way to market.

Inge adored the vast two hectares that the marketplace covered, with the ornate market clock in the centre and the surrounding tall buildings, including two hotels, three cafes and thirteen restaurants. It was the largest village in the lowland area, yet it had a city-like character. Due to the very fertile environment, the town was heavily dependent on the wellbeing of the surrounding agriculture. With very little industry, the population was made up of merchants, shopkeepers and various tradespeople. Inge took an exacting interest in all that she saw and everything her informative Grandmother told her.

"You are not like other children Inge,"

Helene smiled as she spoke to Inge. Helene went on to talk to Inge about her Opa (Julius), whom they both missed dreadfully. She spoke of their courting days when Opa took her to the latest movie in Königsberg. They were always silent movies, of course, and yet sitting for just a few pennies watching that big silver screen gave her a glimpse into another world. She spoke about how they had shared their hopes and dreams as a young couple.

She confided things in Inge that she would not discuss with her daughters. Tears welled up in Helene's eyes as she spoke. Her face wore a forlorn look as she described her pain at losing the only man she had ever loved. Inge voiced her hopes that

"One day *I* will meet a man that will make me feel the same way that Opa made you feel Oma, I will not settle for anything less than perfect love, someone who will show me love every day and never make me sad."

"I hope you do Inge my darling, I hope you do," smiled Helene.

Anita and Herbert were pretty well living full time in the apartment in Königsberg. Out of season when the Hotel was closed, Inge would join her parents in the city at the weekend. Anita and Herbert would take Inge to look at the Schloss and watch the boats on the river and the lake. Inge grew accustomed to jumping on and off trams and eating out once or twice a week. She mainly came to enjoy the famous dish from the city, Königsberger klopse; meatballs served with a white sauce with capers, beetroot and boiled potatoes. Her parents took her to see movies and visit museums; her cultural upbringing was central to both parents. With little intention of having another child, Anita piled her academic ambitions onto her daughter, albeit not accompanied by very much real emotional love. Fortunately for Inge, her father made up for his wife's deficiencies in this area and smothered the little girl with abundant love and affection.

During the school holidays, most evenings were spent in the apartment listening to the radio and Anita would teach Inge the piano. She could be brutal if she missed a note and the piano lid would slam down on Inge's hands if she were not quick enough to move them away. Such were the attempts to instil an aspiration for accomplishment in her daughter. Anita felt determined that her daughter would benefit from a good education and fulfil the dreams and ambitions that Anita once had for herself.

Politically, the people of Prussia were beginning to regret the power they had transferred to Germany all those years ago, as they felt powerless to influence the mood of the nation. It was in the last 12–18 months that the party had witnessed such a rapid rise to power. Although Hitler lost the election in 1932, he gathered support from industry leaders. His right-wing political views were by now well formed. Hitler enjoyed heavy backing from influential industry leaders petrified that communism might take hold in Germany. Being rather dull and lacking personality did not hold back Hitler. As he stood before an audience, something took control of him, and he projected himself outwardly and incited his audience to rapturous adoration through his energy and belief in his ideals.

In January 1933, when Hitler was appointed Chancellor, head of the German government, many Germans believed that they had found the Redeemer for whom they felt their nation searched. At least his portrayal as a cultured gentleman who loved children and dogs worked to convince the masses that he was the man to lead the country into better times.

Conversely, it was a cause of great concern among the inhabitants of the city of Königsberg with their considerable Jewish community. The anti-Semitic undercurrents coming from Germany were tangible, and recently many were feeling persecuted and fleeing to the United States and Great Britain. It was a source of great foreboding that the Nazi Party had taken control of the country. East Prussia did not (on the whole) hold with the same populist beliefs, and many Christians even saw him as the Antichrist. It would be accurate to say that Anita and Herbert held strong views that this man could be the Antichrist. They felt powerless facing the growing hypocrisy that enveloped the country they thought they knew. The couple thought it was incumbent upon them to do their best to live as close to a normal life as possible for the sake of their daughter and their sanity. In spite of what they heard on an increasingly regular basis, none of their concerns were discussed when Inge was within earshot.

The family had word that Walter, who was now married to Betty, had a son Harald. Although Walter's activities gave the family cause for grave concern, Helene still wanted to see her grandson. On these family visits Walter would often seem defensive and elusive and when and if politics was brought into conversation it would inevitably evolve into a fiery argument with Anita at the helm.

Walter was not afraid to defend his position in the SA and insisted that at the end of the First World War, Germany had been stabbed in the back and sold down the river by the rest of Europe with the Treaty of Versailles. The two siblings simply could not agree on the new politics of the day and in general the rest of the family would leave the room.

Walter regularly accused Anita of holding communist views and such was the intensity of the arguments, it soon became apparent to the family that with each quarrel, hostilities between Walter and Anita grew stronger. They resorted to communicating through black stares, and their long looks were cold and bitter. Helene held mixed emotions, she was sad that she saw so little of her son, and his growing family and particularly at Christmas. Yet she too felt a growing mistrust between Walter and the rest of the family and she questioned herself, feeling stunned that her son could follow the path of evil as they saw it, and this disturbed Helene greatly.

Over the next few years, Walter and Betty had five children, Harald, the eldest was born in Rauterskirch, followed by Ursula, Gerhard, Peter and Jürgen who was born during the Second World War. Betty whose maiden name was Krohnert originated from Danzig. She loved her husband very much and was a dutiful wife and even though she had not been brought up in East Prussia, she was content that she was provided for and her husband had a career he loved.

The family settled in Neukirchen where Walter was a driver for the agricultural Minister for their area in East Prussia it was recognised that as he was an early party member he should be rewarded with the relatively prestigious role of chauffeur. Excitement radiated out of Walter everyday as he absorbed the respect that was bestowed upon him from the military and ministerial personnel that he came into contact with on a daily basis.

The sand dunes in Rosehnen, Cranz

The front of the Hotel Blaue Möwe

Dining Room of the Blaue Möwe

The 'Robot' that the Russians built after they knocked down the Schloss.

The seafront at Cranz

Greta holding
Günther

Inge Aged 4

Lotte and Adolf Keller

Chapter 12

As each December crept round, Inge continued to build her lifetime's memories around her most special time of the year, Christmas, and the following is Inge's homage to her childhood Christmas's, written in her own words;-

"December was such a special time to me, there was always snow, always. The double-glazing units in the flat served as a means to decorate the windows, placing cotton wool and twinkling lights behind the sliding window. On 6th December was St Nicholas' Day, and on the evening before I would put my shoes in front of the fire and St Nicholas would come and fill them with small presents in the shoes like chocolate, sweets, biscuits and small toys or fruit. That was the beginnings of the big build up to Christmas of course, and at school, I made an advent calendar and put chocolates behind each door. I would open a door of the calendar every day and felt the sheer excitement that a child always does at that time of year.

The front room was out of bounds to me during the final week before Christmas, and often I was told to spend more time in my bedroom or go to bed as my parents were busy in the front room and the door would be locked. When they were in the room I sometimes tiptoed up to the door and could smell the freshly picked apples and the Pine Tree. The excitement was palpable. On occasions Frau Mallke and her three children, Hilde, Herta and little Gerhard would pop round to take me sledging, the children would whisper together about what would happen when Christmas comes.

One year on Christmas Eve, as usual, I was sent to bed in the afternoon, I woke up suddenly and opened my eyes to find Father Christmas was lying next to me, my heart nearly skipped a beat, and then he left leaving some pfeffer Küchen on the bedside table. When I got up I went running to tell Mutti about it, but she would not believe me, so I ran to fetch the pfeffer Küchen to prove it!

At last, it was here, and I got dressed in my best frock and Mutti announced that Father Christmas had left the front room door open so we could all go in and he might come back later. On the grand piano sat a Christmas tree with real candles on it, under the tree was a Bunter Teller (a plate of Christmas cookies and sweets). I trembled; not knowing how to cope with the excitement of the moment and then Mutti sat down and played 'Heute Kommt der weihnachtsmann' on the piano. Mutti was so creative at this time of the year in making Christmas special with thoughtful touches with decorations and presents. She failed to express love for me in words or hugs, yet she went to great lengths in other ways. The renditions would continue with 'Stille Nacht, Heilige Nacht' and then Mutti would always have to go next door to help Frau Mallke with something, so Papa would take over and play the violin while I ate all the goodies from my Bunter Teller.

Suddenly there would be a knock at the door and Papa would tell me to open the door, I would say

"No you open the door," and the fight continued until I opened the door half hiding behind Papa. Father Christmas stood before me and in a grumpy voice said

"Does Inge Tollkühn live here?" My Papa would reply

"Yes come in" Father Christmas walked into the lounge and sat in the rocking chair, and I had to go and say "Hallo" to him, he asked me if I had been good and looked at my fingernails and asked me if I bit them. He had a ruler in his hand and said to me that if I were bad or had bitten my nails, he would smack me with it, but he never did smack me. Then I had to recite a poem or read from the Bible about the story of Jesus's birth, and then he would open the sack with all his lovely presents, one year there was a sledge, one year a set of skis or skates and one year a dolls house or new clothes. Then Father Christmas had to go because he was so busy and Mutti missed him every time; I could never understand why Father Christmas was so little, other children would argue with me saying that he was big! When he had gone, I would play with my presents and stay up till pretty late, there was a big dinner, and after that Herr und Frau Mallke would come in with all their children and we would play. I never remember what the grownups did, and I never remember going to bed either, Papa said that he always found me asleep among my presents.

On Christmas day all the kids were out with their new gear, sledges or skiing, Papa would hire a horse and all we kids would be towed on our sledges one behind the other, there were bells on the horses' reins, and it would pull us for miles in the snow. After that, we often had a snowball fight and then a hot juice from the stalls in the park with a pfeffer *küchen and then go home, with red cheeks and the snow sticking to our coats and gloves, and Mutti would have a big dinner ready. Sometimes Oma would be there, sometimes Tante Lotte und Onkel*

Adolf, Tante Grete und Onkel Otto or even Tante Behin, (Papa's sister). They are
the most wonderful memories I have.

The winter was her favourite month, with welcome visits to the ice rink where
Inge soon learned to skate on her own. When Herbert and Anita took her
skating, they sometimes took Frau Mallke's children as her husband was
frequently away. The eldest, Hilda, attended school locally, and as Inge was
still going to school in Kaukehmen, they spent only their weekends together.

The following year it became apparent to Anita that the school in Kaukehmen
was not serving the needs of Inge in regards to her musical abilitiy. Anita and
Herbert considered that the time was right to integrate Inge into a school
in Königsberg. The concerned parents took advice from the Mallke family.
They were, of course, quite biased in their viewpoint as their elder children
both attended the local school. So, the following term, it was decided that
Inge would benefit from being placed permanently at The Hans Schemm
Schule in Königsberg. Inge quickly settled in, mostly because having spent so
much time in Königsberg she had made a few friends. Not least Hilde Mallke
who self-appointed herself as Inge's school buddy helping to initiate her into
her new school life. They laughed about how the teachers mistakenly called
Inge, Ingrid, and how frustrated she felt if she was called 'Inga' with a hard
'G' because her name should be pronounced with a soft 'G' Inge.

Inge enjoyed the views from their top floor flat in Königsberg, in particular from sitting on her bedroom windowsill. To the left, she could see a park
and a large hill, while straight ahead she could see two swimming pools, the
one on the left was for children and the one on the right was for adults. A
wooden pier divided them, and in front of the pools, there were about 50
yards of sand consigned for the children to play. Close by there were changing huts and a couple of cafes. Inge begged her parents to take her, and her
Papa often did.

When the winter months came, the pools were iced over. Papa and Onkel
Adolf took her skating, and each held her hands, so she skated between them.
In reality, they dragged her round and kept her upright. However, on occasions, her legs would slide in all directions, and they all laughed as they
slipped to the floor. She loved every minute of the undivided love and attention she received, and there was always music too, booming out from large

speakers at the edge of the ice rink. Even as a little girl, Inge appreciated the loveliness of these times, with music playing in the background, children skating, lots of laughter and the snowflakes falling. It reminded her of a picture postcard.

Frau Mallke permitted her three children to visit the ice rink on one occasion with Inge and her parents. Inge and Hilde enjoyed each other's company and convinced each other they skated better when they both held hands. Anita and Herbert looked after the other two children while keeping half an eye on the two older girls. After they had circuited the iced-over pool a few times, they could hear their names called. Hilde and Inge obediently skated back to the adults, still talking and arranging to walk to school together on Monday.

The two families did see quite a lot of each other. Frau Mallke and Anita had much in common. When her husband was home, the Mallke's were keen to hear some of the political opinions from someone they considered to be more informed than most, Herbert.

They talked about how they were witnessing a worldwide depression. And how Germany was not exempt from the unrest felt across many countries, especially after the Great War where the people still felt the humiliation of their defeat 15 years earlier. They all agreed that the Weimar Republic Government was weak and the people had little confidence in them at this time. They were all apprehensive about how these circumstances were providing the conditions for the rise of the new leader Adolf Hitler and his organisation, the National Socialist German Workers' Party, or Nazi Party for short. They discussed the events of the previous summer, in Königsberg at the Otto-Braun-House. Anita shared with the Mallke's that she had a brother in the party and he had joined the Hitler Youth, shuddering as she explained that they were now almost completely estranged from him. She denounced her brother to her friends in the strongest possible terms. It was apparent to all that Hitler was a spellbinding speaker and convincing in his demeanour. Consequently, he attracted an extensive following of Germans anxious for change. At the Cathedral of Light in 1937 there was an enormous gathering where Hitler spoke to rapturous applause as he promised the disenchanted an improved life and a restored and glorious Germany.

Walter Saul was in the audience.

Chapter 13

Inge's school in Königsberg, the Hans Schemm was renowned for its results with pupils, and Inge was a studious girl. Her friendship with Hilde blossomed, and they spent most of their time in each other's company. Their parents too were firm friends. Although Anita did not like to spend too much time in inconsequential conversation, she had time for Frau Mallke. She was an educated lady and held the same life values as Anita. Equally, she was a Christian as was Anita yet both had Jewish blood and Jewish friends. The distinctions between religions meant little to either in that their underlying belief was in God and Heaven and the need to be a good disciple to Jesus on earth. The fact that the Jews held differing views about Jesus did not influence how they interacted with them. Their measurement of a person was in the way they interrelated with and treated others. They had many discussions about how the Nazi party were using adverse propaganda about Jews to incite hatred, and they had little time nor understanding of it.

Nevertheless, Königsberg was witnessing change, particularly among the Jewish community; many of their shops now confiscated. All Jews were ordered to wear the sign of a Jew. Frau Mallke had a Jewish friend who owned a haberdashery store; she told Anita how her shop had been set on fire the previous week. Also, her children had been rounded up and sent to an all-Jewish school. The divisions were palpable between the communities. It became a great concern to Anita when the authorities informed her that she should no longer accept Jews in her Hotel in Cranz. She categorically refused to do that. Herbert received the standardised sign they were issued and indicated that it would be hung on the veranda of the hotel. Within fifteen minutes of the instruction being handed down, Anita took a hammer to the sign and threw it away.

Herbert wished that she had not done that when during the next morning's radio bulletins came the announcements that Germany was to reject the

Treaty of Versailles. The significance of this move was not lost on Herbert, he knew that under the treaty of Versailles Germany had promised not to arm itself again or build an air force. At the end of the First World War when Germany officially surrendered on November 11th 1918, the treaty was signed. However, Germany was never really happy about one particular clause. Clause 231 was known as the 'guilt' clause and stated that Germany had to bear the responsibility for causing loss of life and damage to property during the war.

Walter and Betty sat listening to the news, Betty bit her lip nervously as she looked across to her husband. Walter adopted an air of reverence as he listened intently to latest developments in rejecting the Treaty of Versailles. The relationship with Walter and the rest of the family had all but broken down now. Walter's views on the direction of Germany and how the Nazi party were on a new path would never coincide with the opinion of the rest of his family. Anita no longer spoke of Walter and would walk out of the room if his name was mentioned, the tension quite palpable. Helene felt tremendous pain. Her voice would tremble at the mere thought of her lost son and she longed to see Walter's children. His family was growing and Helene had word that Betty was pregnant again. Desperate to reach out to Walter yet too afraid of her own daughter's reactions, Helene learned to cope with her grief and feelings. Confused as she felt, Walter was still her son and always would be.

Anita and Herbert sat in silence listening to the broadcast and exchanged concerned glances while rigidly gripping the arms of their chairs in tense forlorn resignation of the events as they heard them. Conscription was going to be reinstated, and Herbert knew it was only a matter of time before he was called to serve in the German Army. The prospect horrified him, not just because he found the possibility of military service objectionable. The whole regime of the Nazi party and Adolf Hitler was utterly abhorrent to him.

Although she was somewhat hostile to the changes being foisted upon them, Anita was mindful that her mother still bore the Jewish name of Saul. Over the last few months, Helene had made an acquaintance with a new gentleman friend called Albert Mertens. This widower in the village in Kaukehman had assumed the responsibility of tending to Helene's garden. He did quite a decent job of keeping it close to the high standards that Julius always espoused. Anita had noticed their growing friendship and embraced the opportunity to bluntly ask Albert if he might consider asking Helene to marry him.

Albert felt quite taken aback. He viewed Helene as a friend, and his intentions were nothing more than that. He explained this to Anita, but Anita had an agenda, she needed to persuade Albert to ask her mother to marry him. It was a way that she could avoid potential persecution if she were to change her name. Albert thought about it for quite a few minutes; Anita had struck a positive chord with him. As Albert stared straight ahead until his eyes dropped down to the wedding ring he still wore as he twisted it with his fingers. Then back into the middle distance as if seeking assurance or confirmation.

Anita leaned on the handle of the spade Albert had been working with in the garden and indicated that a response was necessary straight away. Albert glanced across at Anita as she stared at him. He felt somewhat unnerved by her straightforward approach and domineering stance. After what felt like an eternity to Anita during which no words were spoken, Albert broke the silence.

"Well Junge Frau, you have a smart head on your shoulders. I am not a young man. However, your mother is a good woman. It is not likely that I will be a husband to her in a normal way. That side of my life is over with I am afraid. That said, I would marry your mother and give her my name, she is a good cook, and I can tend her garden. I think that is a fair deal. Now, what happens next? Do I ask her, or shall you tell her?"

He offered a knowing grin to Anita as if compelled to submit, which undoubtedly he had, of course. Anita departed to speak to her mother and prepared her for the impending proposal. Fortunately, Anita had the foresight to dress up the suggestion. How Albert was too shy to ask, what a good idea it would be and how he needed someone to look after him and so did she, he would make no demands on her and she would be rid of the name Saul.

They married within a month, little ceremony followed, and both families were happy to see the match. Helene's papers were changed promptly along with all efforts to eradicate the name, Saul. Helene was left feeling underwhelmed by the proceedings, not the way a bride should feel on her wedding day she thought, even given that it was the second time around for both of them. There was no report in the newspaper of the wedding as there had been when Lotte was married; the authorities now banned newspapers. So as Helene took Albert's arm as they married, they agreed to remain good companions and no more.

Chapter 14
2002 Kuckerneese (Kaukehmen)

Inge had made it clear to Werner who had organised the trip for all the ex-Prussians, that she would not make the trip with them if they did not go to Kuckerneese. Such was the significance of her returning there once more.

Inge was the only person on the coach who had connections to this town, and yet everyone demonstrated extreme patience and empathy at her insistence that the tour went 'off-piste' to accommodate her. This request was far from a whimsical notion; the desire to return burned inside her, as a bird must return to its nest. Talking of birds, one of the sights that struck me was the vast number of storks nesting on the chimney pots, in this part of what is now White Russia. They are an incredible sight.

The day started with a coach drive as usual, but this day we were travelling close to the Lithuanian border. The decision was taken to visit the border itself, or as close to it as we could. We stood by the bridge spanning the River Russ that divides the two countries; it was a stark reminder of the divided cultures and the challenges that the war brought to this area of East Prussia. On the drive to Kuckerneese, we saw shantytowns at the side of the road. It looked like people were living in abject poverty in makeshift houses made with corrugated roofs or planks of wood to protect them from the elements. We stopped in a small town and saw that local people were selling essential homegrown items on a low wall adjacent to a building. They opened up cardboard and newspaper, lay it on the top of the wall and then placed a few measly cabbages or potatoes and even a couple of chickens on the cardboard to sell. The locals observed us with significant misgiving, strangers encroaching on their accepted way of life. It all felt like a forgotten land and was much the same when we finally arrived at the once prosperous and vibrant market town of Kuckerneese or Kaukehmen.

The town was in substantial disrepair, with plaster partly torn from the external facades of most of the buildings, many of which overlooked the once-thriving marketplace of busy shoppers. Decades ago people wandered in and out of the cafés and restaurants, which were now deserted and their architecture was crumbling.

The dusty ground in the marketplace on which we stood was quite bleak. Initially, it was difficult to imagine people walking from shop to shop and sitting chatting on benches watching all the local activity. At the same time, however, one glance at the marketplace tower looking down on us somehow told its own story. It completely contradicted the first impression of desolation, as it remained intact after all those years. The trees had survived and although overgrown, they lined the marketplace, as they always did, like soldiers on guard.

The baker and the butcher's shops were pointed out to us, and for once, nobody made a quick dart for the cemetery, as we had with all the other town stops. These cemetery visits were a procedural drill repeated almost everywhere we went. Of course, if one was to step back and consider the reasons behind the activity, it was clear. The party needed to find their relatives, parents, grandparents, aunts, uncles and cousins whom they buried decades before and not had the chance to visit since. It was quite heart-breaking to witness.

Inge's mission was primarily to find her Oma and Opa's house (Helene and Julius); she was wholly focused on her quest. Having gone through the niceties of explaining which were the various buildings, she started to walk. She did not look back to see if anyone was following; she knew just where to go. Our guide and translator walked with her. Most of the rest of the coach party followed in hot pursuit, keen to witness the sight of their friend potentially reunited with her much-loved childhood home of her grandparents. Inge was well aware that as we reached the house, she may need to convey the reason for our visit to the new inhabitants of this former House of Saul.

Sure enough, as Inge reached the picket fence which was surprisingly still intact although no longer white, rather a faded grey wood, which looked in desperate need of a good lick of paint, Inge held back for a moment. Recognising that Inge was keen to see inside the building, the interpreter went to speak to the inhabitants, an old Russian couple, man and wife. She explained to the couple that Inge's family once lived there and Inge had spent most of her early years living with her grandparents in that house. The little old lady listened intently, glancing over at Inge as she heard the story. Slowly she started to cry and exclaimed to the interpreter how sorry she was that she was living in Inge's house. It was a touching and thought-provoking moment.

The interpreter, in turn, listened to the old couple's account of events after the war. They explained that the Soviets had broadcast to the people of Russia that they should come to this new land. They should make a fresh start; there was good agricultural land and beautiful houses in which to live. The tears rolled down her cheeks as the old lady explained the story. Inge put her arms around her as if to reassure her that she bore her no grudge and she too was very emotional.

After a few moments, the lady scuttled into her house, leaving her embarrassed looking husband to point out their prized hens and chicks. When she returned, the old Russian lady had changed into what was probably her best dress. The humble soul then welcomed everyone into her home, and we, Inge's immediate family, respectfully entered. Inge pointed out where she and the other children used to sleep when they visited. The old lady and her husband watched us in bewilderment. The lady had removed the scarf from her head. The gentleman wore a thick dirty grey shirt buttoned up to the top and large jam jar bottom glasses. His long wrinkled face bore little expression, and when he opened his mouth, his rotten teeth made me wonder how he managed to eat. What must he have been making of this invasion into his personal space on this hot sunny afternoon?

Stairs that once led to upstairs bedrooms were now blocked off as the house had since been divided into several cottages or flats. The air was stifling, and the surroundings gloomy. Concrete floors showed little evidence of a rug, nor were there any soft furnishings within sight. The paint was peeling off the walls, and old worn curtains hung loosely at the small windows. The kitchen table looked as though constructed from rough building planks. I felt embarrassed that we were invading this couple's space and thoughts of our home slipped into my mind. How lucky and privileged we were to live in a comfortable home back in the UK, I must take nothing for granted in future. I wondered if they had grandchildren that came to visit and what they thought about how their grandparents lived.

We went back into the bright sunlight, and each took deep breaths. Although hot, the air was at least circulating outside. We admired the baby chickens in the garden and Dennis, my husband, was invited to pick apples off the tree that once belonged to his great grandfather. The kitchen garden was still a large part of their food source as it had been for the Saul family many decades earlier.

Very mindful of the abject poverty we witnessed each of us rustled in our bags looking for any food or sweets we might leave them. Naturally, we gave them some roubles in recognition of their kindness in showing us around their home. A photograph opportunity followed, and after about forty minutes, the interpreter beckoned us out. We needed to be mindful of the time and not least, the immense tolerance of the rest of the coach party, some of whom were patiently waiting outside the picket gate from where they watched events unfold. Others were wandering around the town while we all visited my mother-in- law's former home.

A local lady who had watched us in the garden as she passed by and waved to us, beckoned us to follow her. She lived in appalling poverty, even worse than what we had just witnessed. She put down her basket of recently picked beans and opened a rusty fence to show me her chickens with lots of chicks; she was so proud of them and was desperate to share them with us. It never fails to astonish me how those people with the very least in the world are the happiest to share. They show immense pride in what they do have – a lesson there for us all I daresay.

The guide pointed out other landmarks in Kuckerneese as we strolled back to the coach in the searing heat of midday. We each comforted Mum in one small way or another as she linked arms with Dennis, my husband, needing that extra bit of support after a very emotional visit.

It was time to climb aboard the coach once more, and thankfully the next planned stop was lunch. En route, we passed rivers where we could see women washing their laundry as in times gone by, while their children played and swam nearby in the water. It was thought-provoking to imagine how this once prosperous land had been permitted to fall into such decline. It felt almost as if the Russians had taken what was not theirs, so in response, the land turned its back on them and forbade the new inhabitants the privilege of flourishing. I partly jest of course as in reality the reasons will hold far more complex political wranglings than I am equipped to unravel. A good historian would no doubt communicate in a couple of carefully articulated paragraphs. Nevertheless, it was a sad sight to see.

After about 30 minutes of watching local life through the glass of a moving vehicle, we arrived at a roadside restaurant and were soon sitting under sun umbrellas and sipping a large beer; time to reflect, take stock, some photographs and discuss the next destination on our trip.

Chapter 15

Herman and Henriette Tollkühn did not feature heavily in Inge's life; she had few lasting memories of spending time with them. When Herman died, there was not a resounding shock in hearing the news. His paintings in the Königsberg Art Gallery were auctioned off along with his house and all its furniture. Herbert had no idea that Henriette was planning to return with her daughter to Italy and wanting to be rid of everything to make a clean break. Apart from Behin, there had not been a great deal of contact with Herbert since his marriage to Anita. Herbert had to accept this fact. Consequently, he turned his attentions to his wife and family even more than he did before.

Inescapably Inge would have to do piano practice on the baby grand piano over which was an oil painting by her grandfather Herman Tollkühn. Anita had been swift to claim this beautiful piece. The picture made a great impression on Inge, so much so that Inge would remember the picture her whole life long. Recalling every detail of it and often wishing that she could emulate her grandfather's style, precision and attention to detail. Mostly Inge would prefer to play out in the street with Hilde, and the political undercurrent had little effect on the two playmates. They made other friends and felt blessed to share each other's company so close to home. Anita would wave a white towel out of the window, and that was the signal to come in. Inge obediently returned home.

The Hans Schemm Schule was a highly disciplined house of education and compliant with the authorities of the day. One morning an assembly was called, and Inge and Hilde along with their peers gathered in the school hall as instructed. They were expecting some VIPs for the day. A few of the children from each year were selected. Inge was one of them. Each chosen child was ordered to form a line in the road just outside the gates of the school and stand still until someone arrived. It seemed to take an eternity in Inge's opinion, and it was nearly lunchtime. Her tummy was grumbling, and she started to shuffle her feet impatiently. One of the teachers shouted for her to remain still. Suddenly the loud engine noises of one or two large cars could be heard driving closer and closer. Inge squinted in the bright sunlight to see who was in the vehicle. Inge was at the far end of the line. It was difficult maintaining her position and looking down towards the line of cars to see who was coming.

Everyone appeared to be in uniform and Inge could not decipher one person from the other. Until one of them, with a little black moustache, seemed to be standing in his vehicle, then he promptly stood down and walked in front of everyone else. He stood for a moment and spoke to the headmaster and some of the teachers and then slowly he walked down the line of children, and one by one he shook hands with them. Inge was the last hand that he shook before he went back towards his car. As he left he raised his right arm upright at an angle in front of him. Some of the men in uniform did the same, and then he entered the vehicle, and slowly the entourage moved off down the road and out of sight.

After this encounter, the children were told to go in for lunch very quickly as the rest of the school were already eating. They needed to join their afternoon classes as speedily as possible. That afternoon, Inge and Hilde linked arms as the two ten-year-olds made their way home from school. Both felt that they had been a part of an extraordinary experience that day and not knowing really what to make of it. Inge could not wait to tell Anita what had happened,

"Mutti, Mutti, today a man came to our school, and he was in uniform, and he had a funny little moustache, and I had to stand in line, and he shook my hand. Who was he, Mutti?" Anita turned on her daughter and replied brusquely,

"Well, you shook hands with the devil, and your hand will drop off!"

Inge described her mother's words to me on the many occasions; how she felt alarmed and confused and looked down at her hand. There was no explanation as to the identity of the man, and the matter was not discussed again. Yet, every day poor Inge woke up and wondered if that would be the day that her hand would drop off.

It was many days later that friends told Inge that the man who had come to her school that day was Adolf Hitler. The reason for his visit, they later learned, was to investigate the land and surrounding territories and fathom the advantages of gaining access to East Prussia. Its amazing Baltic Port of

Königsberg did not often freeze over in the winter, and this was a key factor in transporting corn and other produce over to Germany. His problem was, of course, that Poland stood between Germany and East Prussia. This was an issue he felt he needed to resolve.

Chapter 16

Helene continually struggled to come to terms with the monumental blow received from Walter's actions. She questioned her own parental skills as she also witnessed Anita's apparent lack of maternal instinct, yet Grete had it in abundance. Both Helene and Herbert did their utmost to compensate for any love and hugs that Inge did not receive from her strict mother. Inge experienced her mother's sharpness on many occasions. Anita would be quick to chastise her the minute she stepped out of line, and yet Inge never answered her mother back, not once. Helene watched and said little, not wanting to upset the status quo as she loved her children and grandchildren equally. She and Inge loved the times when they were able to help take care of little Günther. As far as Anita was concerned, Inge remained in awe of the way that her Mutti handled matters of business and held such strong views on things that Inge failed to understand as a child and her respect for her mother never waivered.

Everyone else pretty well fell into line with Anita too. At the hotel, in the summer months, Lotte and Adolf frequently complained of being overworked. Once they even voiced an opinion that Anita should play a more significant part in its running. They were met with an exhaustive and protracted response, and Anita completely validated all the reasons why she needed to be in Königsberg, mainly for Inge's education. In the end, the Kellers would be left feeling selfish for having spoken out and meekly backed down from their position on the subject, as they would on most topics. Herbert often cringed as he listened to his wife when she started to rant and he and Helene would take Inge out of the room if she were within earshot. Grete and Helene would merely share a knowing glance and then fall in line with everyone else.

Inge, luckily, enjoyed sports, because the school was insistent that all the children should be physically fit. Inge and Hilde both became members of the school running team. They would run in small groups around the playing fields belonging to the school, but she excelled at the 200 metres. The name Tollkühn means 'superhero' and her school friends would loudly cry out to Inge,

"Come on Superhero, you can win!"

Increasingly with each year that passed, they would be encouraged to run against members of other schools. Often they travelled over to Marienburg, Osterode and up to Kurische Nehrung, a spit of land 98 kms long which separated the land from the Baltic Sea. This long thin curved dune made for challenging terrain and offered a fantastic training ground. While the northern section was under the control of Russia, the southern section linked to the mainland and was close enough to Königsberg to make the training manageable. There was a hope that Inge would be a part of the national running team.

In the Summer of 1938, the community in Kaukehmen unexpectedly received the news that the name of their town was changing to Kuckerneese. This change was after the demise of the small domain nearby of the same name. It took the population some time in accustoming to the momentous change. While some took the view that it was social evolution, others decried the loss of their identity and significance within the wider area. Only the Town Council had any say in the decision to change the name, resulting in a degree of irritation within the community. The pronouncement was arbitrary, and that was that.

The Jewish population in Königsberg prior to the rise of the Nazi regime was approximately 13,000. Now, along with the Polish minorities, the Jews were classed as _Untermensch_ (socially inferior). By 1938 the Jewish population had shrunk to just over 2000 and then came a devastating blow. The new Synagogue of Königsberg, was destroyed during <u>Kristallnacht</u> , (the night of broken glass). This was when the <u>Sturmabteilung</u> <u>(SA) stormtroopers</u>, took it upon themselves to destroy anything that was Jewish. The German authorities just looked on and did not intervene. In the following days, another 500 Jews left the city.

Just as everyone was adjusting to that lightning bolt of local news, an envelope was delivered to the top floor flat at 28 Schleiermacherstrasse, Königsberg. It had a military stamp on the front and addressed to Herr Herbert, Erich, Gerhard, Tollkühn. The postman handed it to Anita as she was leaving to meet Inge as she came home from school. She stood for 30 seconds on the staircase to their flat, just staring at the letter as if might disintegrate in her hands. Her heart pounded, and she felt cold beads of perspiration on her whole face and neck. As she continued to look at the envelope, her hands shook until Inge came bounding up the stairs,

"Hallo Mutti. I ran all the way. I am so hungry. Do we have cake? I am soo hungry,"

Anita failed to respond. Inge looked at her and tilted her head to one side as she looked at her mother intently before being ushered inside the flat and told to wash her hands before tea.

Within the hour, Frau Mallke arrived with her children. She knocked on the door exclaiming that she wanted to share some news with Anita; many of the men in the street had received their conscription papers. Anita had an inclination of what she was going to say, and so they sent the children to Inge's bedroom to do some homework. On cue, Frau Mallke informed Anita "My husband has received his conscription papers into the army." Anita did not respond and just nodded towards the dresser where the letter sat propped up, waiting for its recipient to come and open it when he arrived home from work. Frau Mallke clutched her face with her hands. In response, Anita placed her arms around her friend's shoulders to reassure her but also to comfort herself.

Both women appreciated the hopelessness of the situation; the political climate was out of control now. That week even more Jews had fled before the inevitable rounding up. They discussed the Polish people who were receiving similar persecution.. Why? They couldn't accept that this was all the actions of one irrational man, Adolf Hitler, and to think that he was Austrian. How could he represent East Prussia? The Prussian people were above this nonsense.

"For goodness sake, we speak our dialect, we do not think like those people in Germany" announced Anita.

"Did you know that the Bornstein Family fled last week into France, and their father served in the last war. What does that tell you?" Responded Frau Mallke.

Looking up to the ceiling, Anita clasped her hands together, looking or hoping for guidance from the almighty. Her eyes flicked between her friend and the envelope still sitting on the sideboard in silent attendance.

Herbert had little time to come to terms with his orders. It was common knowledge that some men who had not cooperated with and accepted their orders were bundled off to concentration camps. The Otto-Braun-House had been requisitioned and became the headquarters of the military. In turn, they used the house to imprison and torture opponents. Herbert had to report there at the end of the week. Herr Mallke received orders detailing his movements in advance in guarding the Russian border, he already knew that, but Herbert was unsure of his destination.

Chapter 17

The family gathered to pray, share their thoughts and express their concern for each other. All the men were expecting that they would receive their orders. Otto and Adolf were waiting for a letter any day now, and the prospect of military service was a real concern to Adolf. He was a gentle soul and loved all God's creatures. What might they expect him to do? Adolf didn't want to be trained to kill; that was not in his nature. He knew that any unwillingness to participate would only result in the worst kind of punishment. Adolf hoped and prayed that his baking skills might save him from any potential combat situations.

There was so little time for the family to come to terms with the events unfolding before them. So much needed to happen in such a short space of time. Anita and Herbert talked late into the night about all the possible consequences of what the current political climate might unveil. Everyone dismissed any likelihood of having to face actual armed combat. They surmised that Adolf Hitler wanted to show the rest of the world that Germany was now stable again. He needed to show strength to the Russians who had forces close to the border with East Prussia, and that Germany refused to be placed on the back foot any longer after their humiliation at the hands of the allies at the end of the Great War. As they endeavoured to draw their conclusions, they looked at each other in turn. Fear and resentment was written all over their faces; no need to express their sentiment in words.

Kuckerneese was uncomfortably close to the Russian border, and Königsberg no longer felt like it offered the protective shelter it once did. Fortunately Herbert was permitted quite frequent contact with his family as he underwent his training in military service. He conveyed his wish for Anita and Inge to take the family from Kuckerneese and move to the relative safety of the Harz Mountains in Northern Germany until he was more sure of the political situation with Russia. He knew people there who would help them find a flat to rent, possibly a job for Anita and a school for Inge. Initially, this seemed a ludicrous suggestion, but on consultation with the rest of the family, all agreed that to have a bolt hole for even a short time seemed a sensible decision. Lotte, Helene and Grete would all visit at a moment's notice and the decision would at least satisfy Herbert while he was away from his family.

Inge was distraught to be leaving her long-time friend, and they promised to write often. Anita assured Frau Mallke that they would be the very first people to be invited to their flat in the rugged terrain of the Harz Mountains once they had settled into their temporary home. True to her word, they were requested to visit within five weeks of arriving in the mountains. Autumn leaves were falling from the deciduous trees of rowan, silver and downy birches. The greenery was taken over by the magnificence of the spruce trees all around them.

The children spent their days in the forest and played happily; they felt carefree and somewhat removed from the world that was starting to close in around them. As they played a dull greyness descended among the trees, and a crisp autumn breeze prickled their faces while they collected pinecones and explored the forests. They searched the area trying to work out where the ski runs would soon carve between the trees.

Their mothers sat and drank herbal tea and exchanged views, news and concerns for their husbands, both of whom were now stationed on the Russian border. Frau Mallke brought news that most of the Jews were now leaving the city. Anita felt grateful that her mother no longer bore the name of a Jew. Thoughts of her brother entered her mind; what part was he playing in all of this? She blinked slowly as though to shift the vision from her mind.

On the Russian border where their husbands were, reports indicated that there was no significant movement of Russian troops in the area. The women felt optimistic that the current climate would settle and life would hopefully resort back to normal within a few months.

Helene and Grete were over in Cranz and wrote frequently, and at the end of the short visit from the Mallke family, mother and daughter were alone in the Harz Mountains. Inge went to school, and Anita had a job locally, helping to organise a library and music room for the visiting schools in the holidays; she enjoyed the role immensely. Winter was drawing in, and she knew that as soon as the first snows bore a firm enough base, the early skiers would be out in force.

Inge quickly learned to ski and due to her sporting aptitude rapidly became a proficient skier. She was fearless and would undertake ski jumps which were more suited to far more advanced skiers. Inge started to take risks with these ski jumps and one day she fell badly. She managed to ski home but complained to her mother that she had a deep pain in her thigh. Anita put hot and cold compresses on the offending area and told her to slow down on the skiing for a few days. After a week, the pain did not subside and became increasingly worse; the next day, Anita took her to the doctor. On examination, the doctor told Anita to take her immediately to the hospital. He was diagnosing osteomyelitis, an infection of the bone, which can often cause the bone to die, and was at that time considered to be incurable.

Anita speedily bundled Inge into a taxi; there was no time wasted as they negotiated the hairpin bends through the forest so that she could reach the nearest hospital. The reception team admitted her with a degree of haste. Her mother worked with the nursing staff to relax Inge and settle her into a ward. Anita strived to comfort her daughters' growing anxiety. After a short while sitting with her and talking positively to her in her usual matter of fact way, Anita left for the night and promised the frightened young girl that she would return in the morning. Inge felt like she could survive anything if she had her mother's love.

The nurses were starting to perform their rounds and ask everyone if they would like a hot chocolate before bedtime. Suddenly the Consultant scurried onto the ward; he wanted to examine Inge. Nursing staff quickly drew the curtains around the bed, and the ward sister stood in attendance as the surgeon poked and prodded Inge's leg. It was a painful experience as he was ham-fisted in his procedure and saw an injury rather than a patient. He looked carefully at her charts, announcing that the infection in the bone was significant. He was very sorry, but he was going to have to amputate her leg the next morning.

Inge felt petrified and cried as the Consultant left the ward swiftly, having delivered his bad news. Inge knew that she needed her mother's support and so quickly collected herself. She pleaded with the nurse, "Please, please, get a message to my mother." Fortunately, Inge chose to beseech a nurse with compassion, and so the nurse did send a message to her mother. At 11 pm that evening Anita arrived and brought with her a great big bag. When Inge realised that her mother was going to stay with her the night, she felt comforted and started to relax just a little.

At 6 am the following morning, the theatre staff arrived to take Inge down to the operating theatre. They had hardly made it through the double doors onto the ward when Anita took her big bag and started to beat the staff with it. Incensed as she was, Anita used all the force she could muster to fight the two men away from her daughter. Anita aimed high and then low with the bag, making it clear that she meant business. After a few minutes of being at the receiving end of these incessant beatings from Anita, much like a wild animal protecting her young, the hospital staff called the police.

The police insisted on being impartial and contended that the whole case be referred to the courts. In the process, they wanted to know everything about Anita. Why was she currently residing in the Harz Mountains? Was she hiding from someone or something? They insisted on examining all her papers and even her marriage certificate; soon spotting that her maiden name was Saul. The next questions proceeded, was she a Jew? Hours of interrogation followed and eventually Anita, who was quite bombastic in her arguments, managed to convince the authorities that she was a Christian and not a Jew. When she was able to recite large sections of the New Testament, the name was of no consequence she assured them of that.

So, the court date was set, Herbert was called to attend and granted temporary leave from his duties, and Anita and Inge were so grateful and comforted to see him. While Inge remained in hospital, husband and wife participated in the court hearing the following day. The judge decided that three of the best consultants in Königsberg had to examine Inge and each had to reach the same conclusion that she should have her leg amputated, before the operation could go ahead. The Consultants were summoned, and in the event, there was no such collaboration of views! And with medication, the infection slowly subsided. While damaged, and leaving a permanent hole in the femur, the bone slowly started to recover, and her leg was saved!

Inge's recuperation benefited further from spending the summer months in the mountains; receiving visits from family and hearing the latest news. Anita and Inge were happy there; they both loved it so much. Only by listening to odd snippets of the news reports, they heard that Germany had signed a pact with the Soviet Union. This came as quite a shock to most people, as both countries came from the opposite ends of the political spectrum. On August 23rd, a Treaty of non-aggression started, and this gave them terrific comfort that Herbert would soon be home. The pact was intended to provide Stalin with the opportunity to rebuild his forces. While neither party trusted each other, they agreed that if there were a war, they would split the

European territories between them afterwards. The pact meant that both countries could breathe easier.

However, Germany marched on Poland on September 1st. The next news they heard was that England had declared war on Germany two days later. Their world as they knew it appeared to disintegrate before their eyes, it was the worst possible news, and Anita felt even more determined to be near her family so they returned to Königsberg the very next day.

Chapter 18

The family made the trip over from Kuckerneese and Cranz to welcome Inge and Anita back from their self-imposed exile in the Harz Mountains. It had been a long period away and given Anita much time to reconcile her thoughts about the political climate as well as to nurse her very poorly daughter back to health. The hole in her thigh would never heal they had been told, but at least she still had her leg, it had been touch and go, and everyone celebrated the good news. Grete and Günther, along with Helene and Lotte were relieved at their safe return and questioned Anita's decision in going in the first place. They were met with Anita's fast response as always and wished they could retract their remarks, but too late. Anita did not give up her elongated diatribe on the subject of parental decisions and how she knew best and the numerous threats in Königsberg at the time of their departure.

Otto and Adolf were summoned to the Russian frontier; Adolf had his wish and was on mess duty, which suited his disposition. The pact that Germany and Russia held meant that the men defending the Prussian border with Russia were remote from the rest of the war. And generally day to day there was little news of what was happening outside of their kingdom. The family shared the story that the entire Zomm family had made their escape, and at that time, they were not sure where they were. The news had distressed Helene greatly; she was concerned for the health of her elderly father and her brothers would all have been in great danger had the Nazi army found their whereabouts. Helene declared that she was relieved that she no longer bore the name Saul. The women members of the family stood together and poignantly nodded in silent agreement.

Inge resumed her schooling at the Hans Schemm Schule and was welcomed back like the 'superhero' her name depicted. Hilde hugged her, and everyone wanted a first-hand account of the leg episode as children often do and wanted to see the evidence of the hole in her leg for themselves. Inge felt comforted to be loved by so many people, and it gave her the fresh confidence that she needed. A spirit, which her mother invariably managed to dissipate each time she harangued her daughter for some misdemeanour or other.

As the months passed, they strived to settle back into some normality. The war was happening far away from them, and there was a detachment, which stemmed from the fact that only propaganda reached them. The expectation was that the war would be over sooner rather than later. One Thursday afternoon Anita suggested that they should go up to Cranz at the weekend, it had been a long time since they were there. Anita was keen to see how the hotel was bearing up and how Lotte was coping. There were hardly ever any guests visiting, and she wanted to survey the situation for herself. Anita met Inge from school, and they caught the next available train to Cranz. Bags in hand, Inge was excited, and she looked forward to the fresh air that only Cranz could offer. Even in autumn, the weather was sunny, and the days still felt reasonably long.

On arrival, they faced overgrowth in the garden that Adolf would never have permitted just a year earlier. Lotte greeted them warmly, and her home help was dutifully present to make sure that the house looked presentable. There were no wages to pay her anymore. She just held a strong sense of loyalty and Anita was grateful for her devotion. The Hotel cat came running towards them, his chest vibrating with every purr and rubbing up against Inge's legs as he did so. Inge remarked that he looked thinner,. She sat and stroked him and it felt good to be back. Following a warm meal washed down with a bottle of Riesling, the two sisters sat and talked about the war, the business or lack of it and pondered over the possibilities of shutting the hotel up altogether. They decided that it would not be wise to decide on a whim, and they should retire for the night before they embarked on the second bottle that sat so temptingly on the sideboard.

Inge awoke early and volunteered to collect brötchen for breakfast. She was eager to help with the chores so that she could go to the beach as soon as they were completed. Inge noticed that her mother was in a good mood and so she was even more keen to please her. She was happily going about her chores when they received a visitor who had heard of their arrival the previous evening. The Bürgermeister was interested in talking to Anita about her plans for the hotel. As town mayors go, he was probably one of the most interfering. He saw it as part of his duties to establish the intention of all the businesses in the coming months.

Life was indeed far from ordinary, and the Bürgermeister felt it was his responsibility to build the town plan. He would then share it with everyone else, and no doubt make himself look efficient in the eyes of the authorities. After 15 minutes in Anita's company, he began to regret his eagerness. The poor man considered he had been in a metaphorical boxing ring with this profoundly bright yet highly dogmatic lady who was yet only in her early thirties. He spent the next 20 minutes doing his utmost to extract himself from the meeting. He felt she had questioned his interpretations of the war. As much as the gentleman tried to assure her of his intentions, she verbally battered the unfortunate man until he managed to beat a hasty retreat.

Anita sat back in amusement, having watched the Bürgermeister shuffle his way out of the house. Then she called Inge and told her that as soon as she had eaten some lunch, she should go and spend some time at the beach. Inge did not need telling twice, and after gobbling her food, and promising her mother she would not be late, Inge wandered into the front garden, breathing in the fresh air and blinking against the bright sunlight. Thoughtfully looking at her surroundings, and feeling thankful for a beautiful day, she made her way across the lawn. As she walked, she noticed how large the cherry trees had grown and slowly made her way through the small copse of trees. Delicate cobwebs hung between the branches and gently caressed her face as she disturbed their silky webs. They tickled her nose, so she started to walk with her arm outstretched to push them aside until she eventually wandered out into the openness of the beach.

The sand was relatively warm in the afternoon sun, and Inge took off her shoes and socks as she combed the terrain for amber on the beach. She diligently searched between the dunes, showing immense patience in her endeavours. Inge was determined to uncover a more significant piece than the one she had clutched in her hand from her previous find. She knelt onto her knees and sifted the sand between her fingers as she absentmindedly reflected on the morning's events. Inge hoped that when she returned to the Hotel later, that her mother's mood would be equally agreeable as when she left.

Inge so enjoyed the peace and tranquillity that the beach in Cranz offered, she felt safe, and the war was a long way away. Inge had little understanding of the war and questioned it even less. In her mind, the less she knew, the less there was to feel concerned about; unless she thought something was affecting her family.

Inge's coat was undone and flapped in the breeze. A shiver came over her as she looked out to sea at the glistening of the sun on the rippling waves. Inge turned to her left peering along the coastline and squinting in the bright light. The sun was lower in the sky now, and she casually observed the gentle sway of the trees in the breeze in the distance.

As she watched her surroundings, she could see the silhouette of a man with the sun behind him. He was strolling across the sand in her direction. Inge could not decipher who the man was, yet knew he must be coming towards her. He did not deviate in direction, moving steadily closer, not faltering. Then as the shadow grew larger and just as she was beginning to feel a little unnerved by this man, Inge realised his identity and jumped up and started to run towards him. "Papa, Papa, Mein Papa," she tearfully cried out as she ran towards her Papa and gave her father the biggest hug. He was sweeping her off her feet, almost with a single-arm action. Herbert swung her round in a circle, just as he used to when she was a little girl.

Herbert was granted weekend leave, and he had been able to get word to Anita just three days ago. It all made perfect sense to Inge now, why her mother had been in such good humour. Her father wanted to know all about her leg recovery, and their time in the Harz Mountains. Inge asked him about what his duties entailed. Herbert assured her that there was little for him to do. He was responsible for defending the Prussian border against the Russians, and because they had made a pact, he thought it highly unlikely that he would see any action as far as the rest of the war was concerned.

Father and daughter sat on the sand together for over an hour talking, sharing their life's experiences. While Herbert spared Inge details of what he was experiencing, he took time to explain the bright side of army life, even if he did have to exaggerate the few good points as he saw them. Herbert made sure to remind Inge what a beautiful girl she was and how proud her Papa was of her. His brave little girl, how much he missed her, and she was so special.

Inge lapped up the sheer love and adoration her father exhibited. It had been a long time since she was made to feel so worthy of the respect he showed her. Her mother was critical of her daily and rarely was she allowed to hold an opinion of her own. So to have her father ask her questions and be interested in her point of view, was quite confidence building in Inge. She rose in stature, gleaming as he bestowed compliments and approval upon her. Inge wanted this time with her father to never end. Just the two of them walking and talking on the beach and sharing the last year or so together.

As the sun started to set, they strolled back to the Hotel where Mutti was waiting with Tante Lotte and dinner was ready to be served.

Saturday was a relaxed day where the family talked and tended to small jobs around the hotel and went for a long walk. Sunday, after attending church, was spent relaxing, playing board games and chatting, and of course, Monday was a school day. So, on Sunday afternoon after they had all enjoyed a hearty lunch, the family packed their bags and bid farewell to Lotte. Anita's dutiful sister was planning to shut up the hotel in the next few days and head back to Kuckerneese. It was a long walk back to the main station in Cranz, with few words spoken, and Herbert seemed somewhat detached. Anita considered he was heavy in thought and reticent to discuss his imminent departure back to barracks. His leave was only for the weekend, and nobody wanted to think about what happened next. Moreover, Herbert was forbidden to discuss it; as a consequence, nobody discussed anything at all.

As they approached the station, Herbert stopped and said to Anita that he would catch up with her in a few minutes. He wanted a couple of moments alone with Inge. As this father-daughter bond was nothing new to Anita, she grudgingly agreed and told them to hurry up, or they would all miss the evening train to Königsberg.

Suddenly Herbert turned and took hold of Inge's hand and said,

"Meine Liebe, I want you to have this." He removed his wedding ring from his finger and gave it to Inge. She looked up at him feeling confused and asked him,

"But why, Papa?" He replied that he had no need of it while in service and he wanted her to have it, and also his watch. Herbert carefully removed his watch from his wrist, and by now Inge was entirely at odds with his actions, which were quite out of character. "Listen," he said, "none of us knows what is going to happen in the coming months and I want to know that you are looking after these for me while I am away. I have no need for them where I am going, and I want you to look after them for me until I come back."

Inge accepted his reasoning and agreed that she would look after them for him as she looked up at him in complete admiration. Herbert smiled in response and squeezed her hands as she clutched the three treasures, her amber, her father's wedding ring and his watch. She held her poignant gifts tightly in her hand close to her heart.

On arrival at Königsberg station, Herbert sensed the atmosphere in the city was changed, and he noted the damage to various buildings that were previously owned by the Jewish community. With a deep breath and a determined smile, he guided his family across the road and along the streets leading to Schleiermacherstrasse. This return was his first visit since receiving his papers, and it was an emotional return to the home his family had shared from the very beginning. It held so many happy memories. He watched Inge as she climbed the stairs and recalled the little girl who had attempted to run up the stairs two at a time. Now, she had turned into a young teenager, and he could see the woman she would one day become and viewed her with such pride.

It was Herbert's greatest wish to escort Inge to school the next morning, which he did. She took hold of his arm as he walked her to the front door in full uniform. Then came the moment of goodbye. Inge clung to him as he took hold of both her arms and assured her that he would be home just as soon as he was granted leave again and that he would write as often as he always had in the time since his conscription. He kissed her forehead, clasped her hands and clutched them to his lips. Again she embraced her father, not wanting to let him go until he pulled away and tenderly pushed her towards the main entrance door. Herbert backed away slowly, not leaving her gaze and blowing her a kiss as she became swept along with the morning rush into school. He kept watching, till she was no longer in sight, then gently wiping away the damp tracks down his face, he slowly started to walk back to the flat where Anita waited to bid her farewells.

Inge was disinclined to permit her schoolfriends to see that she was so distressed, they, of course, had no idea that he was her father and immediately the girls wanted to interrogate her as to who was her gorgeous boyfriend? How did she get such a good-looking lad? Where did they meet? The irony of the suggestion lightened the moment somewhat for Inge, and she chuckled as she replied that he was her Papa. How could they think such a thing, yet secretly she was quite thrilled that all her friends were so admiring of her father. Then the school bell rang, and they all walked briskly towards class, Inge swallowing the lump in her throat, and eagerly scouring the crowd for her friend Heidi. She needed to share the weekend's events with her dearest friend.

Chapter 19

Following Germany's triumphant march on Poland, the Nazis turned to France, which they quickly occupied also. Walter Saul was among the early German soldiers to arrive on June 14th 1940, the government had been overwhelmed and departed on 10th June. As the soldiers paraded down the Champs Élysées, Walter chauffeured one of the military generals, glorifying with everyone else in the brilliance of the swift defeat of Paris. The Nazis were feeling confident in their progress, as they had beaten France into submission in just six weeks. It was a massive shock to England and the rest of Europe. However, Hitler knew that his expanding army needed resources and so, searching for more oil, they invaded Northern Africa too.

Of course, they knew that Ukraine had plenty of oil beneath their soil, but this was in Soviet hands. The allies had built a successful blockade of goods reaching Germany, and the people were beginning to suffer. In World War One, the most significant cause of defeat was not military power but a blockade of food, leaving the German people in near starvation. Hitler knew this and did not want the mistake repeated.

In Russia over the last few years, the Red-Banner Baltic Fleet was developed, previously relying on Tsarist warships. The Soviets expanded their fleet in the 1930s and subsequently used their newfound capabilities to threaten the Baltic States. They even attacked Norway when they refused to sign a "pact of mutual assistance." The parents of one young sailor, Alexander Marinesko, were proud to witness their son climb the ladder in the Soviet navy. He was promoted in March 1936 to Lieutenant and then to Senior Lieutenant in November 1938. By mid-1940 Alexander Marinesko was appointed Commander to what was declared the best submarine in the Baltic Fleet, the M-96. His future was undoubtedly secure, and he relished his position among the naval hierarchy of Imperial Russia.

Alexander Marineskui was born in 1913 in Odessa in the Ukraine of a Romanian father who was a sailor and his mother a Ukrainian peasant woman named Tatiana. His father had fled to Imperial Russia after beating up an officer and being condemned to death for mutiny, Marineskui then escaped and ended up settling in Odessa, Russia. Alexander's father proceeded to make his name sound more Russian by changing it from Marineskui to Marinesko. Having lived among Bulgarians, Romanians, Gypsies, Armenians, Russians and Jews, he carried a strong Yiddish accent that he was well aware of but never managed to erase.

From a young age, Alexander's strong links to the sea determined his maritime future; his father influenced him considerably talking about his sailing travels. Alexander had barely reached the age of 13 when he graduated, such was his determination, although he would have preferred a merchant sailor role, destiny took him to the seaworthy technical school from where his future was sealed.

The Soviet high command of the Baltic Fleet decided that the M-96 which Alexander Marinesko commanded, should be sent initially to the Caspian Sea to serve as a training boat. This order, however, could not be accomplished because of the German blockade of Leningrad, and in the early days of the war, Alexander saw no significant action. He performed his duties in good faith and became a candidate for Soviet party membership. But Alexander had one particular problem, not so rare in Russia in those days; he liked to drink. The fact that he had a couple of failed marriages behind him may well have exacerbated his fondness for drink.

Russia and Germany made their pact with their fingers crossed behind their backs, and neither had any intention of sticking to it. Each wanted to invade the other, and it was a case of who goes first. However, Hitler thought it made sense to march in the opposite direction before he attacked Britain. With the vast lands and the coal and oil reserves that Russia could provide, he decided it was time to break the pact.

Hitler had no qualms about invading Russia, and he was riding high on euphoria following successes in France and North Africa. He decided that he would reach Moscow in six weeks, undermine the leadership and take over the country. Hitler felt sure that Russia did not have the appetite, arms, or ammunition for war. Significantly he was becoming increasingly dependent on Russian natural resources – it was time to pounce, and so he did.

Nazi Germany betrayed Stalin and attacked the USSR in June 1941, known as Operation Barbarossa; Germany had been planning an attack for the last year under the code name Operation Otto. This German front became the most significant invasion force in the history of warfare and Hitler did not reckon on the Russian population fighting hard for their survival. The Russians paid a high price for their resistance, there were some appalling atrocities handed out to the Russian people, and approximately 15% of the population lost their lives. The Battle for Stalingrad (now St Petersburg) cost the lives of over a million of the city's inhabitants, many starving to death. The loss in German lives was approximately 800,000.

Hate for the Germans grew with every new account of their misdemeanours. They reportedly captured over five million troops and did not adhere to the 1929 Geneva Convention. The majority of the captured red army troops were never returned alive and just left to starve to death in various camps as well as over a million Soviet Jews who were gassed in the Nazi death camps. The reports incensed the Soviet hierarchy and following a redoubling of efforts, they commenced a push back on the Germans.

Alexander encountered misfortune in August 1941 when he became embroiled in a drinking and gambling spree. His name appeared on the list of those who participated in the drunken frenzy. He was ordered before a tribunal and sentenced to ten years in the camps. Fortunately for Alexander, the authorities issued a delay of execution and immediately sent him to the front.

Chapter 20
Summer 1941

By wanting to remain in Kuckerneese, Grete and Helene had become a concern for Otto and the rest of the family. The Zomm side of the family who had been such a strong support in the past had fled. Otto had been home on leave the previous month and shared his concern with his wife. Otto had been on the Russian border where things were relatively quiet until he returned from leave, and then everything moved up a gear. Otto formed part of a follow-up section advancing on a small Russian village in late June of 1941. Their commanding officer had given the order to advance and extinguish any resistance. This advance was the first time that Otto saw any action.

Many men in his battalion appeared dehumanised as in searing heat, they moved forward at pace. Each was bearing the look of remorseless machines, under the weight of their uniforms and backpacks. They fired their weapons indiscriminately, trampling over homes and gardens, playgrounds and even a school. A few of the soldiers took it upon themselves to kill any Russians they thought to be Jews, including women and children, slashing them with blades. There was no truce in this battle because only one side played the game of war. No captives; they were too much trouble. If they screamed they were silenced. Many of the women were violently raped.

As Otto and his troop arrived and saw the devastation, they were horrified at what lay before them. In a village much like Kuckernesse at home, soldiers he served with had committed the vilest acts. Russian women violently gang-graped and then any Jewish women immediately killed. To be Russian was to be a communist in their eyes and so everything was 'fair game' to many German Soldiers. When following his comrades into a Russian border village, Otto became terrified on seeing the vision before him; it was beyond his comprehension. Otto stood looking all around to absorb the full impact of the massacres and began to shake uncontrollably. He was physically sick and endured an epileptic fit on the spot. Otto had not experienced a seizure since a little boy. His fellow soldiers stretchered him to the nearest field hospital.

He did not recover, as one would typically expect. He was uncommunicative and lay in a makeshift bed in the field hospital quite motionless. His body remained rigid and tense; the doctors decided he should be sent home to recuperate.

Grete was reluctant to ask about the minutiae of his experience in Russia, sensing a deep reluctance on Otto's part to talk about it anyway. Otto spent much of the time since arriving home sitting in a rocking chair, swaying backwards and forwards. He said little but held Günther close to him. He held him so tightly on occasions the little boy became frightened of his father and later refused to sit on his knee, which upset Otto greatly. Grete was at a loss on how to relate to him; she stroked his hair gently like a mother to her child. Otto gained comfort from this, and so she regularly stroked his head and massaged his shoulders. Not knowing what to say but sensing that these small gestures were offering some relief in his anxieties. With each day, Otto became stronger, and each evening he looked forward to their special time together when Grete would massage him and console him. Their intimacy increased, and their nights became passionate. Often a little too much so for Grete – she saw a difference in her husband. Gone was his gentle lovemaking; he was a changed man, an impassioned man who took her in a tempestuous frenzy on increasing occasions.

After his month's leave was up, Otto was instructed to report the army doctor, he hoped to be discharged from duties, but that was not to be. He was declared fit and showed no signs of any repeats of his epileptic episode. He even tried to argue with the doctor that he did not feel well. Otto was still suffering headaches and the after-effects of the seizure, but the doctor threatened that he would be reported for insubordination. Otto had better pack his bag. He was going back to the front.

Grete and Helene listened to what news they could, and Grete was extremely anxious about her husband as he prepared to leave, as he had regressed to the man he was when he came home. She felt Otto had no will-power to fight if he needed to. Their departure had been highly emotional, and little Günther needed to be restrained by his Oma while his parents said their goodbyes; there were tears on all sides. Otto tried hard to be strong, and Grete sobbed so hard she felt her heart would break.

Otto begged his wife to move further away from the border, even though the fighting remained on the Russian side. He said that there was too much uncertainty with this madman Hitler; they all felt like pawns in a game of chess, never knowing his next move. Otto implored her again as the pickup wagon pulled up outside their house and it was time to go. Otto did his best to stand up straight in the presence of a senior officer who appeared with a driver. He straightened the jacket of his uniform and bit his lip hard as he mounted the vehicle and forced a slight smile towards his family. Grete held Günther up to wave goodbye to his father as the waggon moved off and soon turned the corner, and they were gone. Lifting a shaking hand to wipe away the tears, Grete set to immediately in occupying Günther. She led him towards his swing in the garden and gently pushed him forwards, grateful he could not see her tear-stained face. After a few minutes giving her time to gather her composure, she started to prepare them a meal of bratwurst and bratkartoffeln. They all loved their potatoes done that way, and Günther adored his German sausage.

Lotte took on Otto's biddings and obliged her brother in law in begging Grete and her mother to leave Kuckerneese. The situation close by in Lithuania was too volatile, and they were extremely close to the border. Eventually, Anita made the same case, and they agreed that they should go to stay with Anita and Inge in Schleiermacherstrasse. From there they would decide on the next course of action for them all.

Day to day life in Königsberg was so far relatively unscathed by the war. Food was now rationed. There were still reports of Jews being rounded up and marched off to camps away from the city. Nobody knew exactly where, but they felt confident it wasn't a holiday camp. Other occupants sometimes took up the remains of Jewish shops. But more often they were left as a stark reminder to everyone that the Nazi's operated a zero-tolerance policy where Jews were concerned. Anita felt sure that possibly some remained, but perhaps they were staying hidden, well that was the rumour she heard anyhow. However, she dared not repeat it unless the wrong ears heard her.

School continued as usual, and Günther was at school now too. He needed it as well. He was spending too much time in the company of older females. Even his cousin was a female. He missed his father, and his behaviour was often irrational. Helene said that it was down to the recent episodes with his father's homecoming. Grete was increasingly feeling out of sorts too, Lotte and Anita took it in turns to walk him to school, and when they returned, they frequently found Grete had gone back to bed.

This routine carried on for about a fortnight before Helene trudged her daughter to the doctor. Upon examination came the discovery that she was pregnant again. Grete was far less happy this time at the prospect of having a baby than when she was expecting Günther. Now they were a country, no, a world at war. How could she bring a child into the world under these circumstances? The four women sat her down that evening and assured her that they would, of course, support her and whatever the future held, they would face it together. Grete was feeling detached from the situation; she wanted Otto to be with her. But for this damned war, life would be everything she could ask for.

The next discussions centred on whether or not they should write to Otto and tell him that he was to be a father again. They weighed up the pros and cons; would it make him more fretful being away from a pregnant wife and his growing son? Or would it give him hope and a reason to come home and stay well while he was away from them? The ultimate decision lay with Grete, of course, and she desperately wanted to share the news with her husband. But as she decided not to just yet, she spent the evening writing a long letter full of news and positive things about living in the City and how well Günther was getting on at school. Grete talked about how much they looked forward to his next leave and she might have some good news to share with him. He should be sure to take good care of himself, she closed with sending her love and prayers and assured him he was in her thought's night and day.

She posted the letter the next morning and looked forward to an appropriate reply quite expecting that it might take a couple of weeks to reach him. But depending on his duties, he may not be able to reply immediately. Two weeks became three, became four, and six weeks later an envelope arrived. It had the stamp of the Third Reich and addressed to Grete. She opened it where she was in the hallway in anticipation. As she read the letter, the colour drained from her face. Anita ran to steady her as she started to sway and began to faint. Suddenly, as though she had regained a mountain of strength, she let out the worst bloodcurdling scream her family had ever heard and subsequently started to bend double. Everyone else in the flat came running. Frau Mallke ran consecutively from next-door wearing her apron; she was in the middle of baking, with her hands covered in flour. As Anita grabbed the letter from her hands, she saw the words "Regret to inform you... killed in the line of duty defending his country."

Otto was dead, and she was pregnant. What was Grete going to do now? She collapsed in a distressed heap on the sofa; her head fell into her mother's lap as she pulled her knees up into her chest. Both her sisters clutched her arms and shoulders, stroked her head and did their best to comfort her even though they too were utterly distraught. Frau Mallke dusted her hands on her apron and announced she would collect all the children from their schools and take them to the park. She busied herself, making everyone tea, which they didn't drink. As she reached for the door handle, she confirmed they would be home early evening to give everyone time to come to terms with the news and decide the best way to break it to Günther. Nobody offered up an objection, and Anita nodded to her in agreement and gratitude.

After a further four weeks of living together in the flat, they collectively agreed that the flat was just not big enough. Both Helene and Grete, in particular, were missing Kuckerneese desperately and had word from neighbours that the town was not under any threat and life was continuing as usual. Helene and Greta decided that they would travel back to their home and resume as near normal a life as possible. Moreover, being in Königsberg felt profoundly unsettled with daily reports of Jewish arrests and unpleasant encounters with Nazi officers. Anita shuddered at the thought of her husband having to wear that uniform; it went against every belief she held and represented nothing short of complete evil to her.

The family held a memorial service for Otto; there had been no repatriation of his body. Anita and Lotte shuddered as they concluded that there might be nothing left of him to bring back. Sharing that belief privately, of course, and were certainly not going to tell Grete. The two sisters also considered that as the war was escalating, and with the sheer numbers of reported causalities, it might not be feasible to bring home every poor soul. Either way, the war was repugnant in their eyes, and they prayed for Hitler's defeat every day.

Chapter 21

The whereabouts of Anita's and Frau Mallke's husbands was uncertain, which was a worry to them both. The Russian front was bearing the brunt of activity for the East Prussian Soldiers stationed there, and this was a cause for concern to Anita and the family. Inge would ask about Papa all the time, and Anita pacified her with reasons why his work prevented him from taking leave or writing very often. Her stories were entirely plausible to Inge, Due to the lack of available written news as papers were banned, and nobody particularly wanted to listen to the rants of Hitler and his cronies on the radio too often.

Anita felt that she and her compatriots were helpless in their situation; they felt no more akin to Hitler than any of the countries that were fighting him. In daily life, Anita became more vigilant, and she disliked the way that German soldiers patrolled the streets of Königsberg, observing the locals as they did so. Anita would often wonder if she might come across her brother, they had heard so little about him, just snippets from Betty. Just in case Anita made every effort to avert her eyes. It was challenging for her to reconcile her husband wearing a Nazi uniform knowing he hated it, but thinking of Walter choosing that path, was quite frankly beyond her comprehension. She hoped and prayed every day that Herbert was not in the thick of it on the Russian border, but deep down feared that he probably was. She shuddered to think that her husband was forced to fight a war he did not believe in and wore a uniform he despised.

The authorities placed sanctions and rations on the people of Königsberg, and more and more, it became a daily fight for fresh produce. Anita would queue for hours when the butcher received a delivery. She needed to plan her and Inge's meals very carefully – instinctively wanting to provide a balanced diet and eternally grateful to her mother for bringing homegrown garden produce on her frequent visits to see them. Helene and Grete were becoming uncomfortable with life in Kuckerneese and as the months rolled on they became increasingly aware that their proximity to the Russian border made them vulnerable. That was the dichotomy they encountered every time that they spoke to Anita about the war; it was unavoidable, and Anita would raise the issue at every opportunity.

The day before Grete went into labour in April 1942 with her second child, Frau Mallke received the dreadful news that no family ever wants to hear. Her husband was reported killed in Russia; his body was to be repatriated. Anita was a dutiful friend and looked after her younger children Herta and Gerhard while Inge comforted her friend Heidi as best as a young teenager knew how to do.

Anita was torn between her friend who needed her desperately and the news that her sister Grete was heavily in labour. Although she appreciated that their mother, Helene and Lotte were on hand to help and look after Günther. "Why oh why do these calamitous occasions always happen at the same time" thought Anita? For a few days, the war took second place to all the other events that were happening. Anita did her best to stay in touch with Kuckernesse, and to support Frau Mallke whose own family took several days to appear on the scene. When they did, it alleviated Anita's responsibilities to her friend somewhat. She made a trip to Kuckernesse, leaving Inge to stay with Hilde and her family at Hilde's request.

On arrival in Kuckerneese, the third day after the birth, Anita was met with the happy scene of her sister with her new-born daughter; she called her Marianne. She was a beautiful baby, and her big brother Günther grinned with pride. Grete took one look at Anita and changed from a picture of complete contentment to bursting into tears in seconds. It was as if she had held it together until her younger strong sister, who always had all the answers, finally arrived.

Grete went into a profoundly distressed state, the baby blues took hold, and she wailed for her dead husband. It was a pitiful sight and one which her mother and sisters felt ill-equipped to cope with. Except to comfort her as best they could, hold her tight and rock her. All this they did while taking care of Marianne's basic needs and trying to coax Grete to breastfeed her child. The baby's tiny outstretched hands reached for something to hold. Anita offered her little finger, and the child grasped her tightly. Unusually for Anita, she felt an immediate bond with the little girl. She hadn't remembered feeling the same sensation when *she* was a new mother.

That night Anita stayed with her sister, offering every comfort that she could and at the same time ensuring that the baby's needs were fully attended to. The following day Anita sat with Grete and offered to pray with her. In her prayers she asked that Grete should be given the courage to handle what lay ahead. She asked God to guide her and affirm in Grete that she was more than capable of looking after both children even though she was widowed. Thousands of other women had done so before her, and in these difficult times, Grete would do the right thing and muster up the energy to surround her children with love and support. She asked God to remind Grete that she had the love and support of her family, and how much confidence the good Lord had in Grete. He would not have sent her these challenges if she was not able to handle them.

The prayer session seemed to do the trick, and Grete appeared to find inner strength. The sorrowful state which consumed her started to lapse. Consequently, her mother and sisters piled on her lots of positive reinforcement and praise and Grete began to gain vigour and thanked Anita for her wise words and guidance. Spending time with her new-born daughter, feeding her in the rocking chair and watching Günther play at her feet, brought a renewed comfort. With every day, Grete felt more able to face a future as a single parent and a widow.

In Königsberg as Inge and Hilde went on long walks, the two girls watched in amazement how their beloved city was starting to lose its identity. A few British bombers had managed to infiltrate the anti-aircraft fire and dropped bombs on some regions of the city. They linked each other's arms as they looked around them, taking stock of the damage to the buildings. The skies were grey these days, and few birds sang, there was a gentle humming in the distance, and the girls quizzed each other to establish its origins.

So much was changing in their city. Friends they once knew had left their shops boarded up, and the playground was empty of children. The once immaculately swept street bore evidence of dog mess – testimony to the rumours that many had been abandoned along with stray cats. Rubbish was strewn awkwardly on street corners. One day as the two girls idled along the road adjacent to the park area leading to the lake, they fell upon an old lady they once knew as working in one of the local restaurants. The lady was Jewish, and they were surprised to see she was still in the city, and they enquired as to why she had remained. The lady pulled them towards her and grasped them tightly. She started to recount what she believed might have happened to her family and most of her friends who had not managed to escape. She was living every moment of her life in constant fear. It was a frightening account of cruelty and genocide before eventually, she drew breath and paused with her story.

Inge asked how she could have possibly learned of their fate; it crossed her mind that perhaps this lady was overly embroidering her tale. The lady answered that the information was third hand but had no doubt that it was true. A compassionate officer in the army with no loyalties to Hitler had witnessed events in a concentration camp. He received orders to transfer to another post in East Prussia, rather than become a fully-fledged member of the 'SS'. He then managed to get word back to his family in Königsberg. They had been devastated to hear this news, and far from being Nazi sympathisers, they shared the distressing account with trusted friends.

As the lady finished offloading onto the young girls, she stopped and appreciated for a moment the enormity of this information on their young shoulders. She apologised briefly before relaxing back on the bench where they all sat, looking right and left and behind them to make sure that no one had overheard their discussion. The distraught lady looked utterly spent and dried the tears that had fallen on her face as she spoke. Heidi temporarily put aside her grief as they tried to comfort this lady in her moment of need as she had recounting horrors of enormous proportions.

The young girls were shaken by what they had heard and offered to walk the lady back to her house. She thanked them for their kindness and politely declined. She was in hiding and had no intention of divulging her address to them or anyone else. Inge and Heidi respected her requests; they completely understood the situation and wished her luck, as they bid their farewells. For a moment after they departed the park area where they had met the lady, the two girls fell silent, both absorbing this new twist to this horrific war. Should they tell their mothers and family members? What would their reaction be? The girls decided that they would inform them, but not immediately. Heidi needed to support her mother and other siblings through this terrible time before she could heap even more incredible information upon them.

Four weeks later, the Mallke family gathered for a funeral service, and Anita and Inge joined them. The family concluded that they were one of the lucky ones to be afforded the privilege of being able to bury Herr Mallke. The funeral party slowly left the church after the service and as dusk was falling there was a power cut, and the lights of the city gave way to a beautiful starlit sky. As the party stopped and stood to look upwards, it felt like a message from their loved ones that they were there and looking down on them.

Chapter 22
2002 Rauschen and Cranz

We walked the short distance to the station from the hotel in Königsberg. A couple of little mafia boys walked with us for the first part of the journey, ever hopeful of a small hand-out, or perhaps a request with which they could assist. Notably, we passed several clothes shops, and while the windows offered no tempting displays, on peering through the doorways, it was easy to note the rows of hanging garments. I hasten to add, designed for narrow hips and wasp-like waists. Do I sound sickened with jealousy by this fact dear reader? Oh, yes, I suppose I probably do!

Fortunately, all the party were in good health, although there was a variation in the walking speed of some. Particularly with my poor sister-in-law, Marianne, who was in the early stages of needing a hip transplant. We all assembled on the wide platform in time to watch the 11 am train arrive as it passed through the tunnel halting at the station in Königsberg and then heading for Rauschen. The train appeared to be about 15–20 years old and was functional in design. No soft seats but relatively clean, probably cleaner than we might expect to see in the trains in our large cities. Looking around the train at all the notices in Russian, I wondered what the trains of the Prussian era might have been like; nobody remarked that they were any different really. One or two thought they could have even been the same trains. I wasn't too sure about that although I was well aware that Prussian engineers had been ahead of their time in terms of rolling stock and their tram network in particular.

Visiting these two towns was a key destination for Mum; the time she spent there had very significant memories. Her day trips to Rauschen and picking amber off the beach in Cranz, the proximity to the hotel, the small local railway station that was pretty well personal to the Blaue Möwe and of course the significance of this area during the flight, which, you are yet to hear about.

On arrival at Rauschen station, which is the end of the line, we disembarked and gathered to await instructions on the next leg of the journey, and what time we were all to reassemble. Yippee, we are by the seaside, and it felt fresh and clean and airy being so close to the seashore.

Our little party consisting of Inge (mum-in-law), my sister-in-law Marianne and her husband Leith, my husband Dennis and me stuck together here. Each visitor, of course, carried their personal recollections, some of mum's I just described, but for many in the wider group, Rauschen had been a childhood holiday destination, and for them too it held particularly happy memories.

As we had already been informed they would be, the trestle tables were in abundance, and each stallholder haggled for our business. Mum stood for ages carefully examining the jewellery, rings, bracelets, necklaces and earrings galore. All in various shades of dark amber to pale yellow, some translucent almost, some very cloudy, the choice was endless. Most people bought a few trinkets to take home for family and friends. Or maybe to add to an already bulging collection as was the case with my mother-in-law! Marianne loved the chance to shop too, and we each took our time wandering along the tree-lined road. Framed by the small market stalls shaded from the hot midday sun and edging our way through a constant flow of people.

Rauschen (now known as Svetlogorsk) was on a cliff, and so we needed to access the beach via the funicular. It was a fantastic sight, watching these little boxes carrying people to the beach, all with a sizeable circled number on the outside and taking just two people at a time. They were a little unnerving if I am frank. Poignantly this town too formed part of the historical story of the flight, as so many people made their escape along this coastline.

We all made our way along the crowded beach, with sunbathers galore. We concluded that perhaps it was a local holiday as countless people were lapping up the sunshine. On reaching the promenade, we couldn't fail to notice once again the amber jewellery sellers, eager for our trade. After a rest and a small libation, we assembled back at the station where we boarded the coach which took us to Cranz.

To use the now Russian name of Zelenogradsk was not something that I overheard from any of the party, to be honest. Yet that had been the name of this town for over fifty years. Even as I write this story now in 2018–19, I only know the town as Cranz. Even though I have only heard about it over the last 43 years of knowing my husband, it will always remain Cranz to me. So I can completely understand how the Prussians who used to call this home must feel.

Incredibly most of the buildings had remained intact post-war, and I admired the architecture here too. Albeit dotted in between some post-war, modern buildings, characterless, contemporary and cold looking; much like anywhere else in the world, one could argue. The roads were newly spread with tarmac. It was still a popular holiday destination; multitudes of people lay along the beach, and Mum was on a mission to venture further along the coast nearer to where the Blaue Möwe once stood. We were not sure if the building still stood or not, but keen to find the spot either way. We trolled up and down the promenade until finally appreciating that we were way off the spot. As with each venue we visited, Mum would stop and look and go into deep thought. Often, she would recount the times she spent there, but here the memories were of the night they had to flee. The detail came flooding out, each minute detail of the episode. We had heard it a hundred times, but here looking over the beach and the sea, it was easier to imagine the way it would have been on that bleak January night in 1945. We would stand with her and listen to her recalling the horrors of the events and respecting how real the pain still felt to her after 55 years. I was mildly amused to watch the Russian ladies standing on the beach in their bikinis, their arms outstretched lapping up the sun's rays. Someone remarked that this was Russian sunbathing. They did it standing up. I just thought, what the heck, let me lie down on the beach any day, who wants to stand for hours?

The Russians had done a reasonable job in keeping the town looking respectable, and there was less evidence of neglect and dilapidation as with other towns and villages we visited. I suppose this was an area of economic affluence due to the proximity to the seaside. One or two of the side streets hid the remnants of what would have once been homes to a Prussian family and perhaps were less worthy of loving care and attention all these years later, or maybe the inhabitants were not in a financial position to manage their upkeep. Either way, it was sad to see the plaster crumbling off the outer walls and the paint peeled from the doors and window frames.

I just had to take a photograph of a clock on the promenade, still with the sign of Kranz (as some did spell it). How refreshing to see that some residue of the past has been respected. After lunch, we assembled back with the coach, and once everyone was back on board, we moved off towards The Kurische Nehrung, a favourite and tranquil holiday destination of today, albeit the Russians now call it Kurshskaya Kosa and more commonly known as the Curonian Spit. Gosh, it must have been one heck of a task to strip the names of each town, street, alter all the signage on the roads, complete denigration really of all that the country had previously stood for. It will have taken some organisation. A railway connects all the towns and thanks to the Prussian railway engineers from 100 years ago, the Russians in that area now enjoy a good communication network.

We stopped at a forestry area and were again greeted by the trestle tables of amber and took the opportunity to buy ice-cream. We were grateful for the refreshment and the shade. The temperatures were well into the 30s. Mum and I sat among the trees, kicked off our shoes and sipped bottled water for a few minutes before venturing onto the beach area. Kurische Nehrung is more of a holiday destination than it was in Prussian times, quite upmarket and the beaches were immaculately clean. It was amusing to witness once again the Russian sunbathing ladies, dotted all over the beach, standing up, arms out stretched.

A short visit to a bird sanctuary gave us a new perception of the conservation efforts in the area. Small birds were captured in nets and then checked and tagged and then set free. All explanations were, of course in German, so I only grasped the basic principles, but my husband or mother-in-law explained anything of any real significance. Lunch was followed by a long walk across wooden planks laid on sandy ground and dunes, heading towards the sea. Eventually, we reached the top of the dunes, which meant climbing a wooden platform and then down long steps onto the beach. It was an exertion for some. However, the beach was stunning, and the short time we spent there was worth the effort. Now the area has been designated a UNESCO world heritage site. Almost 100 kms long and 380 metres wide, the area separates a large lagoon from the Baltic Sea.

Chapter 23

1943–44 The War Escalates

Helene's husband, Albert, ensured that the garden in kaukhemen was well tended, and he and Helene enjoyed their companionship. Their marriage gave the family comfort knowing that she was less likely to suffer persecution by the Nazis as she had lost the Jewish name of Saul. She even watched over Albert's, grandchildren, who were much younger than Inge and Günther, and she missed more frequent contact with Walter and Betty and longed to see their children. They sat and played in the garden, secured by the white picket fence and since Grete had given birth to Marianne, Helene's days were quite full. She still missed Julius dreadfully and frequently cried to Albert, who consoled her without hesitation. Helene had no desire to fulfil her marital duties, but she did appreciate the benefits of having a man to look after, and he, in turn, looked out for her. They felt relaxed in each other's company, and while they did not share a bedroom, every other part of their lives entwined as with any other married couple.

Marianne was a pretty girl; she had long dark hair; her mother refused to cut it and spent hours plaiting it and brushing it for her. Anita would scorn her frivolous behaviour, as she saw it. Grete took no notice and Marianne would sit patiently enjoying the pampering. Anita encouraged Inge to read books to Marianne. Even though the child was only two years old, Inge could see that without pictures, a book was boring to a child, so she sat and drew picture stories for her. They spent hours together, sometimes even Günther would join in and help his little sister colour in the illustrations. Often the drawings would be of their mother and father, including Otto who was never far from their minds and he would be spoken about as though he was in the room.

Grete was always comforted when that happened. In the two and half years since Otto had died, Grete had kept herself busy. Working with other widows, had formed a group to support the children who had lost their fathers. Most of the wives had precious little sympathy with the Nazis, but they also had little knowledge of their many atrocities in Russia. They were protected from the full accounts of the brutalities and, the authorities played down such reports as propaganda and misrepresentations of the truth.

Hilde and Inge had shared their knowledge about the Nazi atrocities with their mothers. And while they rejected their account as too farfetched at the time, in the last year or so further news had reached them from friends in the Jewish community to substantiate those reports. They now held such information in higher regard.

Inge was becoming increasingly concerned for her father as the family had not received any letters for over four months; the fact that he had not been allowed home on leave for so long was even greater cause for concern. Where could he be? His letters never divulged his exact whereabouts. He indicated that he had not seen much action in his last letter and was working in an auxiliary role, which gave them some comfort. It felt like an eternity since she saw him, and she would sit for hours and admire his photograph dreaming about him coming home and the war ending. When she was with her friend Heidi, Inge was the epitome of discretion and would not mention her beloved Papa. Her friend, however, was an astute young lady and could sense Inge's reluctance to discuss her father, she understood only too well the closeness of their relationship. So Heidi frequently took the initiative, bringing him into their conversations. In response, Inge shared her concerns that there had not been any letters for some time and Heidi did her best to assure her friend that all would be well. He was unlikely to be so unlucky as her father, yet quietly she became as concerned as her friend.

Finally, in spring 1944, a letter arrived at the flat in Königsberg, marked with the emblem of the Third Reich. The colour drained from Anita's face, as she sat down to open the letter, expecting the worst but hoping for the best as she recognised the handwriting to be Herbert's. Also, it confused her as it had an Italian postmark on it. Anita wasted no time in opening it, thinking as she did so that it may relate to her sister-in-law Behin or mother-in-law Henriette. Oh – the thoughts that were going through her mind in quick succession as she grappled with the envelope. She breathed a sigh of relief when she realised the letter was from Herbert.

"Inge come quickly; we have a letter from Papa." Inge ran into the front room where her mother sat studying the letter, scan reading each line before she would turn to her impatient daughter to give her a synopsis of the content. Inge sat close to her mother, who read out loud the section that Herbert had written to his daughter. Herbert explained that he was in hospital in Italy, he had shrapnel wounds to his leg, but that he dared not complain to Inge after all that she had gone through when she nearly lost her leg. Herbert did not know if he could come home or how long he would be in the hospital for, he missed them very much and loved them both dearly; they should not worry about his safety. Herbert was safe where he was, and hoped to see them soon.

Both Anita and Inge read and reread every word half a dozen times before turning to each other and questioning the fact that Herbert was in Italy. They could not understand it. He had been deployed to the Russian front to protect their homeland from the Russians in case they should decide to invade, God forbid! Perhaps Herbert was sent to Italy because he was half Italian and could speak the language, but how long had he been there? Did his mother and sister know that he was there, had they seen him? The questions kept coming and coming. It occurred to Anita that it would be worth trying to make contact with her erstwhile mother in law, but although she had promised a forwarding address none had been forthcoming.

The relief Anita and Inge felt on hearing this news was palpable. They continued to discuss every connotation of how and why Papa was in Italy – feeling such relief that he was fit enough to write, yet concerned that he was only telling half a story. Or perhaps he was secretly going to be sent home to recover? Might they expect him back any day now? So many questions, the letter had only said so much, and of course, they had to appreciate that the messages were probably all intercepted and scrutinised before posting. Hence there were no explicit details about the location or any ongoing manoeuvres.

Inge started writing a lengthy letter back to her father, and Anita did the same. With letters posted the following day mother and daughter took a train to Kuckerneese to share their joy with the rest of the family. There was other news, too on their arrival. Betty was soon to deliver their fifth child. Helene gave the update without looking at Anita. She quickly slipped into a deep rage about all the time that Walter was allowed leave that he could parent another child, while she rarely even heard from her husband... how very wrong it all was, her face contorted with rage. In the meantime, Helene trundled off into the kitchen muttering that this was good news nevertheless and they should reward themselves and she set to making a käse Küchen. Inge felt jubilant at the prospect of one of her Oma's astounding cheesecakes. While they all waited for it to bake, she played with Günther and Marianne in the garden, drawing pictures and singing songs from school.

Their relief at hearing the news that Herbert, albeit injured, was comparatively safe in Italy was relatively short-lived. A few short months later, the splendour of the East Prussian countryside was interrupted in this summer of 1944. It was a beautiful summer with long days of sunshine and light late into the evening. The landscape took on a whole new dimension that year; the crops stood firm in the fields as if obedient to the farmers, many of who were now the womenfolk who took control of the agricultural responsibilities within the rural areas.

Anita sat in the park behind the apartment in Königsberg. It was lunchtime, and she had worked hard all morning organising things in the apartment for Helene, Grete, Günther and Marianne to arrive in the evening. A light salad was prepared and sat ready to eat in their small fridge, and she knew her mother was bringing some strawberries from the garden. Inge was eager to taste the season's first crop; they were hard to come by now in the city.

Anita enjoyed the sensation of the sun on her face; she relaxed on the bench, closed her eyes, folded her arms, and lapped up the warmth. For a short time, she forgot the war; today was quiet, no German aircraft overhead. There was little activity in the city, and her thoughts took her back to her school days when she had not a care in the world and everything to look forward to. Anita's boarding school had taught her so much, and she had a lot to thank her grandmother for paying her for her education. Anita knew she had not met the expectations of her family from an academic standpoint. Yet she was aware that the tutoring she received had held her in good stead. She had a good head for business, and without her expensive education, she would not be in that fortunate position. 'If it were not for Inge and the war, I might be a successful pianist now,' Anita thought, 'possibly part of a large orchestra.' Her thoughts drifted further as she imagined the prospect. It had been such a long time since Herbert had last taken her to Salzburg or Vienna. She adored their romantic weekends in Vienna. They were such fun.

Anita's contemplations wandered more deeply into the past and happier times, while the sun offered a comforting blanket for her to dream. Then her logic became shrouded by her inner senses, the part of her where her intuition lived – the area of her innermost thoughts that did not always make sense at the time, but did more often, afterwards. She did not always like to feel those thoughts, but they were there all the same. She saw Herbert in hospital, but he was in Königsberg and still wearing his Nazi uniform. He was in pain and his arms were outstretched, calling her to help him, but when she reached out to him in her mind, he moved further away from her and so did Königsberg. The city she loved crumbled, as the vision shrank and faded and turned misty grey. Feeling confused by these visions, she wanted to reject them, but they repeatedly happened until she forced herself to come out of her trance-like state and shouted out loud "NEIN."

Anita shuddered and opened her eyes to look around her, just in case she was being observed. Blinking against the bright sunlight, Anita looked purposefully ahead. Her face was expressionless. Without moving, she started to recognise the thoughts within her. Everything was the same as when she closed her eyes – but nothing was the same. She experienced feelings within her that she did not want to accept.

Anita shivered to admit that Herbert was ill and needed her, but there was nothing that she could do about it. Also, this city of Königsberg, such a big part of her life, was calling out to her. "Things are not the same; they will never be the same again; this is my last summer, my dying summer." With a jolt, Anita sat upright and straightened her top as if to pull herself together. 'What nonsense was she thinking, for goodness sake woman, get a grip of yourself, you have responsibilities, things to do, people to look after, be gone you horrid thoughts'.

Anita took some deep breaths as she started to walk purposefully across the park to the short road leading to Schleiermacherstrasse. When she arrived back at the apartment, she heard the phone ringing, so she ran to answer it. Sensing that it had been ringing for some time, she spoke breathlessly

"Hallo...?"

"Anita, is that you?," came the voice, and she replied,

"Yes, is that Lotte? Are you alright, what is the matter?" Anita concluded from her tone of voice that there was something wrong, and she was correct in her thinking. Lotte babbled out the story about how their mother was desperate to get in touch with Anita and let her know that they were planning to leave Kuckerneese right now. They should be with her within the hour.

Grete was particularly anxious they should go after their village had been trampled over by herds of cows stampeding across the Lithuanian border. They were blundering over the countryside, mowing down crops and hedges. By the time the cattle had reached Kuckerneese, they seemed calmer, but they were eating everything they could, trees and bushes and feared all humans. For those able to get close, it was clear to see the terror in the eyes of the animals. The locals concluded they had been startled by gunfire as the Russians were burning villages in Lithuania. The people hardly had time to make their escape.

Some of the farmers reported large numbers of animals, people and wagons winding their way over the border and into East Prussia. The farmers were offering refuge in their barns. Some were carrying small children, and many were ill equipped to make the journey on foot. Anita started to shiver, fresh from her recent imaginings and feeling the shock from what her sister was saying. She quickly needed to absorb the information, assess what they all knew and decide on a course of action.

"Right, the family should not delay in leaving," Anita said.

"Anita, they have already left, Albert insisted they go, but he won't leave his own family, because they want to stay. They do not believe the Russians will venture further than Lithuania, but I am not too sure. So I am glad that Mother and Grete and the children have made the right decision. Now, are you ready for them, shall I come over too? We are open at the hotel, but only have a couple of elderly ladies in residence, I can leave them with the staff."

Anita thought for a moment and then decided that Lotte should stay at the hotel and look after things there, it was not necessary to come rushing over. It was agreed that Anita would telephone her just as soon as they had arrived, told their story and settled in.

Anita replaced the receiver and stood for a moment trying to take in the enormity of what she had just heard. She reached for the kettle in the kitchen to make a cup of tea, and was shaking as she lifted the teacups out of the cupboard. Just as she decided to sit down and pray for strength in what lay ahead, a sharp banging on the door was followed by it being flung open, and the clambering of small feet across the bare boards in the hallway.

"Tante Nita, where are you?" Both Günther and Marianne were rushing to greet her, followed by Grete and then Helene who looked as white as a sheet. Anita reached over to her mother, gently guiding her to a chair and then sat on a stool beside her. Grete and the children sat on the settee as slowly Anita took control and told her mother and sister to remain calm. They were going to have a strong cup of tea or coffee and take stock; nothing would be discussed until Inge came home from school and took the children away into another room.

The rest of the family soon came to understand that others were starting to leave, no longer were they believing the Nazi propaganda about how they would be victorious and defeat the Allies. News had got out about what the Russians had done to the people of the towns of Nemmersdorf and Goldap and they were not willing to run the risk of the Russians reaching them too.

Walter was now in Norway as an adjutant. By September 1944 he had become very friendly with one of the Generals there. During one of their many conversations, the General said to Walter, "Where are you from?"

Walter replied, "East Prussia near Tilsit, just 7kms away in fact."

The General swung round to Walter and said through gritted teeth,

"Get your family out NOW, don't waste any time. I will give you leave, but get them out as soon as possible." So, Walter did not waste any time. He wrote his wife a letter, in which he desperately implored her to leave East Prussia as soon as possible. It was expected that there would be a massive attack from the East by the Russians; he had information that the Russians were massing on the border.

It was now early October, and Betty did not immediately heed this warning. Two days later, at night, between the Memal River and Neukirch, the Russians dropped paratroopers as a preliminary attack to seize bridges and destroy any installations they could. The very next day the village was closed down as the HG Division (Hermann Göring), rolled through in Panzer tanks and other armoured vehicles. They were the Elite Luftwaffe land combat troops; the men in this division were considered to be the cream of the crop. The same morning the locals heard that the paratroopers had shot and killed the local postman.

The HG went on the attack, and they found quite a few of the paratroopers hiding in the hay bales. In those days in East Prussia the hay was stored on high vertical stacks and so could be 15–20 ft high. When the HG discovered that they were hiding in the hay bales, the HG just drove by shooting into the hay. It took two days to mop up this mini invasion, and after they were sure it was safe, the HG came by every house to let the locals know that it was safe to come out again.

That HG division made an impression on Harald, Walter and Betty's eldest son. They were all young men with brand new Panzer tanks, equipment and vehicles, the whole village turned out for them. All young men with an insurmountable challenge in going to try to hold the Russians back. But they certainly cleaned up on the Russian paratroopers! Harald and his friends played around the HG tanks and for a dare, he dropped inside one of the tanks and the lid closed on him. Harald said that he couldn't breathe and passed out inside the tank. The soldiers came back and saw Harald laying there and picked him up by the collar saying to him, "You will never serve in a tank division as you are claustrophobic." Harald ran home feeling very distressed. This whole episode was enough for Betty, and she made the decision to go; it took little more than a day to pack up, take the children and head for the train station.

The station in Neukirch had only the narrow-gauge railway. Hence, they loaded up into cattle cars as much as they could take and after a two-day journey the train stopped just outside Dresden. It was pouring with rain, and the children were hungry and petrified that the British bombers might come over during the night. Dresden was amassed with refugees already. Thousands were already on the move from the east, and it quickly became apparent that they were not likely to be processed anytime soon. Thankfully after another interim stop, they were registered and assigned to a farmer and his family. They came with a horse and buggy and picked them up and took them to their home in Topseifersdorf in Saxonia, 7 kms from Dresden. There were four families living in the large farmhouse, and each family were designated two rooms. It was hard to adjust; they had little furniture and few of their belongings, but they were safe, and Betty drew her children in close that first night in Topseifersdorf.

Chapter 24
Background to Alexander Marinesko.

Marinesko's career, continued along a rocky road of ups and downs. On 12 February 1942, a German artillery shell hit his submarine (M-96), causing considerable damage. Then while patrolling the Finnish coast in August the same year, Marinesko spotted a massive German artillery barge, the SAT-4 Helene. He saw his opportunity to shine and launched a torpedo. Afterwards Marinesko reported that he had sunk the vessel and recorded that the boat equated to a displacement of 7000 BRT (overall volume). It was later found to be only 400 BRT, much smaller tonnage.

In October, Marinesko subjected his submarine to significant risk, he prematurely returned to base without warning because Soviet patrol boats almost committed an own goal and attacked M-96. Only by sheer chance was tragedy avoided. His catalogue of misdemeanours was halted when later the same month M-96 with Alexander Marinesko at its command was sent to attack a German headquarters and 'capture' an Enigma coding machine. As it happened, only half the unit returned and without the device, yet amazingly it was considered that Marinesko had completed his task successfully! This act resulted in him being decorated with the Order of Lenin and promoted to Captain Third Rank (lieutenant-commander), all quite astonishing really. Once again, he was admitted as a candidate member to the Communist Party. However, the divisional Commander noted that his subordinate (Marinesko) was inclined to frequent drinking – in effect, his card was marked. Nevertheless, Alexander Marinesko was successively appointed as Commander of the S-13 submarine. This promotion formed the most significant part of his destiny.

In 1943 Marinesko almost did not go to sea as he performed various desk duties relating to the replenishment of personnel for the Baltic submarine fleet. The problem with life on the shore was that it was fraught with many temptations, which he found hard to resist. On two occasions that year, there were reported accounts of his drunken behaviour, and he spent time in the guardhouse. Subsequently he was issued with penalties from the communist party, none of which served to deter him from one day bouncing back and rebuilding his reputation.

***

In Königsberg, Anita carefully gathered in news from whatever source she could. She passed the information discreetly to her mother and sisters; they were mindful not to frighten the children. For now, school life continued as usual for Inge and Hilde, they were now of course in their final year and fast turning into young women. Helene made a trip back to Kuckernesse, against the advice of her family it has to be said. Anita was not party to the decision and was furious when she discovered what her mother had been planning. The trains were still making journeys to the eastern frontier towns, and so Helene made the trip. Also, she was concerned for Albert and needed to know he was safe.

Albert was not in good health, and he knew that should he have to flee he would most likely be a burden on who ever he was with. Albert wasn't thinking straight, as all trains were fully functioning, and that would be the most sensible mode of transport in an exodus. So, he let everyone believe that he was determined to stay for other reasons, in particular the love of his home village. Albert was emphatic to all that would listen that he wanted to help those that chose to stay, and he had no wish to leave. When Helene arrived back at her home, she collected an old pram from the loft and placed as many precious family items into it as she could. Mainly photographs and other irreplaceable items, including some jewellery and fresh produce from the garden, much of their stock of bottled fruit and vegetables and pretty well anything that had been of sentimental value and was small enough to carry. Helene was a capable lady and took no risks. She had been in touch with Albert, and he told her it was safe, but better not to bring all the family back.

Helene was perplexed at Albert's stubbornness, and he and Helene had a bitter argument for a good 20 minutes. Eventually, she was forced to accept that Albert flatly refused to budge at that time, and she had to leave swiftly as the last train that day was departing for Königsberg. The hordes of people making for the station meant that Helene might not even gain access onto the train if she were to delay her departure any longer. Albert hugged her, promising that as soon as he could, he would come to her in Königsberg, but Helene knew that he was lying. She could not afford any more time in fighting him, and so she hugged him back and turned her pram around to face the direction of the station. Helene had to move quickly. There was no time to waste. With one last casting glance on the home she had shared with her family for many decades, she made her way across the marketplace and onwards to the station. When she arrived, she was not surprised to discover she was one of the last passengers to make it onto the train.

Consequently Helene was made to travel in the guard's van with the luggage, boxes, crates and other travellers grateful to gain admission on this relatively short but desperate journey. Helene was numb with grief and anxiety at leaving Albert. Not in the way that she felt after Julius died of course. Albert had only ever had her best interests at heart, and Helene was sad to think what his fate might entail. She comforted herself by tucking in her treasured cargo in the pram; all safely covered with a blanket as if there were a baby inside. Helene even lifted the hood so that nobody could quickly peek inside. Not that anyone had the time or inclination to look into anyone else's affairs. Everyone had only one thought now, for themselves and the people they loved most in the world, to be safe.

***

Betty and her children had only been in Topseifersdorf for a week when she decided that she could not live without more of her valued possessions. She wanted her bedding given to them as a wedding present, her fluffy pillows and blankets among other things. So she asked another of the refugees to help Harald look after her five children, one of who was a baby, Jurgan, just a few months old. The farmer, and owner of the house where they lived, found out what she was planning and stormed into the kitchen where Betty was collecting provisions for her journey.

"You are a crazy woman! How can you take such a risk? How could you leave your children, this is madness. If something were to happen to you, what would happen to your kids?" Betty would have none of it; she wanted her possessions, and that was that and left with the farmers' shrills ringing in her ears. She left her eldest child Harald in charge of the family while she was away. Her journey was perilous but fortunately, mostly by train – she was lucky. She collected the items she needed from what was once their home, looking around a room full of memories, visualising the children playing with their toys on the rug by the hearth, wondering if they could ever return. For the first time, Betty felt a moment of fear, as she longed to get back to her children. The house was empty and the silence felt almost tangible like a ghost. Betty packed what she needed in a trunk and set off. She was fortunate that there were soldiers nearby and they helped transport her belongings to the train. The journey back was more complicated with a massive trunk, struggling and repeatedly needing to ask for help as she agonised over what she could not bring with her on the numbing train journey back to her children.

Only a short time later East Prussia was locked down.

Chapter 25

It was increasingly difficult for the population of Königsberg to absorb the snippets of information that reached them. The war had raged for the past few years and decimated other parts of Germany, but on the whole, until recently, the war had primarily passed by Königsberg. There was little industry in the area, and given that East Prussia was at the extremities of their aircraft's operational range, the British strategically left it alone. The population's experience of the war mainly lay with the loss of their husbands, sons, brothers and fathers. All of that changed on the nights of 26th and 27th August. Anita had been taking an evening stroll with Frau Mallke, something they both did from time to time. It was an opportunity to chat about their various challenges, managing parental responsibilities and family issues. They also used these chats to discuss contingency plans in case the war should escalate and gained a degree of comfort as, between them, they drew up a shortlist of possible actions should the need arise.

It was well past dusk when Frau Mallke and Anita parted company on the landing of their flats and wished each other a pleasant night's sleep. Two hours later, their world felt as though it was exploding around them. It very nearly was. Some 174 RAF Lancaster Bombers raged their fury, the City centre being their intended target. The lead aircraft overshot its mark, and as a result, the majority of the bombs fell on the east side of the city, unfortunately in a residential area. The multitude of flashes and explosions ripped through the city. Only four of the British bombers were shot down and the population, being unaccustomed to the noise and fury that surrounds an air raid, were particularly unprepared and utterly terrified.

Anita and her family, along with the Mallke family, took refuge in the cellars of the apartments. Their unrehearsed assemblage was exercised on instinct and with minimal protest from the children, quite surprisingly. After the all-clear siren was heard, they sat motionless for a moment, before slowly yet cautiously making their way back up to their apartments. Inge slipped into her mother's bed, and Grete's children all slept with her that night. Their actions were met with no objections from either mother, both wanting to be in a position to move their children swiftly downstairs again, should another raid occur again that night. Two days later their fears were realised when 189 Lancaster bombers succeeded in hitting the city centre. Nearly 500 tons of ordinance, a mixture of incendiary bombs and the high explosive was dispatched onto the beleaguered city and tore the heart out of the devastated old town. The old timber buildings were a tinderbox in the hot August night air. It was as though someone had poured oil over certain parts of the city and the very soul of Königsberg cried out in pain.

The terrified inhabitants of Schleiermacherstrasse sat huddled together in the cellars of the apartment blocks; they had only candlelight to witness each other's terrified faces. The younger children whimpered to the shushes of their mothers who cradle rocked them as best they could. The older children and Inge included held their hands over their ears as if to block out the sounds of the bombs being dumped in what seemed like an endless tirade on their beautiful city. Anita hummed a soothing tune, and Frau Mallke softly mumbled the words to the song in reassuring unison.

As the sun rose and the silence once again descended on the city, the families slowly and ever so gratefully climbed the stairs to their respective apartments. From there they could view the distant damage that had been dispensed by the bombers like a pent-up giant fury. A realisation crept over Anita as she began to appreciate that they were slowly being sandwiched between the British air attacks and the Russian threats on the Eastern Front. Still, the official advice was to stay put.

The German Army argued over where to build their defences along the East Prussian frontier. The result was that they often made trenches in poorly sited positions. The decision had been taken to use upended concrete pipes to create one-man defensive positions across the extent of the frontier. These defences were positioned 12 miles behind the border. The intention was to protect East Prussia from any invading Red Army, and the construction was the brainchild of Erich Koch. The result was to become a costly exercise, not even completed before the Russians advanced. The disastrous monolith was to be known as 'The Erich Koch Wall'. He, in turn, declared it to be a great success. Even the local army leadership urged for the evacuation of the population, fearing that this would soon be an operational zone. Koch refused to approve any evacuation and even went as far as to order that if any civilians were found trying to flee, they should be shot. It was his view that if there were civilians still in the area, the soldiers would fight harder to protect them. In the meantime, the Russian artillery decimated the Eastern frontier towns of East Prussia.

The reports from areas where the Russians had temporarily retreated were bloodcurdling in their detail. Those who were able to flee recounted stories of rape, torture, inhumane acts upon women and children; and immeasurable suffering for anyone trying to escape. They had no choice but to leave their dead loved ones behind and took little more than their deeply scarred recollections of events, as they had unfolded before their eyes.

As the autumn gales gave way to the winter frost, the frontier activity died down, and many took the opportunity to go back to their homes and collect what they could. The villages and farms in the area formed part of a no-man's land of inactivity. Here the cows stood, their udders dried up from not being milked, and as the grasslands became frozen, they slowly starved to death. One by one, the sick neglected animals fell to the ground.

After the onslaught of the August bombings in Königsberg, it was eerily quiet in terms of warfare, and the city's preparations for Christmas were made, almost as if there was no war. For some, this felt alien and disrespectful to those who had lost their lives and homes. To others, there was an air of anger and resistance to demonstrate to the Soviets that the East Prussian people were stronger than they and life will go on.

Anita and Inge were increasingly concerned at the lack of response from Herbert since his last letter months earlier. They could only imagine what was happening and wondered if he were still in Italy. They considered that no news meant that Herbert must have recovered well enough to be returned to duties and while they gained small comfort from that prospect, it was also a new line of questioning in their minds as to where he may have been sent; was Herbert back on the Russian border? They prayed that he was not.

Anita took Inge out into the city. She was determined that they would have a Christmas tree and, although there were few to be found, there was a market stall which had some. The specimens looked quite spindly and hardly up to the usual standard they were accustomed to seeing in previous years. Anita took on the responsibility of making Christmas as special as she could for Günther and Marianne who was still little more than a toddler, and this was possibly going to be the first Christmas that she would remember.

Having made their selection and with the tree trunk firmly placed under her arm and Inge delicately holding onto the prickly treetop, they started to make their way home.

Anita walked quickly, mindful that she and Inge needed to be back before nightfall. The city was shrouded in darkness now each night in case the English bomber planes were in the vicinity. Inge struggled to keep pace, her bad leg was painful in the cold weather, and it ached more than usual. As Anita crossed the cobbled road with Inge just two steps behind, she heard a scream. Inge let go of the treetop as she had tripped over the cobbles. She was propelled across the road towards the curb, she landed on her side and narrowly avoiding falling on top of the tree itself. Her bad leg, hip and elbow bore the brunt of her fall, and she screamed out in pain. Anita, realising that her daughter was quite badly hurt, for once did not accuse her of attention seeking and jumped to her aid.

A young man saw what had happened and ran towards them to offer help, as he did so Inge could see that his face was severely scarred and the closer he came, the more she realised that he had lost an eye, his cheekbone was gone and half his chin on the left side of his face. Suddenly Inge became more concerned for the young lad who came to her rescue and less interested in herself. Inge stared at the unfortunate young man who quickly caught her gaze and clutched his face with his other hand in embarrassment.

Anita chastised her daughter with a glare, for her lack of discretion and thanked the young man for his kindness. Inge then came to recognise the young man from school. He had left the previous year. Gosh, she thought, this poor chap must have gone from school to war and within a short space of time had virtually lost half his face. Suddenly the gravity of the war came crumbling down on Inge and she felt as weak as a kitten as she hobbled home, holding onto the arm of this once attractive and otherwise able young man, who held on tightly to the end of the Christmas tree with his other hand, ensuring that his right side was next to Inge.

When they arrived back onto Schleiermacherstrasse, the young man helped them both up the stairs to their apartment. After refusing any refreshment the brave young man who had introduced himself as Hans turned to Inge and wished her a Merry Christmas. He gently and respectfully bowed his head to Anita as he shook her hand, then turned and walked back towards the city. Immediately Inge felt ashamed at the way she had handled the situation. She was not sure if the young man had recognised her from school.

But Inge had undoubtedly remembered him and hated the fact that she had shown such shock and discomfort at seeing him. Poor boy, how could she be so heartless, she thought.

The whole episode left an indelible impression on Inge. Her mother reverted to the caring, concerned and doting parent she had known when she was so ill in the Harz Mountains when she had osteomyelitis. Inge suddenly appreciated that when she was sick, she could draw on attention from her mother. She witnessed a demonstration of love that otherwise did not appear to be present in her under normal circumstances. Mindful that a reoccurrence of the osteomyelitis should be avoided at all costs, Inge was ushered to bed with a hot water bottle and a warm bowl of broth.

Chapter 26
My Summary of Our Trip in 2002

Our trip was littered with recollections of times gone by; with no doubt, memories of atrocities not far from the minds of the people with whom we travelled. One thought that struck me was that we were consistently greeted warmly by a new generation of peoples in Russia who had no first-hand account of the war on which to draw. Undoubtedly, they too, had received passed down memories of the massacres from another point of view; unquestionably there had been many. Neither did they make constant references to what was probably the largest exodus of humans at that time. Moreover, the recollections focused around the lives they led, the schools they went to, their homes and lifestyle. In other words, it was the happy memories that were most prevalent, and I suppose that is the way that it should be.

One thing is for sure there are never any real winners in war. And here over 55 years later we witnessed one time enemies of the people in our party, now entertaining them. One such evening brought home the diversities that divided these two peoples. Whilst at the same time wholeheartedly embracing them in the form of a Russian singing and dancing evening. It was wholly compelling to watch, and with many laughs. Even my husband was persuaded to join a line of gentlemen who were coerced into playing a musical instrument. The leading lady built a small orchestra, and slowly they worked in unison to accompany the professionals and manage a half-decent tune.

No animosity existed anymore between the two peoples that I could see. There was, however, a degree of resentment it is fair to say, particularly on our daily travels as the Prussians rediscovered their homeland and noted its differences, destruction and disarray. Substantial sadness was still felt too. Particularly with my emotional mother-in-law, but most now bore an air of resignation and acceptance that times had changed and life had moved on. They had homes now in other areas of Germany, Denmark, Sweden, England and Canada. I think we all realised that continually looking back prevents one from moving forward, and it is impossible to go back. Learning to accept what is, rather than what could have been being an essential lesson for all to learn.

Given the unique circumstances under which this party of people had experienced a massive diversion in their life's path was understandably difficult to comprehend. Many would pine for their homeland until their dying day, Inge included. Others like Mutti made a noble transition into a new life, in a different direction, in full and accepted knowledge of the fact that they still had their lives, and for that, they could be considered lucky. That made their appreciation of being alive so much more fundamental.

The coach party took their seats on the vehicle in readiness to depart Königsberg most for the last time. After a few quiet moments of reflection and gratitude, they grasped the song sheets as if in a scene of defiance, unity and no doubt immense comfort, and sang their old school songs again, tissues in hand, but looking forward as they started the long drive home.

Chapter 27

Ten days into the new year of 1945, Anita was clearing up after her niece and nephew. Grete was less bothered about keeping on top of housework, and Anita was all too aware that there were six of them living in quite cramped conditions. Seven recently since Lotte had joined them also, having shut up the hotel for winter. It was a particularly cold day, having snowed all the previous night. There was over four and a half feet of snow on the roads and pavements outside. Residents were forced to make strategic openings in the wall of snow that lined the street, just so that people could cross the road, rather like tunnels networking across the road and down the street.

It was a Thursday morning, and Anita received a letter. Once again it bore the postmark of the Third Reich, but this time she did not recognise the handwriting. It was the only letter that the postman handed to Anita that day and he offered a sympathetic half-smile as he gave her the envelope. Anita bit her lip, her hand started to tremble, and she denied herself the thoughts that had immediately sprung to mind. No, she told herself, this was not going to be, all will be well, and she carefully placed the letter on the coffee table. For several minutes Anita sat and stared at the envelope as if willing it to self-combust, and the contents hold no lasting consequences.

Helene walked into the room and quickly gathered an accurate assessment of the situation. As she moved towards Anita to sit next to her, Lotte also stepped into the room.

"Anita, Inge will be home from school in a few minutes, you need to read the letter before Inge arrives." Anita glanced at her watch and nodded to her sister in agreement; she took the letter and a knife from the drawer. With one swift action, she slit open the envelope and removed the contents. Anita felt her heart thump inside her chest pounding louder and louder as she read the words to herself. She read the words three times before the tears in her eyes prevented her from reading anymore. She handed the letter to her mother and sister, both of whom had gathered the contents without uttering a single word.

Lotte clutched hold of her sister, and Helene flung her arms around both daughters as she absorbed the magnitude of what was happening within her family. At this moment, Helene became the strong one and took charge of proceedings. She walked into the bedroom where Grete was playing with her children and with a knowing glance, told Grete that Anita needed her to be strong, that she had received a letter. Placing a firm hand on her daughters' arm, Helene looked her firmly in the eye and said:

"We ALL need to be strong for them now Grete."

Helene was fearful that her eldest daughter might crumble on hearing the news, and regress to how she was three years ago after Otto's death. Grete took in some slow deep breaths and managed to control her emotions. Her mother was right. She needed to support her young sister and Inge, oh Inge, what were they to do about telling Inge?

Twenty minutes later Inge arrived home from school, Hilde was by her side, and they had planned to do homework together at Hilde's apartment, she only called in to say where she would be.

"Nein Inge." Anita said firmly,

"Please Hilde, could you go home to your mother and tell her we will need her in about an hour's time. We have some family business to attend to right now, and I need Inge to remain home with me." Both her sister's and mother were in awe of Anita's calm approach to the situation. Anita then turned to her family and said,

"Please, will you all leave us?" They dutifully left the room, reminding her they were only in the kitchen and would be there whenever she needed them.

Inge was now very suspicious of the mood in the apartment and stuttered as she asked her mother what the matter was. Her mother placed her right arm firmly around Inge's shoulder and guided her to the settee, pressing down on her arms as she moved into the chair.

"Mutti, its Papa, isn't it?" Inge felt the tears welling up in her eyes as she asked the question. Her mother nodded. With that Inge started to wail and hid her face in her mother's chest as she did so. Anita rocked her daughter and cried with her, the two of them, swaying and crying for what felt like hours, but in reality, was only a few minutes, until the point when Inge asked how she knew? Anita showed her the letter, and Inge read it over and over again, each time the sobs shaking her whole body. This could not be true. He died serving his country. But he died last October and in Italy. How could he still be in Italy? Why was he fighting in Italy? So many questions, so few answers and no ways of finding the truth.

Inge received comfort one by one from each member of the family. She felt like she was living in a nightmare, that this wasn't real, she would wake up, and her Papa would walk back in through the door. The lump in her throat felt as though it was growing to meet her heart rising in her chest. Inge's stomach churned with hunger, yet she could not eat food. The very thought of eating made her want to throw up. As she crumpled to a small heap in the corner of the living room, Inge became reminded that her mother too must be struggling to absorb the news and so she went back over to hug her. Anita felt stiff and with both hands, held onto Inge's shoulders as she pushed her away and told her that they all had to be strong now, these were hard times they were facing, she must stay in control and not let her emotions run away with her.

Inge felt somewhat startled at hearing this and wiped away her tears and looked at her mother trying to work her out. How could she be so cold? Inge knew her mother was resilient, but she was not ready for this show of strength. On entering the room, Helene recognised the situation and offered all the comfort her granddaughter needed. Shortly they invited in the Mallke family to hear the news. They had been through the same torture themselves and every offer of support was made. Hilde took hold of her friend's arm, and both of them walked off into the corridor of the apartments, even though it was cold. Hilde recognised that Inge needed some space away from the older women in the family and Inge appreciated her friends' thoughtfulness. Hilde also knew of the bond between her father and her. Nobody loved Inge like her Papa. Inge couldn't imagine receiving love like that again her whole life long.

Life was rudely interrupted once more on 13th January; the window panes rattled as artillery in the city started to manoeuvre. It was unnerving for the local population. They were up until now uninformed by the authorities and more significantly, told to stay put. They were actively discouraged from leaving; no harm would befall them. They were safe; the German army had everything under control, the people were advised. In truth, this was about all they were told. That night, as dusk fell, three or four aircraft dived down from the sky and began to fire on the railway station and the airfield. A dogfight unfolded in the air, and almost as quickly as it started, it was over.

By the 17th January, the Russians had broken through the barricades in several areas and started to advance. The border area was a sea of flames by night, and the senior hospital doctors began to bring all the patients down to the ground floor in case they needed to evacuate them in a hurry. Anita knew some of the doctors and nurses and offered to help them when, a few days later, the decision to leave was taken. The patients were relocated to a private house in Pomerania, and only once they were on their way did Anita return to the apartment. She was grateful to keep busy, now knowing that she had been a widow for about three months. Yet only hearing the news a few days ago was a painful fact for Anita to absorb.

There was a phone call at the apartment; it was the home help at the Hotel. She rang to let the family know that all was well in Cranz. She had heard some devastating stories about the East, and from Königsberg as well. She was keen to understand how the family were coping. Her kindness extended to an offer to open up the Hotel again for them to come over; she felt sure that they would be safer there. As the call completed and Anita replaced the receiver, a family conference developed on the topic of going to Cranz. Anita was adamant that was the right solution. Grete and Helene wanted to stay put. Lotte felt that they should be headed west and away from the possible Russian advance.

In the absence of a collective decision, Anita concluded that she would go out onto the streets, to see what she could learn from the local people. Lotte said she would go with her and together they set off down the road. There had been a thaw in the last couple of days in the absence of more snow. For that everyone was very grateful. The streets were clear, and as they walked to the end of Schleiermacherstrasse and turned left after they passed the Hans Schlem Schule, she noticed a rather well-dressed lady at the side of the road talking to a soldier. The lady caught Anita's eye as she was surrounded by antique furniture; it looked like an entire house worth of stuff.

Noticing Anita and Lotte staring at her, the lady beckoned them over and asked if they could help her find some removal men. Anita asked,

"Why are you standing here with all your furniture?"

The woman replied, "I had to flee my burning village. These pieces of antique furniture are all that I have left in the world. Some kind soldiers agreed to help me." Once in Königsberg, the soldiers said that they could go no further and the lady would need to find a removal company. Anita bluntly informed her that she had little hope of finding removal men now; she should leave her furniture and look after herself.

The poor lady looked at Anita and burst into tears, and she repeated; "This is all I have."

The soldier had by now taken his opportunity and escaped the situation. The lady explained that her husband had fallen and she had no children. Her furniture was all that she had in the world since the Russians had burned down her home. Anita took a sharp intake of breath and suggested that perhaps one of the military vehicles might help her as they passed by. Lotte felt great compassion for the lady and attempted to hug her. Anita, at this point, pulled Lotte away and wished the lady well. There was nothing that they could do to help, and they needed to be on their way.

The two sisters made their way back up Schleiermacherstrasse, past their apartment, and towards the city. There were many people around, including soldiers. Lotte asked Anita why she thought so many were in one place at that time. Just as they were taking stock of all they could see, heavy aircraft appeared on the horizon at low altitude. Every soldier dived for cover into all the houses around. Only the civilians were still standing in the roadways and pavements. Very soon a significant noise overhead could be heard, banging and spraying what looked like fireworks all around. Then the realisation set in. These were not their aircraft, it was the Russians. They circled and started to fire at the station as they had a few days before. No doubt they wanted to finish the demolition of the station that the Allied forces had started a few months earlier, and then abandoned. Yet still, there were notices on the station walls to say that they needed to get a special ticket to travel west. The trains were for guns. The people could move and travel again when victory came.

Anita had seen enough. "Come on Lotte, we need to get back to everyone." The two sisters scrambled to their feet after their scare and walked at pace back to their apartment. When they arrived, they were met with "Did you hear that? What is happening? Should we be leaving?" Anita calmed everyone down, and just as the discussion about what to do next began, Frau Mallke and her three children stood at the door, desperate for a friendly ear and the offer of some comfort in the situation.

Chapter 28

After much deliberation and no small degree of argument, it was decided that they would depart for Cranz in two groups. All leaving at the same time would be too convoluted with all the children. Anita would go first with Inge and the Mallke family, and then Helene, Lotte and Grete and her children would follow the next day. That way, they would not all be packing at the same time, and anything that was missed could be brought by the second tranche.

The first group made their way to the station to catch a train to Cranz. Most people were headed west, and the queue for tickets was horrendous with no certainty that everyone would be granted a ticket. On their way in Anita noted the furniture left abandoned on the plaza in front of the station, and recognised it as belonging to the lady she had met the previous day. She must have enlisted some support as far as the station but had not been able to transport it any further. So there it all was lying in a heap abandoned, and it was probably worth a great deal of money. The lady was nowhere to be seen. She must have taken their advice, and possibly the opinion of anyone else she had spoken to, and left with what she could carry. "That pretty well says everything," Anita muttered.

People were attempting to send trunks on any trains that they could book them onto. Increasingly more people were in the ticket queue and no return tickets were being purchased as far as Anita could tell. Once again there were loud noises from above and everyone dashed for the underground shelter. Sharp firing noises sounded all around. Glass was shattered on the outside windows of the station, including the glass roof. It showered the desperate travellers with splinters of glass, but thankfully no direct hits as yet. Once the all-clear sounded, the Tollkuhn's and Mallke's made their way to the front of the queue. Having heard that the train to Cranz was departing in 15 minutes, there was no time to spare. They must be on board that train.

Anita started to feel concern that she was leaving first. Should she not have let her mother and sisters go before her? No time to debate the topic now.

They needed to run to the platform, past the hordes of people sitting on and standing around large trunks and suitcases. The military was all around, but there seemed no organisation on their part, almost as if they were no longer following orders. Anita and her party travelled quite light in comparison to the others, and she was grateful for that as they started to run onto the platform. Everything was taking twice as long as it normally would, all pushing and grabbing. It was most unlike the refined Prussian people, Anita concluded.

Anita was holding onto Inge and Herta, and Frau Mallke had hold of Hilde and Gerhard as they steadily made their way towards the train. The two older teenagers thought the handholding was a little excessive until they witnessed the crowds of people congregating on the platform. Then they agreed that they must not be separated. Just seconds before the whistle blew, they boarded a carriage. There were no seats, but that was not a problem. They were all just grateful to have safely made it onto the train.

The journey was noisy, cramped and as some passengers were carrying dogs and cats in baskets, it was smelly and quite stuffy, even though the temperature outside was drastically dropping. Women held their children tightly, and some of the little ones grew restless sitting on their mother's knee for the duration of the 35 km journey. The journey felt much longer than usual, but eventually the train slowed down as it reached the end of the line. People started to grapple for hats, scarves, gloves and luggage and the train shuddered to a stop.

Cranz had a blackout when they arrived, and it took some time to decipher the best route to walk. It seemed to take an age, but about half an hour later, they were walking into the hotel and deciding on the best rooms to sleep in. Anita made the decision that the middle bedrooms were the only ones where there was a complete blackout facility. Plus the chimney ran up between them making it warmer than the other bedrooms. They all assembled in the kitchen where a light meal was appreciated with what the housekeeper had left for them. After further discussions about security they decided to just use the larger of the two rooms and felt happier having made that decision. And to have a low oil lamp for light in the room gave them all a degree of comfort. Bed beckoned, and they all slept soundly for the first night in a week.

Helene was delighted and relieved to receive the phone call the previous evening, which confirmed their safe arrival. It came just in time too, as when they woke up the next morning the phone lines were dead. Grete stood by the phone for a good fifteen minutes repeatedly trying to make another call to Cranz, but to no avail. Helene told her to stop wasting time and carry on packing as they needed to be making a move. A neighbour brought word that the road to Danzig (which is now Gdansk in Poland) was under attack and that there were dogfights in the air between the German and Russian aircraft. Bullets were sprayed into the night sky, scattering like sparks of destruction and anyone trying to make an escape on foot needed to run for cover.

Grete was still buttoning up Marianne's overcoat when her mother insisted that she wear a second and even a third if she could. The forecast was for heavy snow, and they needed to prepare themselves for some seriously low temperatures. Günther was crying because he wanted to take his toys and Lotte said no, he had to carry food and clothes and be ready to help push the prams. One was full of precious items brought from Kuckerneese, and the other pushchair was for Marianne. Helene was just about to get utterly exasperated with Grete when suddenly she announced they were all ready to go. "At last," exclaimed Helene, "we really must go, NOW."

The 20-minute walk to the station took much longer as the snow was starting to fall again. Marianne didn't want to go in her pushchair and said that she would walk instead. Finally, Lotte picked her up and tied her into her pushchair amid screams and tantrums from the three-year-old. On arrival at the station, Lotte squeezed through the crowd and made it to the ticket office – while those around her tut-tutted and shouted expletives at her for jumping to the front of the queue.

When Lotte asked for three adult and two children's tickets to Cranz, the ticket salesman looked up at her and shook his head. "No way are you going to Cranz by train now; the authorities have cancelled all trains to there."

"What?" said Lotte. She was filled with rage at the prospect of them not all being able to get to their planned destination.

"Your only hope today…" The ticket salesman looked up and down his list, "Yes, your only hope today, is to go to Marienburg if you want to go west that is?" Lotte took a few seconds to take in this news, by which time the ticket salesman was becoming impatient. He had a queue to try to appease and Lotte was not helping him to respond positively to this marauding crowd of people desperate to leave Königsberg.

"Ok then, right, three adults and two children please to Marienburg."

Everything was starting to happen at a quickening pace, and just as she was gathering up her tickets and change, Lotte was wondering how to address this change of plan to her sister and mother.

In the time that Lotte was gone buying the tickets, Helene overheard that there was only one more train leaving that day and it was going to Marienburg. There were no trains to Cranz. The rumours were that the authorities did not want the people to give up and accept that the Russians could overrun them. They wanted them all to stay, soldiers and civilians alike. There had been no orders to evacuate. As Lotte reached her mother and sister and started to tell them the story, they were quick to accept what they already knew. The best thing to do was to find the platform as swiftly as they could. The train was leaving in less than 20 minutes.

Within the next ten minutes the ticket office became boarded up, and no more tickets were being sold. Lotte and Grete looked at each other in relief and, at the same time, wondered what they were going to do when they got to Marienburg. Never mind, they concluded, the time to worry about that was once they got to relative safety. First of all, they had to make it onto the train, and that would be no mean feat!

Just as they made their way onto the platform another airstrike was happening overhead, the children started to cry, and people began to run in all directions, many of them for the underground shelter. Helene looked all around her and told her daughters to remain where they were, as she quickly realised that if they ran and became separated or got stuck in the underground, they were at risk of not catching the train. So they stood firm, and made their way further to the front of the platform. Concentrating on this took their thoughts temporarily away from the reality of what was going on in the skies above. After a few minutes, the noises of the aircraft overhead ceased. Everyone heaved a sigh of relief and Helene took a sharp intake of breath. As she did so, she appreciated that she had been holding her breath for what was probably a good couple of minutes.

The train arrived on the platform. Immediately the crowd transformed into a densely packed uniform mass, slowly shifting forward in the direction of the train's doors. Helene told Lotte to help her onto the train with Günther and the pram. Grete was just a step behind her with the folded pushchair under her arm, her suitcase in hand and holding Marianne by the other hand. It was complete pandemonium, every man for himself and every woman too for that matter. Common courtesy didn't apply anymore, as people were pushed and shoved in all directions. Suddenly Grete felt herself being elbowed sideways and, with the weight of the tide of people, she was powerless to force herself back again.

One moment she was a second from putting her foot on the step of the train, and the next, she was moving sideways and backwards. By now Helene and Lotte were safely aboard and looked around to see where Grete was. They panicked, as they could not see her. Grete called out to them, but the noise was horrendous, everyone shouting and yelling, hats falling off heads and being trampled on, whistles blowing, and the train getting ready to leave. In blind panic Grete pushed passed a lady to get back to where she had been, close to the door of the train, as she did so Grete felt Marianne's hand slip from hers. She screamed, my baby, my baby. Grete turned, and as she did so, a kind gentleman with his wife lifted her daughter and passed her to Grete. In those few seconds more people pushed passed Grete and removed whatever chance she had of reaching the door to the train.

She clutched her daughter tightly, and as she turned around, the doors closed, the final whistle blew and the last thing she saw was the distraught face of her son, mother and sister in the window of the train. Günther was screaming for his mother. Helene was crying, and so was Lotte as slowly the train started to pull out of the station. The scores of people left behind were yelling their last farewells to their loved ones. The heartbreaking scene was like a living nightmare to Grete, and her heart thumped inside her chest. Her rapid breaths became shallower as she started to go into a deep panic.

The elderly gentleman and his wife, who helped her, took note of the situation and appreciated what had happened. For their part, they had accepted that they were not going to make it onto the train and so stood back. In the end, the elderly couple decided their age was a barrier to this selfish madness they witnessed. The couple reached out to Grete as the tears fell down her face whilst she watched the train disappear in the distance, getting smaller and smaller until it could be seen no more.

Betty Saul and her 5 children

Betty and Walter on their Wedding Day

Inge and Harald

Inge pointing to the cellars where they hid at their apartment in
Schleiermacherstrasse, Königsberg.

Anita In her 30's

Nazi Rally in
The Cathedral of Light
C. 1937 25

Inge in the Market Sq in Kaukehmen

Inge at her Grandparents house

Inge and Me, lunch in the forest

Dennis Russian Dancing

Chapter 29

In Cranz Anita, Inge and the Mallke family were asleep in one bedroom upstairs in the Blaue Möwe . All went to sleep feeling shattered. Even though there were six of them they felt very alone in the big hotel. No electric lights were allowed, and so there was just a small flickering oil lamp in an ancient baby lantern that lit enough of the room that they were not all in the pitch black. When someone needed to go to the bathroom, the lamp was taken with them, and the room remained in pitch darkness for the time they were gone. They soon adjusted to a routine of going in two's, that way the lamp was taken away less frequently.

The next morning, they all woke up to see another two to three foot of snow, the temperature was 28 degrees below zero, and there was ice on the inside of the windows. Inge started to scrape the ice so that she could look outside. It was a complete whiteout as the snow was coming down in spades. Anita could hear trains passing the hotel and surmised that people were heading west from Cranz along the coastal railway. It was a relief to know those trains were still running, but she needed to know that her mother and sisters would be making the journey over today from Königsberg. Since the phone lines were down, she had no way of knowing what time they would arrive.

The day moved slowly on, and the children played games and Inge and Hilde worked hard to occupy the younger children. Frau Mallke and Anita talked quietly together. They felt concerned that the weather was closing in so quickly. As the day drew to a close, Anita ventured into the kitchen where they had spent most of the day. It was warmer in there with the wood-burning stove, and even though there was a degree of concern that they might in effect be sending out smoke signals, they felt confident that they were far enough away from the main town, and any other towns come to that. "Who would notice a hotel set among the trees on the edge of a beach with a railway line on one side of it", said Anita, trying to stay positive.

It was getting late at the end of the day, and still; there was no news from

Helene, Grete and Lotte; had they caught a train? Everyone in the hotel could hear the 'stalinorgel' which was what everyone called the Russian missiles as they landed close by. Anita was determined that she would go to the little railway station near the hotel, as they could hear the trains even though they doubted that any were stopping, Inge went with her. Anita wanted to know from anyone leaving if the news was good or bad. Were the Russians still advancing towards Königsberg? They were terrified in the dark; every tree appeared to resemble a man lurking in the woods. The snow squeaked beneath their feet and caused a deep echo, sounding like people were walking behind them.

They stood for what felt like an eternity for the next train. Their faces prickled from the cold, and at last, a train arrived but did not stop. The train travelled slowly from Cranz, as it was only a little steam train, but it was packed, and people were stood on the steps of the train, and some were hanging on the outside of the train like bats. People shouted from the train,

"Get away, the Russians are only an hour away from here." Anita shouted back

"Where are the trains from Königsberg...? Someone shouted in reply, but the train was passing now, and she just made out the response

"They stopped this morning, no more..." And the voice trailed off.

Anita and Inge were alarmed and distraught in equal measure to learn that there were no trains from Königsberg since the early morning, plus the Russians were advancing. Inge turned to her mother and said, "Mutti, what are we to do now?" Anita replied,

"I just don't know." With a heavy heart and her mind working overtime trying to fathom what had happened to the rest of her family, Anita took Inge's hand. They walked back to the Blaue Möwe through the woods. The snow began to fall straight and steady from a sky without wind. It was landing like soft feathered crystals, becoming one with the thickening darkness, descending on the ground, layer by layer. Both Anita and Inge clung to each other and Inge could feel her mother's tension. For the first time in her life, Inge recognised the need to acknowledge her mother's fallibility.

As they walked in through the door of the Hotel, Frau Mallke and Hilde were waiting eagerly in the hallway. Anita ushered everyone into the only warm room, the kitchen. There were the remains of their lunchtime broth on the stove, and both Inge and her mother were grateful for the instant warmth and comfort that food brings in anxious moments. Herta and Gerhard were huddled together on the small settee with a blanket over them, half in slumber. The return of Inge and Anita disturbed them, and they seemed to sense the fraught atmosphere. Even though they could not decipher the low-level conversation, they could detect the undercurrent of anxiety in the room.

The decision on what to do next was to be made at first light; they recognised the need for sleep in everyone. Anita and Frau Mallke ushered all of the children, including the two teenagers, into their beds, tightly packed as they were. The two women went back downstairs to ensure that the stove was adequately stoked to last the night and review what provisions were left for the next day. The two friends spoke few words, both feeling the angst of the other, and not wanting to add to their level of fear by making more of the situation that night. They too retired for the night, they needed to sleep, and that was imperative.

Sleep was not easily achieved; the noise of the bombs, the shooting of machine guns sounded as though it were coming from the garden; it was so close. Everyone huddled closely together that night; they all prayed that God would protect them. In the early morning, the gunfire seemed to subside a little, and they arose early. As they looked out of one of the front bedroom windows, they could see over to the beach. The landscape now disfigured with snow, at any other time, it would have been a fairy-tale picture. With no leaves on the trees, they saw clearly, an unending black snake of people walking, bent over, not looking right or left, nor appearing to speak to each other.

Inge opened the window to see if she could hear anything, but no. They were moving forward in complete silence along the snow-covered beach. A long line of people, all dressed in black or dark winter clothing, standing out clearly against the snow. Some people had a horse and cart, others, little handcarts; others had sledges to transport their belongings or children or both. It was clear that some had a bag around their neck to carry their cat or dog in. Inge shivered, not because of the cold blasts coming through the window, more the sense of feeling terrorised by the silence. Hundreds of people were walking together in a black mass through the snow, but no noise at all.

Just Inge and Hilde remained upstairs now as they moved to see what they could see on the other side of the hotel. There were still trains passing, but these were coastal trains leaving from Cranz. The passengers were all packed to the roof with children, parents, people, belongings, and whatever animals they could take. Suddenly on the other side of the hotel, from nowhere, came planes, flying very low over the water's edge. Then they began to machine-gun the black mass of people on the beach as they dived for cover on the ground. The planes then climbed up and flew away again. The girls ran to see what had happened, but there followed a stillness; there was quiet; those who were not hurt just got up and started walking again in silence – hardly glancing back at the black dots of people that remained motionless on the beach.

As Inge pulled the window closed, she wiped away the wet streams down her face. She had not realised she was crying. Pulling a shawl around her shoulders, she held Hilde's hand tightly as they moved down the stairs. When they reached the half landing, there was a loud banging on the locked front door. Anita shushed the younger children and beckoned the older girls to be quiet, and she went to see who it was before opening the door. "Ach du meine Gute," Anita screeched. She had the shock of her life. It was Grete with little Marianne. The sisters clung to each other for precious seconds before Anita ushered Grete into the kitchen.

Grete told her story, how they were told there were no more trains to Cranz and so they planned to take a train to Marienburg. They became separated. Grete expressed the sheer panic that she had felt at losing her family. The elderly couple who picked up Marianne had looked after her in her plight, and just as they were planning another route via the road, in whatever vehicle they could enlist, they heard that the Cranz trains were reinstated. It started to make sense to Anita, even though the story was frightening to hear and distressing for Grete to recount. She comforted her sister as best, she could, making her warm tea and offering her whatever food there was available.

Anita decided to pop outside and check that the stove was not throwing out too much smoke that could be spotted from the air. They were meticulous about not showing any sign of light, but the smoke was less easy to control. As long as they kept a hot fire, there would be less smoke, and so, someone was always on log duty to ensure it remained hot. The older ladies discussed that apart from the snake of people along the beach, they were not a target while they were in the hotel. There were only six houses in Rosehnen, after all and they were just summer houses mainly for people in the city. The English bombers, they concluded, would need to come in over the 'Ostsee' as they called it, otherwise known as the Baltic, to drop bombs on them.

Inge remarked to Hilde, "Mutti seems happy to have her sister here with her now."

"Jah, the three of them are in deep discussion now, have you noticed them?" The three older ladies remained in heavy conversation for most of the day.

"What do we do now?" they were overheard to say and that remained the main topic to be discussed, unsurprisingly. Hilde and Inge occupied the smaller children, especially Marianne who was entirely withdrawn after her ordeal. Inge played drawing games with her while Hilde played Snakes and Ladders with Herta and Gerhard.

The evening started to draw in, and the kitchen blinds were taped to the windows and Anita went down the back steps to close the outside shutters securely. The children watched on sleepily as the snowflakes, silver and dark, started to fall obliquely against the night sky. There was no electricity now; they only used an oil lamp and cooked on the stove, living between the two bedrooms and the kitchen. The bedrooms they used held the advantage of housing the stove chimney up to the roof, and were, therefore, warmer than the other bedrooms.

About twenty-five minutes later and for the second time that day came a fierce, unrelenting banging on the front door. Everyone stood still in the kitchen, daring not to speak nor move. Again, the door banged, and it became clear the person or persons wanted to be answered. Anita crept out into the hallway and through the two thin panes of frosted stained glass, and could see the silhouette of two men in uniform. They went towards the front door together; the single oil lamp being carried by Anita. Then they heard German voices and so opened the door.

There stood two German soldiers saying, "Please, please let us in." So, of course, they did. The two soldiers welcomed the warmth of the kitchen fire, and as they drank hot coffee, they told their story about how they had run away from their company. The German command was breaking down, and nobody had any trust and faith in their decision making any longer. Worse still, the Russians were advancing; they were probably only 20 minutes away and they needed to get away from here. There was real fear in their voices as they spoke. Anita looked at Grete and then Frau Mallke, and then glanced over towards the children as she exclaimed that she did not want to go. They were now quite a large group, and she couldn't contemplate a mass exodus with everyone.

Grete resented the decision made without consultation, so did Frau Mallke. A big argument ensued as the children watched on, frightened but placing their trust in the fact that whatever decision was made would be in their best interests. After a heated ten minutes, they all agreed that they should go. So, they put on warm clothing, as it was night time now and each day was colder than the last. The wind was howling around the Hotel; it was bitterly cold.

By the time everyone had layered up their clothing and was ready to go, the weather had worsened. It was now blowing a gale. The group left the Hotel, huddling closely together and holding hands. It was hard to know which way to go as the familiar landscape was covered behind the dense white swirling blizzard. It would be easy to feel disorientated, but the women felt somewhat supported in having two soldiers with them. Anita was holding Marianne; the pushchair was too heavy to push in the snow with her in it. Grete started to scream as she dragged her child along. Inge was pulling her mother, and Frau Mallke held on tightly to the younger of her children, unable to carry much else as there was nothing more important to her than holding onto her precious offspring.

A blizzard hardly seems an adequate word to describe the conditions to which the world outside had surrendered. Worse still, the gunfire became louder, closer; they couldn't hear each other speak anymore. And it was so cold, Inge started to shiver.. Any exposed skin would sting as body warmth was sucked away by the wind. The arguments regarding Marianne continued. Above the howling wind and gunfire, Anita abruptly stopped and shouted: "We are going back to the house, we have to die, and that is it, the children can't travel in this weather."

The two soldiers grabbed hold of Inge and Hilde and started to pull them away, saying,

"They are young, they have their whole lives ahead of them, we will take them with us." Anita grabbed Inge and forcefully dragged her away.

"If I die," she screamed, "she is dying with me". Frau Mallke beckoned Hilde towards her and Grete held her little girl tightly. She was screaming above the noise of the storm, "Let us go back in the house." After all, the fighting everyone gave in, and along with the two soldiers, they made their way back to the hotel.

Away from the vicious storm, the discussions resumed, and ultimately, they decided that they would go in the morning and be better prepared. It would then be 25th January, a date not lost on Inge as it was her Papa's birthday and he was foremost in her mind. As they sat and talked, the soldiers explained more rationally about the situation. In the event, they were in the fighting line, and so they should at least try to get away to the next town because the Germans would advance again and then we could all go back home. That made sense to Anita and Inge as they knew that Helene (Oma), had of course been living close to the Lithuanian border in Kuckernesse. The Russians had advanced and then retreated from that area. The weary assembly drank hot soup. Anita set to and made German (black) bread as she knew they would need all the sustenance they could muster on their impending flight. Then everyone tried to sleep.

Chapter 30
The Flight

Loud shells dropping all around crudely awoke them; it felt like the fight was right on their doorstep. This time everyone dressed more warmly, Inge donned two pairs of her fathers' long-johns. On top of that, went ski trousers, three jumpers and coats with a fur lining. Anita got a rucksack for herself and found another for Frau Mallke; that way they had free hands. In them, she put some honey and syrup, a jar of pate and anything else she could fit in. Everyone helped in getting a sledge ready for Marianne. Anita wrapped her up so that they could hardly see her face. Last of all they wrapped her in a feather duvet. Anita locked the door and said there was no point in loading everyone up with any more as they would be back in a couple of days.

The party set off embarking on an exodus with no idea where they were headed – only west. They marched in unison across the garden, winding their way around the snow-laden trees in the woodland. Before they had moved a hundred yards towards the beach, Anita stopped, her foresight once again prevailing. She decided to run back to the hotel; the rest waited. She returned with some sizeable white bed sheets. "We will not go with the crowd, we will be too easily spotted by the planes, we will hold back, and when the planes come over, we will place a sheet over our heads." As they made their way through the snow-laden dunes, Inge looked ahead at the long snake of refugees making their way along the beach.

Inge moved as though in a dream. This was surreal. Her Mutti was just three or four paces ahead of her. Anita bore so many layers of clothing that with her small stature she looked to Inge like a big round ball with little legs at the bottom. She smiled to herself for a millisecond and then the cold hit her in an icy blast.

The beach was of course thickly covered in snow, but much worse, the Baltic Sea was frozen for about half a mile out. The refugees took full advantage of this fact and used the sea as a transportation road. There were far more people travelling that morning, some moving with a wagon and horses, trying to take as many possessions with them as they could. A road ran adjacent to the beach, and some of the refugees travelled that way. When the planes came in, they could see the road quite quickly and so those refugees were an easy target, as were the black snakes on the white beach. Each time they heard the planes coming, Anita shouted, "Cover," and everyone put their white sheet over their head so that they could not be spotted from the air.

The bitter cold was penetrating even their thick layers. Inge wore a scarf wrapped around her face and felt her breath on the inside of the woollen cloth immediately evaporate, making the scarf feel increasingly wet. The outside of the scarf she knew was frozen solid. Snowflakes landed on her eyelashes, her eyes being the only uncovered part of her body. She hated the stinging feeling in her eyes and wished she could close them, but they were her guides in the poor visibility. She blinked continuously to help protect them from the cold and fearful her eyes might freeze.

As the day wore on and they made moderate progress, the soldiers decided to make their own way and bid them all farewell, wishing them luck. They shook hands with Anita and remarked that she was an amazing woman. Every so often, Anita would insist that Marianne should be made to walk and so took her off the sledge. Marianne was crying because it was snowing and she didn't want to walk. The howling wind was unbelievably cold and whipped each snowflake into a projectile that stung any unguarded skin. Temperatures were lower than minus 30 degrees. They took it in turns to hold Marianne and the other younger children's hands as the wind was so strong that they had to fight for every step. Grete was furious with Anita for making Marianne walk. Inge ran to her mothers' defence, "Tante Grete, Mutti is only thinking about Marianne, she might freeze to death if she just lies on the sledge."

Inge's argument got lost on Grete, and she and Anita became so angry with each other that Grete put Marianne on the sledge and said that she would go on her own. Slowly Grete walked away from the main party, Inge looked at her Aunt and then at her mother, alarmed at how they both were so stubborn. Inge stared at her Aunt's footprints as she walked away, but the swirling storm of screaming snow was so dense that before Grete had marched many yards, the prints were covered. The visibility was terrible and the wind so loud, she was lost in the storm and could no longer be seen by any of them.

There was no time or opportunity to regret or reflect, and the party continued to walk onwards. Now there were only six of them and Anita calculated that made them less of a target. She was too angry with her sister at that moment to feel any sentiment. Anita then remembered that Grete was carrying the black bread. First she felt annoyed and then her compassion for her sister crept into her thoughts and she was grateful that Grete had sustaining food for herself and her child. They had walked for hours along the coastline just past Rauschen. Anita knew the geography well and knew that they must start to change direction and cut across the peninsula. Otherwise, they would end up walking further than they needed to.

They left the familiar coastline behind them and headed inland, the bitterness of the cold biting harder with each hour that passed. The group walked over snow-covered roads, devoid of colour; all around them felt like a giant white page. Nothing looked familiar, and no comfort could be drawn from recognisable surroundings anymore. Instinct drove them onwards, survival instinct mainly, but nothing could guide them back from where they came. Intuition drove them south-west towards relative safety. Their energy levels dropped as the dusk started to fall upon scenery that under any other circumstances could be described as hauntingly beautiful. But to the party of weary travellers, this bitter January night felt unforgiving and cruel. They were more sheltered now by trees, and yet they still held tight hold of their white sheets in constant readiness.

It started to get darker and darker, and Inge turned to her Mother, "Mutti, couldn't we just go into the next house that we pass and ask if we could stay there to get warm and dry, just for a short while, could we Mutti, please Mutti?" Anita turned to look at Inge and slowly nodded; it was impossible to interpret facial expressions under the swathes of scarves and hats. Even their eyebrows and lashes were covered in frost and snow.

They spotted a beautiful looking house, and it reminded Anita of her parent's home. It had a white picket fence around the boundary and a path up to the front door, which had been recently cleared. There was a flickering light through the chintz curtains, and Frau Mallke knocked on the door. Each already felt the benefit of the shelter as they stood in the porch, and waited patiently for someone to come. Anita spoke out to them, hoping that hearing Prussian voices would put them at ease and answer the door. But nobody came to the door, and after a few minutes Anita decided to try the door handle, it opened.

They had no insight into the horror that awaited them as they set foot in the house. The décor was elegant, but there was a broken vase lying on the tiled floor below the hallway table where it once stood. Anita shouted "Hallo," closely followed by the others almost in unison. There was no response to their calls as they moved forward on the carpet runner into the inner hallway, which led to the kitchen. Anita held a tremendous sense of premonition, she knew not why, but her heart was sinking into her stomach. She reached out to Frau Mallke to hold the children back. Anita walked into the kitchen alone.

Nothing could have prepared Anita for the sight before her eyes. She screamed out loud, clutched her chest and turned around with outstretched arms to try and prevent anyone else from entering the room. Too late, Inge and Hilde were peering around her to see what had caused the gut-wrenching scream that Anita uncharacteristically emitted. A mother and her three children were sitting at the kitchen table; they were dead, with their tongues nailed to the table. Herta and Gerhard were spared the sight, but the two older girls and their mothers bore witness to the real horrors of what one human being can do to another. There was no time to provide any degree of dignity for the unfortunate family. Nobody knew for sure if the perpetrators of this heinous murder were still in the area. They moved out of the house, their hunger and fatigue almost overtaking their sense of disgust, but self-preservation drove them onwards. There must be a safe house in the area.

Frau Mallke led them down the road towards another house that stood away from all the others. It was in darkness; Frau Mallke wasn't sure whether this was a good omen or not; she walked up to the front door. Behind them, they heard the crisp footsteps of heavy boots in the compacted snow. Anita turned and saw two German soldiers standing at the gate to the garden. They were different soldiers to the previous ones they had encountered. The men pronounced that they had also left their company and nobody knew what was going on. All the German soldiers were now running. The Russians had already been in the area and then moved onwards; nobody was sure where they were anymore. Anita explained their recent encounter at another house. The soldiers spat in the snow in disgust, before moving in front of Frau Mallke. They wandered into the house ahead of the group. Nobody questioned their actions. The soldiers returned to the front door, proffered a nod of authorisation and beckoned everyone in.

This time the owners had left in time, that was clear, and their house lay intact. It was a relief to feel warmer and dry away from the relentless cold. In the kitchen was a reasonable stack of food, so they set to and made a meal on the stove for the eight people in the house, everyone sat at the table and enjoyed the hot food. They all took it in turns to use the bathroom facilities, and it was good to feel clean again. The two soldiers told Anita and Frau Mallke that they should head for Danzig (Gdansk) or Gotenhafen as there were ships there that would take them to safety. Anita listened without speaking as the soldiers talked about some of the horrors they too had seen, they were just like the refugees now, there was nothing left to fight for no instruction from above, it was every soldier, man, woman and child for themselves.

As soon as the food was eaten and everyone had freshened up, each found a bed to sleep in – the children sleeping top and tail. Nobody questioned the fact that they perhaps should keep walking through the night, they were just so exhausted, nothing was more important than sleep, and within seconds of each head hitting the pillows, rest fell upon them. Not, however, before Inge thought of Oma, Tante Lotte, Tante Grete, and Marianne. She prayed they were safe in their escapes and that one day they would all be together again.

Inge had shared what was probably the master bedroom with her mother, and they both awoke early. Inge looked inside the drawers and saw some lovely frilly underwear. She was tempted "Look, Mutti, we could take some to change into later." Anita chastised her irreverence towards other people's belongings,

"No, how would you like it if someone were to take something from your room?" So, they just filled their bags with food from the kitchen. Everyone started to prepare to go outdoors again and felt refreshed from a comfortable night's sleep. One of the soldiers handed Anita a piece of paper and said, "Look, if you ever get out of East Prussia, here is my parents' address, they have a farm in Schleswig-Holstein. Try and get there and they will help you; they are good people. Anita looked down at the piece of paper, carefully folded it and placed it in her pocket; she looked up at the soldier and nodded a thank you.

Frau Mallke had already set off with her family; she was keen to make a start and conscious that Gerhard being the youngest might hold up the party, so she made a head start. As she reached the end of the road, which was a T-junction, she met with hordes of people travelling on horseback, or with horses pulling carts and wagons and even a few German tanks, thundering along, leaving heavy tracks in the snow. Everyone took full advantage of the tracks, which enabled walking at a quicker pace. Frau Mallke turned and shouted to Anita and Inge "We are turning right, the road ahead is straight, you will catch us up..." Her voice echoed in the snow and as she turned her head to move forward. Anita was not impressed that her friend did not wait and it left her with an uncomfortable feeling. Inge said that she felt anxious that they were going without them. Anita assured her that they would soon catch them up.

As they walked to the boundary of this small town, there was evidence of people having broken into the little shops and plundered what they could take. Further along the road, lay evidence their loot had been too much of a burden to carry as they ran. Jewels lay glittering in the snow, testament to the fragility of the nightmare they were experiencing. Stacks of goods and food were left thrown to the side of the road as people had quickened pace to make their escape. Witnessing this, made Anita quite anxious as she realised that the Russians must indeed be as near as everyone was claiming. She turned to Inge and said, "Inge we must run too."

As the pair started to run, the two soldiers had by now moved well ahead, hearing the sound of distant aircraft coming in from behind them in the East. Anita concluded that they must surely be Russian aircraft. They were now on the very edge of the town, and she knew they would be more vulnerable on the open road, especially as she could see ahead that there were fewer trees in the area to shield them. Instinctively Anita grabbed Inge and dragged her behind the wall of a house. The planes would not see them there. Others ran for cover where they could find it, some just ran along the road, not appreciating that meant they were an easy target.

The machine-gun fire was loud and terrifying, and the Russians had a clear field of fire. They knew they were massacring civilians, in their view the Germans were now experiencing what they had done to Russian civilians – tit for tat. Anita and Inge clung to each other for dear life, heads down in self-protection while they both silently prayed to God to be spared. As quickly as the nightmare unfolded, silence returned except for the distant screams of a woman ahead of them. Anita clutched her chest, "Poor woman, she must have been hit, God bless her and anyone else that was in the firing line, come on Inge, we need to keep moving, the next section of the road is open, we need to be careful." Both Inge and her mother took the dozen or so steps back onto the road. A painful sight greeted them, fresh blood drained into the snow from the victims of the gunfire, but worse still were the bodies of people who had fallen earlier, their bodies frozen in the snow, some women still clutching their frozen babies. Inge let out an audible gasp as she looked at the ghastly sight.

Anita instinctively knew they needed to move on quickly from this area and navigate the next section of road, which was so exposed. The two moved quickly, half running, half fast walking, not daring to look closely at the bodies laid strewn along the road edge. Concluding that these people must have travelled through the night and become too cold or tired to carry on, heaven knows what circumstances took them to their frozen state. As wagons passed them, people on foot begged for a lift, some took pity on the elderly, but this was survival – survival of the fittest.

Anita's heart started to thump in her chest as she looked about a hundred yards ahead of them. She recognised her friend Frau Mallke, nursing what looked like one of her children and screaming. Anita knew this scream from earlier. Inge just ran towards them, her pulse racing. Frau Mallke looked up towards them as Hilde ran to meet Inge, clutching her friend and burying her face in her friend's snow-covered chest.

Anita quickly gathered what happened from the scene before her; little Gerhard lay lifeless in the arms of his mother, who was kneeling on the road. Herta stood behind her mother, arms wrapped around her neck. Frau Mallke rocked backwards and forwards, tears pouring down her face and wailing uncontrollably; she was covered in the blood of her child. Anita reached towards her friend, needing to check if there was life in the child, but no, Gerhard was dead, a bullet wound in the back of his head confirmed that. Anita needed to think quickly; they could not afford to stay where they were, nor could they carry a dead child on their journey. Anita started to pry Gerhard from his mother's arms, and was met with massive resistance. Anita pleaded with her friend to let him go; they needed to save the lives of everyone else.

Frau Mallke just kept crying, "My boy, my boy, my only boy." Wagons rolled onwards – others cast a sympathetic glance as they trudged passed – most just kept on walking.

Eventually, Anita physically shook Frau Mallke into listening to her. She had to help her to appreciate that she had to look after Hilde and Herta. There was nothing they could do for poor Gerhard; she had to let her child go. Anita promised that they would come back and collect him when it was safe and then give him a proper burial. At last Frau Mallke reluctantly agreed to this suggestion, but letting Gerhard go and leaving him at the side of the road was the cause of unimaginable grief for the pitiable woman. Everyone was crying, but no one would stop and help them, not even a family on a horse and cart. There was no time to mourn the dead right now.

The party moved on slowly, to begin with, Frau Mallke repeatedly looking back to comprehend her motionless child lying in the snow at the side of the road. Then Anita took her gloved hand and placed it on the side of Frau Mallke's face to prevent her from turning around. "We must walk quickly, you have two daughters who need you – look at them now – they are alive!" The words were brutal but at that moment brought a sense of reality back in the mind of Frau Mallke. who then took tight hold of her younger daughters hand while Hilde linked her mother's other arm in support and active encouragement to move forward.

Chapter 31

All around them lay silver and gold glistening in the snow, among the dead bodies. Inge concluded that they had plundered the jewellery shops as they had seen earlier and then been gunned down en route. Their pillage had served them no benefit in the face of an enemy intent on execution. Nobody stopped to pick it up. Seconds counted in the flight to escape the Russian armies. Time no longer held any meaning; it was a fight to the next place of safety, and for them that meant Danzig. Russian tanks had passed before them, past the dead or dying civilians who had been shot from the air, not stopping, not considering anything other than the need to advance.

Frau Mallke remained distraught at the loss of her only son, as they walked at pace. Her two daughters stayed close by her side, and Inge walked with Anita. Their heads bowed down as they headed into the wind and driving snow. They were feeling grateful for their fur-lined boots as they sank into the deepening snow, so cold it blew into deep drifts like a barrier formed by a ferocious vortex. Then came the distant hum of aircraft again, everyone dived for cover, this time the only shelter available was an open ditch. There were already dozens of dead bodies, both soldiers and civilians lying in there. Others lay wounded. Everyone prayed for the few minutes it took for the aircraft to dip down over the road, release their arsenal and then climb back up into the skies. With no time for dialogue, everyone looked out for their nearest and dearest to ensure they were unharmed and then scrambled to their feet to join the multitude of refugees. Just a few yards from where they had laid, a grenade had landed. It blew off the leg of a young German soldier. Inge was the nearest person in his line of vision. She stopped to look at him for a moment; he reached out and grabbed her by the leg, "Please don't leave me here, help me…." Anita dragged her away.

The blizzard continued unabated, snow blowing down in a horizontal blur and icicles hanging like ferns of frost from the fences of the houses as they passed by. The snow creaked underfoot, yet there was silence all around them in between the bursts of gunfire and the occasional rattle of horse's reins pulling wagons, creaking under the strain of the weight of furniture and trunks of clothes. Others travelled with just the clothes they stood up in were indicative of the haste in which they had been forced to leave.

The sombre group marched forward as quickly as they could, Anita drove the pace and hunger was now foremost on everyone's minds. They elected to divert into a grocery store; there was little left, just a couple of packets of biscuits and jars of jam. Anita took what she could, praying to God to forgive her sins as she did so. She put what she could into her rucksack, then reached for Frau Mallke to do the same with hers. Frau Mallke stood motionless; Anita swung her around so she could access the buckle of the rucksack. Frau Mallke stared ahead bearing a vacant expression and just obediently moved as instructed, much like a puppet on a string. Hilde recognized her mother was not functioning as she would normally and moved to steady her and offer reassurance.

With no time to waste the group left the relative warmth of the shop and moved towards the road again. As they did so, two army tanks made their way in their direction. The group watched it cross a field and head towards the road where they stood. They were the only refugees in sight at that precise moment. They faced real danger now. Anita quickly analysed the situation and instructed the party to stand still and stay calm. It was an order. The tanks drew nearer and as they did so, Anita glimpsed the markings on the tank. She had never seen a Russian tank, yet these markings looked familiar. As the tanks drew closer, Anita could witness the turrets rotating in their direction, and their guns pointing directly at the group. Panic descended upon all of them.

The two tanks stopped metres from where they stood and only when the soldier stood up from the turret did their fear start to subside. They were German tanks. As the Icy fingers of the storm whipped her cheeks, Anita lifted her gloved hand to her face to pull the scarf around her head more tightly. As she did so, she moved towards the soldiers now descending their tank, the familiar German language sounded so comforting in that panic-stricken moment. The soldiers said that they were making their way to the Frische Nehrung, a spit of land, which separates the Vistula Lagoon from the Baltic Sea. They needed to reach Pillau, a seaport town on the northern part of the Vistula spit, with a short stretch of sea between it and the rest of the spit. Ships were docked there and should be able to take them to safety if the sea close by was not frozen.

There was no doubt that the water in the straits would be frozen and they would be able to cross easily. With no time to waste, they offered to transport them. There was a feeling of relief beyond words for Anita and Inge. Frau Mallke, nodded her agreement, her face set in a catatonic stare. One of the soldiers asked if she was all right, Anita explained the devastation they had experienced earlier in the day, losing Gerhard. Hilde squeezed her mother's arm, and Herta held onto her other gloved hand tightly.

The Mallke family boarded one of the tanks, and Anita and Inge boarded the other. It felt good to out of the severe cold, but nothing prepared them for the noise and the lack of free-flowing air. There was little space and Anita developed a newfound respect for the soldiers who travelled in these things day in day out.

Above the booming thunder noise of the engines, one of the soldiers told Anita that they must head for Danzig or Gotenhafen; there are ships there that will take them to safer areas.

"You aren't the first soldiers to tell us that. How do you know?" The soldier did not reply immediately and after a few seconds just tapped the side of his nose with his forefinger, as if to say "Don't ask questions." Anita was quick to respond,

"Do you think that at this point, there should be secrets like that? Who cares about Hitler's little secrets anymore? Prussian people never asked for this war, and now we suffer more than the German people, don't you dare imply that I shouldn't ask questions. I would be willing to question Hitler himself if I could meet him, if he is even still alive, that is!" Her face emblazoned with fury. The words packed a powerful punch, and the offending soldier shrivelled before her.

Inge sat in silence; she knew better than to even look at her mother when she went into one of her furies. Equally, she appreciated that, within her mother, there was no small degree of pent-up rage. The beleaguered soldier happened to flick her switch in a moment when she felt less vulnerable than in the previous days.

As they drove onto the top part of the peninsula, the road was long and straight, making the journey less bumpy, although the atmosphere felt charged in the tank. Inge felt grateful that they hadn't been turned out after her Mothers outburst. The soldier was, however, suitably ashamed and remained quiet, and after a few hours, they arrived in Pillau. The port was used by many of the armed forces who had been transported to and from this port; it was of considerable military importance. The tanks both came to a standstill on the quayside. Quickly the group from both tanks disembarked, these armoured vehicles could go no further, but their passengers still had a treacherous crossing to make as the Vistula lagoon was completely frozen over.

Frau Mallke, having spent the entire journey in tearful mourning, expressed sincere gratitude for their lift and became quite animated as she wished her driver and his companions well. Anita stepped out of the tank, looked straight ahead and left an embarrassed Inge to display appreciation for their assistance.

Chapter 32
Treacherous Steps

The scene before them was hard to imagine. Hundreds of people flocking to the edge of the frozen straits. Some took their time to consider their passage, and then make their way across the few hundred meters to the safer ground of the Frische Nehrung. The journey along the spit would take them very close to Danzig, and then if necessary on to Gotenhafen where there were ships.

The old, the young and the infirm were strewn across scores of carts, interspersed with furniture and small animals, their bewildered and desperate faces lay testimony to the horrors they had witnessed and the terror at what lay ahead. The situation was confused, people were weighing up the risks of taking a cart over the ice, but for some, there was simply no choice. Elderly and disabled family members were incapable of walking the distance to the Frische Nehrung, they had to stay on their carts, and their horses had to pull them.

The whinnying of horses could be heard all around as if they knew their choices were limited, and yet the risks were high. Frau Mallke looked round to see where Anita was; she was by now reliant on her friend to guide her next move. Inge noticed that everyone was wearing black, it seemed, and they stood out against the whiteness that surrounded them. Anita gathered the party together; they stood in a tight little circle to pray while holding onto each other, heads down. "God protect us, guide us to safety, take pity on us, Lord, help us to reach the other side of this frozen water to the Nehrung... Amen."

Anita looked up first, "We must be quick, dusk is falling, and there are hundreds of people trying to get over the ice. Go quickly. We need to run for our lives!" They were travelling light with little more than rucksacks on their backs, and so they were free to move their arms to build speed with momentum as they walked at pace. The snow-covered ice became exposed in parts with all the people walking on it, making the journey even more treacherous as they slipped underfoot. They held onto each other, looking straight ahead. In the cross wind, it was difficult to hear if someone spoke, so it became futile to try.

Then they heard the noise of horses pulling carts, Inge moved to the side to let them pass, dragging Hilde and Herta to walk away also. Suddenly, the horrific sound of horses whinnying and screaming as the weight of the cart broke the ice. The cart sank in seconds, throwing its passengers into the unforgiving icy water. Arms flayed as the screams of people cut through the wind, begging for help. Inge looked one way and then the next, her mother looked ahead. "We cannot stop, they will drag us down, the ice is too dangerous". The horses tried to swim, but couldn't lift themselves out of the icy sea; the sight was horrific, the screams deafening. Anita stared ahead, Inge's face crumpled as she focused on the noise of the horses above the wind and people's cries for help.

Frau Malke was petrified and just kept walking. They all altered their direction many times, zigzagging to avoid the carts as they sank, and people and horses drowned before their eyes. It was every man woman and child for himself or herself. They continued to silently pray as they walked, praying that they would not be next. Anita quickened her pace, and that drove everyone forward. They started to run, remaining together and negotiating the other people around them, never losing sight of each other. Anita focused her sights on reaching the Frische Nehrung. It felt like an eternity, and then they realised that as they were climbing slightly, they must now be on land.

They stopped for a moment and took stock of their situation; the wind now silenced like a scolded dog. Anita pointed towards the group of trees ahead of them, and they all obediently moved in that direction. Inge couldn't determine which was worse at this point the unrelenting cold, the fatigue, the immense hunger, or the main fear that gripped all of them, dying, but there was no time to ponder over any of these things. Within moments their legs took on new vigour, they had to keep moving.

The people around them walked as if programmed; nobody looked at anyone else, only those they were with received eye contact, a nod or an encouraging word. Everyone made their way in one direction, heads down, not looking back at the nightmare they left on the ice. Each person, lost in their thoughts, focussing on their perspective of their destiny. Sporadically a horse and cart overtook them. "One of the lucky ones," Anita remarked as one passed. Her thoughts swiftly turned to their journey ahead.

The darkness made their journey even more challenging; some people stopped and huddled together for warmth in the snow under a tree. Anita watched the actions of others and knew that to avoid shelter was suicidal. By now, Herta was crying and whimpering, the cold was biting, and their hunger grew worse with each dragging step. Frau Mallke remembered the soldiers had given her some black bread in their tank. She swiftly swung her rucksack around and rummaged for the meagre offering that each of the group wolfed down with gratitude.

The need to find shelter and get some sleep became prevalent in Anita's thoughts; she looked around anxiously between the trees. Hilde, then said, "Why don't we build an igloo?" Frau Mallke scowled momentarily, until she heard Anita exclaim,

"Yes, of course, good idea, that is what we should do." With minimal direction from the older women, the group gathered some full pieces of wood with which to dig out and pat the snow. Careful to leave the opening away from the wind, the five of them worked furiously for the next 50 minutes until, as if by miracle, an igloo emerged. Rather haphazard-looking but the science was correct, and it was large enough for them all to shelter away from the storm. Herta was hardly able to stand up by now, and Frau Mallke took a position in the shelter with her younger daughter in her arms. The other three gathered together as best they could and, with heads against shoulders and others on knees, the party were grateful to lie down and rest. Even if sleep eluded them, the rest was appreciated.

Each lay huddled, wrapped in their blanket of thoughts amid the silence of the woodland that surrounded them, protected against the wind, and sheltered from the snow that gently fell all around them for the next few hours. Daylight greeted them all with the stark comprehensions of their situation and reminded them that this was a reality, not a dream, and they needed to recommence their journey, and soon. Herta whined and complained that she was hungry; her mother hushed her and rummaged for a last morsel of bread in her bag. Each took a turn to relieve themselves under cover of trees before making their way back the few meters to the pathway that led along the Nehrung towards the mainland. Soon, a swarm of people greeted them walking the same route. Few even looked up as the group of five females joined the crowd, all moving in the same direction.

In the morning half-light, the trees glistened with their fresh layer of snow and in the sky rolling clouds of multi-grey threatened to release their next discharge. The narrow spit offered little protection from the Baltic winds, being less than half a kilometre wide in parts. As far as possible they tried to keep to the more sheltered side by the lagoon. After most of the day fighting against the wind and cold, they saw the familiar shape of the timber-framed holiday homes. They knew that they were reaching the lower end of the spit. Grateful for the opportunity to shelter out of the bitter wind, they joined other groups of people harbouring in one of them to rest for a short while. Any food was long gone, but at least they sat in relative warmth for about an hour. Long enough to recharge and prepare for the next stage of the journey.

While they rested, Anita entered into conversation with a soldier who was fleeing with a young family which may or may not have been his own. He said that he had heard that the ships were setting sail no later than 30th from Danzig or Gotenhafen. Tomorrow was 28th, and they had about 70 kilometres still to go. "You must not waste time," he said, "we are done for, the Generals are giving up, and the Russians have superiority over us – keep going, don't look back and run for your lives."

Chapter 33

Anita was starting to panic. She bore the brunt of the responsibility to guide herself, her friend and their children to safety. Time was not on their side. They needed to quicken their pace, but hunger was now prevalent in their minds as well as exhaustion. The group made full use of the remaining daylight marching onwards. Ahead, hues of red hung in the sky between the clouds as slowly a dark canvas descended with no stars to be seen nor a moon to guide them. Anita stopped for a moment and prayed as the darkness crept over them. The spit was wider here and she felt guided to swerve off the main road and walk through dense woodland. Inge knew better than to question her mother's motives for moving 'off-piste'. Frau Mallke was just happy for someone else to make the decisions. Anita was unsure she was taking the right choice when she looked up to see flickering candlelight about 150 metres in front of them. As they drew nearer, they could see a smallholding with a barn and a quaint little timber-framed house. The only tracks in the snow were the footprints to and from the barn; the drive to the house was like a soft white fluffy blanket of virgin snow. They moved closer to the house, not daring to speak in the quiet of the woods and conscious that every crunch of the snow echoed all around them. Cautiously they looked into the window with the light and saw a man leaning over something; they could not see what.

Anita told everyone to hold back, and only she would knock on the front door. She knocked twice, waited and then knocked again. Eventually, the man answered, he was distressed and stood with his arms hanging limply by his side. Anita instinctively knew that they were entering a world of grief. At that precise moment, Inge and Hilde wandered into the eye-line of the old gentleman; he turned and asked how many there were of them. "Five," Anita said. The gentleman's' reply was straight to the point.

"My wife is dead, she is in here, I can't leave her, she has been very ill, but you are welcome to come in out of the cold."

Anita turned to the others, who each nodded in agreement. Each faced the dilemma of experiencing the human need for warmth and the prospect of food versus the probability of confronting a dead body and her distressed husband. Everyone respectfully lowered their heads as they entered into a large but only room in the downstairs of the house. There was a log burner, which incorporated a stove and held the embers of a fire, a large dresser, a small and ageing pine table and four chairs. A curtain lay drawn across the back of the room. Anita imagined it led to the kitchen. A lady was lying on the settee; her smooth, waxy face looked ghostly grey. Frau Mallke whispered into Anita's ear,

"She looks like she has been dead for days, which would account for the unpleasant smell in the air." Anita took charge and politely suggested that they cover her face, for the sake of the children. Her grief-stricken husband reluctantly agreed as he brushed her cold face with his hand and gave her the dignity of a shroud.

Following this act, the gentleman appeared to start to accept the fact that his wife was dead. As he collected himself, he remembered to be hospitable and offered them all a hot drink, and after placing a log on the fire, he started to reheat the soup on the stove. Food had never tasted better, even though it was out of a tin. Other food in jars was randomly placed on the table. Although there was nothing fresh, they were so utterly grateful to the gentleman for his generosity.

"My name is Klaus," the gentleman felt it was time he introduced himself appropriately. His formal introduction was at odds with his general distraught condition.

"I wish we were meeting under better circumstances." It was a difficult subject to broach but Anita, being her direct self, asked about the deceased's passing. He told them that when everyone was told to evacuate, he refused, his wife had cancer, and they knew she did not have long to live. The gentleman did not want to subject his wife to the vagaries of a journey to who knew where when she was already dying. She had died two days ago, but he could not leave her, and as there was nobody to call, and no help came, he decided to place his destiny in the hands of God. Anita asked if they could all pray together, and they did, praying for the departed and asking for strength for the living. It was clear to see that Klaus gained a degree of comfort from this.. As they lifted their heads, Herta could be seen in the armchair fast asleep, too exhausted to concern herself that she lay just two metres from a dead body.

A tearful Frau Mallke recounted the sad story of Gerhard's death. Then as eyes began to droop, Klaus helped carry Herta and guided the party upstairs to the two small bedrooms. He offered his bedroom up for Anita, Inge and Hilde and a second with a single bed, which Frau Mallke shared with Herta. On wishing them a good sleep, Klaus remarked that they were too tired to discuss plans for the next day. He promised to wake them at dawn, understanding the importance of an early start. He descended the stairs to spend another night with the love of his life.

Daylight broke through the curtains and for the first time in what felt like months, sunshine stroked Anita's face as she turned to blink towards the light. The stark recognition of where they were brought her bolt upright in bed, she shook the young girls awake and told Hilde to wake her mother and sister. When Anita reached the only downstairs room, which led to the bathroom, she could see Klaus still asleep in his chair.

The water in the bathroom was cold, but Anita still appreciated the bar of soap and the opportunity to wash, she quickly beckoned the others to do the same and took the liberty to light the stove and make some coffee. Klaus awoke and for a few moments sat and just stared at his wife, now respectfully covered in a sheet. When he stood up and turned around towards the kitchen area, Anita greeted him sympathetically with a smile.

"We need to talk, Klaus; you have to leave; it isn't safe to stay. The Russians are moving closer, I doubt they will come onto the Nehrung immediately, but they may do unless they retreat entirely and it doesn't feel to me like they will do that. There are ships in Danzig and Gotenhafen, they will take us to safety, but we don't have long." Klaus thought for a moment, then he turned and put on his coat and hat and fur boots,

"I need to go and feed the horses." Anita held onto those words,

"Horses? Do you have horses? Do you have a cart as well?"

"Better than that," came the reply as he disappeared out into the small yard towards the barn.

Anita stared after Klaus; her mind was working overtime now; this could be the answer to their prayers. She called the others downstairs and explained the situation to Frau Mallke, who was quick to agree that this could be an excellent solution for them. The main stumbling block as they saw it was the corpse lying on the settee. Would Klaus leave her and if not, would he allow them to take his horses and cart?

Anita and Frau Mallke cheekily took what food was left in the cupboards and made a concoction of a meal on the table, carefully, considering which items would be suitable to take on the journey. Deciding the biscuits and meat pâté were the better options, the rest was laid out for their breakfast. As Klaus re-entered the room after feeding his horses, he glanced at the table, and Anita apologetically explained their actions. Klaus waved his hands,

"No need to explain, you are a sensible woman, and you think logically, not like me. I am an oversentimental old man with no life left anymore." The girls all said at the same time,

"Yes, you do have a life, you must come with us, please"!

Klaus sat at the table with the group and Anita noted that the extra heat in the room since they arrived, plus the additional logs placed on the stove was turning the bad smell into a putrid stench, they needed to leave soon. Klaus was not unaware of the fact either, and as he sat, he became more animated. "If you help me bury my wife, I will take you with my two horses. I have a sledge, built for a driver and four people, but I am sure you will all fit in, it will be a tight squeeze though." They all replied in unison,

"Yes, Yes, of course, we will."

The grim task of digging through the snow to the frozen ground below took time, as the spades weren't made for such conditions and two of the three broke. Klaus held his head in his hands and Anita, aware of the time this was taking, came up with a proposal.

"Why don't we do the best we can today, cover her with snow and then when the Russians retreat you can come back and give her the burial that she deserves?" Klaus considered this solution for a moment and then grudgingly agreed. Together they moved the corpse, now easier as rigor mortis had passed, and quickly the adults buried the lady in a shallow snowy grave.

Klaus took his time gathering his belongings to take with them. It was now well past 9.30 am, and they needed to be making headway. Frau Mallke helped him as much as she could, gently coaxing him with sympathy. Anita helped to take charge of the horses, a dapple-grey and a bay; slender in build and, while both were nearing twenty years old, Anita could tell they were healthy and robust as she noted their muscles under their well-groomed, sleek coats. The sledge was homemade; Klaus explained he used it to collect logs and provisions in the winter. The horses were bridled, and a harness rigged with chains attached to the sledge. Klaus was proud of his construction with his little driver's seat carved into the front; the internal dimensions of the vehicle looked to be more appropriate for children. Conditions were going to be very tight indeed, but everyone was so grateful, they packed inside, adults sitting on one cheek, arms wrapped around daughters and blankets carefully laid over them all, their bags tucked away on the floor.

After what felt like an eternity to all concerned, they set off. Herta was excited and squealed when the sledge jolted as the horses took their first few steps pulling a heavy load. There had been no discussion about the route they would take. Klaus, shouted back that he had to be careful if they were to encounter a downhill run, as the sledge might speed up and slide into the fetlocks of the horses. He knew the route to take; it was cross-country, avoiding the steep banks of the snow-covered roads. The relief among the party was palpable; to be moving at trotting speed meant that they might make the bulk of their journey before it got too dark. Inge took in the countryside, feeling so sorry for the poor people they passed, trudging through the snow all moving in the same direction.

Every one of the party sank into deep thought, at last allowing themselves a little time to think about their loved ones. Each looked back at all that had happened since this dreadful war had escalated to this point. Inge thought about Tante Grete and Marianne; had they made it? What had happened to Oma, Tante Lotte, and was Onkel Adolf still alive? They had not heard to the contrary. She wondered about her cousins and Tante Betty. She fleetingly wondered about Onkel Walter, looking at her mother in guilt as she did so. Anita too, was thinking about her mother and sisters. Her thoughts also went to more joyful times, with Herbert and her grandparents, the times when they had all be together in her parents' cosy home. Also the happy times when she had visited her grandparents and the Zomm family. Where were they all now? How sweet and chaotic those days now felt as Anita realised she had shut out those thoughts of loved ones. What was to become of the beautiful Kingdom of Prussia she loved so much? What was the point when communication was reduced to clenched fists and guns, where common sense had disappeared, and our young men had become pawns in a battle of fascism and dictatorship. Anita recalled the time almost two decades ago when she first heard of Hitler, how he considered himself to be righteous and superior. She knew then that no good would come of that man. How right she had been.

It soon became darker and started to snow again; the weather was indifferent to their needs right now. Inge shivered as she glanced over to her mother, who remained unflinchingly deep in thought. The branches of the fir trees swayed under the weight of the snow, and everyone pulled their rugs closer to them.The kind old gentleman who had taken them this far was nervous about driving his horses over the next stretch of frozen water. Inge sensed his fragile emotions and completely understood his predicament. She knew how much his horses meant to him, and they were now even more precious to him since the death of his wife.

The large snowflakes rested on their clothes and rugs, and Klaus brushed it from his hat and shoulders. The horses looked forlorn, Inge thought, and were quite tired. Lost were their well-groomed manes, and frozen snow clung to them like stalactites. The wellbeing of animals was always prevalent in her mind, Hilde squeezed Inge's hand, and the two girls shared a sympathetic and encouraging smile. Frau Mallke held her younger daughter in what felt like a cradle hold to Herta. She recognised that her mother was equally comforting herself and no doubt thinking about her little brother. Tears were futile now. The survival of the living was prevalent in everyone's minds.

Suddenly Klaus pulled his horses to a stop. He turned around to look at the party as they shared curious glances.

"I can take these horses no further today; we are now on the outskirts of Danzig. I have a friend who lives close to here, and I want to stay there tonight with my horses if he hasn't already fled. I know we will be safe there. You still have a few hours before it gets dark. I am so sorry ladies. I can offer you no more today."

Frau Mallke was the first to take the initiative and speak, and Anita was grateful for that, as for once she was all out of ideas. "Thank you for your kindness, we are so thankful to you, but we are concerned for you too, Klaus," she exclaimed,

"Nein, Nein, you must not worry yourselves about me, what will be will be, but you have young women, and they deserve a life and an opportunity to make a future. You two…" he pointed to Frau Mallke and Anita. "You must guide them to Danzig and get there before dark, and the weather closes in, even more, go now, go!"

The group were already in dismount as he spoke. They recognised that no amount of persuading was going to make an ounce of difference to the mindset of this old gentleman. Without wasting too much time on formalities, they bid their farewells and wished each other good luck and Godspeed. They gathered up what they could carry and wrapped their blankets and rugs around their shoulders against the harsh winds and razor-sharp icy blasts that now blew in sideways off the Baltic Sea.

Making their way across the frozen river, they stayed close with shoulders hunched and barely aware of what lay beneath their feet. The two mothers were protecting the younger ones against the fierce winds, which whipped their cheeks. All walked in a circle around Herta, protecting her as best they could. As they started to climb the bank on the other side of the river, each recognised the black dots ahead were people, and so gathering pace, they soon found they were among other refugees. But nobody spoke; everyone who had reached this far had a story to tell, but no energy to share it. Every effort went into putting one foot in front of another as they trudged through the snow. They had to reach their destination. They knew the ships would soon set sail. Just as dusk was falling, Herta looked up from her protected position and saw the dim lights of Danzig. She shouted, "Look, look, Danzig, we are nearly there, come on we need to hurry." They all thanked God for the sight of a large town and with a renewed energy began to quicken their pace. Determined as they were to reach their destination before nightfall.

The other refugees started to flock together, so many young children and older adults so few men, except for soldiers and men in tanks, who joined the multitude in increasing numbers. Anita, Inge and the Mallke family were walking along a road, surrounded by evacuees. Mainly women, pushing prams, and many pulling small trailer carts with possessions or other children or very elderly relatives with their other hand. Others were fortunate to have horses pulling carts laden with refugees, most of whom were children. Many were attempting to carry far more possessions than they ought to risk taking, but everyone had the same intent. Some of the more able-bodied soldiers helped to transport small children. Women walked with children too big to carry, but not yet adult. They stumbled with each exhausting step. A sharp yank or pull from their mother reminded them that they had no choice but to keep going. Even tanks were driving past laden with refugees. Inge remembered their journey on a tank. It seemed so long ago; time was now immeasurable. She winced as she recalled her mother's brutal outburst towards one of the soldiers.

As night fell, bringing a silent blanket of darkness, the fuzzy, dim lights of Danzig grew closer, even though there was supposed to be complete blackout at night. What few lights they could see drew them-reassuringly closer to safety. As they reached the city, they heard rumours among the various groups of refugees and that there were no ships left in Danzig. Everyone's hearts sank, this could not be true, they had been through so much, travelled so far, why were there no ships? Why had the authorities not considered the vast number of refugees taking flight from East Prussia? The truth was even more disturbing; Hitler did not want anyone to flee, that would mean accepting inevitable defeat. So instead, they caged people's thoughts in fear. The Nazi's wanted men, women and children to stay and fight till victory was finally theirs, such was their delusion.

Anita began to feel incensed but controlled her fury until there was confirmation of the rumours; maybe there was one last ship to sail and other people had also mentioned ships being in Gotenhafen. The crowd dissipated somewhat as they reached the quayside. Hilde asked the question about where all the people had gone, did they not want to find a ship? Then reality dawned. They looked up and down the harbour, no big ships, only small fishing vessels and tugs, nothing capable of aiding their escape. Frau Mallke started to cry, "This is it; we are not meant to get through this, we will all die, either be shot or freeze to death!" Anita glared at her friend,

"What about our children, are we going to give up, they deserve a chance, we have come this far…" A young naval lad overheard the conversation and interrupted Anita.

"You do have a chance, if you hurry, there are ships still to set sail in the next couple of days, but they are in Gotenhafen. You need to keep travelling another 20 kilometres." Anita thanked the young man and turned to her party,

"We have time, we can get there tomorrow, but tonight we need to find somewhere to sleep."

There were people everywhere, all wanting to find somewhere to rest. Slowly someone started to take control and guide them into a large shed/loading bay. It was where the cargo was stored before being loaded onto the ships. They were out of the worst of the wind, but it still felt raw, only a concrete floor and certainly not suitable to lie down and spend the night. Hilde and Inge wandered around and soon spotted some empty hessian sacks piled into a corner of the building. They quickly went about making a softer bed to lie on with the empty sacks. They smelt terrible, and nobody even wanted to imagine what they had been used for, but in their desperate circumstances, they knew they needed to make the best of what they could find, and this was it.

There must have been about 50–60 people sleeping rough in that large shed that night, little opportunity to rest. The youngest fell asleep in utter collapse. Just as Anita started to close her eyes, she heard a kerfuffle as someone wandered around with a large pot of soup, no cups or bowls. Each person was allocated a swig from the large metal spoon. It was watery, but they were grateful for the warmth of the broth. It wasn't enough to satisfy their hunger, but it gave their shrinking stomachs some degree of nourishment, and they were very thankful. The soft wind whistled round the building lulling its beleaguered occupants were hugging together for warmth, most already fallen into an exhausted sleep.

Dawn brought a welcome gap in the storm, the snow lay high and heavy on the ground. Everyone needed to know what to do next, and most were moving around with the dawn to grab an advantage over the others. Nobody knew if there was enough room on the ships leaving Gotenhafen – but clearly that was where they needed to be.

Chapter 34
The *Wilhelm Gustloff*

The ship, *Wilhelm Gustloff* was named after a well-known agitator in the Nazi party, who was particularly active with new troops of the Hitler youth. A lofty man with a receding hairline, he stood tall and proud in his Nazi uniform. Gustloff gave speeches in Berne and Zurich and spied for the third Reich. He passed on names of any Germans who refused to attend his parties in Switzerland, where he was known as the Dictator of Davos. He met his end in his study at the hands of a Jewish medical student called David Frankfurter who sat waiting for him as he entered. It was a highly planned assassination, and Frankfurter reportedly handed himself in. He confessed to the following, "I fired the shots because I am a Jew, I am fully aware of what I have done, and I have no regrets." Again he repeated this at his trial.

In death, the Nazis inflated Wilhelm Gustloff into a figure of greatness. His coffin draped in the swastika flag with the deceased's armband, cap and dagger also lying across the coffin. Two hundred party members gathered as the last salute resounded over the corpse. He became a martyr.

In the previous year, there was a rise in the German labour front after the disbanding of the labour unions and the new doctrine could be heard 'Strength Through Joy'. Workers were encouraged to take holidays and trips to the Bavarian Mountains, thousands were encouraged to take these trips, and the costs were very low… an imaginative way to build people's loyalty! One of these ships was the Dresden, used to cruise the Norwegian fjords. When it hit a granite ledge in Karmsund, it began to sink. Fortunately, all lives bar two were saved, but the full Strength Through Joy project became at risk after that.

In January 1936 a new passenger ship was commissioned for the German Labour Front and its 'Strength Through Joy' project. It cost 25 million Reichsmark to build and was designed to reward factory workers with state-paid holidays. The Ship was built to carry 1460 passengers with 489 cabins and just over 400 crew. The main difference with this Ship from any others was that it would not have any class distinctions and would encourage German unity among the passengers.

Initially, there was a plan to name the ship after the Fuhrer. However, there was a member of the Reich present at the memorial service for the murdered party member, Gustloff, in Switzerland and the decision was made to name the ship after the martyred comrade. So, plans were laid for this new ship to be called the *Wilhelm Gustloff*. Her namesake's murderer was sentenced to life imprisonment. After he had served nine years and the war situation had radically changed, he asked for clemency and was denied by the Swiss Supreme Court.

The very idea of a classless ship was a new concept for the many passengers who all enjoyed eating together in one dining room. On the 5th May 1937, the ship was launched, watched by thousands of support workers. Frau Gustloff swung a bottle of champagne against the ship and called out, "I name this ship the *Wilhelm Gustloff*." This was proudly watched over by members of the Third Reich and the Fuhrer himself and all presented the Nazi salute. The ship gleamed white from bow to stern and set sail as passengers waved flags and handkerchiefs. The shore was lined with an expanse of people watching, waving and showing their admiration at the sheer magnitude of this incredible feat of engineering.

It stood eight stories high with spacious sun decks and varnished walls and a top sun deck. The lounges were all panelled in wood, and there was a beautiful ballroom and music salon. The walls were decorated in old master style oil paintings, and pictures, mainly of the Fuhrer. Below the waterline lay the deep swimming pool, exquisitely covered with mosaic tiles of mermaids and sea creatures. The top deck housed 22 lifeboats, all fitted to crane-like devices called davits, used on a ship for supporting, raising, and lowering lifeboats in an emergency.

From 1938–39 the ship took a total of 80,000 passengers on countless voyages all over Europe, and in 1938 it answered a distress call from an English ship, the *Pagaway*. She was crippled after she lost her manoeuvrability when much of her cargo slid overboard. The *Pagaway* started to take on water and slowly sink.

The incident happened between the Netherlands and the Dover Straits and the *Wilhelm Gustloff* was the nearest ship to answer the distress call. Her lifeboat number one was launched with a crew of 12, but being only powered by oars she struggled to come alongside the vessel in heavy seas.

The lifeboat itself looked in need of rescuing, and so lifeboat number six was launched with a crew of ten. As it had a motor, it was better placed to assist. After first taking back its Crew from the first lifeboat it ventured back to help the *Pagaway*. All 17 of it's seamen jumped into the sea and were rescued by lifeboat number six. A Dutch tug boat arrived to assist, but it was too late for the *Pagaway*, and she sank. The lifeboat number one from the *Wilhelm Gustloff* was so severely damaged she was set adrift and washed up on the shores of Terschelling, an island off the coast of the Netherlands, on 2nd May.

In 1939 the ship was requisitioned by the Kriegsmarine (German navy) as a hospital ship, and subsequently, The *Wilhelm Gustloff* became a floating barracks, and a U-Boat training school for naval personnel at Gotenhafen. It was repainted from hospital colours to standard navy grey to reflect its new role. She remained docked there for the next 4+ years. In 1942 she stood next to the SS *Cap Arcona* which was used in the filming of the German version of the *Titanic*, and many of the *Wilhelm Gustloff* training division acted as extras in the movie.

Operation Hannibal was an initiative to help with the evacuation of German troops under the Russian advance and of course the refugees who were now fleeing, having been told to stay put by the German authorities. The exodus soon took on epic proportions; millions ran for their lives; their protectors abandoned them while fleeing themselves. Senior members of the Nazi party were in total denial of what the rest of the world was starting to realise was unfolding in the east. Innocent refugees with no appetite for the war in the first place where now left to their own devices; their only sin was to be German.

Herbert Tollkühn

Inge aged 17 in
Summer 1944

Alexander Marinesku

The Railway Station in Königsberg

Winter in Cranz

Carts laden in their escape

The Wilhelm Gustloff – Ready to
Set Sail 30th January 1945

Chapter 35

Tired and exhausted Anita and Inge, Frau Mallke and her two remaining children arrived in Gotenhafen. There was a queue of people in the street leading to the dockside for the last remaining ships to leave. Obediently they joined the back of the line, which moved, slowly towards the dock area. Eventually as they turned a corner of the street and feeling the icy blasts of the sea, a magnificent ship stood proud before them. The *Wilhelm Gustloff* was the superliner of its day, and next to it stood the Hansa. Inge looked up at the ships funnels as they moved closer, craning her neck to see the upper decks. She turned to her best friend, and they both grinned with excitement and gratitude. Further along the Gotenhafen Oxhoft piers were two other smaller ships, *Oceania* and the *Antonio Delfino*. They had made it; they had arrived at their destination, and were safe.. Thank God they all said, thank God.

The *Oceania* and the *Delfino* were both overladen with refugees. Although they eventually made it to their chosen destinations safely, Kiel and Copenhagen, most people wanted to be aboard the giant ship. The *Wilhelm Gustloff* would be safer. On the quayside, there was absolute mayhem, tens of thousands of people were swarming upon Gotenhafen, many trying to reach the ships gangway. Anita shouted above the noise, "stay together, we need to stay together, look over there we must report to someone, so they know we are here".

"Ja," shouted back Frau Mallke, and everyone surged forwards as they spotted what looked like an area where people were registering their arrival. Anita watched what seemed to be some process or procedure and noted that some people had a ticket in their hands. Holding no such card herself, she asked another prospective passenger what the system was. "Join the queue," was the abrupt reply...

There must have been a thousand people in a queue before them, and it was a desperate situation. Volunteers were recruited to assist the elderly, infirm and young children as they waited to board the ship. Some of the women naval auxiliaries attempted to help treat the children. Frostbite was common among the multitudes waiting on the quayside, and Vaseline was administered at will. Some women arrived still holding their dead babies, reluctant to let them go. Frau Mallke took pity on them; she knew and understood their pain. Silent tears fell down her cheeks as she watched an auxiliary grapple to snatch a frozen baby from the clutches of a despairing mother; her screams were lost in the turmoil.

There were many military personnel making the voyage also, including a large contingent of female naval auxiliaries. Some of the military personnel decided to cast off their uniforms and disguise themselves as refugees, no doubt thinking they would have a better chance of being accepted on the last ships to leave Gotenhafen. In spite of Hitler's deluded assurances of inevitable victory, the multitude of refugees running from the approaching Russian army told their own story. Even the German Naval authorities had hastily appropriated any naval vessels in the area to help with a massive evacuation of refugees, in apparent disregard of any orders from above.

Food was scarce, and people were plundering the local houses for whatever they could find, many were at the point of starvation. Confusion reigned in every direction, the smell of desperation hung in the air like a vapour. People held on tightly to whatever meant the most to them in the world, be it a child, mother, father, sister, or just a small suitcase of precious items. Many men in their middle years were denied access onto the ship, the reason given, that they may still be able to help in the final stage of the war effort. There were many painful goodbyes.

There was still a thirsty, hungry and freezing mass of people trapped outside the quayside. Eventually, they forced their way forward through the quayside gates. The Tollkuhn's and Mallke's were swept forwards towards the *Wilhelm Gustloff* as the mass swayed behind them. The women moved with the tide and quickly made their way to the gangways and joined yet another queue. Here and now – on the 29th January, no further records were being kept of the numbers making their way onboard the Wilhelm Gustloff – they had run out of paper.

As the group reached the top of the ramp and boarded the ship, they were issued with a lifejacket, which they each put on immediately as instructed. There were people everywhere like a physical wall before them. No order was apparent, and people were seeking warmth and a space to sit or lie. On the decks they pushed their way through to the doors leading to the inside of the ship – it was evident that the whole ship was full to the ramparts. It seemed there was not an inch of space for the party to sit together and be warm and dry.

The ship had been in dock for three days, and the early arrivals had the benefit of cabins and enjoyed the luxury of a comfortable area to rest and wait. For the thousands that arrived in the days that followed, the wait to board was painful. In the final hours, the previous orderly registration process broke down, and eventually, the authorities lost count of the numbers of people when they reached 6050. After that, they had no idea of the names of the later arrivals. There were Germans, Prussians, Latvians, Poles, Lithuanians, and Estonians as well as Croatian volunteer soldiers who had been pressed into duty to supplement the ship's crew. All eagerly making their way on board.

Anita turned to Frau Mallke and said that everyone would make for the upper decks, so if they were smart, they might find space in the lower desks. Accordingly, they made their way down to the lower decks. Every lounge was full of people, and they were told at the door that no more would be allowed in. Everyone was now measuring their lives into the next few seconds. The ballroom was strewn with mattresses and makeshift beds; it was reduced to little more than a dormitory. The walls had been stripped of the beautiful artwork that had previously adorned the music rooms, lounges and library. It was stuffy and hard to breathe with all the people scrambling to make space for themselves and their families. Children were crying, and babies were screaming for food and milk.

Inge, who was beginning to feel dislocated from the here and now, noticed a heavily pregnant lady clutching her stomach as she tried to squeeze through the crowds of people. She was quickly directed to the maternity ward area, next to the room where all the severely wounded soldiers were laid – their moans and screams penetrated the maternity ward. Already since embarkation began, four babies had been born; for the midwives, it was quite simply – business as usual.

Hilde nudged Inge to look out of the window as they passed through a corridor on the very edge of the alleyway, they saw the crowds of people still on the quayside and even more clambering up the gangway. The pushing and shoving knew no bounds, and occasionally a mother would lose hold of her child's hand, and the child would fall between the harbour wall and the hull of the ship – there was no point in screaming – nobody came to help.

Inge shook her head and again thanked God for the fact that they were safe aboard the ship. She felt they were among the lucky ones. In the girls' attempts to look outside, they had lost sight of their mothers and panic set in. Oh no! which direction had they gone in? Left or right, with all these people it would be difficult to see where they were. Then Anita pushed her way back and saw her daughter, and she shouted harshly for Inge and Hilde to join them and not to take their eyes off their mothers again. The girls dutifully obeyed and watched where they were going like hawks.

All around them were the continual messages coming from the public address system asking for parents to go and pick up their lost children from one station point or another. Each level they went down felt as full as the last until they came to the lower deck, which housed the swimming pool. They were now, below the waterline, and there were no windows. Naturally, the swimming pool was empty of water, and people were starting to make camp in there. Anita decided that it was a safe and sensible place to settle so they made their way down the mosaic steps of the pool and turned to reach a corner of the swimming pool. They all collapsed into a heap together and laid out what blankets they had to make themselves as comfortable as they could. Frau Mallke smiled at Inge and Hilde, "No more wet feet or cold hands, we are safe at last." It was now in the early hours of the morning, and many of the exhausted passengers were already asleep – as best they could manage to sleep. Anita told the girls they should sleep now while they could, and all five of them tried to close their eyes. Shutting off their ears to the constant noise of people and crying children both near to them and in other parts of their deck, was not so easy. Each said their prayers of thankfulness and hope for their safe crossing and landing in the relative safety of Germany. At least they would be further away from the dreaded fear of the Russian invasion.

As they tried to settle down to sleep, there was a lot of rummaging around them, and soon nearly 300 female naval auxiliaries were clambering down to try and join them. They too were included in the evacuation and some found refuge in what space remained in the swimming pool, further along from where Anita, Inge and the Mallke family were lying. They soon removed their close-fitting jackets. Some even removed their caps, which were perched on top of their hairdos and marked with the swastika. By now the swimming pool was well and truly full of individuals. It was stifling hot and cramped, and the smell was not pleasant, but still, people remained hopeful. They were safe onboard their rescue ship, their salvation, and they were grateful, so very appreciative.

Chapter 36
Mutti's dream

Sitting silently, Frau Mallke was thinking of little Gerhard and so were Herta and Hilde who each dripped tears from watery eyes in memory of their brother. Hilde imagined his lifeless body lying at the side of the road now frozen solid, no doubt covered in snow, invisible to anyone who passed. Herta watched her sister and tried hard to quench her tears, wanting to prevent the sobs from affecting her breathing. Each gasped for air, as they could restrain themselves no longer. Their mother held her face in her hands, unable to hold back the emotion of leaving her son behind – poor Gerhard, just another body at the side of the road. Inge was thinking about her father, wondering where he lay. What of Oma and Tante Lotte, darling little Marianne and Tante Grete? Where are they tonight? Anita prayed for God to guide and help carry them to safety.

All around people tried to settle small distressed children and the elderly struggled to get comfortable in the limited space with no soft cushions. The atmosphere felt sticky and hot, a complete contrast to the bitter cold that everyone had previously endured. Eventually they each fell into a deep, deep sleep. During her exhausted sleep Anita had a dream that they were in the swimming pool and she dreamt that all their possessions were with them and that their coffee table from home was floating in water in the pool. In her dream, she was choking from water in her lungs; she sat upright; there was water all around them, and she felt sheer panic. Anita awoke from her dream as a scream tore from her chest. Her dream felt real and quite distinctive, the experience was hard to capture in words. It felt like they were all drowning, and they needed to escape, the vision was stark and clear to her, and she was seeing it again and again in her mind's eye even now that she had awoken.

Frau Mallke looked to Anita and asked "Anita what is the matter?", Anita wore a ghostly expression, ashen white and staring into the middle distance. Not responding to her friend at all, Anita turned to Inge, grabbed her arm, saying:

"We have to get off this ship." Inge looked at her mother in complete disbelief and said,

"Why Mutti, why? We are warm and safe and out of that terrible cold, why?"

"I have had a dream, Inge, I dreamt that our coffee table was floating on water and we were going to drown."

Everyone turned and looked at Anita in complete amazement. Frau Mallke tried to reason with her. She reminded Anita that they were all tormented by the cold and the torturous experience they had all endured. She would be mad to want to disembark this ship. They were setting sail in a few hours, and soon they would be in a safe area, why would she want to jeopardise all that based on a silly nightmare?

No amount of persuading would change Anita's mind. She was getting off the ship, and Inge was going too. She wanted her friend to bring her two daughters with her as well. Frau Mallke looked at her girls, the younger one still sleeping.

"Hilde," she said, "do you think we should leave this ship, I don't!" Hilde looked at the pained expression on her friend Inge's face and replied,

"No, me neither, I think we should all stay here."

With that, Anita started to gather her belongings and grabbed hold of Inge's arm to force her to stand. Frau Mallke looked on in quizzical fury,

"My dearest friend, please rethink what you are doing, this is madness, we are safe, don't base your actions on a silly dream, please think of Inge, she doesn't want to leave either."

"We must say our goodbyes if you refuse to come with us."

Anita was determined and not waiting to debate the decision anymore. Frau Mallke was in despair of her friend. She told her,

"There is no way that I am prepared to risk the lives of my two girls by taking them off this ship, Anita. You are crazy, but if you insist on leaving, there is nothing I can do to stop you, I know you better than that."

Herta was now wide awake and coming to terms with what she was hearing; she reached out to give Anita a massive hug, then she swung her arms around Inge who started to cry. Her mother scorned her for her display of emotion and told her to be quick; they were not to be on the ship when it set sail.

Heidi and Inge embraced in a tight hold and kissed each other's cheek, promising to get in touch as soon as they arrived in Germany. Anita remembered the address she was handed for the farm in Schleswig-Holstein and shared it with Frau Mallke. The two friends wished each other luck and Godspeed in their journeys. Inge felt distraught at leaving her friend and family; her bottom lip quivered as she waved her goodbyes as they made their way through the packed swimming pool up to the steps and back to the area where they had boarded.

Incredibly, people were still arriving and poured into every available space that they could find. Facing the human mass in front of them made her mother's decision even more bizarre in Inge's mind. She questioned her mother again as they made their way through the crowd of people. Anita would not reconsider her actions. "We have to leave Inge, I had a dream, and we are getting off this ship!" Her words remained steadfast, and Inge was only too aware that her mother's disposition was unlikely to alter. It was for Inge to come to terms with what she was being told to do.

After many minutes spent fighting the tide of people, needing almost to hold their noses as they stepped over older people who had not been able to make it to the toilet, as well as babies with dirty nappies and no hope of them being changed. Finally, they reached the gangway. There were countless people still trying to get on board, no sign anymore that anyone was check-ing who arrived on the ship. Anita concluded that the authorities could have no idea just how many people were on that ship, but it felt to her that there must be at least ten times more than the ocean liner was ever designed to carry. People stared at them, quizzing them as they crossed on the gangway. Why would anyone decide to leave the ship they were so desperate to board?

It was dawn and the cold prickled their already chapped faces as they reached the quayside and slowly made their way into the sheltered areas where yesterday they queued with everyone else. Inge looked back at the ship in disbelief, their salvation was before them, and her mother made her leave both the boat and their friends. A soldier who was about to board the ship asked what on earth they were doing in leaving? Anita snapped, "Mind your own business, and get on that ship if you wish, but we will not be sailing with her." He shrugged his shoulders and started to board without a backward glance. Nobody cared that these two women were making possibly the worst decision of their lives. "Mutti, what do we do now?" asked Inge. Anita stood for a second in deep thought. Inge knew better than to repeat the question at that precise moment. Anita glanced over to some rolling stock on the railway line close by them.

"This way," came the instruction to her daughter, "we go this way." Anita, stern-faced, walked with purpose, her daughter close behind. Inge turned to take one last look at the *Wilhelm Gustloff* and wished all aboard a safe passage, then turned and followed her mother, head bowed in silent disbelief.

Frau Mallke, Heidi and Herta sat incredulous, Herta sobbed uncontrollably, and Heidi felt the corners of her mouth droop and her chin quiver. Anita was the matriarch of their party. She had made almost every decision since they had left Königsberg, but this time she had gone too far. How could she? Inge was a young woman who deserved to live and should have stayed on board the ship with the rest of them.

There was much restlessness among the people in the swimming pool area. Individuals were making a trip to the toilets in relays. The queue was horrendous, everyone needed an early morning pee, and there were just not enough toilets for everyone on board. The military personnel mingled with the refugees; uniforms now disregarded in terms of hierarchy. Everyone now was quite literally in the same boat, and they all felt the same camaraderie. After the toilet logjams came the queues for freshwater. Frau Mallke wasted no time in making the quest for the rationed drink while ensuring the girls retained their cosy corner position in the swimming pool. The next few hours dragged, and the air around them became stale as more people clambered into every available space. Some individuals took off their lifejackets in the heat and used them as pillows.

Then when it felt like the ship would burst with folks and could take no more, the engines started up. There was movement on the quayside, and the heaving of the gangways could be heard from the upper decks, as they were dragged onto the ship. The lower doors were closed leaving hundreds ashore on the quayside, but the *Gustloff* could take no more. A large number of pets and particularly dogs had been left abandoned on the pier and quayside, slowly reaching starvation. They could no longer be trusted, and that made the quayside unsafe.

Finally, early in the afternoon of 30th January 1945, the *Wilhelm Gustloff* accompanied by the passenger liner, the *Hansa*, set sail. They were both escorted by two torpedo boats. Unfortunately, the *Hansa* and one of the torpedo boats developed mechanical problems and could not continue, leaving the *Wilhelm Gustloff* and one torpedo boat to continue their voyage.

Apprehensions were stirring among the officers because the ship had not been to sea for five years. There were not enough lifeboats for all the thousands of passengers that they now knew were on board. At least ten lifeboats had previously been commandeered and used to form smokescreens in the harbour when ships were coming and going and they had not been replaced. There were also disputes between the four captains on board as to whether they should display lights or not.

Two of the captains were younger merchant marines, Köhler and Weller; as such the older naval officers did not treat them with respect. One of these was Friedrich Peterson who had previously been captured by the English as a blockade-runner. The British released him, as in their view, he was an old sea dog and not likely to ever be used for military service at his age. Also, he swore in writing that he would never again take to the seas as a captain, so accordingly he was deported to Germany. Apparently, this was why this man in his sixties was assigned to stationary captain aboard the *Wilhelm Gustloff* when it was a "floating barracks" on the Oxhöft Quay. The other 'captain' was Commander Wilhelm Zahn; he was a former U-boat commander and always had his dog, a German shepherd close to heel. The two groups stayed in different officer's messes and only communicated when they needed to.

The *Wilhelm Gustloff* was still fitted with anti-aircraft guns, and she also carried a crew of 173 naval armed forces auxiliaries, 918 officers, NCOs, and men of the 2 *Unterseeboot-Lehrdivision*, 373 female naval auxiliary helpers, and 162 wounded soldiers. However, she mainly carried around 8956 refugees, of which over 5000 were children. They followed the rules of war, and as such, she did not have any protection as a hospital ship. Few passengers could access the deck to see the ship set sail even if they wanted to. There was not enough room to make the complicated journey from where they each were to the access points to the deck areas. They did, however, feel great relief to be finally setting sail.

Frau Mallke held both her daughter's hands; her face now crumpled with the distress of their parting from Anita and Inge. In addition she had, in the last few hours, held back considerable tears as she finally had the time to contemplate the grief of losing Gerhard. She imagined him lying at the side of the road, cold and alone, nobody to take care of him, offer him a decent and proper burial. She felt a physical pain rising in her chest like an erupting volcano desperate to find its exit point. She knew she could afford no such luxury as to grieve loudly and cry out. The stricken lady held in her pain, but her face spoke a thousand words and she visibly aged before her daughters' eyes.

Shortly after they had set sail and pulled away from the dock, the *Gustloff* could see a coastal steamer heading towards them out of the ice and snow-covered waters. The steamer, the *Reval*, which was travelling from Pillau, was packed with refugees. So overladen that many had to stand on the open deck, shoulder to shoulder. As a direct consequence of the freezing temperatures, many had frozen to death, standing up. The *Gustloff* pulled alongside and let down some rope ladders, and some of the survivors managed to scramble aboard the larger ocean liner and ultimately find warmth in various crevices of the ship's corridors and stairwells. The *Reval* continued into port.

The four captains argued with each other as to who was in charge. The two younger captains wanted to travel in shallow waters without lights so that they could not easily be seen and remain closer to shore – but the area closer to shore was scattered with mines. The ships main captain, Friedrich Petersen, backed up by Zahn made the decision to head for deeper waters where he knew the pathway had been swept for mines. He then decided to activate the ship's green and red navigation lights, which of course made them easier to see in the dark. However, Peterson rejected the advice from all the other captains, that the ship should steer a zigzag course and his decision was final. They now only had the torpedo boat, the *Löwe* as an escort, there was a heavy swell, and the outside temperature was minus 18 degrees celsius.

Chapter 37

In late October 1944 Marinesko again undertook military operations, his reputation was tarnished, and he needed to make an impression. While sailing in the Baltic in open waters, Marinesko spotted and managed to pursue a German transport ship for quite some time, yet after a few attempts was unable to sink it with torpedoes. However, with the assistance of Soviet aircraft guns, the ship was severely damaged and towed to port where it stood in repair until the end of the war.

This was considered a weighty accomplishment at last, and as a result, Marinesko was awarded and very happy to accept the Order of the Red Banner for the part he played in the campaign. Following this welcome career highlight, there came another low point where Marinesko narrowly avoided a tribunal. His submarine received serious damage during a dangerous duel with a German ship, and for many long weeks, his vessel remained under repair in the Finnish city of Turku.

At the end of December, Commander Marinesko took the opportunity to go ashore on 24-hour leave with his crew; they were due to return the next day. However, most had spent New year's night in Hangö enjoying the pleasures of a Finnish brothel. Marinesko with a woman who was the owner of a restaurant, had drunk copious amounts of potato schnapps. Marinesko subsequently disappeared for several days, completely forgetting his obligations, and as a result, he was put on the wanted list. The proposition was for him to be court-martialled as a deserter, which could have been fatal for him, not least because fraternisation between Soviet officers and foreigners was strictly forbidden. However the consequences could also mean that the S-13 would not be operational for some time in the absence of its Commander and so the decision was made for Marinesko to be sent on a mission to prove his competences.

Marinesko was a complex man; he felt hurt and somewhat embittered by events in his past. He knew he needed to restore his integrity and also to restore the reputation of his crew who accompanied him on his New Year's Eve visit to the brothel. They too were due to be punished at a subsequent court-martial, the date still to be set. Once again like a slippery eel, Marinesko resumed his duties with his crew and set sail in his U-boat leaving Hank on January 11th and took up a position near Kolberg on January 13th. During this time his submarine was attacked several times by German torpedo boats. He had something to prove; he knew that if he failed, he would have to leave the fleet forever.

The S-13 was instructed to patrol the Baltic, off the coast of Lithuania, but saw no opportunity for action. His instructions were simple – destroy enemy ships. So after days of fruitless hunting, he ordered the S-13 into the Bay of Danzig where the massive evacuation of German refugees had begun. Deep in the surrounding waters off the Bay of Danzig in the early evening of 30th January 1945, Alexander Marinesko directed his S-13 U-boat to resurface. Russian submarines did not all have radar; consequently, most of their operations happened in daylight. The signaller standing on the coning tower could see two ships leaving the bay. He could see one was a big ship and it looked to him like a troopship, but he couldn't tell what it was carrying. He noticed that one ship stopped, but the other continued to make headway out of the bay. Marinesko made the decision to follow the ship, while maintaining his course above the waterline as the submarine was camouflaged by the snow and blizzard conditions.

The *Wilhelm Gustloff* proceeded to deeper waters and as she did so, the officers heard over the radio that there was a German minesweeping convoy close by. Captain Peterson took the decision to display all the running lights so that they were clearly visible to them. The weather started to close in, and it became quite uncomfortable for the thousands on board that night. The Mallke family held on to each other tightly as the ship started to rock from side to side. The less seafaring passengers among them felt nausea claw at their throats. Soon the pungent stench invaded the nostrils of the passengers not able to escape the sound of heaving from their struggling fellow travellers.

On board, a call went out that there was an important message to hear. Most of the passengers managed to assemble close to a speaker to listen to the Fuhrer. Frau Mallke suggested to the girls that they should move out of the pool area and listen to the broadcast in the corridor as she also was struggling with the putrid smell all around them. Together the family made their way up to the next level. The feeling of nausea was beginning to overcome

Frau Mallke. Today was the twelfth anniversary of Hitler's rise to power, and he reminded the nation of the need to remain steadfast until victory could finally be realised. The tone of the message, they had heard many times before. Everyone listened in anticipation, some in expectation, others in abject disbelief.

It is now 21.00 hrs, and the ship is arriving over safe shallow waters. The crew on the bridge, including Captain Friedrich Petersen, celebrate with a glass of cognac as they listen to the closing of Hitler's delusional broadcast.

In the hospital area of the ocean liner, a lady is being reassured by an auxiliary nurse that they are now in safe waters out of the reach of Russian boats. She pays little attention to the message; her contractions are now only two minutes apart; she wants to push her baby out. The nurse orders her to pant; she is only five centimetres dilated; she isn't ready yet, she hears. The expectant mother pants furiously, supported by other women close by and watched over by her three-year-old son. Only 15 minutes later, the nurse shouts for the doctor; she can see the baby's head; he needs to come quickly.

Out in the bay, the S-13 followed a parallel path to the *Wilhelm Gustloff* like a leopard stalking its prey, aware of its every move, but needing to increase speed to keep up with the ship travelling at 15knots. Eventually catching up with the *Gustloff* it turned at right angles to the liner, having travelled in a great loop around the ship. Marinesko considered his decision to launch an attack above the waterline. He had heard that submarines had a great deal of success in the Atlantic launching this way and he wanted to try it out for himself. An above-water attack means greater precision and visibility as well as being able to hold the submarines speed more effectively. Marinesko gave the order to discharge four torpedoes to the petty officer Vladimir Kourotchkin. The order was to aim for them to hit three metres below the water line and the estimated distance to reach their target was 600 meters. However, the submarine was in poor repair, and the first one failed to discharge. Again the order was given, and one by one Kourotchkin sent the three remaining torpedoes on their way towards the ship he believed to be full of Nazis, the *Wilhelm Gustloff*.

The first torpedo exploded just aft of the bow of the ship and destroyed the crew's living quarters. Many young men were off duty and would have been resting in their bunks, perhaps enjoying a snack. People shouted, "Out, out, we have struck a mine." This was no mine. The second torpedo broke through under the swimming pool. The naval auxiliaries had little chance to escape, and only two or three of them made it out of the swimming pool area. Most were slashed to pieces by the shards of tiles from the mosaics. As the water rushed into the pool, body parts and corpses floated all around, along with empty lifejackets, so randomly used as pillows. The third torpedo tore through the engine room and ripped through the side of the ship right up to the railings. Anyone in the lower decks died within seconds. Even sending an SOS was impossible as the radio room was destroyed. Only the accompanying torpedo ship the *Löwe* was able to send out a distress call as well as the position of the ship. "*Gustloff* sinking after three torpedo strikes."

The renowned author Günter Grass later reported in his book *Crabwalk* that before the S-13 left Hangö harbour, a member of the crew named Pichur, allegedly took a brush and painted dedications on all the torpedoes. The first read 'For the Motherland', the second read 'For Stalin', the third, 'For the Soviet people' and the fourth read 'For Leningrad'. The torpedo which failed to discharge was dedicated to Stalin and was hastily disarmed when it failed. It had been aimed at the area of the ship housing the maternity ward where a soon to be mother lay resting. Just after the last torpedo struck, a poor lady went into labour. A doctor gave her an injection to stop the pains.

Immediately the lights went out, and the ship was plunged in darkness. On the forward deck a ten-year-old child had been sent to bed. He was reading a book, as the darkness fell upon the cabin. The child reached for his torch and as it shone on the title of the book *Der Untergang, die Titanic, The Downfall of the Titanic*. At that precise moment, he knew that the same things were happening to this ship too. He was so scared and feared he might not even be able to escape past the bulkhead door. He virtually sprang out of bed and rushed out into the gangway. Behind him, he heard a terrible bang as the closing bulkhead door hit people as they reached it. The child recognised the need to get to midships. He was lucky. The automatic bulkhead would not reopen on the captains' orders. Those behind it were trapped. Many of those trapped and unable to escape were the Croatian volunteer soldiers trained in lowering the lifeboats. Who knows how long it took for death to take her hold on them.

On the S-13, the successful hits were greeted with modest jubilation. Its commander Marinesko gave the order for the vessel to be submerged, as they were susceptible to the depth charges being so close to shore. The S-13 maintained her position, while above, the *Löwe* circled the *Wilhelm Gustlof* with its searchlights.

Hilde grabbed hold of her mother and sister and shouted for them to run up the stairs to the deck above. Each corridor became crammed with passengers who deserted their cabins in nightgowns, most without shoes. Some remembered to put on their life vests; others ran back when they remembered they should be wearing theirs too. At least a thousand made their way to the promenade decks, but they were encased in glass with no way of escape. The moments inside that promenade deck can only be imagined. Above them, a high-ranking officer was taking his family away from the ship using a motor launch that had been used as an excursion boat on shore trips. Incredibly the electric hoist was working and the launch lowered, half-empty, past the promenade deck where women and children looked out through the glass panels from their imprisoned state. The occupants of the motor launch clearly saw the expressions on the faces of the small children as they descended. Only at the last minute, did someone find a gun to shoot through the glass, to help make an escape. In the end, the sea broke through the glass, but for many, it was already too late.

The stairwells were treacherous, Little consideration was extended to fellow passengers, and small children who got left behind were being trampled on. Young children died on the stairwells, others were squashed in the corridors as thoughtless adults only looked out for their own, or themselves. Everyone wanted to reach the top of the ship, struggling upwards as the ship sank beneath them.

The Mallke family, now in a deep panic, reached the upper decks, all holding hands. They could see that the fire extinguishers had been discharged from their holders, and consequently, foam lay all over the metal stairs taking them to the next level. It was dangerous if not impossible, to mount many of the stairs – but in sheer desperation, Herta took her first steps, carefully followed by Hilde and finally, their mother. Frau Mallke almost made it to the top but then slipped, falling from the top of the metal stairs to the bottom. Both the girls screamed, shouted to their mother, "Mum, Mum, get up." Their battered mother was quite badly hurt, but after a few seconds, she waved her arm and pulled herself up and slowly started to climb the stairs again. They were finally reaching the top, much to the relief of her two daughters. Now they were at the top of the stairs they could look down onto the lifeboats. The first lifeboats were being filled, women and children first. The davits were being activated to swing the lifeboats out and into the water and slowly they descended into the icy sea.

All around them chaos reigned, children lost their mothers, mothers lost their children, they called out their children's names. Everywhere there were cries of those who had lost loved ones. The massive cruise liner had a 15-degree tilt on the port side, and consequently, none of the starboard lifeboats were accessible.

The second lifeboat was full, and the Mallke family were too late and failed to get on board. It probably held a few more people than the 70 it was designed to hold. One of the two davits was working ok but the other one was frozen. Suddenly the lifeboat started to tip sideways and one by one each person in the boat fell into the water, amidst screams of terror. The lifeboat remained hanging from the frozen ropes of its one remaining davit.

The seaman controlling the boarding of the lifeboats beckoned to Frau Mallke, "You're next, come on be quick." A man with a scarf around his neck rushed past them and said, "I need to get on the boat, I need to get on the boat!" The seaman replied,

"NO, women and children only." The pitiful man pulled the scarf tighter around his head, started thrashing his arms and repeating,

"I need to get on the boat" as he pushed harder to forge his way through – the seaman pulled out his gun and shot him.

Frau Mallke gathered up her two girls. She felt stunned by the brutality of the episode as it unfolded right in front of her and ached terribly from her recent fall, but the pain was eclipsed by the need to reach safety. They quickly climbed aboard the lifeboat and made their way to the other end. The pressure to reach a lifeboat became an unachievable dream for the vast majority on board, yet some of the senior officers had already made their own arrangements. Those with their families in the grand officers' quarters took their destinies into their own hands using their guns. As the Mallke family made their way to the other end of the boat, they saw a man in uniform, already sitting there. It was the Captain, Friedrich Petersan; apparently his reason for being there was because he needed to oversee the evacuation. He later admitted that he saw no other way of saving himself – he was not going down with his ship.

They all sat shivering in the boat while it quickly filled with women and children. Then came the time to start winching the davits, and again, one was frozen to the boat. The process stopped this time, and someone shouted out for a knife to help them break free. There were petrified expressions on the faces of all aboard, thinking back to what they had witness happen to the previous boat. Then a young boy, Horst Woit, reached into his sock and pulled out a Swiss knife and handed it to the seaman, then quickly sat back down next to his mother. She looked surprised at his actions; she did not even know he carried a knife, but soon pulled her son close to her. The ten-year-old boys' actions saved the lives of everyone on that lifeboat.

The lower decks were by now filling with water, and the ship started to list badly on the port side. As the ship listed further, the engines cut out one by one, and the screaming moved up a pitch. With the cutting out of each engine, the ship lurched forward and started to list even more – those on the upper decks needed to hold tightly to the railings by now.

As their boat was slowly lowered towards the sea, they looked up and saw the people still on the upper decks, screaming. Some of them, in desperation, jumped into the icy water next to them, then floundered as the temperature hit their bodies and the weight of their clothes made it hard for them to swim, or move at all. It soon became apparent that only about seven of the 22 or so lifeboats would make it into the water, each with around seventy passengers on board.

As the boat was lowered, Hilde, who was closest to the *Gustloff*, clearly saw and heard a family. A man in a Nazi uniform, the only one that Hilde had seen on board the *Wilhelm Gustloff*, stood on the deck looking all around for an escape route. He could not find one. He was with his wife and children. Hilde heard the wife shout at him "Put an end to it, put an end to it." The officer took out a gun, still holding onto the railings and shot his two daughters one by one, followed by his wife, each hitting the deck and immediately sliding across the deck into the sea. Then he turned the gun onto himself. Holding the gun closely to the side of his temple, he pulled the trigger – nothing happened – he had no bullets left. He shouted to another passenger who was also clinging onto the railings for dear life. "Give me your gun," he shouted. The chap replied that he did not have a gun. With that, the officer let go of the railings and slid across the icy, snow-covered deck following his family into the freezing sea.

The Mallke family's lifeboat safely reached the water and was slowly pulling away from the *Gustloff*, which was by now nearly two-thirds sunk. Abruptly, the lights came on, on the upper decks, but within minutes had started to fade, lower and lower until ultimately, they went out. It was pitch black.

Life rafts were discharged, and whole families clambered on board then, instinct taking over and the need to stay together paramount in their minds. People frantically held hands to stay together, but large waves washed over them, and many lost hold of their loved ones. Their fingers slipped as the power of the sea washed them away. Sheer terror lay everywhere. The air temperature was minus 20 degrees, and the sea temperature was just above freezing. In those temperatures, people died within minutes.

In one of the last lifeboats, Doctor Reichter ensured the safety of the new mothers and their infants along with those still pregnant and one who had just had a miscarriage. One woman who had been given an injection to hold off her labour was ushered onboard and witnessed the dislodging of one of the anti-aircraft guns on the after deck. She saw it plunge overboard and land on a fully occupied lifeboat that had just been lowered right next to them. Her lifeboat was swept away from the ship with the surge of a large wave, and soon they were swiftly moving towards the *Löwe*, close by. This was the first lifeboat to reach the relative safety of a larger vessel. In particular, one soon to be mother, Ursula Pokriefke was winched aboard by the sailors over the railings. She lost her shoes in the process and was quickly taken to the cabin of the engineer on duty. Then the contractions resumed.

The ship was now sinking quickly, and the souls left on board knew it; the screams grew louder and louder and as the vessel listed further to port, she took her final bow, and quickly sank amid inconceivable cries. Those in the sea and in the lifeboats screamed too, as if in the act of unity for the last time. Just 62 minutes after the torpedoes hit the *Wilhelm Gustloff*, the ship sank, a short time for such a massive cruise liner.

At the precise moment that the *Gustloff* sank, Ursula Pokriefke gave birth to a little boy; she had a remarkably normal delivery, and her son was born in an engineer's bunk bed. He let out an inordinate cry, almost as though representing the cries of the people sliding down the decks of the *Gustloff*, or being ravaged by the freezing seas. In complete unison with the *Gustloff*'s siren, rather like a death cry, this small child was born, as were others that night, but this one was to survive, and his story told by author Günther Grass, who's influence on my story I acknowledge at the end of this book. As the captain of the *Löwe* turned to note the exact time of the sinking of the *Wilhelm Gustloff*, Paul Pokriefke, fell silently asleep as his mother cradled him.

Herta tucked her head in close to her mother and Hilde looked at all the people in lifejackets in the water. Heads bobbing up and down in the waves, with lifejackets keeping them upright, but their bodies were frozen. Then she started to notice the children and babies. Their short little legs rising up out of the sea were the only means of identifying them; their heads were under the water, being so heavy in comparison to their bodies.

Quickly, those in the water who were still alive used every means within them to swim to the boats. Where there was room on the lifeboats, many were dragged aboard, their lives saved. When each desperate swimmer reached the side of the Mallkes' boat and frantically tried to hang on, many were hit on the head by the paddles of the boats – others were pushed back. Nobody on board the boat wanted to risk being overladen with more people in their lifeboat. Yet people still held onto each other on the life boats like bunches of grapes. The fitter and younger ones kicked others away to prevent themselves from being dragged under the water.

Hilde saw clearly what was going on as she looked into the eyes of a young man who pleaded with her to help him. She reached out to take his hand. But with one short swipe, his arm was swept away from the side of the boat. Hilde turned back and watched as the young man started to drift away from the boat, his arms in the air and lashing out to stay above the waves and keep moving in the coldest of waters. Hilde kept watching until he stopped moving and she could only see the colour of his life vest. It was a cruel but essential act in the survival of the fittest. The lucky ones climbed over others to reach the safety of a life boat if one was nearby. The weaker ones left in the water, did not last long in the ice-cold temperatures.

Frau Mallke ushered her two daughters to the back of the boat, which was covered in a tarpaulin. She wanted them to be safe and felt that it was drier undercover. There were many young children huddled together, and Hilde was probably the oldest. As mothers each attempted to make sure their children were under cover, Frau Mallke was forced back to the other side of the boat. Now there was nothing to do but wait.

As the hours slipped by and daylight started to creep over the horizon, it was evident that those still in the icy waters were all dead. Empty lifejackets littered the surface of the now calm sea. Toys and teddy bears and suitcases floated all around in silent witness to their owners' inescapable demise. Crystals of ice etched the contours of the faces of the people in the water. They remained constrained within the lifejackets which were so well equipped to keep them from sinking, yet inept at keeping them warm enough to survive the freezing temperatures on that dreadful night of 30th January 1945.

On board the S-13, Petty Officer Schnapzev, using his earphones, listened to the noises aboard the *Gustloff* as she was sinking. He heard popping sounds as the watertight doors cracked under the pressure of the water and vibrations from the ship's engines, as they broke free. From the moment that the torpedoes were discharged, the order for total silence had been observed. Yet in all that he heard through his earphones that night, there were no sounds of human voices, no screams, no cries from young children for their mothers – no evidence of the catastrophe they had initiated that night.

The torpedo boat, the *Löwe,* stayed behind and continued to pick up about 200 survivors using ropes from its railings. The lifeboats had trouble getting close to the Lowe as the sea tossed them away with each new wave, resulting in the fraught passengers rising above the *Löwe* and then feeling like they would sink beneath it. The Mallke's lifeboat was among the boats that needed to come alongside the *Löwe.* Only when the boat could maintain the same height as the *Löwe*'s railing was it possible to jump aboard – they only had seconds in which to launch themselves. One by one, the passengers made the jump; then it was Herta's turn; she needed to make the jump at the precise moment the two boats were level. She waited for a second too long, and the *Löwe* rose three feet above her as she made her jump. She couldn't reach the other boat and was washed unceremoniously into the icy sea.

Hilde, ashen-faced glanced at her mother who held her face in her hands, then a split second later, with a shout of "Be careful," it was Hilde's turn to make the jump. Without hesitation, she jumped and made it to safety aboard the *Löwe.* Hilde shouted to her mother "Mum – jump!" Her mother hesitated, then moved to jump but lost her opportunity. She had to wait for the swell of the boat to bring them level once more. Frau Mallke took her chance. To her complete horror, Hilde watched her mother jump into the sea; she didn't even wait until the right moment, it almost looked intentional. Hilde wondered for a moment if it had been. Then the realisation set in, she had just watched her sister and her mother fall into the freezing Baltic Sea. She lost control of her senses and fell to her knees. Hilde was then carried into the sheltered area of the ship, her heart pounding in her chest, the cold creeping over her like an icy blanket. Her thoughts at that moment were to wish death would take her, too; overcome with grief, she no longer wanted to live.

The *Löwe* picked up about 200 people as they surrounded the ship. The captain decided that it was the right thing to do to rescue as many as they could take, even though they ran the risk of being hit by a torpedo themselves. As the last passengers came aboard, the captain looked around, and to his surprise, he came face to face with the captains of the *Wilhelm Gustloff*. They were all dry. All the captains of the ship survived, while thousands under their command and their passengers drowned.

The S-13 then torpedoed the rescue ship too. The captain of the *Löwe* saw them as he stood on the starboard bridge wing, quite well spaced out, but undoubtedly they were torpedoes. There was only one thing to do, order his ship full ahead and hard to starboard. They launched depth charges against the unseen enemy – the S-13 made good its escape. At that moment the *Löwe*'s commander knew that they couldn't pick up any more survivors and they moved away.

Those in the water, still alive, started to cry for help, confused by the fact that nobody appeared to rescue them sooner. The cries came from the depths of each of their souls, but still, no one came. Finally the pride of the German navy, the *Hipper*, arrived in the area with a torpedo boat escort. The *Hipper* already had 2000 people on board and afraid of further torpedoes in the area, she sailed away, leaving widespread incredulity among the desperate survivors. The feeling of despair would stay with those people for the rest of their lives.

Finally, other ships made their way to the site of the sinking, but they were met with complete silence, the water now calm. Just a sea of corpses, toys, and lifejackets floated in the water; even in the lifeboats many of the inhabitants were now dead. One petty officer Werner Fick reached inside to look at a blanket, a frozen blanket, lying next to the dead body of a woman and small girl. When he looked inside, he saw a baby, barely alive. It was a baby boy, wearing a blue romper suit and blue with cold, but still alive. He clutched the baby to his chest, pushed him inside his jacket. He wasn't about to abandon him. The fleet doctor started resuscitation techniques on him and administered an injection of camphor; they did not rest until the little boy opened his eyes. Werner asked his commanding officer if he could keep him. There was little discussion, Werner and his wife had no children, this baby had no parents and no way of finding out who he was. So the request was granted, and Werner took the baby to look after him, the last survivor of the *Wilhelm Gustloff*.

The *Wilhelm Gustloff* was carrying military equipment and personnel, and because of that, it was reckoned to be a fair target in war. The reality is that the vast majority of passengers were women and children. Refugees who were fleeing from a Russian army intent on raping women and then killing them in revenge for the actions of the Nazis just a few years earlier in the war. Their choice was to stay and be killed or board one of the many evacuation ships. Sadly, over 8000 of them were to lose their lives, 5000 of whom were children. The Petty Officer aboard the S-13 who sent the torpedoes towards the *Gustloff*, Vladimir Kourotchkin, had nightmares for many years when he heard that around 5000 children either drowned, froze to death or were sucked down with the ship that night. It was always the same dream.

On April 15th 1912, more than 1500 people died on the *Titanic*. On May 7th 1915, 1198 perished on the *Lusitania* when a German submarine torpedoed it. On December 7th 1941, 1177 died aboard the SS *Arizona*. If you were to calculate the total of all these disasters and then multiply by two, you would still be short of the number that died on the night of January 30th 1945 on the *Wilhelm Gustloff*.

History chose to ignore the plight of so many. Mostly because to be German, at the end of the Second World War, was to be abhorred. What happened to the *Gustloff* has become politicised to the extent that the human aspect of what happened has been buried. Sometimes the truth is more comfortable to ignore. Possibly 9000- 10,000 souls drowned in the icy waters of the Baltic; over half of them were children and babies. I believe their story should be heard. It was the worst maritime catastrophe in history, and yet the world does not know about it. Because there were military personnel on board, the sinking could not be declared a war crime.

The sinking of the *Wilhelm Gustloff* did not bring glory to those who sank her – not for many years at any rate. Many did not even believe that Alexander Marinesko could be responsible for such a sinking. The Russian authorities thought that the air force had bombed it, and that is why no awards or medals were given to him. Also, Marinesko was a difficult person for the party to deal with, temperamental and fond of his drink; so they made sure that he remained quiet. It was many years after his death that Marinesko was declared a hero and is still recognized as one today in Russia.

As for the survivors of the *Gustloff*, they believe that blame should not rest with what happened on 30th January 1945, but what happened twelve years earlier on 30th January 1933, when Hitler came to power. They are under no illusion about that. In present-day terms, a ship sinking of this magnitude would be remembered the world over. But the fact that the *Wilhelm Gustloff* was a German ship at the end of the Second World War, regardless of the nationalities of its passengers, meant that it was fair game to be destroyed.

Chapter 38

Inge and her Mutti, Anita, made their way towards the railway sidings not far from the dock area. They could see cattle trucks all hooked up and ready to go, no carriages for people, just cattle wagons with sliding doors. Anita banged on one of the doors; she could tell they were full of horses from the neighing in the background. Slowly the clunk of the lock being released was met with the slow grating and grinding of metal on metal as the door slid open. She begged the man who answered the door, "Please take us with you, please." He looked behind him as he replied, "I have got ten men, here." He pointed behind the food he had piled up for the three horses. The men looked thin, filthy dirty, many had dried bloodstains on their faces and bodies, and to Anita, it looked like they were soldiers who had discarded their uniforms.

After repeated requests from Anita, the man gave in and allowed them to board his cattle truck. Anita climbed the makeshift ladder, then held out her hand to Inge as she followed her mother. The indication was that they should be the ones to close the corroded iron door. Without help, Anita used all her strength to slide the door closed. The presumed horse owner ushered them towards the ten men.

After around ten awkward minutes where few words were spoken, the train started to lurch forward with a rocking motion. The passengers left standing swayed from side to side as the train inched its way along the tracks at a tediously slow pace. The horses were restless and began to whine as the train rocked backwards and forwards until finally reaching momentum and a smoother ride. Thirst and hunger gripped the women, but their gratefulness at being permitted aboard the train prevented them from making a forthright yet necessary request for water.

The women could overhear whispered discussions informing them that the train was travelling to Yugoslavia. To Anita and Inge, the destination mattered little, only the fact they were moving away from the advancing Russians. Inge, too tired to stand, sat on the urine-soaked wooden floor of the carriage. The smell was putrid. She sidled towards some straw, hoping to create a layer of protection between her bony buttocks and the contents of the wooden boards. Her mother soon joined her. There was little or no conversation. Everyone had the same goal, joined together in grim circumstances, wishing they were anywhere else, yet grateful at the same time to be precisely where they were.

The train travelled only at night so that it was less of a target from the air. During the day it would stop in sidings or an area well covered with trees. The only opportunity to preserve a small degree of dignity when needing to use a toilet was during the day when a few trees might spare their humiliation. While they travelled there was a red bucket which everyone had to share for his or her toilet requirements. There was no dignity offered other than the men would look away as the two women used the bucket.

When the train stopped in sidings, if they were lucky, the Red Cross might be there. They would take the only bucket, swill it out for them and then pour them some hot or at least warm food, usually soup into the same bucket for them all to share.

The train took days to travel through Czechoslovakia, Hungary and eventually into Yugoslavia, their journey's end. On leaving the train, they realised just how alone they were in this baron place and nowhere did they feel welcome. Food was scarce and the cold bitter, and Inge felt vulnerable, not least because they couldn't speak the language. Although Yugoslavia was German-occupied, there was precious little military presence when the train stopped. There were few women on the station platform, and the men looked at Inge inquisitively. She was a helpless pretty girl and would be an easy target for a young man.

Witnessing what they presumed to be German civilian refugees, was a new concept for the Yugoslavian locals and they were not sure how to react to the situation. Anita pulled her daughter to her and scowled at the curious young men. Just as she did so, one of the older men stepped forward and held out his hand to Anita. He wore a rugged expression with deep lines down his face, partly hidden by an old leather cap. He was probably only around 40. Anita noted his awkward demeanour, hunched shoulders, his crimpled face that looked tanned even though it was early February. For the first time in days, Anita acknowledged they had slipped into February, and yet it meant nothing to her, neither the day nor the month.

"I am Sepp. Joseph Hospodarz is my real name, but everyone calls me Sepp," the rugged-looking chap said in perfect German. Anita offered him a smile of relief.

"I am Anita, and this is my daughter Inge. We have escaped the Russian advance on our home in East Prussia" she replied.

Sepp said, "I can offer you somewhere to stay tonight. It is only a single bed and not the most comfortable, but I do have a shower." He paused, "When it works. Who knows we may be lucky tonight." Sepp looked down at his feet and kicked the icy ground with an awkwardness that revealed vulnerability. Anita thought it endearing.

Anita was well aware of just how much they must have smelt, and she needed to consider Inge. She quickly replied: "Thank you, yes we will accept your kind offer." Without speaking, mother and daughter followed Sepp, listening as he berated the snide remarks from many of the locals with a sharp Yugoslavian tongue and a dismissive scowl. He needed to make it quite clear that these two women were not German, moreover they were East Prussian and that was different from being German.

They walked along a narrow cobbled street lined with tall three-storey balconied buildings. A turn to the left and the road became narrower; children played football even though the temperature was freezing. Abruptly Sepp stopped in front of a large wooden door, which was in dire need of a coat of varnish. A pitched roof hung over the doorway, and with two turns of the large mortice key, the door opened.

The two women were so grateful to step into a warm room. A small stove flickered with dying embers. Sepp rushed to place a log on the fire, and it flared up to bathe the room in a vibrant amber glow. The room was stark, and it had three less-than-comfortable looking chairs, each with wooden arms, a seat cushion and a couple of old scatter cushions for back support. The floor was bare boards with what seemed to be a wicker woven rug, worn, dirty, and with threads pulling away at the edges. The once white walls were bare of pictures; in fact, there was nothing that indicated that this was someone's home. Sepp caught Anita's stare, "I know it's not much, I rent this place. It costs me little." Sepp looked thoughtful for a moment before speaking again. "I am a Yugoslav partisan. You need to know that I do not support the Nazis. Our home was bombed. There was nothing left, and I was the only member of my family to survive, I lost my mother, father, brother, his wife and their two children." Again he paused as Anita took one step towards him. "I was out at the time, and I came back and found their bodies amongst the rubble. It took me three days to bury them all. A couple of villagers helped me."

Anita was unsure whether to offer comfort as Sepp turned towards the wall for a moment and wiped a tear-stained cheek; the tracks left a clean line down his dusty face. Anita touched his forearm and Sepp placed his hand on hers, it was momentary, yet intimate, and they both felt it as Anita pulled away. She went on to explain,

"We are Prussians, a different people from the Germans, and yes, I too hate the Nazis". They exchanged a unified nod of approval of each other.

Sepp went on to explain that even though they are so far away from Germany, their village had been eradicated of all its Jewish inhabitants. He described how he had witnessed horrific scenes of women and children bundled onto the back of buses and wagons. One of his friends' wives had her baby torn from her breast as she suckled him because she refused to go with them. The child was thrown some distance, and the woman shot as she started to run to retrieve her child. Sepp paused from his story, aware of the ghastly implications of his words on the young teenager in the room. As if to justify his verbal tirade he went on to quicken the end of his story; "I hate the Nazis, With every lungful of breath, I expel contempt and disgust." His teeth were gritted together as he spoke, and his eyes turned glassy as he gazed into what Anita felt was an empty chasm.

Inge sensed the degree of tension and asked where the bathroom was; she had no appetite for any further embellishments from Sepp. Sepp guided her to the small room at the back of the kitchen. It contained a shower basin with a torn modesty curtain, a toilet with a broken seat and a sink covered with a crusty layer of grime. On the wall hung a full-length mirror, but the back must have been scratched and worn as her reflection looked green and faded. "Much how I feel," Inge spoke out loud. She instantaneously thought that she could at least repay Sepp's kindness by offering to clean it all in the morning, but for now, *she* needed to feel clean.

Inge reached for the tap in the shower; it was rusty and stiff and made a loud clanging noise as she turned it. She heard the boiler kick in as the light flared up and started to heat the water – she heaved a sigh of relief. At that moment Sepp's arm reached around the almost closed door and handed her a towel. Grabbing the cloth with a polite thank you, Inge wasted no time in stepping into the shower and washed quickly. The soap had a horrible smell, but at least it helped her to get clean. As she was drying herself, she observed in the mirror, bites all over her body as she listened from the other room as her mother told their story.

Anita needed questions answering, "Sepp, how can you be sure that we can make safe passage back over to Germany, and how did you learn to speak such good German.?" He informed her,

"I went to find work in Graz in Austria." Anita said,

"Oh, I love Austria. I particularly like to go to Vienna." Sepp looked at her and nodded as he said slowly,

"I once visited there too." He referred back to Graz again, "I knew the Hauptplatz well, which was the main square in the old medieval town of Graz. I loved the shops and restaurants that lined the surrounding streets and in particular the baroque architecture." He described it so well, Anita felt that she had visited the place with him, and she welcomed his warmth towards the Austrian way of life. Sepp used to work on the funicular, which led up the Schlossberg (main hill) to the centuries-old clock tower. It hadn't paid well, but he had gained a love of the language and all things Austrian and German, which was evident to Anita.

It soon became apparent that the bed that Sepp had offered Anita and Inge, was his own. Anita felt grateful, yet embarrassed that he had given up his single bed while he lay on blankets on the floor. The women woke early from their broken sleep, both aching and irritable, particularly Anita.

"You kept me awake all night with your wriggling and taking the blanket off me; I think you can sleep on the floor tonight." Inge knew not to moan when her mother was in this frame of mind. She rushed downstairs to see if there was food she could prepare, maybe that might help her mother's mood. Inge managed to concoct a small breakfast of stale bread, a few preserves and strong coffee. The conversation was a little stilted, and it became apparent that nobody had slept well. After breakfast, Inge was true to her promise to herself and cleaned the bathroom while Anita made the living room a little fresher. Sepp brought in logs from the back yard, and then the three of them sat to discuss what was to happen next.

Inge's mind was not on the conversation in the room. Instead, her thoughts drifted. She dearly missed her friend and presumed that they would all now be safely in Germany and oh how she envied them. How stubborn was her mother; she felt a shiver of frustration at remembering them having to clamber off that ship; a ship that would have taken them to safety instead of catching flea bites on that cattle truck among the horses and lying in the prickly hay on a urine soaked floor. A far cry from her lovely bedroom in Königsberg, or her little bedroom in Cranz. What had become of their beautiful homes? Had the Russians taken them? Were they destroyed? So many questions, so few answers, then it grew too painful to hold those thoughts anymore, and Inge turned to listen to her mother's conversation with Sepp.

Sepp concluded that for Anita and her teenage daughter to attempt to travel alone was too dangerous. Anita listened to Sepp's reasoned argument that he should go with them, to shield and guide them on their journey back to Germany. Inge remained silent as the adults made decisions about what was to be their next move. Initially, Anita thought that Sepp was over-generous and unnecessarily protective of them. Then she slowly began to accept that Sepp had no one in this town that mattered to him anymore and perhaps he was looking for an escape. Recognising they both had needs of a different nature, it took little time for Anita to agree to Sepp travelling to Germany with them.

The plans for the journey were carefully prepared, and Sepp plotted a route. Anita gathered up their clothes as best she could to wash them while they had the chance. She felt embarrassed as she asked Sepp, "Do you have any money for food?." Sepp nodded,

"Yes, a little, we will collect what provisions we can before we leave." Inge felt so grateful to Sepp and could see that her mother gained confidence, knowing that he would be there to support them on the next stage of their journey. Anita turned to her daughter and gave her a reassuring smile, which in turn left Inge feeling energised. If her mother was happy about things, then she knew that everything was going to be all right.

They decided that they would travel later in the week when the weather had cleared. No snow was forecast in the next few days. Their clothes were dried and their modest provisions packed into whatever holdall they could carry. As they prepared to leave Sepp took charge of the map and Anita ensured that they had a hot meal of potato soup and dumplings. It was time to go, Anita watched Sepp as he took one last look at the humble home he had been so grateful to for the previous few months. Devoid of emotion, Sepp closed the door behind him with a deep thud that echoed down the street. Leaving the key under an upturned plant pot on the step, he studied his two escorts "We have a treacherous journey ahead ladies," Sepp called out to them. Anita and Sepp's eyes locked as she responded,

"It can't be any worse than what we have already faced! God is good, he will help us and guide us." Sepp lifted his eyes to the sky in doubt and disbelief.

"Onwards" uttered Sepp, he felt a renewed sense of purpose and responsibility. He needed to ensure safe passage for these two women, one of whom he had begun to feel particularly fond of.

Chapter 39
Helene, Lotte and Günther's journey.

When Helena, Lotte and Günther left Marienburg, they were one of the fortunate few to make it across Poland and Germany using whatever means available to them. They travelled on carts, trains and even army trucks. Part of their journey was undertaken on foot, resulting in Helene suffering quite badly with chilblains and poor circulation. The redness and swelling in her fingers and feet became exacerbated when she warmed them by a fire on the occasions that they were blessed to be near one, but she never complained. Günther constantly asked for his mother, and Lotte and Helene made every effort to calm the boy. They had no idea where she and Marianne where – it was torture for them to imagine what might have happened to her.

With the family dynamics in chaos, Lotte felt that she needed to establish a safe area to stay with her shattered family. The cities were bombed daily, the Russians still advancing, and Germany was fast being reduced to rubble. Where was there that was safe? They were among around ten million refugees who tried to escape the advancing Red Army. Every day was about surviving to see what tomorrow would bring. Lotte noted the worsening conditions as every steam train chugged into the station where they waited. The crowds of people waiting on the platform grew, spreading farther along on the platform. Many were shunted dangerously close to the platform edge when the trains arrived.

There were no fancy suitcases; just sacks strapped to peoples backs mainly. In between the trains arriving, people would mill around the platform, wander onto the tracks dragging their belongings from one platform to another across the railway sleepers. Occasionally a stretcher would bear the weight of some poor soul, injured or dying most likely. Piles of bags, sacks and prams lay together; often children would sleep among them. If they were fortunate, the sun might come out for a few minutes and bathe the weary evacuees in momentary strands of warmth as they stood in patient anticipation. Helene would close her eyes for a few seconds and maybe dream she was somewhere else. All too soon, the cry of a hungry child brought her back into a hellish reality.

At last they boarded a train which was heading to Berlin. It took Lotte, her mother and nephew through a small village. When the train stopped at the little station and only a handful of people disembarked, Lotte, Helene and Günther were among them. Blankensee, just a tiny village in the middle of nowhere felt safer and less risky than taking her family to Berlin, Lotte decided. Lotte was unable to explain what drew her decision to walk away from the station down a country lane, but she felt infinitely guided to do so. Helena shouted to her daughter to slow down; she was unable to keep up with her pace. Lotte apologised and walked back to support her mother. Together with Günther they wandered over the brow of a gentle hill and before them lay a deserted farm on the edge of a small lake. Lotte turned to her mother and smiled, "This is meant to be Mama."

The family spent many weeks living on that farm in a principality south of Berlin. It was evident the people who had lived there previously were Jews, forcibly removed, probably to a concentration camp. They were not the only refugees to discover this otherwise tranquil place. A day after they arrived another family of five joined them. Every bedroom was soon occupied by an entire family, and they each shared all provision and space available to them. All were aware this was temporary, but a welcome respite from the drudgery they had all faced in recent weeks. Experiences were shared among the group; most were from East Prussia with a couple of families from Poland.

Many of the farm animals had survived their owners. Now, these beasts provided a source of food, and thankfully, a couple among the party had the stomach, or experience, for butchery. There was no shortage of cooks, and the growing community shared everything they gathered. Word was spreading fast now among the refugees, horror stories about the atrocities that had taken place in the various camps. Helene and Lotte could barely believe what they heard. Many of the refugees rejected the claims as propaganda, preferring to accept that they were just stories whipped up by the advancing Allies and Red Army.

The group living in the previously deserted farmhouse talked about their next move. At night they hid in the cellar when the English Spitfires could be heard overhead, mostly turning in mid-air, having discharged their arsenal over Berlin. The contingent now living in this farmhouse consisted of women, older men and children. Collectively they established that the

Prussian refugees were mainly heading for Hamburg. It made sense to Helene that they should do the same. If there were to be any chance of finding any family members that could be a starting point. Ultimately they decided the best plan was to stay exactly where they were for the time being while food supplies remained, as long as they did not draw attention to themselves.

Chapter 40
Grete's Journey

Grete was exhausted. Marianne had cried and whimpered for the whole three days she had been aboard the fishing boat transporting them and a dozen other refugees from Pilau to Rostock. A monumental journey in the circumstances, the boat was small, and Grete was in awe of the fishermen going about their duties. Almost on autopilot, the seamen were oblivious to the evacuees strewn across every available part of the boat. There was no food left and only a meagre few litres of water, now rationed by the captain.

Grete felt fortunate she had been driven by tank for most of her journey after being separated from the rest of her family. Consequently she had been spared some horrific sights from the security of the tank. The soldiers were frightened and in flight as much as everyone else. They sensed the end was coming and no longer felt the hierarchy held any degree of command. Once they arrived in Pilau, Grete was unceremoniously invited to disembark and cast on her way. The soldiers did not want the responsibility of a young woman and small child any more than they wished to execute their orders as they made their escape.

Circumstances had led Grete straight into the arms of the captain who took her aboard his boat. With limited vision as she carried Marianne, she had avoided the bollards, but slipped over the moorings. As she had fallen with Marianne in her arms, Grete landed awkwardly to protect her child. Her arm took the full force of her fall, and she was not sure initially if it was broken. A weathered-looking man began hauling her up almost as soon as the ground had come up to meet her. Grete's first concern was of course for her daughter who had taken a bump to her head, but not as severe as the blow to Grete's arm.

After a few moments comforting the screaming child, a pause in the drama permitted introductions. "I am Klaus Fischer, pleased to make your acquaintance," the voice was deep and husky and Grete felt herself stand up straighter.

"Next you are going to tell me that you are a fisherman," chuckled Greta managing to find humour in the moment. "My name is Grete, and this is Marianne, my daughter, thank you for helping me." The man laughed in response,

"Not only am I a fisherman, but I am captain of that beautiful vessel over there." He pointed to an old weather-beaten fishing boat that needed a coat of paint at the very least. "And next *you* are going to tell me that you are looking for a boat to take you to Germany – yes?."

"That is a fact," nodded Grete, "but I am not sure that your ship is really what…" her voice trailed away.

Captain Fischer stood tall and said, "I can assure you, dear lady, that she is more than capable of transporting those who are desperate to escape before the Russians arrive." Now aware that she had offended her rescuer, Grete's hand reached up to her chin as she said,

"Please excuse my thoughtlessness. I would be so thankful to be considered as one of your passengers?" The reply left Greta feeling relieved and grateful.

"Come on, climb aboard, we set sail within the hour." Captain Fischer helped Grete over the frozen snow and towards the gangway of his fishing boat. Little did Grete know that another kind gentleman called Klaus had been so kind to her younger sister and niece also. A common enough name, but in these times, a rare show of kindness. Although feeling more than a little worried Grete placed her fate in the hands of God and determined she could have travelled no further on foot in any case. She looked at the people trying to make their way over the ice and decided that was too high a risk for her and Marianne. Setting sail on open water had to be her only option. What happened next, she decided, was outside of her control.

Never had Grete wished so much that they should reach land. From her crouched position on the inside deck of the boat, she looked through the window. It was as if the wind conducted the rise and fall of each wave and the sea appeared to climb up and greet them. Grete intensely felt the motion of the boat as it was tossed from one wave to the next, and the sense of nausea became unbearable. Grete feared Marianne was becoming dehydrated; she was vomiting continuously, and there wasn't enough water to replace what she was losing. She just needed her to take gentle sips from the metal mug, which held her ration of water.

The sky was dark, blotting out the moon and the stars; nothing from the view out of the window could indicate their position to Grete. Every time someone opened the door leading to the outside deck, the wind and storm blasted inside. In these moments the rage of the elements took over their very being, rendering them gasping for air as the wind and water flooded through the door for those few seconds. The door would close, but as they hoped for a moment of peace, it was broken by the screams of a hungry sickly child.

After prayers were said and reassurances were given, the sea calmed enough for the besieged passengers to sleep. Later as Grete opened her eyes, her child quiet, she checked she was breathing in a moment of panic – all is ok, thank goodness! She looked down on her beautiful face, so peaceful and her heart could almost have burst with the love she felt for this child in her arms and her son who was heaven knows where. Grete could feel the tears welling up and so blinked and turned to look upwards through the window and gazed at the crescent moon ahead of them. With the next swell of the boat, Grete could see dawn breaking. She was desperate to stand and observe their surroundings but equally unwilling to disturb her sleeping child. Grete whispered to the woman next to her,

"Do you mind finding out where we are?" With that the young woman stood and whispered back loudly,

"I can see land, we are close to the shore."

"Thanks be to God," voiced Greta, "thanks be to God."

As the boat docked alongside the pier, everyone started to move towards the starboard side. Captain Fischer, shouted, "Two at a time – do you want her to keel over?" The occupants dutifully stepped back, and one by one were led ashore and down a makeshift gangway. Grete had never been so grateful in all her life to feel terra firma beneath her feet. Each passenger offered extended thanks to the Captain and his crew for delivering them safely to Warnemünde close to Rostock. As Grete started to make her way along the quayside, the captain called to her, "Hey, you, do you know where you are going?"

"No," came the reply, "I have no idea".

"Come with me," said Captain Fischer. Now Grete felt nervous. "My wife will look after you." His rugged face held no expression. A relieved Grete turned and said,

"Oh thank you, yes please, I need to find my family. I would be so grateful for your help, but how can I ever repay your kindness, you have already done so much! And why me?" Klaus Fischer, just shook his head,

"This is war, we all do what we can, yes?" he said, looking at Marianne. "Thank you," she replied, Grete just wanting to cry.

Cramped passengers aboard the Wilhelm Gustloff

The Corner of the swimming pool where they made camp

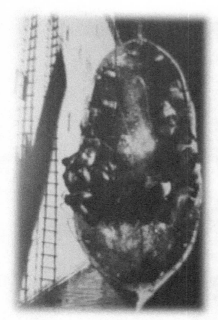

The Lifeboat davits froze and tipped its passengers into the sea

Illustration of the ship sinking

Marinesko was recognised with his picture on a stamp

Climbing the foam covered
steps of the ship to escape

Crowds made an escape
aboard cattle trains

Hundreds of people waited on
the railway platforms for the
next available train to escape the
advancing Russians

Chapter 41
Hilde's Pain

When the rescue boats brought the survivors of the *Wilhelm Gustloff* to safety in Denmark, there was no order to events, no running commentary on what would happen next. There were others who had escaped across the Baltic Sea, hundreds and thousands. The port was black with people, mainly women and children, with an uncertain future ahead of them. Very few families remained intact and were torn apart, most were bewildered and shell-shocked. Hilde felt like she just wanted to die; there was no point in carrying on. Thoughts of her family preoccupied her mind, her girlish childhood spirit now sucked out of her. In the aftermath of the disaster when she watched both her sister and mother fall into the icy sea, Hilde had screamed obscenities long into the night while the crew attempted to calm her. Now there was only a vast cavern where her stomach and heart once lived; she was empty of emotion, devoid of purpose and incapable of rational thought.

Filling in forms and papers was pointless, couldn't they understand, she was now alone in the world? Asking for her home address was futile too; she felt irritated by the authority's stupidity in even trying to ask these meaningless questions. Given a chance right now, Hilde would have chosen the same outcome as her mother and sister. She had no desire; no fight and her sense of survival deserted her. "What is there to live for?" Hilde thought. She wandered away from the relative collective safety of the rescued passengers as they gathered on the quayside that morning.

Leaning against the railing of the boat's gangway from which they had all disembarked, stood an older man in a weathered trench coat. Unshaven and wearing a peaked cap, he blended in well with the travellers, but he only had eyes for one person, Hilde. He watched as she wandered off looking for she didn't know what, but hoping that sleep might wipe clear her memory and take her away from this living hell. That's if she could find somewhere to lay her head.

Hilde's sleek frame stood in the doorway to a bar on the edge of the quayside. Her silhouette with the daylight behind her took the eye of another younger seaman. He advanced towards her, smiled a hello and asked her if she wanted to come in and drink with him. He detected she was Germanic and spoke in broken German. Hilde did not understand Danish, she was alert to what he was saying, but she was too numb to care. Her skin was pale and grey, and she wore a vacant expression that gave nothing away of the nightmare she had experienced in the last few days.

The young man reached out to take her hand, sensing that this was a very distressed young lady – she was quivering, her hands visibly shaking. "My name is Hagen; what is your name?" Hilde looked at him with soulless eyes, "Hilde, my name is Hilde." Hagen was intrigued as to what had occurred.

"Were you on that ship that sank? We have all been talking about it." Hilde nodded slowly, no tears, no hysterics. Her eyes darkened before Hagen and it looked to him as though a shroud of hopelessness draped over her fragile body.

"You must be starving hungry; please come with me. I will get you some food."

Within five minutes, there were a few meatballs in a tomato sauce that sat in front of her. Hilde's desire to eat was utterly absent; even the smell of the food made her want to throw up. Hagen offered her a drink. It was a strong spirit; Hilde didn't know what of, and cared even less. For the first time something took just a little of the pain away and she knocked it all back in one. Hilde nodded in appreciation and the corners of her mouth attempted a smile. Hagen looked astonished and decided that he had done a good thing in helping this young woman; at least he had managed to squeeze some reaction out of her, even if it was only to knock back a large glass of akvavit on an empty stomach. A second was knocked down similarly. When Hagen asked for a third, the barman looked across at the slender body of a young woman gently swaying in her seat and suggested that this should be the last drink, to which Hagen nodded as a subordinate would to his master. Hagen gently tried to coax Hilde to eat, but she pushed the plate back into his direction, preferring the akvavit, which she had started to get a taste for, and the effect that it was having in blocking out her emotions.

A couple of companions joined Hagen, as they too were intrigued by the young girl. As they sat down to join the couple, Hilde managed a forced smile to say hello. Before long, another round of drinks was ordered. The barman now faced a busy bar on his own and paid little attention as to who was ordering drinks for whom. Hilde was increasingly swaying now and giggled as she sensed she was losing control of her balance. The three young men took her to be game for a laugh, and as she slowly came out of her shell, they plied her with more drinks. Hagen was starting to feel uneasy. He recognised that Hilde was distressed and began to feel guilty that he had taken her down a path of alcohol abuse that was not appropriate in a young lady such as her, especially as she had still not eaten any food.

The barman shouted 'time'; they all needed to go home. But what were they going to do with Hilde? The three young men now realised the fun they had experienced in trying to coax Hilde out of herself had got out of hand, and she was now incapable of looking after herself. They took her by the arms and walked out into the cold evening air. One of the boys was behind her, and they stopped to prop her up against a low-level wall. Hilde started to lurch forwards as if to fall.

Conversation between the three boys was louder than it should have been, and discretion was absent as they discussed what they were going to do with her. In the shadows and unbeknown to the group, stood a man wearing a long trench coat with a fur collar, a black peaked cap and a cigarette hanging loosely out of the side of his mouth.

The sky was dark that night, no moon or stars and, with limited light, anyone could blend into the brickwork of the buildings. The stranger kicked at the melted snow now freezing again in the cold night air where his breath quickly turned to heavy moisture in the atmosphere.

Two ladies wearing headscarves and carrying a bundle of clothes wrapped in a sheet observed the scene and felt the need to intervene. One made her move and spoke to the boys, "Is she alright? What is her name?"

"Hilde" came the reply. Within a couple of seconds, the man who previously stood in the shadows lurched forward and reached towards Hilde's arm.

"Hilde, darling, where have you been? We have looking for you everywhere…!" Hagen looked taken aback,

"So you know her then?"

"Of course," came the reply in broken Danish, "Hilde is my niece, and I need to look after her." Relief now swept over Hagen's face.

"Come on, sweetheart, let's get you to safety…" The man kissed her forehead lovingly. Hagen and the others offered to help him to carry her. The man waved them away and said thank you for looking after her, but he would take care of things from here on.

Hilde moaned as she was half-dragged along the cobbled quayside. The man reached under her arm to lift her as close to a walking position as possible. He didn't want to draw undue attention to them both as his intended destination wasn't far. Hilde lifted her head. Everything was swimming all around her. She slurred, "Where am I?" The reply was immediate,

"Don't worry about where you are sweetheart, concentrate on who you are with on this cold night. Soon you will show me lots of appreciation for rescuing you from that sinking ship." Hilde tried hard to keep her head lifted. She attempted to stay awake and aware of her surroundings, as a menacing feeling of foreboding swept over her as she struggled to keep a hold of her senses.

The room she was entering felt plain and cold; she was being placed down onto a small bed; it had no blankets and felt coarse and smelt dirty. A rough hand pushed her hair from her face, and she felt hot, acrid breath on her cold face. Next a tongue searched the inside of her mouth. As she felt a hand reach between her legs, she came too in stark awareness that jolted her back into existence. She kicked and managed to lift herself up a little, but was pushed back and as her head sharply hit the wall behind her, she fell back on the bed in an unconscious state. It took only a short time for the man to violate her body, gasping with pleasure as he did so. He spoke to Hilde, tried to bring her round, but concluded her drunken state had not permitted her enjoyment of the encounter in the same way that it had him. She had better sleep off her intoxication and would probably wake up in the morning and have no recollection of their passionate embrace!

Kissing her forehead once more, he removed his coat and placed it over her. In the morning, he would return and assume the role of the hero who saved her from freezing to death while being completely drunk. He closed the door behind him and wrapped his arms around himself with a simultaneous slapping movement to keep warm. "I should hurry, it's late, mother will be waiting up for me," he muttered. Feeling gratified on two counts, the second being that he had left Hilde tucked up under his coat, cosy and warm, he concluded he had done the right thing and not just left her there with no cover.

The following morning, Hagen arrived back for work on the quayside, and found it in uproar. The body of a young girl had been found in one of the sick bays on the edge of the docks. An unsettled feeling churned in Hagen's stomach. Soldiers and police were all around. Rumours were rife that the girl had been raped. There was clear evidence, he heard. Hagen pushed through the crowd and saw them carry out a body on a stretcher. He begged the stretcher-bearers to be allowed to look at her face. After much pleading, they allowed him to pull back the shroud. Hagen jerked backwards, turning as he did so. He then fell to his knees at the edge of the quayside and leant over to empty the contents of his stomach onto the broken ice of the dock below. Then he knelt back onto his heels and sobbed.

A policeman held on to the coat they had found over Hilde, and a warrant was put out for the arrest of its owner. There was talk that the suspect was a simple man and had maybe been guilty of other copycat assaults before the war started. They would find him, there was nothing more certain. Now they knew his identity there was no escape, and justice would be swift and exacting.

Chapter 42

Betty and her five children received the occasional letter from Walter, but she increasingly worried about his whereabouts, and with the estrangement from the wider family she felt quite isolated. Topseifersdorf is situated close to Dresden, and mid-February saw the Allies' relentless bombing of the city. Harald and his siblings witnessed the white snow on the ground turn to grey as the ash fell from the burning buildings in the city. The children would look up continually as the planes owned the skies above them. On one occasion a bomber came out of its formation and started to circle overhead, dropping lower and lower, over the next village, and when it came down to about 1000ft, it dropped a single bomb that landed about 1/2km away. It missed the village houses and landed in a nearby field. The children ran towards the bomb site and saw an enormous crater, and as they stood, they watched it fill up with groundwater. Harald saw a piece of shrapnel, and picked it up, quickly dropping it as it was hot from the explosion. He needed to nurse his burned hands in the snow before going home to explain to his mother what he had done.

By April 1945, things were going badly wrong for the German army, and the local people would watch the soldiers as they passed through the village trying to escape from the advancing Red Army in the East and the Allies in the west. They were particularly avoiding the Americans who had crossed the border of Saxony en route to Czechoslovakia. Harald could see that hundreds and hundreds of German soldiers were travelling on whatever vehicle they could find, hanging off the sides of the vehicles and offloading their equipment and boxes of ammunition on the roadside and ditches to make their vehicles lighter and faster. Harald and other refugee children from East Prussia stood outside their houses and waved at the trucks as they trundled past. On one occasion, some soldiers stopped outside their home to ask if they had any civilian clothes to disguise their identity. They would stop in the nearby woods and change clothes, hanging their German uniforms upon the trees before carrying on to make whatever escape they could, general direction – west.

On her trip back to East Prussia, Betty had brought all her husband's uniforms and dress uniforms of the SA, including sabres and daggers. Now as she saw what was happening, Betty panicked and so took her husband's uniforms and weapons and buried them in the nearby farmers' field behind the house where he had recently turned over the land. A couple of days later, the local Mayor (Burgermeister) came to warn everybody that the Americans were just a short distance away and everyone should hide and go into their cellars or barns.

Betty would have none of it and said: "If we are going to die, I am not dying in the cellar." So Betty took her five children outside with a blanket and sat outside the house on the front lawn. She waited, and after around two hours the first American tanks came through, three in fact, and when they saw this woman and her children on the front lawn of their house on the main road into the village, one stopped. The hatch opened slowly and deliberately as Betty felt her heart thumping in her chest. The children sat frozen to the spot as they watched a black man come from out of the hatch. He was the first black man that they had ever seen and they could only sit motionless as the man moved towards them. The soldier reached into his pockets and handed the children a chocolate bar, followed by some cans of drink that they had stashed in the vehicle. The tension evaporated in a second, followed by smiles all round as they enjoyed their first chocolate in months. Betty now knew that things would be alright if they had to live under American or Allied occupation, just as long as it wasn't the Russians.

Following the arrival of the Americans, the children often played in the woods nearby with several refugee friends, in particular Harald, who at 12 was the oldest, and of course, there was no school. They came across abandoned German uniforms and had fun trying them on. Some they took home where Betty converted them into coats for the smaller children. One of Harald's friends found a fur hat with a German badge on the front. He showed off to his young friends, parading around in his fur hat, which he wore from that day on. Hunger never left them, and in the absence of fathers the older children took on the responsibility of providing for their families. They roamed from village to village looking for food, often breaking into farm cellars. On finding a more accessible dwelling with external cellar access, they would make the smallest child climb down through the little trap door at night when the farmer was asleep. The child, dangling on a rope to get through the opening and into the cellar, would take what they could and then climb back out again. Nobody dared think what might happen if the farmer caught them. On desperate occasions, they would take what they could from a pit where the Americans threw out their old cans of food, and they would look for anything that was left. This practice was soon halted when they were in the pit, making rather too much noise. A drunken American officer started shouting at them, took out his pistol and began to shoot at them, scattering the children far and wide, luckily the officer did not hit any of them.

The children found ammunition lying around regularly, and when they had collected enough bullets, they would remove the tips of the shells and began to take the powder out to collect the gunpowder. They kept on doing this until the pile of powder was about three feet high. One day a 16-year-old boy decided that the collection was big enough now to create a bonfire and he made up his mind to ignite it to see what happened. He handed the matches to Harald to ignite the powder, Harald threw the match onto the pile, and it didn't ignite. It was probably damp. So an older boy snatched the matches from Harald and pushed him away saying, "This is how you do it." As he spoke, he knelt to the pile of powder and struck a match when ignited, he stuck it into the middle of the powder.

All around them was a massive flash of blinding white. The teenager disappeared into the flames, with his jacket on fire, as was the German army fur hat he was wearing. His whole head was on fire, as were all the children around him. They each ran towards the small stream to throw themselves into the water. The older boy was black with the flames which had burned right into his flesh, His clothes were burned off from the waist up. His younger brother was screaming. The severely injured boy went into shock as he was taken into the nearby barn by the other children. They didn't know what to do but wanted to clean him up. They saw a horse brush and decided to clean off the black soot from his body with the brush intended for grooming horses. As they began washing him, his skin started to fall off. The frightened children kept the unfortunate teenager in the barn overnight, hoping that he would get better, not knowing what else to do. The next morning, the injuries were just too awful, and they needed to call a doctor. The boys didn't see the injured teenager until about a year later, and were shocked to see, that his ears were burned off, as were his lips and nose, and he looked like a skull with skin stretched over it. He had spent a whole year in the hospital.

Chapter 43

Soon after Anita, Inge and Sepp had commenced their long journey to Germany, Anita noticed that Sepp always walked next to her and Inge just a couple of paces behind as if programmed. Little eye contact took place, and Anita glanced over her shoulder frequently to check that her daughter was keeping pace. Other refugees walked the same road, many travelling in the opposite direction. Each had their head down, collars pulled up to their ears, tightened scarfs and bags over their back or shoulder. Once more there were prams; some contained babies and small children, many carried the remnants of a life left behind. Occasionally a face might look up and acknowledge a fellow traveller, often with white tracks down a dirty face if they still had tears to shed.

Once over the border into Austria, the small party of three found a small village with a moderate railway station. On the platform, a large crowd of people waited. Shortly the sea of people flocked to the edge of the platform hoping to get a seat on the train. "Where are you heading for?" Anita asked a small man with a child.

"Salzburg," came the reply," But you will be lucky to get on the train without a ticket, everyone in front of you gets on first." Anita grabbed Inge's hand and led her through the crowd towards the ticket office. Sepp was momentarily stunned at the sudden swift actions of Anita, but he followed her lead. After a two or three-minute struggle to clamber through, they reached the ticket office. On enquiring about tickets to Salzburg, the response was curt, "You are too late, all tickets sold. Some people, without a ticket, will hang onto the outside, but you would be taking a massive risk." With that, the ticket master waved them aside and shouted, "Next! Where do you want to go?"

Inge started to cry, her leg hurt her, and her boots were showing the beginnings of a hole, allowing the snow to seep in and make her feet feel even colder. Sepp scolded Inge for moaning and turned towards Anita, taking her elbow in his cupped hand and moving her closer toward him. The act left Inge a couple of feet behind them, but the gesture said much more to her. Oblivious to the small signals that Sepp was emitting towards her daughter, Anita turned to Inge. She assured her that they would find somewhere to sleep that night. Just as dusk was falling the train pulled into the station. It was a frantic sight watching the desperate mob try and board. The behaviour was brutal, and many got left behind. Some who could not get on board took the risk of clinging to the sides of the train. Anita feared for their chances of survival.

Now feeling weary, hungry and deflated, the three moved away from the station and down a street with just a few houses nestling the side of the road. They drifted towards a building, which looked to be a beer tavern. There were no lights on, and the door was locked. Trying not to draw attention from the few passers-by, Sepp walked around the building and established that nobody was home. He became determined that they would gain entry and turned to Anita assuringly, "I will find some food and somewhere to sleep." Feeling uncertain of these surroundings, Inge reached for her mother's arm and stood close by her side. She was grateful and relieved when her mother permitted this close contact and Anita shot her daughter a rare but reassuring smile. A few moments later Sepp returned from the back of the building and said, "Everywhere in the main building is boarded up. Without breaking and entering it is futile to expect to enter." Anita was adamant,

"No we shouldn't break-in," to which Sepp, replied,

"Right then we have the barn and a pile of hay for the night. That is our lot." Inge's heart sank until Sepp confirmed his intention to go and look for food. Anita and Inge made the best of a bed for themselves, and within 20 minutes Sepp came back with some stale bread and very suspect looking sausage. When Anita asked him where he had found it, he replied that she should not ask questions and eat. All were too tired to argue.

First light saw them moving quite quickly, the respite being short-lived and the sleep one would hardly describe as restful. Hunger was by now a state of being, and nobody dared to mention that they were hungry. Inge ran her fingers through her hair. It was a tangled, matted mess, and as her fingers touched her face, she could feel the open sores that stung in the cold. Another day of walking, another night in desperate search of somewhere to sleep, repeated itself again and again. The mountains soared up all around them now as they negotiated the valleys through Austria. Thankful that they did not encounter many soldiers, they decided that they must also be running. In the half-light of dawn on the sixth day, a man approached them from a farmyard track. He shouted to them, "You lost? Where are you heading to?" Sepp replied in perfect German,

"We are heading for Germany, Hamburg probably, these ladies have come a long way, East Prussia. They are exhausted." Sepp spoke openly in the vain hope that he might solicit support in one way or another.

"Come with me," the man replied. One glance at Anita and Inge confirmed they were both completely shattered. "You won't get there on foot. Going that way is too dangerous. The Nazis are behaving very strangely these days. And you don't want to encounter too many questions – trust me. I have a couple of old donkeys, they don't look much, but they are good and reliable and can pull my cart up many a mountain." He paused to survey the reaction. "Want a ride?" The response was a unanimous

"Yes," and they all turned to follow the man up the rutted track into his little log cabin with a barn and stable attached. Inge noted the logs stacked under the veranda and dreamt momentarily of a log fire. One glance up at the chimney confirmed her dream as she sniffed in the smell of burning logs.

They each introduced themselves, quite formally and with a considered reticence in fear of giving too much away about themselves. The man, whose wrinkled face indicated he was probably around the age of 55 or 60, told them that his name was Jacob. After a few minutes, Anita softened her stance and engaged in conversation, bluntly asking if he was a Jew. Jacob viewed Anita closely before confirming that he was. Immediately Anita told him her family background, how she had changed her mother's name by persuading her to marry again. And how her extended family, the Zomms, had all fled, and she knew not where.

Jacob's story was equally tragic, if not worse. His son and family were all taken, and his wife died soon afterwards. He believed from a broken heart. His daughter was somewhere in Europe, and he hoped and prayed that she had escaped the camps where they now knew so many were taken.

He and his wife had only been spared because his son had hidden them in the cellar when he saw the soldiers coming. There had only been room for two people, and with no time to argue, the couple remained hidden for over two long hours. They were barely breathing, in stifling heat and very little air. When they finally emerged, they had no idea if it were safe. However, they resolved that staying hidden any longer could possibly be worse than whatever fate awaited them when they came up from the cramped cellar. When they arose from the cellar, their family were gone, and in the four years since, they never heard what happened to them. At that point in the story, Jacob broke down. Inge, who was by now well used to coping with grief, flung her arms around the long-suffering gentleman and offered what comfort she could. Jacob appreciated the human contact and consolation.

They devoured a bottle of peach schnapps that night, and all had a good night's sleep as a result, partly due to the alcohol and partly because they slept in beds and enjoyed a good wash. Each of them remarked on each other's sores and bite marks, but with little option other than to put a little petroleum jelly on to soothe them from the cold. There were no medicines to treat their conditions, and Jacob felt embarrassed as the food on offer was either stale, rotten or out of a jar. The only fresh thing was goat's milk, and even the cheese was slightly past its best. However, when Jacob found some potatoes and a couple of onions, which hadn't withered, Anita had managed to put together a respectable käsespätzle.

Jacob was the first to rise closely followed by Sepp, the two men decided on a course of action and direction of travel. Anita joined the conversation to gather news on the plan. Inge wandered out to look at the view from the porch of the log cabin; the sun shone brightly across the valley – it was a beautiful day, almost spring. The air was fresh, and Inge breathed deeply, feeling grateful for the previous days encounter with this lonely older gentleman. Her thoughts went back to Klaus in the forest on the Frische Nehrung and how he had taken five of them on his sleigh. He was so generous and kind. Inge's thoughts continued along the same vein; their tortuous journey mainly. Then she thought about the Mallke family; were they safely in Germany? Yes, of course, they must be. She hoped that Hilde would make contact from the address they shared in Schleswig-Holstein. Maybe in a week or so, they would see each other again. Abruptly an overriding sense of emptiness and loss ambushed her thoughts. Feeling confused by her feelings, Inge blinked hard to help bring herself back into the moment.

At that instant, Inge reached deep into her pocket and felt the large piece of amber, her father's watch and his wedding ring, wrapped in an old serviette. She took them out and allowed herself a few seconds to look at them as her thoughts turned to Oma, Tante Lotte, Tante Grete, Günther and little Marianne. Inge knew that they didn't have the address in Schleswig-Holstein, so finding them would be a bit more complicated. These successive thoughts took seconds to bring Inge back into the present as she continued to appreciate the view. Her mother broke the silence, "Come, Inge, we are travelling over the mountain today, we will not use the donkeys, they would not cope. Jacob has found three pairs of old snowshoes, they will give us a chance to get over the top, and once we are on the other side, we will be in Germany. Today is a perfect day and not too cold, the snow will soften in the sun, and Jacob says that he has done the trip many times."

Inge thought for a moment, "Is Jacob not coming with us?"

"No, he feels he belongs here; this is his home and he wants to make his own plans." Inge accepted her mother's response. With that, she sat on a stool to start to strap on her snowshoes. As old as they looked, they were still sturdy and made with wood leather and rawhide. On enquiring if they knew the route, Sepp and Anita confirmed that they were clear about that and would follow Jacob's instructions to the letter. Jacob made them promise not to deviate from his route, and they agreed. The alternate journey could be treacherous, and although it looked safe at first glance, he insisted that it could take them into dangerous areas of the mountain. Inge shuddered at the thought of what could happen. They knew they needed to be careful. After saying goodbye to Jacob and thanking him profusely for his help, they set off.

The sky was bright blue and invited them to make haste as they clambered over the loose stones on the first part of their journey. Inge wondered if they had put on their snowshoes too soon. Sepp took the lead, closely followed by Anita and lastly Inge. The path was narrow in parts; not even a ski run thought Inge. She was reminded of their time in the Harz Mountains and how happy she had been before her accident. To ski freely was a complete joy to Inge and how she had loved the experience. Now it was different; they could not ski in this area, but instead had to climb up a narrow, snow-covered pathway through the trees. Then they reached the treeline and started to look across the valley at the other mountains rising like sculpted snow-topped peaks reaching for the sky as they glistened in the sunshine.

After a couple of hours, the atmosphere became thinner; they felt breathless, and even though the sun still shone, the air began to feel chillier. Squinting as they reached the top of the mountain, it felt to Inge like she was on top of the world, her leg ached with climbing, and she asked for a break. Sepp suggested they stop and eat the last remnants of the käsespätzle, wrapped in a paper bag, which was now beginning to disintegrate. The flask of hot coffee that Jacob insisted they took became appreciated at that moment. They had been taking sips of ice-cold snow up until that point, which did nothing to help control their body temperature.

From here, their journey was downhill. Where Anita thought it might feel more comfortable to walk it was, in fact, harder to remain upright, as the propensity to slip and fall was high. They did slip on many occasions and so formed a human chain to steady each other until they reached a more gently sloped section of the mountain. By mid-afternoon, they felt relief when a town at the bottom came into view and felt grateful to have the sun behind them, their faces reddened from lack of any sun protection. Sepp's lips were blistered and sore, but he made no complaint. Instead, he was concerned for his female companions, particularly Anita, and he checked on her regularly, turning and asking if she was all right. A series of hairpin bends led them through a forest in the late afternoon. The snow was crisper here in the shade, and with no sun to warm them on the lower slopes, it began to feel very cold as the wind whipped up to greet them. Finally, as the dusk began to fall, Anita, Inge and Sepp walked slowly into a village somewhere in southeast Germany.

Having made the mountainous section of their journey alone, for the first time, they had been devoid of other refugees. Soon they witnessed evidence of other travellers. As they walked towards a small group of people carrying large bags and backpacks, Inge asked where they had come from, and a conversation developed. Each exchanging brutal details of their experiences, no need to exaggerate, quite the opposite, as some things were better left unsaid. The discussion culminated around expectations and ideas about the journey ahead. The people they met had no destination in mind other than to stay clear of any Nazis. Anita wholeheartedly agreed with that sentiment. Looking around, the village was bereft of its young men. Only adolescent boys were apparent. The women looked at the refugees with mistrust and Anita's dialect was questioned. When she explained that they were from East Prussia, one woman turned away. Another older lady remarked, "Well, you are not one of us, are you?" as she walked away leaving them standing alone. Anita and Sepp looked at each other; this reaction was not what they had expected.

Eventually, a teenage girl wearing a scarf and an expensive-looking fitted winter coat moved closer to them, eyeing them carefully. After a few moments of observation, she mentioned: "My family have a summer-house, not used in winter. It will be cold, there is only an electric heater, but it will be better than nothing." Anita asked,

"Will your parents mind?" The young girl shrugged her shoulders, and not knowing what that meant, Anita accepted her offer. They followed the girl without further discussion. After a short walk, as night fell, they went down the path of a large house which was far enough away not to overlook the travel-weary group. Next, they entered a dark little room, full of cobwebs and it smelt musty. The heater was hastily switched on by the girl. It let out a low heat, but anything to take the worst of the chill out of the air was appreciated.

The young girl put her finger to her mouth to indicate they should remain quiet. "Wait here." The instruction was obeyed, and she scurried away. A few minutes later she returned with a small bowl of broth, and passed it to them with some water, "I am sorry," the girl explained. "That is all I can offer. If my father knew I helped you, I would be in trouble." Anita nodded in acceptance but equally wondered why helping someone could be anything other than a good thing. However, she quickly abandoned her thoughts to make them all as comfortable as possible. There were blankets on the small settee which Anita and Inge slept on, while Sepp tried his best to settle into a small soft-backed chair.

In the morning, the young girl was nowhere to be seen, and mindful that her help had been offered illicitly, they made a speedy departure from the summerhouse. There had been nowhere to wash and no toilet. Each did what they needed to do in as discreet a manner as possible. Inge hated the way she knew she smelt; her clothes in particular, she felt. Their brief wash in Jacob's cabin had been quick and rudimentary. The next section of their journey quickened because they were travelling along roads through the valleys. Although the terrain was not always even and often winding, they at least knew they were heading in the right direction – north.

They now needed to beg for food wherever they could; not something that came easily to Anita. She would be happier eating scraps off the floor than having to ask. Some people took pity on them, and others shunned their appearance. One lady told them to "Go back you mongrels, you don't belong here." This hatred brought home a stark reality to Inge. An invading country had cast them from their homeland. Yet their German allies treated them like unwelcome foreigners – what was to become of them? Anita knew that Sepp was once quite a stoic man, yet now he appeared tired and dishevelled.

Although he was doing his best to protect the two of them, he was never-theless vulnerable and quite broken inside. Anita could feel a bond growing between them with each day that passed.

Their best bit of luck came on finding a train station and a stationmaster that was willing to take refugees with no money. Here there was a small contingent from the Red Cross, and they had warm soup and guidance was offered to those who needed it. The relief was palpable among the weary and browbeaten travellers. The Red Cross informed them that there were special camps set up for refugees in and around the Hamburg area. This train was going to Munich. From there they would need to make it to Nuremberg and then onwards up north. The danger was that bombers were coming over nightly; the attacks on the cities made them dangerous places to be. Anita always did the talking, wanting Sepp to remain quiet in case anyone questioned his accent. Sepp and Anita entered into deep discussion. Ultimately they decided that they would avoid the big cities at night and use them as connection points as best they could during the day.

They arrived near the city of Nuremberg, which was the centre of the Nazi regime. Sepp assessed that the city was gearing up for a series of allied attacks he felt would inevitably happen soon. There was news that the Allies were now moving in from the west. Sepp realised that this Nazi stronghold would fight to the last. Not wanting to be faced with too many Nazis, Sepp guided his female companions around the outskirts of the city, carefully negotiating the checkpoints and road blockades.

They saw the evidence of destruction, which took their breath away – some people were still living among scattered piles of concrete. Each kept their heads down as they walked. They were only too aware that their appearance could do one of two things. Either help them to blend into the surroundings or, on closer inspection, invite a series of questions. Fortunately, they were ignored and travelled around the city to the north. Occasionally they would look right or left and note that the shops were mostly gone. The elegant stores were now derelict or reduced to rubble, and the market stallholders that once traded in the open air were no more.

After what felt like an age to Inge, they found the railway station and were thankful it still was intact. From there they scrambled onto a train heading north. This night train carried soldiers, even weaponry. As refugees, they were forced to travel in the cattle car with a few animals and artillery. Inge looked at her surroundings and wondered what these guns had been used for.

Under strict instructions not to touch a thing, she observed that much of the artillery still looked polished. This observation led to a dichotomy of thought to Inge, as all human life around here was anything but polished.

The train stopped at Bamberg, and they dismounted on the orders of the guard. The next few hours were spent sitting in the station waiting room. Their stomachs were empty and they felt cold and close to exhaustion. As a train drew up on the platform, they again forced their way aboard, this time bound for Schweinfurt.

The next stage of the journey would have been to get to Kassel. However, the strategic allied bombings since 1942 had rendered the city almost derelict. With train lines broken, they needed to proceed on foot. Sepp and Anita moved closer together to discuss their next move. Inge, standing to one side, noticed some young soldiers who were chatting on the street corner. Appearing not to be acting under any particular orders, Inge thought they looked tense. She walked towards them and, on seeing a pretty young girl, they started to talk to her, even though she did look a little unkempt. She was soon offered a lift in the back of one of their wagons. However, the soldiers had not banked on a mother and an older man appearing from the shadows and promptly retracted their offer and swiftly departed the scene.

Sepp was furious with Inge for her impetuous initiative. With flared nostrils and glaring eyes, he belted out a tirade of insults, "Do you not appreciate that I was part of the Yugoslavian resistance? You stupid girl, have you no common sense at all. Do you want to get us, or at least me killed?" He was so angry, he looked to raise his hand to strike her, but Anita reached up and blocked his arm from falling back down. Inge bit her lip to try and prevent the tears from falling as she turned and started to walk ahead of them for once. Inge went very quiet for the rest of the day.

Chapter 44

Grete and Marianne spent nearly eight weeks seeking refuge with and being cared for by the Fischer family; they were kind and their home welcoming. Grete and Marianne shared a bedroom; each had their own bed and the room was decorated with soft furnishings that made Grete feel at home. Although Grete was concerned for her immediate family and in particular Günther, she felt weak, needing the benefit of the nurturing that their stay provided. Marianne was not a well little girl; she had suffered from a severe cold, which had left her with a persistent cough. There was little doubt in Grete's mind too that the stress of the journey had taken its toll on her young child. With no children of their own Frau Fischer took full pleasure in providing the best food that they could afford. Although not a wealthy family, they ate well, with bread baked every day. Grete and Marianne enjoyed a varied diet, including some bottled fruit and home grown vegetables from the previous summer. Something that Marianne could barely remember eating.

Grete did as much housework as she could to help repay the kindness of the couple who had fast become her family, not least because she had no idea what had happened to her own. Grete was sitting darning socks for Klaus, when he came home early from his latest fishing trip. He knew the waters well and took great care to avoid the mines, not venturing far out these days; he kept close to shore. As he bounded into the room, Grete saw excitement across his face. "It looks like the Allies are advancing, we need to sit tight because the Russians are moving closer in the East. There are warnings out not to venture far." Grete felt confused,

"But Klaus, you do not look concerned, aren't you worried?" Klaus replied,

"Well, of course, we should feel concern, but don't you realise, this means that Hitler will inevitably be defeated!" He sat down in his chair and looked at the two women in the room. "What this also means is, Grete, you will need to soon think about looking for your family." Klaus sat forward in his chair, his elbows on his knees and he spoke thoughtfully to Grete. "I also heard today that the Red Cross is asking refugees to register their details and there is a desk at the local town hall. I must take you there tomorrow."

The next day they arrived at the Town Hall to witness quite a queue of people waiting to register their details. Even for late March, there was a bitterly cold onshore breeze which curled round them making Grete shiver as she stood to wait. As she reached for her scarf to cover her tousled hair, Grete was amazed to see how many refugees there were in this little village. She seemed not to have identified them from everyone else. Some were injured and bandaged, many bore the scars of battle, and some were soldiers on crutches with lost limbs. Grete thought how they had been forced to follow orders or be shot. Every day they were ordered when to eat, when to sleep, when to shoot. She knew this from Otto's recounting of his experiences. Now their enemy was perhaps going to become their liberator. "Let us hope so," she said out loud. When her turn finally arrived, Grete needed to fill in a complicated form and provide whatever identification she could. She had to fill out a separate form for Marianne; both their details were then telegrammed to Hamburg.

***

Helene, Lotte and Günther were living effectively as squatters in the little farmhouse, in the countryside south of Berlin. Lotte had just managed to settle Günther and the other children in their group when there came a loud and persistent knocking on the large farmhouse front door. It was a Wednesday night in early May when three German soldiers came thumping at their door. One of the two older men answered the door, and the three scruffy looking soldiers entered before they were even invited. "You have to leave now. There is no time to stop and debate what I am telling you. You have to leave NOW!" The old man replied,

"Woah, what is the rush?" The most senior of the soldiers jumped in to say,

"The Allies are advancing fast, Berlin is now cut off, and you are too close to the outskirts to be safe." He looked around the room to see if his words were having any effect. "Worse still the Russians are on the east side of Berlin – now that Hitler is dead anything could happen."

The group all looked at each other in disbelief. "The Führer is dead? When? How?" The reply was brief,

"Murdered some say, others said it was suicide... who cares, he is dead!"

The soldier spat on the floor before looking up. The reaction was a little mixed once the reality of the news had set in. One of the Polish ladies asked,

"So what happens next? What will become of us?" The soldier paused for a moment before speaking, now in full appreciation that he had just delivered shattering news, which would have an immense impact on all of them.

"The truth is that we don't know, but Germany has effectively lost the war, and it's only a matter of time. Berlin is in chaos. You need to move before you get caught up in the aftermath."

Helene, who was by now quite sceptical of everyone and everything, asked, "Why have you even bothered to come and tell us? Why aren't you doing what all the other German soldiers did in Prussia and just run?" The senior officer turned to Helene and nodded in agreement,

"I understand why you would think that, but can you not tell, that I am from East Prussia too. I was sent to fight on the western front. While I was there, the Russians attacked my home town of Tilsit." At this point, his voice broke, "The bastard Reds killed my entire family and burned down our house. I have no home to go back to…. so I won't allow them to destroy any more of my countrymen, or Polish too for that matter." He swept the room with his eyes as he spoke, in the full knowledge that not everyone in the room was from East Prussia. "We knew you were all here; everybody in this area knows about your little commune. In all conscience, we couldn't leave you to whatever fate befell you knowing what you have all faced already." Helene looked him in the eye and replied,

"I respect you for that; it is good to know that all Nazis are not villains."

Trying hard to swallow his anger, the retort was quick and unequivocal

"I, madam am NO Nazi." With that he took off his jacket, threw it on the floor and stamped on it, twisting his foot as he did so and then picked up a random coat he saw hanging in the hallway. There was no time to question, argue or explain further. "Now, we move, Now! I can take all of you in the back of our Opel blitz truck. I have a canvass cover, so you will not be exposed. Come on; we must hurry!" His voice became louder, and it was clear that he wasn't going to accept any argument. Time dissolved before them as each family scurried to pack up the essentials they would need. The smaller children, eyes wide with fear, clung tightly to their mothers. Günther wanted so much to be seen as a brave older boy; he took the hand of a little girl and offered her assurances that they would be all right. She smiled back at him in admiration, as if being comforted by an older brother.

In less than ten minutes, the massive old oak door to the farmhouse was slammed shut. The Opel blitz had benches down either side; the adults sat there. The children either sat on the adult's knees or in a huddle on the floor of the back of this rudimentary military vehicle. Among them were large cans of what they all concluded was spare petrol. Seconds later the wagon was rattling down the tracks of the trail to the main road. It was a sunny day but dark inside their covered vehicle as each sat in wonderment at the speed of their departure and what might happen next. Helene's stomach was doing somersaults and Lotte held her mother's hand in gentle encouragement to stay positive.

The vehicle travelled at speed. They could hear other military sounding vehicles in the vicinity, but their journey continued unchallenged. From the front of the vehicle, the soldiers shouted, "We are avoiding the outskirts of Berlin at all costs. We are heading for Hannover; it should be a safer area. I hope that you are ready for a long journey." There was a loud murmur of appreciation from the back and a distinct thankfulness that they had at least brought bread and water in their rush to escape. The uncomfortable ride took them by Potsdamer Forest, little knowing the significance that this area would have at the end of the war.

Consequently, the journey took nearly seven hours; it was long and tortuous. They continued along minor roads with few toilet breaks and the opportunity to stretch their legs under the cover of trees. Finally, as the sun was setting on this early May evening, they arrived in the outskirts of Hannover, their destination pinpointed by a Red Cross flag which flew over a wooden shack of a building on the edge of farmland. The English forces had already infiltrated the area, and the rescuers were quick to discard all evidence of their uniforms. Having delivered their cargo safely, the men quietly slipped away, hardly giving anyone the chance to thank them. Helene caught the eye of the most senior of them and rushed to acknowledge the risks they had taken, and the heroic act, which had delivered them to a safer place.

The shack was sparse, to say the least. There was a simple bucket for a toilet and half a dozen other refugees already in situ all needing to share it. Their beds were old mattresses on the ground covered in tarpaulin, and the blankets looked to be army issue. Part of the floor was carefully nested with old cushions in an attempt to offer somewhere to sit. The presence of candles indicated the lack of electricity, and there was no stove on which to cook. Nobody mentioned what was going to happen next, probably because nobody knew.

***

Inge had clung on tightly to the piece of paper handed to her by the soldier they met on their escape from Prussia. It contained his family's address in Schleswig-Holstein, near Hamburg. After they had left the area of Kassel, it became apparent that it was essential to find a cross-country route. That way, they would attract less attention to themselves. Their constant hunt for food was desperate, and they were reduced to eating whatever they found on the floor that looked edible. Inge looked at her mother and thought she had visibly aged on that journey. Sepp was always at Anita's side, and it often felt to Inge that he resented her presence and wished he were travelling alone with her mother.

Their journey took them far north, and they heard constant reports along the way about advances from the allied forces in the west as well as the Russians in the East. Anita took advice from other refugees and travellers to steer well clear of Berlin; it might soon be cut off.

April was usually such a happy month for Anita. She thought back to the Blaue Möwe in Cranz;, the cherry blossom would be out now, Oh how she missed her homes in Cranz, Königsberg and her family home in kuckerneese. Constant thoughts of her mother, sisters and niece and nephew, how likely it was that they would be alive? As they reached the outskirts of Hannover, they decided to try and find cover for the night and then carry on with their journey north to Hamburg the next day. Anita persuaded Sepp once again to stay quiet and let her do the talking as they approached a small gathering of local women. One of the groups for once did not shun them. Instead, came the offer of a place to stay and the use of a bathroom. Inge could have cried with gratitude and repeatedly thanked the lady.

The Good Samaritan was a nurse and quickly recognised the malnutrition that Inge in particular was suffering from. Her hair covered in lice, she was advised to shower thoroughly and use an antiseptic ointment all over her body. Anita was the same, and when they saw themselves in a full-length mirror for the first time in months, the shock brought Anita to tears. "The local Red Cross, have small stations in various areas close by, you should go and see if they can help you tomorrow," was the advice they received from the family who's hospitality they so gratefully accepted. The hot food offered tasted better than anything that Inge had ever eaten in her life, and the bed was like sleeping on a cloud of soft cotton. Sleep came quickly and knowing that she had her mother lying next to her gave her increased comfort. Inge was glad that Sepp was nowhere near them that night and for the first time, she admitted to herself that she did not particularly like him – even though she knew that even in declaring that meant it could become a problem for her.

The family's generous hospitality could not extend beyond one night; there was a hasty explanation as to why. Anita considered that they were probably too much of an inconvenience, and even after a bath, they still looked like tramps. With the full expectation that they would continue their march north after speaking to the Red Cross, they moved in the direction they had indicated to find the Red Cross registration point. After about half an hour, they arrived, were greeted with soup and freshwater and invited to complete their details on a form. Anita suggested that they would do that when they got to Hamburg; that was where most of the East Prussians would be heading. "You are safer staying under the protection of the Red Cross for now." The Red Cross administrator was quite forceful in her advice to register there and not to travel further for the next few days. "The roads are strewn with tanks and advancing soldiers, and you should not even consider it." Anita had no appetite to argue.

***

Marianne was increasingly sick, and Grete wanted to take her to a hospital, but where was safe? The word was out now that the war might be reaching the end. Klaus and his wife did not think that Grete should move away yet. Secretly they loved having her with them and Grete relented. So they decided that until there was a significant change of circumstance in the war, they should remain in their remote little area near the coast. Marianne's cough slightly improved and Grete felt that she was now over the worst of whatever childhood ailment had taken hold of her. News of the *Wilhelm Gustloff* had reached the area, and on hearing the news, Grete went into a deep depression. She felt sure that Anita and Inge would have been on board that ship. Frau Fischer did everything possible to placate Grete, but the feeling of loss she had felt when Otto died swept over her again. Grete became convinced she was being a burden and was at a loss to know what to do next. She went for long walks and started to listen to the news more intently. The propaganda was becoming less realistic, and people nearby were able to access the

BBC World Service. With Berlin now isolated on all sides, they heard that Hitler had retreated to his bunker. Then in early May the news broke that Hitler was dead. Grete felt shocked and happy at the same time – surely the end of the war was near?

Chapter 45
The Allies Arrive

The section army officer shouted orders to his regiment. Now towards the end of the second week of April on a bright sunny morning each soldier needed to be briefed on what to expect when they reached their destination. They were the second batch of Forces to enter this area, and they had been on stand-by for the last few days. Stationed at Celle at the Bergen-Hohne Garrison, the accounts of events, which had reached them in the days since Bergen-Belsen was liberated, were shocking. The Germans had told the first batch of liberators that Bergen-Belsen was a typhus hospital. It flew a white flag, and the Germans indicated that any fighting in the area could lead to an escape of typhus sufferers. When they arrived, there was barbed wire, sentry boxes, and a vast garrison building for SS troops. The first arrivals drove up in three or four jeeps, and identified a concentration camp that they believed was a typhus hospital. But they quickly came to appreciate that it was nothing like a hospital.

Dennis Hopper, just 19 years old, had joined the forces in the latter stages of the war; he came from a working-class home in Manchester. Ill-prepared for what he was about to encounter. No amount of army training could prepare young men for the horror and suffering that they were about to witness. One of their key concerns was that there was an outbreak of typhus and desperate attempts had to be put in place to contain it as far as possible. In the previous couple of days, the German officers in charge of this living hell had been led blindfolded through the British lines and were now in the custody of the British army.

The need to enclose the prisoners within the camp was essential in keeping the disease contained. Ironic that, after all their sufferings, their Liberators were forced to keep them prisoners still. Of the 60,000 prisoners found alive, many, around 10,000 were later to lose their lives to typhus. Others were too weak to digest the food they were now receiving. Dennis and his fellow soldiers looked around in horror and disgust. The camp had an atmosphere of death and the dying lay everywhere.

Struck by the sheer numbers, Dennis saw some trying to walk; some collapsed, some had already died and remained where they lay. The stench was pungent and yet everywhere remained eerily quiet. Those with clothes on wore striped uniforms with a coloured triangle on their backs. The triangle depicted if they were a Jew, Roma, Jehovah's Witnesses, socialists, common criminals or gay, each had their coded colour so that the German officers could quickly identify them.

Even though the sun was shining, there was a haze of grey that lay over the barbed wired camp. The ground was dusty, and everything appeared dead. Even the living walked in a ghostlike state, if they could walk at all. As Dennis stood around in stunned shock a scantily clothed, skeletal person came up to him. It was impossible to tell if it was a man or a woman. The person managed to kneel in front of him and kiss his boots. Dennis was nearly brought to tears as he helped up the sick person, being so careful in how he handled them. Only a thin layer of skin covered their bones.

It was established that Bergen-Belsen was used as a collection centre for the survivors of the death marches. Presumably more survived than were expected to and as a result, the camp was a place of massive overcrowding. Subsequently, it became a site of significant neglect and was allowed to deteriorate, particularly in the last few months of the war.

Fellow soldiers looked on with tears in their eyes as they were ordered to help hand out food to those able to take it. They paired off, and each pair took responsibility for a hut, where some people lay dead inside. The stench was putrid. The stew was too thick for most people to swallow, so they watered it down with boiling water. Many would vomit the food back, and if they could keep anything down, there would be diarrhoea to contend with. Dennis struggled in the face of what he came across; every person that was still alive was seriously ill with a perpetual cough. Their skeletal bodies were covered in open sores and filthy dirty. Each morning they would visit every hut and check to see who was dead and who was alive. Sometimes it was difficult to tell. Then they took each dead body out into the open air, from where, Hungarian soldiers along with a few remaining German SS guards had the unenviable job of burying them in mass graves. Dennis took some sense of justice in witnessing the SS Guards being forced to dig the graves.

Dennis's senior officers lowered their tone of voice now in giving out orders. Not surprisingly this relaxation led the lower ranks to question what was happening and why these people were not taken to hospital. The answer was clear.

Nobody could be moved until these people were cleaned up and assumed free of disease. This process consisted of them being hosed and washed down, deloused and put in clean clothes and ultimately evacuated. But the number one priority was to try and get some nourishment into the emaciated bodies.

To Dennis, these people had not only become degraded but dehumanised, stripped of everything which made them human, no dignity, no identity it left an indelible scar on Dennis and his fellow soldiers. Those inmates who survived insisted that the truth be told, "Tell the world, tell the world," they implored. They wished to be the living testament and actual reality of what one human being is capable of doing to another. In the name of what? Nothing which made any sense to those who witnessed the scenes in April 1945 in Bergen-Belsen.

***

In Topseifersdorf there were hazards and war junk everywhere for the children to find as they wandered the countryside looking for food. Harald got chatting to another group of boys one day, generally discussing where they could go to find food. As they often did they were wearing the uniforms they had found in the woods. There were probably about ten to 15 of them all together, when one of them jumped into a ditch and found some grenades, holding them up to show the other boys. Suddenly he shouted to the others to come and see what he had found. In the event the small boy had found a wooden crate and in it was a rocket propelled grenade, about 18" across. The German army would use these on their half-tracks and each vehicle would have carried about half a dozen of them. They are in effect a rocket propelled bomb. The older boys looked closely at the bomb which had been moved and one of them said "Its ticking, it's making a noise – he's set off the timer, this thing is going to explode."

The boys dived out of the ditch as fast as they could just before the device ignited and the rocket took off down the ditch and ended up travelling about 2 kms and smashed in a field just outside a village where the Americans were billeted. The children, still wearing the German clothes they had found made off in the other direction. The Americans could see the vapour trail of the rocket and took off in a couple of half-tracks believing they were under attack. As the children were at the crest of the hill near a forest, they could see the half-tracks coming.

The American soldiers, in turn, were looking at the German uniforms on the crest of the hill. One of the half-tracks had a 50-calibre machine gun and they began shooting at their target. A couple of the boys were shot. They all dived into a ditch as the other half-track raced towards them. They shouted to the other vehicle to stop shooting as they realised that they were just children. The Americans were furious and started to beat up the children as they assumed that they were Hitler Youth who were causing trouble. The children were black and blue and left, hardly able to move, at the side of the road. The Americans took the two children who were shot away.

After a couple of weeks, the Potsdam Conference took place, and the demarcation lines were drawn up. Almost as soon as they had arrived, the Americans left, and the Russians took over the area. Again everyone was ordered into their cellars until the Russians showed up. This time Betty took no chances and went into the basement with her children and waited until the Russians arrived at noon. Once the Russians occupied the area, there was no more fooling around as they had with the Americans. Now the rules were followed, and everyone had to stay where they were told. They thought the difference was like night and day. Anyone that was deemed a Nazi was either taken out and shot or treated very poorly by the Russians.

Topseifersdorf was sited at the bottom of a hill; there was a bad bend just after an old stone bridge as you entered the once pretty village. At the edge of the road stood spiked metal railings which had been there for years. Hidden in the many barns were vehicles put into storage as there was no fuel. One Russian soldier who was clearly drunk on vodka took one of the motorbikes and started to rev the engine showing off to his comrades. He raced off and probably entered the village at about 100 kms an hour as the spectators, including Harald and his friends looked on. The Russian was going far too fast to make the bend and crashed, impaling himself onto the iron railing, splitting his body into many pieces in the process. The children followed the soldiers who ran to see what had occurred. After little cursory glances, and no doubt realising he was dead, the Russians all started chatting and wandered off. About an hour later, a wagon pulled up and flung the body into the back of the truck like a piece of meat. To the Russians life was cheap; everyone had to toe the line or face the consequences. That was the moment that everyone knew they were never going to be in a position to stand up for themselves, they just had to do what they were told, and that was that.

Chapter 46
May 1945

Klaus Fischer came running into the kitchen wielding a newspaper. His wife and Grete were peeling vegetables and preparing the evening meal. "It's over, the war is over, Germany has surrendered, and Hitler is dead." The excitement poured out of him and like early morning sunshine, he glowed. Everyone started jumping up and down, and the exhilaration initially frightened little Marianne, who needed to have the excellent news explained to her, after which she beamed around the room emitting a devilish glee. She became too overwrought, which made her cough again, so Grete needed to calm her down. Klaus turned to Grete, "This means we must try and find your family now Grete. You have waited patiently, and no news has arrived. Surely now the authorities will start to organise things so that family members can be re-united." Grete smiled in response to his positive outlook.

"If they are still alive, Klaus, if they are still alive." Frau Fischer hugged Grete, and they decided that tomorrow they would resume the search.

***

On the insistence of the Red Cross, Inge, Anita and Sepp had moved to an initial assembly centre in Vinnhorst on the Northside of Hannover. There had been little argument or even discussion; each was too weary even to consider attempting to reach their intended destination of Schleswig-Holstein. The completion of documentation was a serious business and the need to prove their identity was a significant step in the process. Also, the names of any family members were recorded. The war finally ending was the basis for momentous rejoicing among the camp, once the news of Germany's surrender broke through the inevitable news cordon. Gossip of Hitler's death gave way to an unearthing of the many horrors that so many had sustained over the last five years. Anita quaked at the thought of her Jewish friends from Königsberg, and the inevitable nightmare they must have experienced.

***

Helene, Lotte and Günther were among the first refugees to arrive in what became Laatzen Camp on the south perimeter of Hannover. They had been there over a week when one of the Red Cross personnel came running over to Helene, "Do you have family members by the name of Tollkühn?" Helene's heart jumped in her chest, "Yes, Yes, Anita and Inge." The woman just smiled, "I think we have them." Helene started to emit short, shallow breaths, "Where, where are they?" The woman continued smiling as she replied, "They are very close by, Hannover in fact, in a small camp just the other side of Hannover." Next came the questions about how they were and when could they be reunited. The reply was noncommittal; "Soon, we will arrange something soon."

On hearing the same news, on one of the rare occasions of her life, Inge witnessed her mother cry; in fact, they both sobbed together. Sepp looked on and stroked Anita's shoulder in thoughtful comforting gestures. In less than half a day, Anita and Inge were waiting for a truck to arrive with the precious cargo of her mother, sister and nephew. The reunion was emotional, each holding onto the other for many minutes, incredulous that they should be found so close to each other. "This is like a miracle," Helene said, "My prayers answered, or at least they will be if we can find Grete and Marianne." Günther became emotional at the very mention of his mother's name. As fortune would have it, Günther did not have to wait long. Within a week the authorities in Hamburg made contact and notified them of Grete's whereabouts.

It was a tearful departure for Grete after all the months she had lived with the Fischer's, and they promised to write and visit as soon as everything was more settled. The journey to Hannover was difficult due to the roadblocks and trains that were not working. The journey took about 24 hours with nowhere to sleep, and Marianne was continually coughing. Grete arrived in the outskirts of Hannover and with other refugees was taken straight to Vinnhorst Camp, which was growing daily. The first person she saw was Günther who ran to his mother and flung his arms around her. Grete's first words were, "My darling boy you have grown so much." Günther then hugged his little sister, and she cried as she was handed round the whole family in a series of hugs. The talking and stories of what had happened to each of them went on long into the night. News of the *Wilhelm Gustloff* led all to believe that the Mallke family were now dead. They prayed together, giving thanks for their safe reunion and from the background, Sepp looked on waiting for the moment when Anita might introduce him to her family.

The Nazi party had complete control over the press and of course the radio stations until the end of the war. On 9th May 1945, after announcing the unconditional surrender of Germany to the Allies, the last remaining German radio station in Flensburg near the Danish border went off the air. The propaganda radio had been halted as a direct result of this crackdown. Accurate up to date information was hard to come by, until slowly, the allies worked together to rebuild the infrastructure of society. Information was increasingly gathered from the BBC world service. The refugee camps were building daily as more and more mainly from the East arrived in the western area of Germany, desperate for help and support.

Anita and her family, now reunited, stayed in Vinnhorst Camp and slowly made it their home. Marianne's health continued to cause concern until she was at last admitted to the hospital in Hannover. Marianne was now seriously ill, and Grete stayed by her bedside constantly. On one particular afternoon Inge found herself alone as Helene, Lotte and Günther were also at the hospital. Anita was doing something with Sepp, so Inge decided she would walk the mile or so on her own to join the rest of her family and visit Marianne.

British soldiers took over patrolling the streets in a similar way to that of German Soldiers just months before. It was a sunny afternoon in the middle of May when Inge walked briskly towards the hospital to visit her cousin. She had recovered from her frail condition after her long journey from Yugoslavia. Returned was the pretty young girl with dark locks of hair. As she passed a closed up shop she caught the eye of a young British soldier, standing in the porchway, smoking a cigarette. Inge hated the smell of cigarettes, she looked straight ahead as she started to pass him, but he called her over. She ignored him. In a split second, he grabbed her arm and forced her into the shop doorway. She immediately knew he intended to rape her, she struggled to break free, and he pushed her hard against the wall, scrambling with her clothing.

Fortunately for Inge, the soldier spoke German. When she shouted, "Stop please I am going to the hospital, my aunt's little girl is critically ill, we are so worried about her, please don't do this." The soldier stopped in his tracks.

"Alright then, I will go with you to the hospital, but if I find out that you have been lying to me – I will kill you!" In silence, they walked the half a mile or so to the hospital, and the soldier followed her in. She walked straight into the ward and saw Tante Grete, praying at the side of the bed where her daughter lay, as if asleep. Her Oma turned to look at Inge as she walked in the room, almost simultaneously, Inge turned to face the soldier. He nodded in acknowledgement that she was telling the truth and then turned 180 degrees and walked out. "What was he doing with you, Inge?" Helene asked her granddaughter.

"It's alright Oma; he just wanted to make sure that I was coming where I said I was." The grave faces around the bed, eclipsed the need to elaborate. Marianne's breathing was becoming more and more shallow. Three of the doctors held a small meeting at the end of the ward; it was clear that they were discussing her condition.

Nobody left the bedside that afternoon, and later that evening, little Marianne who had brought so much joy to the family, lost her fight for life and gently slipped away. After initial screams of denial, Grete became lost in grief and Günther did the best he could to comfort his mother. Nobody could understand why she had died, couldn't the doctors have saved her? So many questions, so little response, other than she had a deep lung condition exacerbated by her experiences over the last few months. They sat with the curtain around the bed for what felt like an age to Inge, each looking down at her perfect pretty little face, no more coughing, no more pain. Anita arrived and did what she could in making practical arrangements in a hopeless situation.

Having sat by the little girl's bedside for as long as the nursing staff would allow, they quietly slid away from the hospital ward. "The war may have ended, but the suffering of so many continues," Anita spoke profoundly, and "I knew many years ago 'that man' was a danger to our very existence. Nothing good has happened in any of his actions, only pure evil. So many millions have died. Now our little Marianne is lost to us too!" She gritted her teeth as she sucked in her disgust. Inge walked alongside her Oma as Anita and Lotte supported Grete back to the camp that evening,

"Oma?" Inge spoke through the enormous lump in her throat that almost prevented her from breathing as she tried so hard to be brave.

"Yes Inge," replied Helene.

"If I ever have a daughter, I promise I will call her Marianne," then the tears fell down her face.

"That's a nice thing to do my darling." They squeezed each other's arms and held on very tightly till they arrived back at the camp.

At the funeral, everyone rallied to support Grete. Inge had only ever known grief like this when the letter arrived to inform them of her father's death. The family all helped to carry the sorrowful little casket and then bury Marianne in the newly formed cemetery on the outskirts of Hannover. Grete's grief was like an ocean coming in waves of uncontrollable sobbing, and she would hardly let Günther out of her sight. The boy often felt a little restricted. He wanted to play with the other boys in the camp and take his mind off the distresses of the last few months. Inge recognised that he needed male friends and time away from all the women in the family. She came up with the idea that was also a solution to another issue in her life, Sepp. He continued to monopolise her mother's time and space, so Inge suggested that Sepp take Günther to play with the other boys and watch over him. Her cunning plan worked, and Sepp was happy to be of use to the family. He knew that would please Anita, and give him something to do.

Inge made friends with some of the other girls in the camp, and they made sure that if they ventured outside of the camp that they were never alone. One day Inge walked to collect brötchen from the bakery. They were issued with a weekly allowance from the authorities, and it had to go a long way. On turning the corner on their way back to camp, Inge spotted the English soldier that had tried to attack her and then went to the hospital with her. He smiled at her in a non-threatening way and started to whistle the tune to, "You are my sunshine, my only sunshine, you make me happy when clouds are grey." Inge glanced in his direction and carried on walking. After that, Inge saw him quite often, and every time he would whistle the tune, "You are my sunshine, my only sunshine." Inge had not heard the tune before and certainly didn't know the words until much later. The song had only been released in 1939, yet somehow she felt the soldier was non-threatening – in a strange way he started to watch over her whenever he was near.

The weeks passed by, and the camp began to grow, their first shacks were replaced with sheds, one for each family and they were located an allotment sized plot. Most wasted no time in planting fresh produce to feed their family, rather than rely on the Red Cross handouts. The food was nourishing, but not always fresh and not what they were used to in their East Prussian home-land and they would talk of their home in the evenings as they sat around an open fire. Confirmation came from many sources about what happened to the *Wilhelm Gustloff*. They all prayed for the Mallke family; assuming they were all dead. They tried to contact the family in Schleswig-Holstein, as that was where they had agreed to meet. When confirmation came that they had not arrived, Inge knew they had all perished, not least because they heard how few had survived. When people heard about Anita's dream, they were aghast. Her family took it as confirmation of Anita's sixth sense, or her messages from God.

Chapter 47

Norway surrendered to Germany in April 1940, and Walter spent his time during the war there as a driver. Towards the end of the war, the German occupation had planned on making Norway one of the last bastions of the Third Reich and a sanctuary for the German leaders. General Böhme was the senior German officer, and he issued instructions to his troops that they should display unconditional discipline and obey orders until the last. In the event on 5th May General Eisenhower sent a telegram to the headquarters of the resistance in Norway to forward to the commanding officer, Böhme, with instructions on how they should contact the Allied forces headquarters to surrender. General Böhme offered initial resistance, but in the end he capitulated two days later. The underground resistance movement immediately mobilised, and Walter was lucky to get out of the country and not be interned in the many camps where the Nazi's were sent.

Walter ended up in Hamburg and fell on his feet mainly because his driving was considered skilled work and the Allies needed drivers so he worked in the British sector driving supply trucks. His wife and family remained in the Eastern side of Germany. It had taken months for the Russians to organise food for the civilians and get the bakeries up and running again. Harald, being the eldest and now a boy of 15 took on the responsibility of searching for food for the family in his father's absence. He would spend all day, picking vegetables and fruit where he could find them. Often he would take the food home and not eat himself just so that his brothers and sisters could eat.

Harald became adept at climbing trees to collect apples that belonged to the farmers along the road. The far branches nearest the road were not picked, and the refugees were allowed to collect what they could. On one occasion, he had collected bags of apples and left them at the bottom of the tree while he climbed up to pick more. He could see a woman stop by on a bicycle. As she lay down her bicycle, she casually went up to the bag of apples and took them. Harald shouted after her, "Hey that is the only food I have!"

but these were desperate times, and people would do what they could to feed their families, including an adult stealing food from a young fellow refugee.

Food wasn't the only thing in short supply, coal was also. In most houses there was just one stove on a tiled plinth or fireplace and that was the only source of heating and often cooking too, but it needed a constant supply of coal. As Harald was the eldest he would walk for many kilometres each day looking for food as well as coal. He usually found coal on the railway, where the trains transported coal to the cities and often coal would spill off them. One day he found a coal train parked on a branch track, so they went back at night to gather as much coal as they could in potato sacks. Harald being a skinny young teenager from lack of food, then had to carry a 50 lb sack of coal back for the family. He took on all the responsibility of the man of the family in the absence of his father and feeding the family and keeping them warm was uppermost in the young teen's mind all the time, especially as his young baby brother who was born in early 1944 was so malnourished they now knew his ocular nerve in his right eye had not developed and he was blind in that eye as a result.

Dreadful conditions at Bergen Belsen
Concentration Camp

The Destruction of the last Hut at
Bergen Belsen

The Sign erected by the English Soldiers
after they liberated Bergen Belsen

Dennis Hopper
(Senior)

Inge about
the time
she Married
Dennis

253

Chapter 48

Dennis Hopper and his regiment continued their work in the liberation of Bergen-Belsen, a concentration camp that was only set up in 1943. It contained no gas chambers, but neither did it have sanitation, electricity or running water. It took a few weeks to rescue the 38,000 prisoners, many of them barely alive. Ten thousand lay dead. Also, in somewhat better physical condition, another 15,000 were in the nearby overflow camp at the Wehrmacht barracks. Finally, on 21st May 1945, the liberation was completed. The last of the wooden prisoner huts was decorated with the German War Flag, and a massive portrait of Adolf Hitler. It was subsequently torched by a massive flamethrower. The whole exercise symbolised the end of the 'Hell of Belsen'. As the hut went up in flames, the Union Jack was raised for the first time in Bergen-Belsen. Crowds watched the destruction of the last hut two days after the evacuation was completed.

The images of Bergen-Belsen became engrained in Britons memories after they saw the newsreels in the cinemas. This emerging news helped justify to many the need for war in stopping these atrocities. Even though Auschwitz was liberated first by the Russians, it was Belsen that was first documented through photography and newsreel, and the British erected a sign there on 29th May 1945 to remind the world what happened.

From the nightmare of Belsen, the regiment felt relieved to be posted to a refugee camp. Their work in Bergen-Belsen was now completed and the camp had been shut down. It would not have been the soldier's choice to deal with the aftermath of the hell of Belsen. They were following orders. The long-term impact of what they saw would never leave them. In late May they were posted to the camp at Vinnhorst. Marching in, they plastered on smiles for the children. An unnatural hush fell upon the camp as they were observed with suspicion and mistrust. The Soldiers soon settled in the camp and christened the people 'the Balt's', Baltic refugees.

It wasn't long before a pretty young girl caught the attention of Dennis.

He unobtrusively watched her as she walked around the camp. Inge caught his glances in her peripheral vision, and one day she turned suddenly and smiled at him. That was the moment he decided to tell her something he had wanted to share since he first set eyes on her.

"Hello, I am Dennis, you are Inge, aren't you?" Inge responded thoughtfully,
   "Your German is good, and you even pronounce my name correctly." Dennis went on to say,
   "There is something that I have to tell you, I am part German, my grand-father was German and went to live in England before the First World War." Inge was not impressed but listened all the same as he carried on his story. "My grandfathers' name was Hoppe, and he changed it to sound more English, he was interned in the Isle of Mann during the great war. In fact, he is buried there.
   "Oh, that is interesting." Dennis was gaining her trust now, and Inge went on to tell Dennis her story. He was fascinated and sat and listened to her for longer than he should, his commanding officer shouted:
   "HOPPER! – Get yourself over here." Dennis gave Inge a wink and said that he would be back later to talk to her again. In turn, Inge felt flattered that someone was interested in her and walked away, swinging her skirt from side to side as she squinted in the early June sunshine.
   The 9th June was Inge's birthday, and somehow Dennis found out in advance. On the morning of her birthday, he presented Inge with a posy of flowers and chocolates he had bought with his ration tokens. His gesture broke through the language barrier; Inge felt overwhelmed, and warmed to his caring like a moth to a flame after all the months of hardship, and without speaking they both sat down on the grass to talk. Dennis told Inge how his Aunt Agnes and Uncle Sam brought him up after his mother died when he was two, and his father died when he was nine years old. They had their own son, and there was a vast difference in the way they were treated. "I hated living with them, Inge, I had a horrible childhood." Inge was as ever sympathetic and wanted to offer comfort to Dennis. She made light of the moment by poking fun at his German, and so as the months rolled by Dennis started to teach her to speak English. The senior British officers gave Dennis some leeway and left him unchallenged in his relationship with Inge. Anita was wise to what she saw happening and warned her daughter that she should not speak so often to 'that soldier' as she called him.

When news that Adolf Keller was alive reached the family, they were over-joyed. He was still in the catering division and was permitted to write Lotte a letter. When it arrived, she read it over and over again. She wanted to come to terms with the fact that the war was over, but her husband wasn't able to go to her. He was fortunate in that he had been stationed in barracks most of the war providing the fighting soldiers with food. For a while, he was stationed at the eastern front. When they started to retreat in the summer of 1944, he was posted to the western front near the Danish border. Now he was moving to a camp as a labourer, labelled a 'disarmed enemy soldier' rather than a prisoner of war. He closed his letter by asking them all to pray for him that he may be allowed to bake for their captors rather than work as a labourer as he had seen how many of them were being treated.

The months rolled on and life began to form a routine of sorts living in the camp, and conditions started to improve. Sepp had continued to ingratiate himself into Anita's affections and suggested that the sensible thing for them was to get married. This proposal came around the time that the authorities were starting to issue compensation payments to all the refugees. Anita was feeling vulnerable after all that had happened. As he persisted in asking her time and again, finally, she relented. Anita being pragmatic as usual, con-cluded that she would be more secure and have extra support to offer her family if she married Sepp, which she did in June 1946. There was a little ceremony, and the marriage took place in Hannover and Anita became Frau Anita Hospodarz.

Within a very short time, Inge began to feel more and more marginalised by Sepp; and as a result, she spent more time with her aunts and Oma. Sepp moved into their hut of course and the room that Inge had shared with her mother now became the marital bedroom. Inge began to sleep on cushions on a bench in the living area, not ideal, nor very comfortable. There was an increasing air of dominance coming from Sepp and Inge wondered if anyone else could feel it, or was it only her that could read the signs? She could see her mother enjoyed the physical attention that Sepp bestowed upon her, but increasingly Inge felt like the cuckoo in the nest.

Inge continued to be 'courted' by her young English soldier and was grate-ful for someone to go to when Sepp lost his temper with her and lashed out. He hit her on increasingly frequent occasions, often for minor offences like being five minutes late back one evening. On another occasion, he lashed out at her because she hadn't included him in her meal planning. Inge was under the impression that Sepp was going to be elsewhere that evening and so did not cater for him. She felt his piercing glare throughout the meal, and did her best to avoid eye contact. Nevertheless, at the end of the meal, he took her to one side, and accusing her of being selfish, he gave her a swipe around the face when no one was looking.

It was the final time that Inge would permit this to happen. She was aware that her mother was turning a blind eye, and this made her feel even more dejected and isolated. The following day Dennis asked her why she had red marks across her face. Inge admitted what had happened and burst into tears. Dennis wanted to take action against Sepp. "No please don't do anything that will hurt my mother, she will never forgive me, please just let it go, I can look after myself." Dennis replied,

"If I ever see him hurting you Inge, I will not be made responsible for my actions. Feel free to warn him if you like. He needs to remember who is in control here now!" Inge snuggled her head into Dennis's shoulder, grateful for the support of someone who cared for her. Especially at a time when she felt she was not receiving the love she needed to be shown by her mother.

Adolf and Lotte were reunited and joined Anita in making plans to build a house in Isernhagen near Hannover. The plan was for the family to live together and support one another. The area of Isernhagen was semi rural and the plot surrounded by fields and woods. An ideal place for Inge to live away from the camp, so Anita thought.

The situation with Sepp failed to improve and Inge's protestations to her mother one day drew little or no sympathy or support. The next time that Inge found herself confiding in Dennis, his response was unequivocal. "Come with me to England; I will give you a better life. You are worth more than this place, I will be returning soon at the end of this tour, and you could come with me as my wife." Inge was astonished,

"Are you serious? I am German in the eyes of the British; they would surely not accept me after the war."

"Inge, I love you. I don't want to leave without you; please think about my proposal; I mean it." Inge was a huge romantic, and this was not the way she envisaged receiving a marriage proposal. However, she promised to think things over. She wanted to consult her family, knowing full well that any thoughts of leaving them all would meet with little support.

"Mutti, I need to talk to you. I have something to ask you." Anita searched Inge's face for any trace of what might come next. "Mutti, I want you to know that I do not want to leave you, but I do not feel able to stay here anymore. Dennis has asked me to marry him, and he wants me to go to England with him." Anita stood up and went instantly into one of her rages. Helene came running to see what was happening, swiftly followed by her other two daughters. Inge was met with universal condemnation from them all. Yet no one appeared to be able to offer any alternatives that meant she might have a better life in Hannover. Feeling completely unsupported, Inge went to try and find Dennis. He was off duty, he had returned to his barracks, so she waited until the next day, when she knew he would be on duty early in the morning.

Inge and Dennis spend many hours over the next few days discussing their options. Nobody supported Inge. Still, she was desperate for her circumstances to improve. Inge couldn't imagine a life where her stepfather resented her, and a mother who turned a blind eye to her beatings. Nor did her mother show her the affection she so desperately craved. Conversations between Oma and Lotte and Grete resulted in them showing her some understanding, and privately they wished her well. Still, none of them would dare go against Anita. After careful deliberation, Inge agreed to marry Dennis and move to England. Inge felt broken inside and believed that she had met a man who could fix her. The marriage between Inge and Dennis took place in the Barracks in Hannover, two people witnessed it – none of her family attended.

Shortly after the ceremony in 1947, Inge packed what little she owned, and Dennis made all the arrangements for her to travel to England. It was an emotional departure, the atmosphere tense and gloomy. Saying goodbye to Tante Lotte, Tante Grete, Günther and of course Oma was particularly testing for Inge. She turned to Anita, "Mutti, please wish me well. Can you not see that I have the chance of a better life in England with Dennis. There is nothing for me here." Anita's reply was succinct,

"I can never forgive you for leaving, but I wish you well. You must keep in touch regularly, promise me Inge, do you hear me?" Inge flung her arms around her mother and confirmed that she would, then boarded the truck that was to take them on the first stage of their long journey to England, feeling she was leaving part of herself behind. Inge waved her goodbyes and wiped the tears from her cheeks, blowing kisses to her loved ones. Dennis squeezed her hand and said, "We will be alright Inge. I will look after you," and the truck lurched into first gear, slowly moving away from the family Inge was leaving behind.

Epilogue

Inge and Dennis started married life in Openshaw, Manchester, a part of Manchester that was a hard, deprived, working-class area, and the consequences of her actions in marrying Dennis soon became clear. A German speaking lady arriving in a city in Northern England straight after the war was like walking into an ambush. Swastikas were sometimes painted on the doorway of their council flat. Also, as with any refugee, taking on a new language, culture and way of life was very difficult for quite some time. Trips home to see her mother were infrequent for the first few years – Anita wrote that she could hardly forgive her daughter for moving away from the family.

Early in 1949, Inge fell pregnant, and on November 4th, she gave birth to a beautiful baby girl. As she had always promised, she called her Marianne. Inge and Marianne were incredibly close. In her early years, Marianne needed elocution lessons so that she could stop speaking English with a German accent!

Blessed with her mother's resourcefulness, Inge ensured that she could help support the family and always work, even knitting or sewing clothes to make ends meet. Their home was basic, and they were very poor. Dennis left the army and went back to work as a 'turner' in an engineering company in Manchester. To make ends meet he also worked several nights as a security guard with Securicor.

Having been an only child, Inge desperately wanted a brother or sister for Marianne. Unfortunately, she suffered one miscarriage after another, nine in total. Then in 1957, Inge managed to carry a baby past the first four months, she was overjoyed. When it came to delivery, she was to discover that her baby was 'blue', rhesus positive, Inge was rhesus negative. Then the news no mother wants to hear, doctors said, "We think your baby is dead." By now Inge was heavily in labour, she was beside herself. She opened the window of the hospital in Manchester and attempted to jump out from the third-floor window. She was crazy with pain and grief and had nobody to support her.

The doctors grabbed her in time and forced her back into bed where on

May 2nd she delivered a little boy – her baby was alive. However, he was indeed blue and needed a blood transfusion immediately. The hospital realised that they did not have enough of a blood match. The crisis continued when the hospital staff got people to go round the local area with a loud-hailer, shouting for blood donations. The situation was critical for days. At home Marianne was cared for by her father and the Brierley family who lived close by.

After about four days in a critical condition, the baby began to gain strength and was out of danger. Only then did his parents give him a name, they called him Dennis after his father and their family was complete. Marianne became a protective big sister, a role she assumed for most of his young life.

Inge was resourceful and always wanted to improve her life in England, as she had been used to a privileged life in East Prussia. She took nothing for granted and trained as a nurse, working in a psychiatric hospital in Macclesfield. She went on to learn management skills working in various shops and ultimately moving into the hotel business. Firstly in Blackpool and ultimately in Torquay, where she owned the guest house that had been the gatehouse to Isambard Kingdom Brunel's home in Torquay. Her empathy with the homeless both in England and elsewhere never left her and she worked for homeless charities and every Christmas would make shoeboxes up for the homeless in her area,

Life was hard for those left in Germany, food remained scarce, and their treatment by the Allies varied depending on which area of the country the nationals lived. After the Potsdam conference closed in August 1945 a deal had been struck which disarmed and demilitarised Germany. England took control of much of West Germany, and The Russians took the East. As a result, many innocent families were separated for many years until unification in 1990. We visited Potsdam, near Berlin in 2018. It was such an enlightening visit to see the room where Joseph Stalin, Winston Churchill, Clement Attlee and President Harry S Truman sat and carved up Germany between them.

Walter's family remained in the East, and Walter sent money regularly. However, the currency changed in 1949, and the money he sent to Betty was no use to her, so the family were once again starving. Betty decided that they needed to escape to the west. This escape was a dangerous endeavour under Russian rule, and she needed to plan the journey carefully. So in winter

1949, Betty made backpacks out of blankets and decided they were going to walk many kilometres to the village of Mittweida where there was a train station. Betty was careful not to book tickets too close to the East/West border, so as not to draw attention to themselves. They arrived at a village where others were planning to do the same. They followed an older man who knew the way through the forest and guided them through the night to West Germany. Americans picked them up and took them to a refugee camp in Hof, Bavaria,. So many refugees were escaping from East Germany that the Americans were boarding them onto buses and sending them back over to the Russian side. After interrogations, Betty and the children were allowed to stay as Walter was in the English sector.

Living conditions were still severe, four families to a hut, but they were warm, dry, and food was plentiful at last. Betty discovered Walter's address and went to find him. The money he was sending had stopped, communication had stopped, and she needed to know why. On arriving at the house, she knocked on the door, and a pregnant woman answered, Walter had started a new life with a new family. Betty hardly waited for an explanation, now knowing their marriage was over. She returned to the camp where they stayed in Moschendorf until she was eventually given an apartment in Essen. Betty did meet someone else and they had a son together. She died in late December 1984.

When Harald finished his Apprenticeship at Friedensdorf in Nuremberg, he worked one more year to make his Meisterprüfung (master painter papers). Two of his friends had emigrated to Vancouver a year earlier and were telling him how beautiful it was there, with lots of work and more freedom. So he made the trip via Frankfurt and Montreal to Vancouver in April 1957, even though he had met and fallen in love with a beautiful girl, Hannelore. Harald saved to bring her over in the following October and they married three months later. In 1959 they had a son, Raymond, and then they had a daughter in 1964. The family made many trips back to Germany every other year. Hannelore was particularly homesick as they both had family who remained in Germany. Harald died in January 2018, and Hannelore still lives in the big house they brought up their family in Vancouver. Harald and Inge stayed in touch, and we welcomed Harald and Hannelore to the UK in around the year 2000. The aching that refugees feel for their homeland lives on in their children, and that is one of the reasons why I wrote this book.

Walter remained with his new family in West Germany, never marrying as his new partner was the war widow of an army officer and would have lost her husband's pension should she remarry. They had three children together, but they carried their mother's name, not the name Saul. Walter never really made amends with his sisters and only had minimal contact with his mother. A lifelong alcoholic very fond of schnapps, Harald saw him the first time he went back to Germany, and it was the last time he saw him too. Walter remained the black sheep of the family and died in 1960.

Anita and the family settled in Isernhagen, Hannover. She officially changed her name to Anita from Anna and having received a support payment made to all refugees, she put the money to good use. Anita started a business as a moneylender. She and Sepp eventually divorced and she took the name Tollkühn once again. Her house, contained three identical floors as many German dwellings do. There were cherry trees in the garden and the cellar housed a beautiful wooden sauna. There was also storage for jars of fruits and pickles, also cupboards full of health supplements. Mutti was so well-read on health, she would regularly send articles over to Inge and keep her on her toes concerning health matters.

Academics, doctors, and solicitors, among others, frequented the house, and regularly wanted to take counsel with Anita. To us, she was always Mutti and as fierce as I found her, she was a character, and there was nobody else quite like her. Mutti would sit all day in her pyjamas and often not dress until four o'clock in the afternoon. On one of our visits, she insisted I cooked a gans (goose) for dinner. I had never cooked a goose before and the experience has stayed with me ever since. The fat I poured off that bird could have greased the engine of a battleship! Luckily the meal was well received and mum tapped my knee with a 'well done' wink.

Helene (Oma), had a room on the ground floor. Adolf and Lotte lived on the top floor of Mutti's house. Tante Lotte loved to cook big family meals for everyone. They would give young Dennis Dunkel beer which was a sweet low alcohol beer. Onkel Adolf worked for Sarotti in the chocolate factory, so there were always loads of chocolates around. Dennis would sit on the window ledge in their kitchen eating chocolate almonds as he watched the deer in the woods nearby. Lotte and Adolf both died in the early seventies, and I didn't meet them. Anita was by then with Heinz, a strong, gentle soul, and although they were never married, he took great care of her until she died. Anita's intuition remained with her, along with an incredibly positive outlook on life, something she instilled in her daughter and everyone with whom she came into contact.

Anita's trust and belief in God was her mainstay, she prayed every day, and her prayers were often answered. Some might say that she understood the power of the universe; her ability to bring her visions to reality was incredible. For instance, she wanted a white Mercedes; she visualised it every day. Then one of the people to whom she had lent money, defaulted on their payments. Anita was not a lady to reckon with, and she took possession of the item purchased with the loan – a white Mercedes. She and Heinz drove to England in that white Mercedes, and there was even a photograph of her with an accompanying story placed in the local paper, the *Congleton Chronicle*.

Grete lived close by to Anita and Lotte, Grete never married again, and Günther emigrated to Canada after his mothers' death. Helene died in 1968 and the next day Inge received a telegram simply saying "Oma is dead will call tomorrow". Inge always kept that telegram.

Sadly for Inge, she soon came to realise that she had married a man who held utterly differing views of life to her own. Dennis Hopper (senior) had little aspiration in life, and lacked the necessary skills a father needs. Young Dennis never had any childhood memories of happy times spent with his father. Once he pushed the child off his mother's knee, throwing him across the room in the process. Such was the jealousy he felt toward his own son. Soon after his ninth birthday, young Dennis came home from school one day and said to his mother, "I don't want to come home anymore Mummy." That was all that Inge needed to hear to make her move. She left her husband and moved back to Greater Manchester, leaving the Congleton bungalow she loved so much and had worked so hard to acquire.

As with many refugees, there was an omnipresent preoccupation with food. In Inge's case, this also extended to clothes. She could never buy just one of something, if she liked it; she needed to buy two, in case she never saw it again. It was the same with shoes. Everything was doubled up, and her wardrobes constantly bulged with items, bargains, wool, books about East Prussia and mementoes of her life.

There were regular trips over to Germany to see Mutti. On Mutti's seventieth birthday, Inge drove over with Marianne in her Triumph Spitfire. Inge was never really forgiven for leaving Germany. When Mutti became older and needing care, there were many discussions about whether she should come to England. By then Inge lived in Torquay and was divorced from her second husband, Peter. Mutti decided that the many hills in Torquay would be too much for her and she stayed in Germany.

Mutti (Anita) spent the final months of her life in bed, non-communicative and needing round the clock care. Heinz was an excellent carer. Following Mutti's death in 1998 at the age of 90, Heinz died the next year. They lie side by side in Isernhagen's cemetery.

So what happened to Inge's two children, I hear you ask? Well in 1968 Marianne married Leith Hutton, they were married for 42 very happy years and they had three children, Jon, Luke and Ben. Regrettably, Marianne developed a severe liver condition. Although she received a liver transplant in early 2009, her disease returned, and we lost her on August 4th 2010. The loss was hard for everyone, particularly Leith. She left two granddaughters. Their youngest son Ben, had a son a couple of years after she died. Ben and his new partner, Olimpia, had a little girl in December 2020; they called her Marianna.

Dennis married me, and we have two sons, Daniel, married to Kirsty and Adam, married to Luping, a grandson Jack and a granddaughter Emily. This story is one I was told by mum countless times in her life. Her experience during her flight from East Prussia coloured her whole life, and the incidents on board the *Wilhelm Gustloff* left an indelible stamp on her identity. She often referred back to what happened, and I am now so glad that three years before she died, we asked our two sons to record an interview with her. Daniel interviewed her about what happened, particularly on the *Wilhelm Gustloff* and Adam, who is in the film industry, did the videoing.

In October 2015 Dennis and I went with some dear friends to Lake Garda in Italy for a short break. While we were there, we searched for the German war cemetery where we knew Dennis's grandfather; Herbert was buried. After a few minutes of searching, we came across the small stone, which marked the spot in the immaculate cemetery, where Herbert lay. In a mark of respect and with no small degree of emotion, Dennis removed Herbert's wedding ring from his finger. He reunited it in the closest way possible to its valid owner by placing it on the stone, more than 70 years since Herbert handed the ring to his daughter to look after for him. It was a genuinely poignant moment for us all to witness.

Mum never really adjusted after Marianne died, her diabetes exacerbated dementia, and four and a half years later, on April 10th 2015, we lost her from Sepsis. She often asked us not to forget her story, and I know she wanted me to write about it. She likened their flight during January 1945 to something out of the film Dr Zivargo; the weather was horrendous. It was often too painful for those who lived through the mass exodus to bring themselves to recount those events during their lifetime. Others told the story to their children, piecemeal, as it came to the forefront of their mind and with the benefit that time brings, in numbing the pain. Most witnessed atrocities too incomprehensible to translate into words. We can only imagine taking flight from our homeland, running for our lives and never being able to return – they were all genuine refugees and the vast majority, victims. May we always remember them.

Well, mum, I hope I have fulfilled your wish. Till we meet again, Wir vermissen dich und wir lieben dich.

Bis wir uns im Himmel treffen.

(We miss you and we love you, Until we meet in heaven)

Four generations of females, Helene, Anita, Inge and Marianne

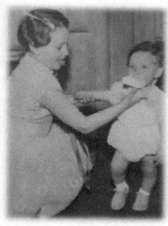

Marianne and Dennis in 1959

Inge with Marianne and Dennis in 2007, on Inge 80th Birthday

Reference and sources

Günter Grass – Crabwalk, First Publication in 2002, published in Great
Britain in 2003 by Faber and Faber . Translated by Krishner Winson.

Gunter had first hand knowledge of the sinking of The Willhem Gustloff
and was born the same year as Inge, strangely he died three days after her.

East Prussian Diary – Count Hans von Lehndorf, a diarised account of the
final days of East Prussia. First Published in Germany in 1963 for English
Translation by Oswald Wolff. Translated by Violet M MacDonald

bildarchiv ostpreussen – www.bildarchiv-ostpreussen.de

no copyright infringement intended

Acknowledgements

To my mother in law, Inge Tollkuhn, for her endless references to her life in East Prussia – we heard you. For the fun, the shopping trips and the coffee and cake. For the love you showed and the memories you shared, we will never forget you.

To my dear friend Pauline Hunt, who, while on holiday in Portugal in 2018 with Pat Clayton and Lorraine Cliff, handed me a heart shaped note pad and a pen and told me to "Start writing this story, and not just talk about it". That was the wake up call I needed and without you this book may still be whirring around in my head.

To my lovely friends Lynn Robinson and Pat Clayton, who, as authors themselves, offered invaluable advice.

To Astrid Pohl who painstakingly looked through many of our German papers and documentation, thank you.

To Raymond Saul – I am so glad we found you and heard the story from your side of the family, thank you for the input.

To (Aunty) Jean Robinson who as a published author herself, painstakingly edited this book and whose input was invaluable, Thank you.

Thank you to my son Adam for designing this books' cover and my husband Dennis for the patience and research input.

Finally to all my family for giving me life's meaning – I love you all.

For More Information about this Story, please visit www.muttisdream.com

CPSIA information can be obtained
at www.ICGtesting.com
Printed in the USA
BVHW031001211021
619524BV00007B/194